THE REFORM'D COQUET; OR MEMOIRS OF AMORANDA

FAMILIAR LETTERS BETWIXT A GENTLEMAN AND A LADY

AND

THE ACCOMPLISH'D RAKE, OR MODERN FINE GENTLEMAN

Mary Davys

Martha F. Bowden, Editor

THE UNIVERSITY PRESS OF KENTUCKY

Publication of this volume was made possible in part by a grant
from the National Endowment for the Humanities.

Scholarly publisher for the Commonwealth,
serving Bellarmine College, Berea College, Centre
College of Kentucky, Eastern Kentucky University,
The Filson Club Historical Society, Georgetown College,
Kentucky Historical Society, Kentucky State University,
Morehead State University, Murray State University,
Northern Kentucky University, Transylvania University,
University of Kentucky, University of Louisville,
and Western Kentucky University.

Editorial and Sales Offices: The University Press of Kentucky
663 South Limestone Street, Lexington, Kentucky 40508-4008

99 00 01 02 03   5 4 3 2 1

Library of Congress Cataloging-in-Publication Data

Davys, Mary, 1674-1731.
    [Novels. Selections]
    The reform'd coquet, or, Memoirs of Amoranda ; Familiar letters betwixt a
gentleman and a lady ; and, The accomplish'd rake, or, Modern fine gentleman /
Martha F. Bowden, editor.
        p.   cm. — (Eighteenth-century novels by women)
    Includes bibliographical references and index.
    ISBN 0-8131-2127-2 (acid-free paper)
    ISBN 0-8131-0969-8 (pbk : acid-free paper)
    1. England—Social life and customs—18th century—fiction. I. Bowden,
Martha F. II. Title. III. Series.
PR3397.D6 A6 1999
823'.5—dc21   99-13687

This book is printed on acid-free recycled paper meeting
the requirements of the American National Standard
for Permanence of Paper for Printed Library Materials.

Manufactured in the United States of America

CONTENTS

ACKNOWLEDGMENTS

~

I would like to thank the following people for their assistance and support in preparing this edition: James Bowden; Anne Brennan of the Hibernian Genealogical Society; my colleagues on C18–L, the eighteenth-century discussion group; Douglas Chambers; Brian Corman; Frans De Bruyn; Antonia Forster; Isobel Grundy; the librarians at Kennesaw State University, especially Beverly Brasch, the interlibrary loan librarian; the librarians at the British Library, the Bodleian Library, Oxford, the Cambridge County Records Office, and Trinity College, Dublin; Dr. Muriel McCarthy, Keeper of Marsh's Library, Dublin; Dr. Raymond Refaussé of the Representative Church Body Library, Dublin; Frances Short; the late the Rt. Rev. H.V.R. Short; The Very Rev. Dr. Maurice Stewart, Dean of St. Patrick's Cathedral; and Patricia Hamilton. I would also like to thank my students, particularly Julie Lieber and Judy Oberste, for reading and responding to typescript versions of this edition. I received travel money from the English Department at Kennesaw State University, my institution, and a grant to fund genealogical research from the Center for Excellence in Teaching and Learning at Kennesaw. I would especially like to thank my husband, Bill Bowden, without whose support I would never have ventured into this or any other project.

INTRODUCTION

~

Mary Davys was born in about 1674, in either Ireland or England. Her parentage, family name, and origins are all lost to us and she herself was not particularly helpful in establishing when and where and to whom she was born. In *The Fugitive* (1705) she suggests her origins may have been English: "when I was in the sixth year of my Age, I began my Ramble, being about that time carried by my Mother into *Ireland*, a place very much despised by those that know it not, and valu'd by them that do."[1] Note that while the lines from *The Fugitive* do not state categorically that she was born in England, they certainly suggest that she was, for her wanderings begin when she leaves England for Ireland. When she revised the book as *The Merry Wanderer* in 1725, however, she makes herself indisputably Irish:

> To tell the Reader I was born in *Ireland*, is to bespeak a general Dislike to all I write, and he will, likely, be surprized if every Paragraph does not end with a Bull: but a Potato's a fine light Root, and makes the Eater brisk and alert; while Beef and Pudding, that gross heavy Food, dulls a Man's Brain as bad as too much Sleep. And I am going to say a bold Word in defence of my own Country; The very brightest Genius in the King's Dominion drew his first Breath in that Nation: and so much for the Honour of *Ireland*, of which I am just going to take a final leave.[2]

Jacob's *Poetical Register* (1719), which was published between *The Fugitive* and *The Merry Wanderer*, gives her birth place as Ireland and lends further weight to her assertions in the later book.[3] If she had any reason to hide her Irish birth in 1705, by 1719 it was public knowledge.

Her birth date has been posited on her assertion of her husband's age and her own at the time of his death: "I once had a Husband, and knew the Pleasure of fine Conversation; he was a Man without exception, whom I lost in the twenty-fourth Year of my Age, and the twenty-ninth of his."[4] We know without any doubt when Peter Davys died; his burial is registered at St. Patrick's Cathedral, Dublin, on 6 November 1698. It is therefore a straightforward arithmetical matter to subtract twenty-four years from 1698 and get 1674 (assuming her birthday did not occur sometime in the next few weeks, before the New Year). But that in itself is problematic, for, according to the records at Trinity College, Peter was seventeen when he entered in May, 1685, making him at least thirty when he died.

Not only was Davys's imprecision about geography equal to her carelessness about dates (she announces at the beginning of *The Fugitive* that she wandered about for eighteen to twenty years before returning to England, making her between twenty-four and twenty-six in 1700 when she left Dublin), but the desire for fact on the part of her readers is further frustrated by her placement of the few hints she gives us. The references to Ireland and England and the beloved spouse do not appear in the dedications or prefaces of *The Fugitive* and *The Merry Wanderer*, where the author may be assumed to be speaking in her own voice. Rather they appear in the body of the narrative, which is at best autobiographical fiction, told by a narrator whose character has changed over the years, as the titles suggest. It is difficult to know whether or not to give any more credence to these personal references than to the wealthy merchant brother in the East Indies, who seems more distinctly a fictional device, particularly since he reappears in *The Reform'd Coquet*. Davys's construction of herself as writer and woman is a topic to which I shall return below, but it is important to point out how effective that effort was, and the extent to which it has governed most of what we know about her.

Of her husband, we can be a little more certain. He was born in Dublin, around 1668, and his father was a shoemaker. He entered Trinity College, Dublin, as a sizar and graduated with his B.A. in 1689 and his M.A. in 1692.[5] He seems to have had an ordinary enough career there, in the company of some more illustrious classmates, including Jonathan Swift and William Congreve. The time of his marriage to Mary is unknown, as are his activities between 1692 and 1694. But in the latter year several momentous events took place. Narcissus Marsh became Archbishop of Dublin in May[6] and at some time that year he appointed Davys as headmaster of the Free Schools attached to St. Patrick's Cathedral, where Davys himself had been a student.[7] Also in 1694, Davys published a book, *Adminiculum Puerile, or An Help for School Boys*, "for the Use of St. *Patrick's*-School," which he dedicated to Archbishop Marsh. The dedication suggests that the appointment to the headmastership was through Marsh's agency: "May it therefore please Your *Grace*, to accept of these *First-fruits* of my labour in this *Station*; and that I may be capable of presenting something more useful, and worthy of Your *Grace's Patronage*."[8] It also suggests that Peter was not new to the business of school mastering. In describing the disadvantages of dictating passages to the students, so that they may take them home and translate them, an authentically weary note of experience comes in:

> But not only so much time, (which may now be better employed) but the labour too was in a great measure lost. For young beginners generally write ill, and when they come home, can scarce read the English, much less the *Latin*, and are more puzzled about the words, than the putting them together, which is a great discouragement to them at first setting out, and daunts many of good parts. Others again omit some sentences, others lose the whole, or pretend so, twice or thrice a week; so that by one miscarriage or other I cannot get that done in twelve months, which may certainly be accomplished in three.[9]

Peter Davys's book was still being published one hundred years later in both Dublin and Philadelphia, making it ultimately more successful than his wife's novels or plays; its adoption as a school text in Philadelphia suggests that it must have been considered a classic grammar book.

Davys must have thought that his career was well set, with his new position and his book, but trouble was not far away. Before the end of the year he was "barred out," a procedure in which the schoolboys barricaded themselves in the school and refused to come out until the faculty allowed certain concessions. What their grounds for unhappiness were we do not know, but the records of the cathedral indicate that Davys himself was not only hurt in the encounter, but was in danger of going without his year's wages: "Then Peter Davys petitioned the said Deane and Chapter that he might have the usual sallary allowed to him as former schoolmasters have had heretofore from the said Dean and Chapter and the rather that by reason of his constant and diligent Industry and attendance of the said Peter Davys then under great paynes by reason of a shott in his thigh which one of those his scholars which went about to Break up and Barr out their master gave him upon his forceably Entering into the Schoole."[10] It is fortunate that the Dean and Chapter agreed to pay his twenty-pound salary because the need for money must have been urgent. At some point between 1692, when he received his degree, and 1694, Peter and Mary Davys were married, perhaps as a result of the security promised by the headmastership. Peter was also ordained a priest in the Church of

Ireland. By December 1694 they were either expecting a child or had one already, as we can assume from a melancholy entry in the cathedral register: on 3 April 1695, "Ann the daughther of Petter Davis" was buried at St. Patrick's. There is no record of her baptism, which may mean that she died at birth, or that she was baptized elsewhere. The story of the Davys marriage as we can plot it through the remaining records is equally cryptic and tragic: the death of Peter in 1698 is followed in February 1699 with the baptism of a "daughter of Peter Davis deceased clke"[11] named simply "Piddy." The name is probably linked to the dialect expression, "It's a pity of a person,"[12] and indeed to be baptized with such a pathetic nickname, a child would probably have been in danger of immediate death. In cases of emergency baptism, the child is sometimes given a stopgap name, such as "baby," especially when the parents are not present or able to specify their wishes; "Piddy" may represent such a hasty decision. She was certainly born after the death of her father because children were generally baptized very soon after birth—the rubrics of the *Book of Common Prayer* advise that they be brought to the church the next Sunday, or as soon as possible. "Mary daughter of Widdow Davis," who was buried on 5 April 1699, was probably this same child, the name in the burial register reflecting the family's wishes. With that burial entry, the author of the novels in this collection emerges from the shadows of speculation into the light of historical fact. "Widow Davys/Davies/Davis" with all its varieties of spellings was a designation she was to keep for life—in the letters of Swift, in the name given when she was licensed to sell spirits in Cambridge, in her own writings, and finally in the entry of her own burial in the Church of the Holy Sepulchre in Cambridge. She maintained her connection through marriage to the Anglican clergy as part of her own self-construction, the writerly self she presented to the world.

After the death of her husband and child, there seems to have been nothing to keep Davys in Dublin. Swift says that "she went for meer want to Engl^{d}"[13] one or two years after he arrived in Dublin in late summer, 1699.[14] Allowing for the fact that his haziness about dates equals Davys's own, leading him to say she had been a widow "some Years" rather than months at the time of his arrival, she probably went to England in 1700. Swift's final words on his friend Peter Davys are "he was a man I loved very well, but marryd very indiscreatly."[15] It is safe to assume that Davys's origins were very humble, even humbler than those of her husband, for she never mentions her family, appeals to it, or uses it to establish her own respectability. Whatever circumstances she came from, however, she must have had some education, if only autodidactically and through her husband, and she obviously was very bright, for her writing scintillates from the first. She either intended all along to become a writer or chose this means of subsistence soon after arriving in London, turning to publication to supply the want that had driven her from Ireland.

In the preface to her collected works she writes that the novel *The Lady's Tale* was her first publication:

> The *Lady's Tale* was writ in the Year 1700, and was the Effect of my first Flight to the Muses, it was sent about the World as naked as it came into it, having not so much as one Page of Preface to keep it in Countenance. What Success it met with, I never knew; for as some unnatural Parents sell their Offspring to Beggars, in order to see them no more, I took three Guineas for the Brat of my Brain, and then went a hundred and fifty Miles *Northward*, to which place it was not very likely its Fame should follow: But meeting with it some time ago, I found it in a sad ragged Condition, and had so much Pity for it, as to take it home, and get it into Better Clothes, that when it made a second Sally, it might with more Assurance appear before its Betters. (179)

For many years, this volume was thought to be lost; but as a result of Frans De Bruyn's discovery of a copy,[16] Davys's Moll Flanders-like description requires some editorial commentary.

While Davys may in fact have written the book in 1700, and might even have packed it into her luggage for the trip from Ireland to London, it was not published until 1704, under the name of *The Amours of Alcippus and Lucippe*. Far from being sent naked into the world, the volume contained both dedication and preface. It is dedicated to "*M^dm* Margaret Walker, *Wife* to *Capt.* Walker, *And Daughter to the Late Honourable Sir* John Jeffreson, *one of his late Majesty's Judges in Ireland.*"[17] With this preface, she begins what would be her preferred approach in her first publications—that of seeking the patronage and approbation of the male power structure indirectly, through women with access to the hierarchy. Margaret Walker's father, John Jeffreyson (1635–1700), was a judge of the court of common pleas in Dublin where he went by appointment of William and Mary in 1690.[18] It is therefore possible that Davys came in contact with Mrs. Walker in Dublin: she refers to the "Knowledge I had of your unexceptionable Temper, when in another Kingdom" (i-ii). She also echoes her husband's dedication to Archbishop Marsh, calling the book her "first Fruits." Her chief concerns are to protect herself from "such as are glad of an Opportunity of showing their own Wit, by being very Satyrical upon that of another Person's" (ii-iii) and to retain her self-respect by avoiding overt toady-ing: "I hope I shall escape the Censure of a Flatterer, since I have (contrary to the Customs of Dedications) omitted those Encomiums which I know to be justly your due" (iv).

Just as the dedication attempts to be a non-dedication by avoiding the usual fulsome praise included in such a document, and suggesting such praise in the process, so the preface is an exercise in satirizing the expected justifica-tions and explications. It is worth quoting the whole essay, because it is very short—which indeed is part of the joke—and because it demonstrates that Davys's wit is targeted at the beaus and the ladies from the beginning of her work:

> I should have saved my self the Trouble of Writing a Preface, had I not known the expectation of almost all Mankind, which is very much disap-pointed without one, and will no more allow a Book Complete without a Preface, than a Lady fine without a Furbeleau Scarf; or a Beau without a Long Peruke. And it is purely to satisfie those, into whose Hands this small Piece may fall, That I have said any thing more than barely the Subject matter; For which I can say but little, only that as it is chiefly design'd for the Ladies, so the most reserved of them may read it without a Blush, since it keeps to all the strictest Decorums of Modesty. But as it it [sic] would look very ridiculous for a Person to exclaim against late hours, when her himself [sic] sits up all Night; So would it be the very Abstract of Impertinence, in me to say I dislike a Preface, and at the same time Write a very long one: To prevent which and the Censure of the Criticks, I shall only with *Sancho Pancho* give you an Old Proverb, *viz: Little Said soon Amended*, and so have done with the Preface. (7–9)[19]

The novel is a first person narrative recounting the trials and tribulations two lovers go through before the inevitable happy ending. When she revised it twenty years later, she presented it as a frame-narrative with a conventional romance scenario. The young woman, now called Abaliza, tells her story to a friend named Lucy, who appears to have inherited the protagonist's discarded name. The hero continues to be called Alcippus, now spelled Alcipus.

Davys's next work, *The Fugitive*, was published after she was settled in York, as the dedication makes clear. Once again in her choice of a dedicatee she attempts to approach her true (male) object of patronage through the mediation of a woman. In this case, the woman is Esther Johnson, known better in this century as Stella, the nickname given to her by Swift. It is almost certain that Davys wished through this dedication to reach her husband's old schoolfellow, for his literary patronage would have linked her with some of the greatest writers of the day. That she is reaching for assistance is clear for she obviously does not know Johnson as well as she did Walker. She describes herself as "one, who, though she is almost a Stranger to your Person, yet has been always an Admirer of those Perfections that make you the Envy of us all." By approaching Johnson she has "left the Circle of my own Acquaintance, for one to whom I am, perhaps, altogether unknown." Her acquaintance is indeed limited: "I had once the happiness here [i.e. in England], to be where you was, tho' among a mixt Company." The meeting would have had to have been some time in 1700 or 1701, the year in which Stella went back to Dublin. Davys's distance was both social and geographic—she was not sure Johnson would know who she was, and initially did not even know that Johnson had gone to Ireland, becoming thereby less useful in providing Davys with the kind of patronage that would link her with the literary circles she wished to join: "When I first design'd my self this Honour, I had not heard of your remove (being then retired into the Country) and I hoped, however, it would have found you return'd." Since Stella had moved to Dublin about four years before, it is evident that Davys was truly removed from her circle of friends and influence.

In any event, the appeal to Stella, and through her to Swift, was unsuccessful. Neither name appears on the list of subscribers for *The Reform'd Coquet*, although Johnson may have subscribed *to The Works* (see below, 90). When Swift wrote to Johnson several years later, he displayed both his attitude towards Davys and a necessity to explain who she is: ". . . have been writing a Lettr to Mrs. Davis at York, she took care to have a Lettr delivred for me at Ld Tr's, for I would not own one she sent by Postt: She reproaches me for not writing to her these 4 Years; & I have honestly told her, it was my way never to write to those whom I never am likely to see, unless I can serve them, wch I cannot her &c. Davis the Schoolmastrs Widow."[20] The preface also indicates the truth of Davys's later assertion about her first novel, that after being paid for it she immediately left London; for while *The Fugitive* was published in London in 1705, the year after *Alcippus and Lucippe*, it is clear that Davys herself was no longer living there. Davys may have been well enough aware of the book market to realize that a London imprint would have more cachet than one from York. (Half a century later a clergyman from that diocese cannily had the first two volumes of his novel printed in York without any imprint at all to disguise the fact that they were a provincial production.)[21] The condition of the book may also reflect the author's distance from its production. The first pages are printed clearly enough, but the typeface gets smaller and smaller as the book progresses, until the print on the last page is about half the size of the type on the first. It is an obvious attempt to save paper, which was expensive, but not an attractive format for any book, nor one an author exerting control over its production would have chosen.

I have already mentioned the substantial changes in tone and implication between *The Fugitive* and its later appearance as *The Merry Wanderer*. The changes are extensive and include everything from proofreading and stylistic revision to addition of new material and changes in the purport of that which is already there.[22] Davys may have had mixed feelings about her revisions, for she does not mention them in the preface, where nearly everything else merits a comment, and very often a short history. *The Fugitive* relates the wanderings of the narrator from one place to another, in each of which she derives some truth or moral drawn from the human condition. In many cases, she herself is both observer of the scene and director of the action, arranging marriages between deserving persons, and punishing foolishness and pride. Both preface and dedication insist that the adventures came from actual experience, although many of them seem to derive straight from fable and legend. The preface, however, reflects what may well have been her frame of mind:

> When Fortune (that Common Gilt, who is fondest of those of her own Character) had toss'd me out of one Hand into the other, for the space of Eighteen or Twenty Years, and had all that time made me her sport, she at last grew weary of her Diversion, and gave me one hearty Cuff to get rid of me, which brought me once more into *England*; and tho' she did not follow me her self, yet she sent after me to let me know her Will and Pleasure, which was, that I must never expect to live a quiet or settled Life, but must with *Cain* (tho' for different reasons) turn wanderer: When I found what was determined against me, I was resolved to bear it with resolution, and disappoint that disturber of my Peace, by letting her see that she had no longer a Power to make me uneasy, and to this end I reversed my own Humour, and from a lumpish melancholly drone, I became of a sudden chearful and pleasant. . . . (viii-ix)

These comments on her arrival in England from Ireland could equally describe her necessity to move once again, this time from London, the center of the literary world in the British Isles, to what must have seemed exile in the North. The personal losses of the late 1690s and the disappointments of the few years in London would be enough to turn anyone into a "lumpish melancholly drone." The determination to challenge ungenerous Fortune by striking out on her own also seems characteristic of the woman who supported herself through thirty-four years of widowhood. Her decision that, "as it was decree'd against me, I Rambled till I met with a Subject for this small volume" ([ix]) displays her energetic transformation of grim necessity into fiction. Or, as she says herself at the beginning of the book, "As Ignorance is the Mother of Devotion, and Necessity of Invention, so may Travelling be properly enough call'd the Mother of Observation" (1). Her satire of English racial prejudice towards the Irish, in the form of a country bumpkin who expects her to be a wild creature with a tail, is neither lumpish nor melancholy.

Before she left London, however, she seems to have written another novel, although it was not published for twenty years, when it appeared in her collected works as *The Cousins*. Its separate publication in 1732 as *The False Friend* has been taken as either a revision or a piracy, perhaps on the authority of William McBurney, who refers to it as the latter in *Four Before Richardson*, without giving any explanation for the designation.[23] Donald Stefanson believes that after revising it in 1725, she returned to an earlier manuscript. Certainly the dedication to Lady Slingsby suggests that it came from her pre–York days: "When I first design'd this little Book for the Press, I was not resolv'd to write a Dedication to it, first, Because I knew I should suddenly be remov'd to a part of the Kingdom, where I had very little Int'rest . . . But Fortune, who had a long time ow'd me a good turn, at last, to my great satisfaction, paid me largely, by giving me the honour of your Ladyship's Acquaintance."[24] I will return to this volume in due time, since it was published in the year of her death, but in the meantime it is useful to note the extent to which Davys attempted to establish herself as a writer in London in the first half-decade after her husband's death. Her departure for York could only have been owing to financial necessity, and not to any hopes she had of furthering her career.

It is not known why Davys went to York specifically, rather than any other county center, nor do we know what she did there. She may have been given an opportunity to fill a position as a lady's companion; she may on the other hand have had relatives there. It could be that her mother was Irish and her father English, which would explain her mother's taking her to Ireland at the age of six. If she did have relatives in York, she cannot have been very close to them, and they themselves could neither have been very welcoming or have represented any possibility for comfort in her life, because York was never her first choice. She went there only after it proved impossible for her to survive in London, and she left as soon as she possibly could, about ten years later, having followed the time-honored tradition of writing herself out of an undesirable situation. When she returned to London in 1716, she had a successful play in hand, and with the proceeds she established herself in a coffeehouse in Cambridge, not back in York.

Defoe's description of York, based on his travels in the first quarter of the eighteenth century, and therefore at exactly the time that Davys went there, suggests that hesitant as Davys was to leave London, it was probably a good choice for many reasons: "there is abundance of good company here, and abundance of good families live here, for the sake of the good company and cheap living; a man converses here with all the world as effectually as at London; the keeping up assemblies among the younger gentry was first set up here, a thing other writers recommend mightily as the character of a good country, and of a pleasant place. . . ."[25] Whatever her hesitations, it certainly seems a suitable setting for an impoverished woman with literary interests. It would be useful to know what Davys was doing and who her associates were, for successful plays are not *sui generis*, and hers was accomplished enough to earn her a solid third night's revenue. Whether she was involved in theater there, or simply spent some time reading and observing plays, she learned well. In addition, she did find herself the "interest" which she thought would be lacking, for the Slingsbys are a Yorkshire family, as are a number of other names on her subscribers' lists.

It is hard to believe that a woman who turned out three novels in under five years should then spend the next decade writing nothing at all, unless her employment allowed her no free time. Swift's statement to Stella that there was nothing he could do for Davys has been commonly understood to mean that he had no money to send, but he might have meant that she was asking for his patronage in getting her works into print, for he did on occasion send her cash. Whatever she was doing, she drops from our sight at this period and is next heard from in the spring of 1716, when her first play, and the only one to be performed, was produced at Lincoln's Inn Fields Theater in London. William Congreve, who was at Trinity College with Peter Davys, had been one of the original patentees of the theater, and while he was no longer associated with it, he may have had some influence. *The Northern Heiress: or, The Humours of York* had the crucial three nights—crucial because the third one was the author's benefit—on Friday, April 27, Saturday, April 28 and Tuesday, May 1. The final night brought in £20 16s in money and £51 3s in tickets,[26] a substantial amount, especially if we remember Peter Davys's annual salary of £20, the sum that the cathedral was still paying its headmaster in the first decades of the eighteenth century. Davys herself says that "The Success it met with the third Night, was . . . infinitely above what I had Reason to expect."[27]

The play is set in York and clearly made a stir there, for according to Davys's preface, some members of the audience, in the expectation of seeing their relatives abused, came ready to defend them:

> The first Night, in which lay all the Danger, was attended with only two single Hisses; which, like a Snake at a Distance, shew'd a Resentment, but wanted Power to do Hurt. The one was a Boy, and not worth taking Notice of; the other a Man who came prejudic'd, because he expected to find some of his Relations expos'd. But both his Fears, and his ill Nature, were groundless, his Family being such as deserve Respect from all, and from me in particular; and if any of the Characters was design'd for any of them, it was only one of the very best.

Wisely following her determination announced in *The Fugitive* to remain cheerful no matter what Fortune chose to send, Davys points out that the gentleman's concern was a kind of backhanded compliment: "I think this angry Gentleman would have shewn a greater Contempt had he said, This is a Woman's play, and consequently below my Resentment" (5).

The publication of *The Northern Heiress* is notable for a couple of reasons. In the first place, it is the only one of Davys's works to be printed with an illustration—not, alas, of the author herself, of whom no image or description exists, but of a scene from the play. Secondly, it contains the most painfully sycophantic of all her dedications. While she had some acquaintance with Margaret Walker and a very little with Esther Johnson, she of course had none at all with Princess Anne, a seven-year-old granddaughter of George I. It is her most obvious attempt to reach the seat of power through a female member of it.[28] Following the usual pattern, she speaks of her inability to do justice to the charms and graces of her dedicatee, but in a particularly cloying way: "To speak of your budding Beauty, your promising sprightly Wit, your affable sweet Temper, and those many Virtues you are so early initiated into, comes still so short of your intrinsick Value, that I only lay myself open to the Censure of the World, for aiming at a Work I have not Skill to finish" (3). The next lines, however, contain an explanation for her approach to the princess, for she speaks of her "submissive Obedience" to the Hanoverians, and her loyalty to the monarch. It is at this point that the prose becomes cloying to the point of nausea: "the Royal King GEORGE has not a Subject within his three Kingdoms, that would do more to shew his Zeal for him, than I would. May he (as now) always shine in the clearest Light: May he continue the support of Church and State: Let his Crown flourish upon his own Head; and may his Enemies meet with that Reward which is always due to Ingratitude, Treachery, and Infidelity; and when Time has spun his Thread to the last Inch, may he again revive in his Heroick Son, your Father" (3–4). Here, in the protestations of loyalty, no doubt lie the reasons for such excess. Short months after the attempt by the Jacobites to overthrow the Hanoverians and place James Edward Stuart, son of the late James II, on the throne, pro- and anti-Jacobite demonstrations were taking place in London. She seems to have believed it necessary to show her loyalty, perhaps to overcome any suspicions attached to her being Irish, in the face of widespread civil unrest.[29]

Once again Davys attempted to make a living as a writer in London. The proceeds from the play would have given her some funds on which to survive for a time, and she appears to have spent it writing. Once again, although she may have published a poem, "Answer from the King of Sweden to the British Lady's Epistle," a reply to a poem by Susanna Centlivre,[30] she was largely unsuccessful. When *The Self-Rival* was published in the *Works*, it bore the motto, "As it should have been Acted at the Theatre-Royal in *Drury-Lane*"; and while *Familiar Letters Betwixt a Gentleman and a Lady* contains internal evidence of having been written between 1716 and 1718, it was not published until 1725. Instead, Davys made a very practical, and as it turned out, a wise decision: she took whatever remained of her third night's earnings and moved to Cambridge where she set up a coffeehouse in 1718.[31] There she remained for the rest of her life. Appeals to the great had not resulted in wealth, patronage, or pensions, and while running a coffeehouse was not without drudgery, she was independent. She seems finally to have found a group of admiring supporters in the undergraduates who were her primary clientele.

The actual site of Davys's coffeehouse is unknown; she was licensed in more than one parish over the years, which may indicate that she moved at least once. Defoe's description of Cambridge indicates its suitability for a woman in her situation:

> . . . as the colleges are many, and the gentlemen entertained in them are a very great number, the trade of the town very much depends upon them, and the tradesmen may just be said to get their bread by the colleges; and this is the surest hold the university may be said to have of the townsmen and by which they secure the dependence of the town upon them, and consequently their submission.

> . . . As for society; to any man who is a lover of learning, or of learned men, here is the most agreeable under heaven; nor is there any want of mirth and good company of other kinds. (107)

Davys was one of those who depended upon the university for its trade, but she received more than that; a coffeehouse was a meeting place for the exchange of ideas, a kind of public salon. An illustration in Ruth Perry's biography of Mary Astell shows a coffeehouse with a woman behind the counter and the patrons engaged in spirited discussion; printed broadsides litter the table and at least one disputant has given up the verbal exchange and resorted to tossing whatever he may be drinking over his adversary.[32] Mary Davys, witty and well-read as she was, would be a worthy overseer of such arguments, and possibly also a source of appeal, despite the fact that the clientele of the eighteenth-century coffeehouses was entirely male. She certainly benefited from whatever exchanges took place, as these last sixteen years proved productive for her writing as well. Her two most substantial works, *The Reform'd Coquet* (1724) and *The Accomplish'd Rake* (1727), were written and published while she lived in Cambridge. Her two-volume *Works of Mrs. Davys* (1725) was published by subscription, and the subscribers' lists to both the *Works* and *The Reform'd Coquet* contain, in addition to the great and worthy, the names of many undergraduates. Here, too, her tone changes, and instead of the dedications to potential patrons, she speaks in a mixture of satire and good-humored admonishment to more general audiences.

In *The Reform'd Coquet*, she states most clearly her gratitude to the young men of St. John's College:

> I come now to the worthy Gentlemen of *Cambridge*, from whom I have received so many Marks of Favour on a thousand Occasions, that my Gratitude is highly concern'd how to make a due acknowledgment; and I own their civil, generous, good-natur'd Behaviour towards me, is the only thing I have now left worth boasting of. When I had written a Sheet or two of this Novel, I communicated my Design to a couple of young Gentlemen, whom I knew to be Men of Taste, and both my Friends; they approved of what I had done, advised me to proceed, then print it by Subscription: into which Proposal many of the Gentlemen enter'd, among whom were a good number of both the grave and the young Clergy, who the World will easily believe had a greater view to Charity than Novelty; and it was not to the Book, but the Author they subscribed. They knew her to be a Relict of one of their Brotherhood, and one, who (unless Poverty be a Sin) never did anything to disgrace the Gown; and for those Reasons encouraged all her Undertakings. (5)

The past and the present combine in this passage: she is valued for her abilities by her friends and she is supported for the memory of her husband by the members of his "Brotherhood." *The Accomplish'd Rake* also contains a tribute, both in the name of its protagonist, and in the choice of university to which John Galliard's tutor wishes to send him. It is Cambridge of course, his father's school, we are told, where, Teachwell tells Sir John, there are "a great many worthy Gentleman of the first Rank tugging with pleasure at that very Oar [scholarship] you have so lately mentioned" (135).

The coffeehouse did not make her wealthy, and the work did not allow her much leisure to write, but she had escaped the destitution of her earlier years. Towards the end of her life, however, when all must have seemed settled, came the only public attack she received in an age that reveled in such attacks. In July, 1731, *The Grub-Street Journal*, a weekly newspaper that supported Pope in the war of the dunces, published a letter purporting to be from Davys herself, requesting membership in the society of the grubs, who were the hack writers who earned a perilous living doing translations, writing pamphlets and satires, very often publishing anonymously to avoid libel suits. Why Davys should be targeted at this point is a mystery; Pope clearly did not classify her with his other dunces or with Eliza Haywood, the most popular and prolific female novelist of the day, for he subscribed to her works. Her last work, *The Accomplish'd Rake,* had appeared four years before, and no known more recent production had made her name suddenly visible. Nonetheless, the letter contains all the scurrilous and suggestive accusations that she had spent her life attempting to avoid.[33] She is linked to Ned Ward, "a late Brother of ours" who ran a tavern not a coffeehouse, and whose journal, *The London Spy,* explored the darker aspects of London city life in full and vivid detail. She is made to describe herself as "a perfect Mistress in the finesses of love," a satirical echo of her own desire expressed in the preface to her *Works* to "restore the Purity and Empire of Love." Her generous compliment to her friends in Cambridge becomes a description of the visitors to a brothel: "my house was not only filled with Freshmen and Under-graduates; but learned M.A.'s and reverend D.D.'s have received not a little delight and profit from my instructions." Lest anyone should miss the joke, the editor has thoughtfully supplied a footnote: "*Mrs.* D. *wrote several bawdy Novels, and the Northern Heiress.*" The letter is signed "Philo-Grubaea," lover of grubs.

The response is without a doubt in Mary Davys's own distinctive voice; stylistically it contains the typical run-on sentences evident in her writing, but more importantly it exemplifies her sharp wit and her determination to present herself as respectable and in charge. To the accusation that she had trouble collecting payment from her patrons, she gives a firm denial; to the suggestion that she provided other services, she disdains to answer, except to say that the letter is compounded of a mixture of dubious wit and pure malice. She also shows a confidence in her writing earned through the modest successes of the previous decade: "The *Novels* may e'ne fight their own Battles[,] all I shall say for or against them is, that they are too unfashionable to have one word of Baudy in them, the Readers are the best judges and to them I appeal." What is equally significant for biographical purposes is the description she gives of her own condition: "Tho' my Hand trembles and my Eyes are allmost blind." Within a year she would be dead, and this letter indicates a slow decline rather than a sudden illness. Also notable is the way in which she refers consistently to her coffeehouse in the past perfect tense: "As for the Licquor you speak of, had it been Eleemosynary it wou'd have had no fault and had I never desired to be paid for it I should have had none neither." As we will see, she appears to have died in poverty, and we might speculate that, given the debilitating illness, she may have had to give up her livelihood.

She is equally hampered when it comes to writing, as the opening of her letter suggests, and therefore the appearance of her final work requires some comment. I have already stated my belief that *The False Friend* was not a piracy but was published with Davys's authorization. Especially if she were strapped for cash and in ailing health, publication would be a source of funds. Given the nature of her ailments, it would make sense for her to pull out an old manuscript rather than attempting a new one. The preface is a carefully tailored version of the preface to the *Works,* retaining only her discussion of the writing of novels and eliminating all references to specific works. The dedication to Lady Slingsby, to which I have already referred, would certainly have been written at the time of publication, since it describes the writing of the book some time in the past, and the changes in her circumstances since then, specifically her acquaintance with the dedicatee. It is the most direct and personal of all her dedications, and draws on a lifetime of experiences: "I cannot forbear to say, that among all the Observations I have made at all times, and in all places, I never met with any Person of your Ladyship's Quality."[34] Her reference to Divinity being Lady Slingsby's usual form of reading connects her once more with the church; her insistence that her books contain "nothing inconsistent with Modesty" (2:407–8) reiterates her separation of her own writing from the customary salaciousness of many contemporary novels.[35] Thus the dedication would indicate that the book was indeed one whose production the author had overseen, and not a piracy. In addition, while Davys was certainly impoverished at the end of her life, there is evidence that she had some source of funds in the year of her death; an entry in the accounts of St. Patrick's Cathedral suggests that she sent money to Dublin in the spring of 1732: "Rec: from the Rev. the Dean and Chapter of St. Patrick's Dublin the Sum of Five pounds Sterl; for a large Oxford Bible on Imperial paper Re'd 8 April 1732 by Order of Mary Davys."[36] The money may have come from payment for the copyright of her book.

Davys herself is buried at the Church of the Holy Sepulchre, better known as the Round Church, in Cambridge, not far from St. John's College, and close to her coffeehouse since her license lists her as being in Holy Sepulchre parish.[37] Her admirers who go there looking for her, however, will not find any sign of her; Holy Sepulchre parish has been amalgamated with St. Michael's and the building itself is now used as a brass rubbing center. There is little sign of the graveyard, for the town has encroached on the property. In any event her grave would not have been marked, because there was no one to arrange for a stone. But the church itself, built by the Knights Templar, is in good repair; the heavy ceiling beams terminate in carved wooden angels who variously hold musical instruments and books of music. They look down on us today as they did on 3 July 1732 when the words of the burial service were read over the body of "Mary Davis, Widow."[38]

After her death, Jonathan Swift received a letter from one Thomas Ewin of Cambridge who claimed to be the residual beneficiary of her estate. Swift was appalled for a number of reasons: for one thing, Davys had a sister, Rhoda Staunton, who lived with a lame child and was supported by charity from St. Patrick's Cathedral; yet all Davys gave her was a mourning ring and her clothes. Swift sensibly had the ring and clothing converted to money, bringing a total value of less than five pounds.[39] Why, he asks, very reasonably, would a woman leave money away from a starving member of her own family? And why bequeath her goods to a man who has the temerity to blackmail the Dean of St. Patrick's by offering for sale some of his old letters to the Davyses, and threatening to publish them if the Dean refuses to buy them? Ewin also apparently asserted that Davys had claimed to write *A Tale of a Tub*. All of these exasperating circumstances should be borne in mind when we read Swift's final words on Davys: "she was a rambling woman with very little tast of wit or humour, as appears by her writings."[40]

Ewin was a known usurer in Cambridge although it is quite possible that Swift did not know that—he attributes the scandalous things the man says to his being drunk when he wrote the letter—and his control over Davys's estate could indicate that she was in debt to him at the time of her death.[41] I have not been able to find either a copy of the will nor any record of its having been probated; simple wills did not need to be proved, and hers was probably simple.

The gaps and silences in the scant record we have of Mary Davys's life are obvious, and the extent to which what we know has been controlled by Davys herself is striking. Some of the gaps were of course beyond her control: there is no portrait of her because she was too poor to sit for one; and she could not have known that Ireland would experience a revolution in the twentieth century, in the course of which the Public Records Office in Dublin would be burnt to the ground, in all likelihood taking the record of her marriage with it. Even should that record have survived, the early marriage registers did not necessarily contain the birth name of the woman; they were more likely to say simply "John and Mary Jones." But her own disinclination ever to mention her own family, much less reveal her family name, ensured that the identity she took on with her marriage is the only one she has. Swift's remark about his friend's indiscreet marriage suggests that she herself may not have wanted to reveal her origins, for to do so might have undermined the designation "by a Lady," which she placed on several of her books, and which she strove to maintain throughout her life. It may well be that what we know about her is precisely what she wants us to know and no more, a situation far less satisfactory for the biographer than for her subject.

Davys's writing is distinguished from that of many women of the period. While sexual encounters, rape, and seduction are present in the plots, the scenes are not explicitly erotic like Haywood's; and despite the political commentary in *Familiar Letters*, she does not write *roman a clef* in the style of Delariviere Manley's books. On the other hand, although her novels are framed in a strict moral universe, they are not overtly religious like Penelope Aubin's. The disputes in *Familiar Letters*, even when they address Catholicism, are more about political than religious values, and while transgression is punished, the agency of punishment is as likely to be society as providence. Her prefaces display a deliberate construction of the self in line with her writing: independent; loyal to the king, as befits a Whig; virtuous and supportive of the Church of England, as befits the widow of one of its clergy; and wanting to be associated with the Irish Ascendancy rather than the native Catholic Irish. Her self-construction appears to have been accepted by her contemporaries. Apart from the satirical letter in *The Grub-Street Journal*, there was never any suggestion of loose living, no doubt a result of her own strict control over her behavior. Far from appearing in *The Dunciad*, she could point to its author's name on both of her subscription lists. She wished to have patronage, not protection, and her approach therefore was never directly to a man but always through a female intermediary. Before her she had the prospect of Aphra Behn's reputation, both its positives—playwright, poet, and novelist, supporting herself by writing—and its negative—the scandalous reputation that attached itself to a woman whose domestic life was not regulated according to what the age considered strict virtue.[42] Her approach also demonstrates the influence she thought women had over the men in their lives, a belief she displays most desperately in the dedication to Princess Anne attached to *The Northern Heiress*, and far more gracefully a few pages later in the Prologue to that same play:

> From her own Sex something she may expect;
> 'Tis Women's Duty Women to protect.
> For Pity, Ladies, let her not despair,
> But kindly take the Suppliant to your Care;
> Let her from you but some small Favours find,
> The Men will be out of good Manners kind.
> (lines 23–28)

Her final dedication to Lady Slingsby reflects most clearly her belief that women could and should support one another, for here she was approaching a woman whom she knew, and through whom she does not seem to be reaching for any male support; Lady Slingsby herself was sufficient.

The Reform'd Coquet (1724)

The Reform'd Coquet tells the story of Amoranda, an essentially good but flighty young woman whose unfortunate tendency towards coquetry and carelessness of her reputation is tamed by Alanthus, the man who wishes to marry her. In order to effect the reformation, the handsome lover disguises himself as an old man, called Formator, and moves into her house as her guardian and guide. It is the first work we know Davys to have written after her move to Cambridge, and her longest to this date; only *The Accomplish'd Rake* is more extensive, and it is no more elaborate. The preface suggests that she may have returned to writing out of financial necessity: "Few People are so inconsiderable in Life, but they may at some time do good; and tho I must own my Purse is (by a thousand Misfortunes) grown wholly useless to every body, my Pen is at the service of the Publick, and if it can but make some impression upon the young unthinking Minds of some of my own Sex, I shall bless my Labour" (5). Whatever the reasons for its creation, it is an accomplished work and shows no sign of being turned out mechanically merely for monetary reward. The dedication is addressed generally "To the Ladies of Great Britain" rather than to a particular lady from whom Davys might expect patronage; and in contrast to the flattery usual in such a document when the writer is seeking support, it contains words of admonishment and advice. She holds up her heroine as a model who, "when the Lightnesses of her mind were removed . . . became worthy of imitation" (3) and suggests that the ladies who read the book for "an hour or two of agreeable Amusement" (6) follow her example: "When you grow weary of Flattery, and begin to listen to matrimonial Addresses, chuse a Man with fine Sense, as well as a fine Wigg, and let him have some Merit, as well as much Embroidery" (3). She thus indicates her intended audience, who are young, unmarried, potentially giddy and impressionable young ladies.

The book was her first published by subscription, that is the collection of money from supporters in advance of publication to pay for the printing. The subscribers received a copy of the book and their names were printed in a list that they could have bound in the front of the volume. It was a method of ensuring publication that was widely used—Pope's edition of Homer is perhaps the most famous contemporary example—but an unusual approach to publication for novels at the time.[43] As the second novelist to make use of this mode of publication, Davys was in the vanguard of innovation. An examination of the subscription list explains the absence of a potential patron on the dedication page, for the list represented each of the social strata: the nobility and gentry, the clergy (in addition to those obviously designated "The Reverend" there are also two listed as "Dr. Anonymous" who are probably clergymen as well), the literary world, and a long list of more ordinary folk, many of whom were probably her undergraduate patrons.

The novel, while innovative and well-crafted, also reflects her previous work. Although it is not, like *Familiar Letters,* an exclusively epistolary work, Robert Adams Day includes it in his discussion of epistolary fiction, which he defines as "any prose narrative, long or short, largely or wholly imaginative, in which letters, partly or entirely fictitious, serve as the medium or figure significantly in the conduct of the story" (5). Indeed, Davys's writing is always efficient, so that all thirteen letters in the volume, like the dialogue, are not ornaments to the plot but essential devices for furthering the story. Unlike many of her contemporaries, she has little indirect discourse. The characters speak directly for themselves, demonstrating the extent to which the drama has influenced her novels.

The preface to the *Works* (1725), which precedes the text of *Familiar Letters* in this edition, is Davys's clearest articulation of the use of dramatic technique in narrative fiction: "I have in every Novel propos'd one entire Scheme or Plot, and the other Adventures are only incident or collateral to it; which is the great Rule prescribed by the Criticks, not only in Tragedy, and other Heroick-Poems, but in Comedy too. The Adventures, as far as I could order them, are wonderful and probable; and I have with the utmost Justice rewarded Virtues, and punish'd Vice" (87). In the prologue to *The Northern Heiress*, several years before both *The Reform'd Coquet* and the *Works*, Davys also alluded to the rules of the critics, specifically Aristotle, in the works of learned writers:

> . . . you Poets know, whose Brains
> Having at last produc'd with mighty Pains,
> Pieces in which not one Rule was forgot
> Of all that mighty Aristotle wrote;
> Nature in all the Characters observ'd,
> And Time and Place to Nicety preserv'd.

She had then excluded herself from this august company, claiming to have little learning and only one language.[44] But of course she has already demonstrated her familiarity with the rules, and she does so again in this novel. Like the letters and dialogue, the various subplots and interpolated stories— Callid and Froth, Lord Lofty and Altemira, Biranthus and Arentia—all work towards the purpose of the story, the "reform" of the title. They allow Amoranda to be placed in multiple dangers, which are held to be the consequence of her own over-trustfulness and carelessness, without resulting in actual rape, which would have prevented virtue's natural reward, the happy ending.[45] While Altemira's story has a technically "happy" ending—marriage to her seducer— Lord Lofty is such a loathsome character that the only happiness we can imagine for her is the restoration of her good name. The marriage, from Lord Lofty's point of view, is punishment for his mistreatment of Altemira. The wicked are chastised with a severity that verges on parody; to take all these deaths seriously would be to undermine the comic intention of the book.

Davys's use of the summerhouse is a good example of dramatic technique incorporated into the structure of the novel. Indeed, apart from its dramatic uses, its placement is rather odd: surely an estate would have a quieter, more private setting for a retreat than the side of a highway. But it can easily be imagined as a functional stage set: it is on two levels, which allows Callid and Froth to be overheard by the housekeeper when hatching their plot. Both the listening servant and the plotting beaus are visible to the audience, or the reader, but the beaus are of course oblivious of any auditors. Its front windows allow it to be used as a little theater itself—we can look in at the various scenes going on there, such as Formator and the footman beating the beaus or Lord Lofty attempting to seduce Amoranda. Froth and Callid can thus also suggest to Amoranda that she sit in it to watch "a Dance of Shepherds and Shepherdesses in the High-way by Moon-light, just at the Summer-house window" (24). The proximity to the highway allows the most dramatic delivery of all the letters: "a Gentleman rid by, and threw in a Glove at the Window; *Amoranda*, at whose foot it fell, took it up, and found there was something in it, which she conceal'd, but was much surpriz'd at the Action" (19). The glove contains a letter whose contents are a declaration of love, but there will be many adventures and many more letters before the mystery of this one and the man who delivers it will be revealed.

Davys's use of cross-dressing can also be linked to the theater and the breeches roles in plays like Wycherley's *The Plain-Dealer* and *The Country Wife* or Farquhar's *The Recruiting Officer*. In fact, however, her use of the device is quite different from that of the playwrights whom she obviously read with affection. There are also significant differences between media that make crossdressing on stage and on the page two very different devices. One aim of the breeches roles in plays—the display of women's legs, a novelty in a theater where actresses themselves were a novelty—was impossible in the nonvisual medium of print. The audience perception also changes. There is no doubt that everyone in the audience knows that Fidelia in *The Plain-Dealer* is a woman dressing as a man in order to attend her lover. Similarly, few of the characters and none of the audience are fooled by Margery Pinchwife's appearance in her brother's clothes in *The Country Wife*; yet the novel reader sees only as much as the author will let her, and is no more knowledgeable than the characters. Thus, while we may have suspicions about some of the little gentlemen in both *The Reform'd Coquet* and *The Accomplish'd Rake*, we do not truly learn their identities until they are revealed to the fictional characters.

More importantly, cross-dressing is connected with transgression in

Davys, in ways it is not in Wycherley, Dryden, or Farquhar. In *The Reform'd Coquet*, Altemira becomes emaciated from grief and dons men's clothes after her femininity has essentially been burned away by her experience of multiple betrayal. Despite the fact that she is essentially blameless, she has been "ruined" by her trust in Lord Lofty, and wears the clothing of a man as a kind of penance until her reputation can be restored. In the same way, Davys's use of male cross-dressing in some ways invokes the role of the stage dame but is fundamentally different in purpose.[46] The episode in which Formator and a footman, both in women's clothes, attack the unsuspecting Callid and Froth is farcical—particularly since Formator is already one level deep in disguise. Amoranda unknowingly enters into the masquerade by promising another kind of exchange of roles: "if you happen to be worsted, we'll invert the Custom, and instead of your delivering the distress'd Damsel, she shall come and rescue you" (27).

The story of Birantha, however, bears little resemblance to stage farce, and is rather linked entirely with trangression. The rape attempt is disturbing, not humorous, because Birantha/Biranthus is far more competent than the fops and appears much more likely to be successful. On the stage two women in full dress fighting with each other might have a slapstick appeal; but without physical presentation to lighten the mood, the threats are quite horrifying: "This minute, by the help of thy own Servant, I will enjoy thee; and then, by the Assistance of my arm, he shall do so too" (59). Biranthus's ending reflects his transgressive behavior. He is put out of his misery by one of the Stranger's servants, a fate no gentleman would expect or desire, and is left lying dead still in the dishonorable woman's clothes. The betrayal by Biranthus and Arentia is surrounded by imagery of the fall of man, which emphasizes the sense of transgression and further distances the incident from the world of the stage dame. Biranthus's several disguises link him with Satan's shape changes in *Paradise Lost*, as does his decision that both his interior and exterior must be hidden. He is "resolved to disguise his Mind as well as his Body" (57), the former with rhetoric, the latter with petticoats. Biranthus and Arentia are called devils by the narrator (58) and Biranthus a viper by Amoranda (59). Arentia becomes the voice of the tempter, as she urges Amoranda to comply since she is being offered the choice of forced marriage or outright rape. But Amoranda, while she shares with Eve the vulnerability that comes from separation from her mentor, recognizes and rejects the rhetoric: "Peace, Screech-Owl, *said* Amoranda, thy Advice carries Poison and Infection in it; the very Sound of thy Words raises Blisters on me, so venomous is the Air of thy Breath" (59).

Finally the serpent claims his own, for Arentia, who brought the tempter into the garden, dies from the bite of an adder.

In addition to the dramatic influence in this novel, there is a connection with the world of fairy tale and enchantment, which is not developed until the end of the novel, with the arrival of Lady Betty, Alanthus's sister. Lady Betty has come looking for her brother, who seems to have disappeared: "I fancy he's got into *Fairy-Land*, he lets me hear from him, but will not tell me how he may hear from me" (82). When Formator is revealed to her as the long-lost brother, she faints: "she not expecting to find her brother there, and seeing him all of a sudden turn'd from an old Man, whom she had never seen before, to a brother whom she knew not where to find, she thought herself in some inchanted Castle, and all about her Fiends and Goblins" (83). Amoranda has a dual role in the fairy tale world. She is the enchantress, keeping Formator/Alanthus captive and transformed ("There, there's the Inchantress, who by a natural Magick, has kept me all this while in chains of love," says Alanthus), and a type of imprisoned heroine herself. As in the fairy tale "Beauty and the Beast," it is necessary for her to love Alanthus as Formator before she can see him in his true shape and thus move towards the "happily ever after" ending. The spell is broken when, being attacked by Biranthus, she calls for Formator, and Alanthus appears.

But that happy ending is itself problematic. Amoranda's character is developed in a careful and some ways conventional manner. Like many heroines, she is an orphan, whose mother dies of grief shortly after her father, leaving her alone and without direction at a critical point in her life. She has been raised in a sheltered place that has prevented her from learning the ways of the world, thus making her even more vulnerable. Davys also establishes the roots of her behavior in her flawed upbringing: her parents encourage her tendency to vanity, "under that mistaken Notion, of everything looking well in a Child" (13). But unlike many heroines in works of this nature, she has, in addition to beauty and charm, a quick wit and some of the best dialogue in any novel of the period: "Pray, my Lord, have done, *said* Amoranda, for I freely own I am not proof against Flattery, there is something so inexpressibly pleasing in it— Lard! you Men———— Come, let us catch some Fish, and divert the Subject. Hang the Fish, *said my Lord*. Aye, said Amoranda, for we shall never drown them" (17). It is unfortunate from a twentieth-century viewpoint that her "reform" directed by Formator/Alanthus through the incidents in the book should involve silencing and fear and be observable in her growing suspicion of other people. The girl who ignores a warning about the lecherous Lord Lofty becomes afraid to allow first a puny man, who turns out to be a woman, and then an obviously respectable lady into her house: "*Amoranda* had a just compassion for the unfortunate Man, and saw his Lady's Journey retarded; but the late Attempts which had been made upon her, made her afraid to desire her to come in" (69). By the end of the novel, the masks and disguises are gone—in Alanthus's words, "we are now barefac'd, and know one another" (83)—but all Amoranda's sparkle has disappeared with them. In the final happy scene she is utterly silent. Her last words, to Alanthus's sister Lady Betty who wants an explanation of her brother's white beard, are "Lord *Alanthus*, and Mr. *Traffick*, are the fittest to give your Lady-ship an account, which I leave them to do, while I beg leave to go and dress me" (83). Having left her story in the male hands of her lover and guardian, she leaves the stage. When she returns and Alanthus makes his formal pro-posal, her answer is not recorded.

Part of the problem lies with the character of Formator, whose tendency to priggishness is obvious in his acceptance of Mr. Traffick's request, to mold the niece into the perfect woman as a preliminary to marrying her. To Amoranda he seems initially a killjoy; and his behavior in leaving her apparently to be raped by Biranthus, with the words, "Well, Madam, I am sorry for you, but I am no Knight Errant, nor do I ride in quest of Adventures; I wish you a good Deliverance, and am your humble servant" (60) in order to teach her a lesson, is not only priggish but outrageous. When Amoranda later challenges him about his desertion, he admits to conflicted feelings: "I was resolved, if pos-sible, to cure you at once of rambling with Strangers: in order to which, I put on an Air of Cruelty, which Heaven knows! my Heart had no hand in" (80). But the reader may feel that his words are too little, too late, especially since he shows a sadistic pleasure in her pain (80-81), and Amoranda in turn seems only too quick to enjoy it (80).

The fairy tale framing allows us to suspend judgement in part on the shortcomings of his character. He is also partially redeemed through the ob-servations of Maria, Amoranda's clever, older relation, for although her sharp eyes penetrate his disguise very quickly, she nonetheless finds him attractive, and takes the beard away with her so that she can ask potential suitors to wear it. Pictures of perfection are not easily drawn and many of us share Jane Austen's reaction to them; accusations of priggishness against Richardson's Sir Charles Grandison demonstrate the difficulty that even the greatest writers have in portraying virtue. But like the problematic nature of Amoranda's reform, the concept of Formator as perfection is bound to be questioned by twentieth-century readers. Did Davys really believe him to be so (would she choose him as a husband?) or was she reflecting the demands of the literary marketplace and her own desire to establish herself as a writer of texts that restore the "purity and empire of love"? And finally, are we supposed to see in the young man who puts on a fake beard and a lisp a spoof on the whole idea of Mentor? He certainly presents a much less dignified appearance than Athena does when, disguised as a wise man, she arrives in Ithaca to aid and strengthen Telemachus, who has to cope with his mother's unruly suitors. Davys's other writing suggests that she has enough familiarity with the classics and gift for satire to make that reading a possibility, or at least a subtext. At this distance an "authoritive" reading is both impossible and undesirable, but the wise reader will keep all these possibilities in mind.

Familiar Letters Betwixt a Gentleman and a Lady (1725)

While *Familiar Letters'* sole publication in Davys's lifetime was in her *Works* in 1725, there is sufficient internal evidence to date it from her days in London between 1716 and 1718. Donald Hal Stefanson (1:xi, xii) believes it was begun in the fall of 1717 and finished in 1718. He bases his date on the announcement of the birth of an heir to the Hanovers in the text (95), which he links with the birth of a son, George William, to Prince George on 2 November 1717, and "the 'Glorious Revolution' of 1689" (xii n. 5). On the other hand, because William III landed on British soil on 5 November 1688, the twenty-eight years of Whiggish rule referred to in the text might direct us to 1716. Furthermore, the child was born on 20 October, not 2 November 1717.[47] Whatever scheme one uses to date the work, it clearly comes from the London years, as the references to Flamsteed and the Reduction of the Light Horse indicate; it may have had several revisions whose chronologies have not been made consistent in the final version. There would also have been good reason not to publish it, for George William was born with a congenital weakness— a polyp in the heart—and the plaudits and good wishes for the birth of the first Hanoverian son born on English soil would have fallen rather flat in the face of the child's death in February, 1718. By the time Davys published the Works, however, William Augustus had been born (1721) in good health, and thus the compliments could flow without apology. In any event, the tributes to the so-called British heir are pure Whig apologetics, since the succession to the throne continued through the eldest son, German-born Frederick, who did not himself rule, but whose son became George III.[48]

Robert Adams Day includes *Familiar Letters* in a list of the four novels that "represent the highest development of letter fiction before Richardson."[49] He draws attention to the realism of the text, Davys's "sense of humor and an eye for physical detail" (187), and the fact that the letters are dated at adequately-spaced intervals to allow them to arrive at their destinations through the post as it then operated (203). While not noting the serious divisions between the two characters, he commends the tone of the letters for emphasizing wit over passion: "A pair of correspondents like Artander and Berina, who manage to be witty instead of passionate while conveying the impression that they entertain tender feelings for one another, is a refreshing innovation . . . The very lack of stress on conventional passion in the letters, combined with their playful tone, makes them perhaps the most realistic letters in early English fiction" (187, 190). Their wit makes Artander and Berina particularly good company; it also suggests that their text is somehow different from the other fictions into whose company they are generally gathered. Ruth Perry describes the typical epistolary process: "Certainly within these novels, characters use their letters to re-live moments they have spent together. Not concerned with narrative progress, they describe to each other the episodes they have lived through together, dwelling on them in loving, repetitious, detail."[50] While this description is an accurate characterization of many epistolary novels, it does not describe *Familiar Letters*, where we know almost nothing about the correspondents' lives before the book and the correspondence begin.

We know that they have been in the city together, that Artander has left for his family seat in the country, and that they have agreed to be platonic friends rather than courting lovers—a situation that suits Berina much better than it does Artander. There is no dwelling on their moments together, although there are some complaints about the separation from Artander, and a reference to previous political disputes. Instead, they discuss politics, argue, describe their friends and visitors, all in the witty manner that has delighted its readers ever since. The anomalies in the book, which set it apart from the epistolary fiction of the day, also lead us to other readings. Lindy Riley's article, "Mary Davys's Satiric Novel *Familiar Letters*: Refusing Patriarchal Inscription of Women" is quite right in describing the novel as satire, although I believe she is wrong in describing it as a reverse conduct book.[51] Its satire is aimed at society rather than at exclusively gender issues. The vignettes interspersed throughout the letters paint a picture of social situations—fashion, miserliness, love, faithlessness, the pains of marriage, and death. They underline how broad a net Davys is casting. That she asserts a female Whig as the voice of reason and stability suggests where she thinks the answers to society's ills may lie.

Davys sets up a relationship between a man, Artander, who is both Tory and mildly misogynistic, and a woman, Berina, who is a Whig and reluctant to accept the restrictions of the past, both for women and for subjects of the crown. It is significant, however, that the conduct advice she rejects is from what she calls "one of those modern Creatures call'd a *Prude* . . . being the oldest Lady in the room" (94).[52] Her reason for rejecting the injunction to cease writing to Artander is not that she feels that women should no longer be restricted in their correspondence. Rather, she rejects the "modern" and prudish idea that all relationships between men and women are sexual and makes a more ancient claim for her ties with Artander, that of friendship. She bases her decision to go on writing within the ancient and classical locus of the demands of friendship: "A Friend is not worth calling so, who dares not run the risque of so trifling a Censure, to maintain so noble a Character."[53] After a brief reference to Artander's letter, in which he describes a woman taken to task by her husband-to-be, she goes on to what will be one of the central concerns of the letters, the Tory/Whig argument, in which each tries to convert the other.

Politics and religion share the same close relationship in this text as they did in eighteenth-century England. Davys's connection with the clergy is a part of her writing persona and demands that she support the established church. Stefanson mentions that she does not seem to be particularly religious and that she makes fun of the pious. But the pious she makes fun of, particularly the woman in *The Merry Wanderer,* are dissenters, and she upholds the centrality of the *Book of Common Prayer,* as her use of November 5 makes very clear. By announcing the birth of the prince on November 5, instead of closer to the actual birth, Davys chose to link the continuity of the Hanoverian succession with two other significant events in English history, both of which confirmed in the minds of the British people that the maintenance of a Protestant monarchy was under providential control. On 5 November 1605, the Gunpowder Plot, more commonly known to us as Guy Fawkes Day, was uncovered; in 1688, William of Orange cannily arranged to land on English soil on the same day. The Gunpowder Plot had been a day of required observance in the church since 1605; after 1688, the commemoration of the Glorious Revolution was added to the service. Thus the choice of the day is deliberate, as is no doubt the day on which the correspondence begins, November 1, All Saints' Day, on which the church recognizes its unity through the ages in the community of those who have gone before.

Berina's support of the Whigs throughout the encounter, which she also describes as providential ("heaven had designed me for what I am" [97]) is a repetition of anti-Catholic and anti-Jacobite rhetoric as it was expressed in the public press and in the sermons of the day. All the parish congregations as well as the Houses of Parliament convened to commemorate the Gunpowder Plot, according to the rubrics of the *Book of Common Prayer*, and to hear a sermon that rehearsed much of what Berina asserts in her letter of November 10. The catalogue of Catholic atrocities, including Mary Tudor's persecution of the Protestants and the Irish Rebellion, was standard fare, aired in pulpits all over the country. Artander's responses—his defense and hagiography of King Charles and his repudiation of Cromwell's people, whom he calls "King Killers"—are equally those of the Tory supporters of the Stuart monarchy and divine right.

Davys, stalwart Whig and Hanoverian as she has demonstrated herself to be in her dedication to *The Northern Heiress*, deliberately presents the Tory as inconsistent, changeable and untrustworthy. For example, Artander offers to subvert the Church's construction of marriage, in which the woman promises to obey her husband: "you shall find I will out-do your own Wishes, by giving myself up so entirely to your will, that your least Inclination shall be a Command" (117). Just as he goes against their pact and speaks to Berina of love, linking it with friendship in a way that she has previously rejected as prudish and modern, so he cannot be depended upon to follow through on his principles and match the absolute monarch on the throne with one in the family. Having used the Bible to support his Tory argument (99), he proposes to subvert scripture in order to win Berina's hand. Finally, he displays his cowardice: rather than reject a marriage proposal outright, he invents a mortal illness to explain his inability to accept it.

Davys is satirizing the political argument by diminishing it to the level of a quarrel between lovers; but she is quite serious in the description of marriage that she gives Berina to articulate:

> . . . the Promise you make of inverting the God of Nature's Rules, and being all Obedience, is no Inducement to me to become a Wife: I shou'd despise a Husband as much as a King who wou'd give up his own Prerogative, or unman himself to make his Wife the Head: We Women are too weak to be trusted with Power, and don't know how to manage it without the Assistance of your Sex, tho' we oftenest shew that Weakness in the Choice of our Advisers. The notion I have always had of Happiness in Marriage, is, where Love causes Obedience on one side, and Compliance on the other, with a View to the Duty incumbent on both: If anything can sweeten the bitter Cup, 'tis that. (117-18)

There is nothing ironic in Berina's tone; what she says is consistent with her support of the King, who was also head of the church. Like her anti-Jacobite rhetoric, it reflects the Church of England view. She sees marriage as a mutual contract between husband and wife, much like the contract worked out between king and people: "When we swear Allegiance to a King, 'tis conditional; as long as he keeps his Oath, we'll keep ours. When God Almighty commanded our Obedience, he commanded his Care and Love" (100). The same *Book of Common Prayer* that mandated the commemoration of November Fifth and obedience in marriage also required that the King be prayed for at every service. Thus Berina's rejection of marriage because it too much resembles slavery is not representative of her rejection of women's obedience in marriage. On the contrary, she accepts the terms of the contract, but chooses not to enter into it herself, and therefore cannot accept marriage with Artander or anyone else. In doing so, she, unlike Artander, remains firm in the principles she espouses at the beginning: "I hate a Yoke that galls for life" (96). She is linked in her views of marriage with early feminists like Mary Astell, although given Astell's high Tory sentiments, it is unlikely that they would have much else in common. It should be remembered that Davys did not remarry, and instead chose to live thirty-four years a widow. Therefore it is probably significant that she places the words of the rational, clear-eyed Whig in the mouth of a woman, and one who fears love because she equates it with blindness and loss of control. The extent to which the satires of politics, gender, and belief, are intertwined in this novel is clear from the dynamics of the correspondence, for Berina is no more able to refrain from talking about politics and current events than Artander is from speaking of love. It is a reversal of gender roles; it also implies that the Whig/woman is more serious-minded than the Tory/man.

Day believes that Berina's laughter at Artander "grows fainter as the correspondence ends" and that "the reader is left to assume that a marriage will take place" (188). But does the reader assume any such thing? Certainly one eighteenth-century reader did so and wrote a couplet on the subject,[54] but that very couplet invokes the god of love who, represented as a blind and blinding boy, is very much a presence in the novel. Artander and the reader beware: we may be misreading the heroine. Many of my students assume that when Artander arrives in town, Berina will welcome him as more than friend, but there are dissenting voices. One student thought that Berina would set him straight and send him away; another thought that she would probably marry him, but it would be, in the student's own words, "a complete waste." Given the necessity for obedience and the expected role of the wife in the eighteenth century, the student saw Berina's brilliance snuffed out by marriage. She had not read *The Reform'd Coquet,* but she seemed to intuit Amoranda's silencing.

Davys's pattern of allusion is particularly strong in this short work; she draws in all the sites of reference that she invokes in the longer works. The density of allusion also marks it as somehow different from the other novels, and helps us to see her strategy. It is probably no coincidence that among the writers to whom she refers most often are Swift, Congreve, and Farqhuar, all of whom went to Trinity College, Dublin, the first two at exactly the same time as her husband. In addition she refers to Cowley, whom Ruth Perry describes as a favorite among the women of the late seventeenth and early eighteenth century, although Davys is more drawn to his love poems than to the celebrations of retired life; retirement was not something she was ever able to enjoy.[55] The many classical references announce Davys's claim to be an Augustan wit, although her status and gender denied her a classical education. Two Scriblerians, Pope and Gay, subscribed to her work, and in *The Accomplish'd Rake*, the Belinda story is a deliberate revisioning of Pope's *Rape of the Lock.* Cervantes' hero Don Quixote and his companion Sancho Panza also appear; they were favorites among the wits of the day, particularly the Scriblerians to whom Swift belonged. It is as if, isolated both socially and geographically (after 1718) from the intellectual center, she is nonetheless attempting to write herself into it, creating in her work an association that mimics the connections of friendship and writing between the members of the Scriblerus group, to which she could never in actuality belong.[56]

The Accomplish'd Rake

Like *The Reform'd Coquet*, the story of Sir John Galliard is one of transformation and education. Here again Davys carefully sets up the protagonist to be a prime candidate for reform. His father dies when he is young, leaving him, like Amoranda, without a strong moral force in the family. While Amoranda's mother is physically weak and dies, leaving her orphaned, Sir John's mother, Lady Galliard, fails him morally. The psychological preparation is very astute in a pre-Freudian age, for Sir John's antipathy towards women, the vice that especially requires reform, begins with sexual betrayal by his mother when he finds her in bed with his footman. At that point he leaves the house in disgust, rejects Cambridge and the groves of academe, and instead takes the high road to London. Given the eighteenth-century pastoral/urban dichotomy, one might say he chooses to go to hell on his own terms. When at the end of the book he returns home, his mother reveals her complicity in his actions by quoting Cowley's "The Welcome." Superficially the poem seems entirely appropriate for welcoming home one's long-lost son, with its prodigal son imagery, but it is in fact the speaker's welcome to his own heart. She admits, through the poet's voice, that her own actions have initiated and participated in the progress of this particular rake.

Once in London, he falls into all the well-known vices: gambling, whoring, dandyism, falling into bad company, and spending his inheritance on luxuries before he gets it, so that he is obliged to go into debt. Particularly he attacks women, even the daughter of Mr. Friendly, his surrogate father and the man who cares most for him in the world. Attractive women are there for him to take, to seduce, to enjoy and to discard, regardless of their social status. He suffers all the usual ills of a man in his situation: he is sick, hungover, infected with venereal disease, cheated and in debt. Eventually he goes too far and rapes Mr. Friendly's daughter. From then on, even he is able to see how everything he does blows up in his face (sometimes literally) and he is forced to go home and face the consequences.

The novel repeats many of the techniques of *The Reform'd Coquet*. Here as well, letters play a significant role in furthering the plot. Of particular note are the double-talking letter from a jealous husband that lures Sir John into a trap (214) and his mother's deceptively breezy note from home which reveals to him that Nancy Friendly has given birth to a child who looks suspiciously like himself (212-13). Davys also uses the breeches role in a similar manner as before, to mark transgressive behavior; the "little gentleman" called Venture-all dresses as a man to solicit Galliard's attention, something she could not do as a woman. Yet while Venture-all appears to accomplish her goal of producing a child for her husband, her approach is transgressive in Davys's world and is not rewarded. She is not able to convince Galliard to impregnate her until she takes off her mask, and he complies only because she is beautiful; the resulting child is a girl, not the son and heir she had hoped for. When she proposes marriage, again assuming the male prerogative with male dress, he refuses her. Catherine Craft-Fairchild, in *Masquerade and Gender*, includes Davys in her consideration of the "Darker Side of Masquerade": while female cross-dressing results in empowerment, it also "seems to be a cautionary tale warning women against the dangers of female desire."[57] For her actions nonetheless confirm the roles that society dictates: "If transvestism is a woman's effort to 'move up the patriarchal hierarchy,' such a move only confirms the terms of that hierarchy and privileges 'man' at the expense of 'woman'" (45).

Among the several seduction plots, the rape of Nancy is a critical point in the reformation of Sir John, since from then on he is beset by misadventure, experiences qualms of conscience, and is eventually led to offer marriage to her. Nancy's experience is thus more important than the seduction stories in *The Reform'd Coquet,* which are designed as a cautionary tales for the heroine. The tone is significantly different from the story of Altemira and Lord Lofty—the rape is more violent, the girl more vocal, and there is no question of her ultimate happiness being fulfilled; as she says, not even marriage will restore her good name entirely, for "the good natured World knows my Fault, and it will be sure to keep it in continual Remembrance" (225). But as in the case of Altemira and Lofty, we may be compelled to question Sir John's fitness as a husband, since nothing in his previous behavior has led us to expect him to be faithful. Indeed, he hastens the marriage lest he lose his nerve, and the author admits that she has set spies upon him to make sure that he behaves. Nonetheless, the story has been resolved in the time-honored way; Sir John has returned home, faced his duties, and been granted an heir to boot.

The parallels with *Clarissa* are obvious and illustrate the way in which Richardson's novel builds upon and transforms the amatory fiction which preceded it; Davys is just as surely a forerunner of Richardson as she is of Fielding. We have a virtuous woman betrayed, raped while drugged, her life apparently ruined, and her family distraught.[58] As in *Clarissa,* this action becomes the turning point in the central male character's life, after which nothing is the same. The differences between the two lie in Clarissa's recognition of the essentially tragic nature of her situation. She refuses to marry Lovelace, although her family and Anna Howe want her to; and instead of pregnancy, a child, and redemption for both by marriage, she and Lovelace die, in very different ways that reflect their roles in the story. Like Clarissa's, Nancy's mind becomes disordered by the event—she says that "Peace is become such a Stranger that if it were to make me a Visit I should look surprised and cry I know you not" (224). Even when she is recovered she does not want to see or meet with other people. Her concern with whether or not her door had been locked on the night of the rape anticipates Clarissa's language, and her revelation of what has happened to her is linked to the unlocked door: "Perhaps (replied the poor Lady in Tears) they broke it open when they could not awake us; but be it how it will, I fear I am ruined past Redemption" (169). Twenty years later when Clarissa describes her own catastrophe, the room is transformed into her own body: "when all my doors are fast, and nothing but the keyhole open, and the key of late put into that, to be where you are, in a manner without opening any of them."[59] Davys's world is still a comic one, however, although in Nancy's pathetic cry that "No one has done this," there is a growing recognition of the potential for tragedy.

The character of Belinda is also crucial to Sir John's reform, because she presents him with the salutary experience of a smart, attractive and articulate woman who does *not* find him irresistible. Of all the women he meets, she is most his equal. Her name is significant, for she clearly represents a reference to, and a reversal of, Pope's character in *The Rape of the Lock*. It is only after the reference to ombre, the game that proves fatal to Belinda's hair in Pope's mock epic, that the narrator rather disingenuously gives her character a name, "the common name of Belinda." However common a name it may be (and it stands out among the other characters" names—Jenny, Nancy, Dolly, Sarah, Betty, Margaret) there is only one other Belinda connected in contemporary minds with a game of ombre. Miss Wary, like Ariel and Pope's Clarissa, attempts to warn Belinda against this particular man, if not against men in general. Having established the connection, however, Davys reworks the entire encounter.

Like her predecessor, Belinda is beautiful, vivacious and involved in London society; unlike her, she is not superficial. Even when Sir John manages to get her alone in a coach on a deserted road, he is not able to carry out in actuality what the Baron does metaphorically—Belinda does not lose a lock of her hair or anything else. What is more, she has paid some attention to Miss Wary: "But how resolved so ever *Belinda* was to reject Miss Wary's Counsel, it put her upon her Guard, and she kept a constant Centry at the Door of her Virtue" (188). The celestial powers of Davys's world do not desert a lady when they see the image of a man in her heart. The greatest change, however, is in her articulate use of rhetoric: where Sir John expects a wrestling match, he gets a debate, and one the lady wins, as she could not have won the physical encounter. She does so by suggesting, in her anger and not realizing how close to the bone she is cutting, that his mother is less than virtuous and that he is a footman's bastard, since he is not behaving in a way that indicates nobility. Sir John is vanquished; he was "never so stung in his life before" (193). The encounter has the extraordinary and unique effect of changing his feeling for her; it "is now turn'd to Esteem and Respect, which shall for the future regulate all my actions towards you . . . I am ashamed of what I have done, and, which is more, you are the first woman who has ever made me so" (194). She is also the first woman with whom he has a relationship that is neither sexual nor predatory; her influence prepares him for the remorse and sense of responsibility which will result in his returning home to acknowledge his son and marry Nancy. Nancy, too, wins him by the force of her rhetoric.

While it is always dangerous to speculate on personal parallels, this novel contains several distinct instances that suggest that although Davys did not put her name on the title page or at the end of the dedication, she nonetheless left her mark in the text. I have already mentioned her reference to Cambridge and the use of the name John, which is given to the hero, as well as to his Cambridge-educated father, Mr. Friendly, the surrogate father, and the "Little Mackroon," the child whose presence in part effects the reform of Sir John's character. Teachwell, the man of "worth and learning," clergyman, scholar, and teacher, who dies tragically young, is surely a tribute to Peter Davys, who was all those things. He is of "sober mild Behaviour, affable to all, but very industrious to bring his new Charge to a Sence of those Rudiments which Neglect had made him a Stranger to" (133-34). This novel also contains most of the few instances in which Davys discusses children in an emotional way. Venture-all's brief note to Belinda announcing the illness of her daughter, "whose Life is hers" (187) is full of pathos: "*MY trembling Hand is now imployed to tell you, my dear Child is extremely ill, and you well know I share the Malady, fly to see it while alive and help to comfort a distracted Sister. P.S. Dear* Bell *make hast*" (186). Sir John's reaction to the first sight of his own son is also notable, for it cracks his supposedly disinterested façade before he overtly accepts the boy as his own: "Sir *John* at Nature's Call, ran to meet it, took it to his Bosom and embraced it with a Father's Love" (224). Perhaps at the end of her life, Davys was finally able to think of her daughters without pain; in this work, we see her tribute to all she has lost.

Notes

1. *The Fugitive. Containing, Several very pleasant PASSAGES, and surprizing AD-VENTURES, observed by a LADY in her Country Ramble; being both Useful and Diverting for Persons of all Ranks* (London, 1705), 2.

2. *The Merry Wanderer,* in *The Works of Mrs. Davys,* 2 vols. (London, 1725), 1:161–62. By "brightest Genius" she of course means Jonathan Swift. Some of the material in this introduction has previously appeared in my article, "Mary Davys: Self-Presentation and the Woman Writer's Reputation in the Early Eighteenth Century," *Women's Writing* 3, no. 1 (1996): 17–33.

3. [Giles Jacob], *The Poetical Register: or, The Lives and Characters of the English Dramatic Poets. With an Account of their Writings* (London, 1719), 286. Ann Arbor: University Microfilms, 1970.

4. *The Merry Wanderer, Works,* 1:221.

5. *Alumni Dublinensis: A Register of all Students, Graduates, Professors and Provosts*

of Trinity College in the University of Dublin (1593–1860), ed. George Burtchall and Thomas Ulick Sadleir (Dublin: Alex. Thom and Co., 1935). All information about Peter Davys's academic career is from this volume.

6. Typescript of the journal of Archbishop Narcissus Marsh (1692–94) in Marsh's Library, Dublin; entry for 26 May 1694. Marsh's son Jeremiah, who wrote a commendatory poem for Congreve's *The Old Batchelor,* was at Trinity at the same time as Peter, another example of the important contacts to be made there. I am grateful to Dr. Muriel McCarthy, Keeper of Marsh's Library, for allowing me to see the journal.

7. *Alumni Dublinensis* lists Mr. Torway as Peter Davys's schoolmaster; John Torway was master of St. Patrick's School, as well as being himself a graduate of Trinity.

8. *Adminiculum Puerile* (Dublin, 1694), dedication [2].

9. *Adminiculum Puerile,* preface, ii. The preface is set entirely in italics; I have reversed them. Marsh's Library in Dublin, which was founded by Archbishop Marsh, has a first edition of the book that is probably the presentation copy. Although the title page is damaged, its verso shows the remnants of an inscription, concluding with what looks like "Davys"; the volume is corrected in several places by the same hand. I am indebted to Rex Cathcart, *"An Help for School Boys": The Choir and Grammar Schools, 1431–1991,* St. Patrick's Cathedral 800 Series, no. 1 (Dublin: St. Patrick's Cathedral, 1991) for revealing to me the existence of Davys's book in Marsh's Library, as well as Davys's petition in the Acts of the Cathedral. It is notable that the book's title quotes Davys's own. I am grateful to the Very Reverend Maurice Stewart, Ph.D., Dean of St. Patrick's, for giving me permission to examine the Acts.

10. Entry for 8 December 1694, *Acts of the Cathedral Chapter House,* vol. 6, St. Patrick's Cathedral, Dublin. The cathedral records are in the Representative Church Body Library in Dublin.

11. "clke" is short for "clerk" or clergyman.

12. It can also be spelled "peety" and is described as "an expression of compassion." *The English Dialect Dictionary* (London: Oxford Univ. Press, 1970).

13. Swift to Benjamin Motte, 4 November 1732, *The Correspondence of Jonathan Swift,* ed. Harold Williams, 5 vols. (Oxford: Clarendon Press, 1965), 4:84.

14. Irvin Ehrenpreis, *Swift: The Man, his Works, and the Age,* vol. 1, *Mr. Swift and his Contemporaries* (Cambridge: Harvard Univ. Press, 1962), 261.

15. Swift to Benjamin Motte, 1 February 1732–33, *Correspondence,* 4:107.

16. Frans De Bruyn, "Mary Davys," *Dictionary of Literary Biography,* 39:131–38.

17. *The Amours of Alcippus and Lucippe. A Novel. Written by a Lady.* (London, 1704), dedication [1]. I am grateful to Frans De Bruyn for sharing his photocopy of the text with me.

18. F. Elrington Ball, *The Judges in Ireland, 1221–1921,* 2 vols. (London: John Murray, 1926), 2:9, 58–59.

19. The original is in italics, which I have reversed. The spelling of Sancho Panza's name is Davys's own.

20. Jonathan Swift, *Journal to Stella,* ed. Harold Williams, 2 vols. (Oxford: Clarendon Press, 1963), 2:625, and note on that page. Williams refers to a possible visit Swift

made to Davys in York in May, 1709, but Irvin Ehrenpreis, Swift's biographer, states categorically that he stayed with his dying mother in Leicester throughout the month of May (*Swift: The Man, his Works and the Age*, vol. 2, *Dr. Swift* (Cambridge: Harvard Univ. Press, 1967), 346. In the letter to Benjamin Motte cited above, Swift mentions that he spent an hour with Davys in her coffeehouse in Cambridge, which would have been after 1718.

21. Melvyn New, introduction to *The Life and Opinions of Tristram Shandy, Gentleman*, ed. Melvyn New and Joan New, 2 vols. (Gainesville: Univ. Presses of Florida, 1978), 2:822.

22. See Donald Hal Stefanson, "The Works of Mary Davys: A Critical Edition," 2 vols. (Ph.D. diss., Univ. of Iowa, 1971), 2:555–650, for a full collation of the two versions.

23. William H. McBurney, *Four Before Richardson: Selected English Novels, 1720–1727* (Lincoln: Univ. of Nebraska Press, 1963), 236 n. 3. I described the book as a piracy in my article, but have since changed my mind in the light of new evidence.

24. *The False Friend: or, the Treacherous Portugueze. A Novel. Interspersed with the Adventures of Lorenzo and Elvira. Carlos and Leonora. Octavio and Clara*, in Stefanson, 2:404.

25. Daniel Defoe, *A Tour through the Whole Island of Great Britain*, ed. Pat Rogers (Hammondsworth, England: Penguin, 1971, 1986), 520.

26. *The London Stage 1660–1800*, 5 parts, pt. 2, vol. 1: 1700–1729, ed. Emmett L. Avery (Carbondale: Southern Illinois Univ. Press, 1960), 400. The total for "tickets" is the amount raised before the performance through sales to the author's friends and patrons. Since there was no advance box office, Davys would have been responsible for soliciting the sales herself, an experience that no doubt came in handy for the subscription sales of her novels. The rest of the money would come from sales on the day of the performance. I am grateful to Brian Corman for this information.

27. *The Northern Heiress: or, the Humours of York* (London, 1716), 5. Italics reversed.

28. See Cheryl Turner, *Living by the Pen: Women Writers in the Eighteenth Century* (London and New York: Routledge, 1992), 104–5, for a discussion of dedications, whose tone she describes as varying "from dignified appeals to the more precious and obsequious declarations." She notes Davys's satire of the convention in her dedication to *The Accomplish'd Rake*, but that book came a decade after this somewhat obsequious essay.

29. Fuller discussion in my article, "Mary Davys: Self-Presentation and the Woman Writer's Reputation."

30. See the biographical note for Davys in *Eighteenth Century Woman Poets: an Oxford Anthology*, ed. Roger Lonsdale (Oxford: Oxford Univ. Press, 1989), 102–3, and *The Poetical Register*.

31. Davys first applied for a license to sell spirits in Cambridge in 1718; see William H. McBurney, "Mary Davys: Forerunner of Fielding," *PMLA* 74 (September 1959): 349 n. 7.

32. Ruth Perry, *The Celebrated Mary Astell: An Early English Feminist* (Chicago: Univ. of Chicago Press, 1986), 293.

33. See the Appendix, below, for a complete text of the original letter and Davys's response.

34. Stefanson, 2:406.

35. The Slingsbys were a Yorkshire family, of Knaresborough and the Red House near Marston Moore. This particular Lady Slingsby was probably married to Henry Slingsby, who is listed as Mr. Henry Slingsby with his wife as subscribers to her works. He became Sir Henry on the death of his father in 1726. Another subscriber was Mrs. Barbara Slingsby, who might have been a daughter or sister; Barbara was a family name. Edward Cokayne, *Complete Baronetage*, 2:430–31.

36. From *The Register of Accounts of the Dean and Chapter*, St. Patrick's Cathedral, Extraordinary Payments, no. 49.

37. McBurney, "Mrs. Mary Davys: Forerunner of Fielding," 349 n. 7.

38. Holy Sepulchre burial register, Cambridgeshire County Record Office, ref. P21/1/2.

39. This is a particularly pitiful amount in the light of Perry's assertion that in 1719 it cost the poor-tax £10.18s.6d to provide a widow with one set of very basic clothes (Perry, *The Celebrated Mary Astell*, 287). Either Davys's clothing was very sparse and in poor condition or Ewin cheated Swift (and this is quite within the range of possibility).

40. Swift to Motte, 4 November 1732, *Correspondence*, 4:84.

41. McBurney, "Mary Davys: Forerunner of Fielding," 355 n. 27. McBurney suggests that Ewin may have been her landlord. The letters, if they ever existed in Ewin's possession, have disappeared.

42. For a good brief discussion of the dilemma women writers faced, see Jeslyn Medoff, "The Daughters of Behn and the Problem of Reputation" in *Women, Writing, History, 1640–1740,* ed. Isobel Grundy and Susan Wiseman (Athens: Univ. of Georgia Press, 1992), 33–54. For book-length treatments see Cheryl Turner, *Living by the Pen*, cited above, and Jane Spencer, *The Rise of the Woman Novelist: From Aphra Behn to Jane Austen* (Oxford and New York: Blackwell, 1986).

43. It is the first book Turner identifies as being published in such a way in her "Catalogue of women's fiction published in book form 1696–1796," although Robert Adams Day notes one earlier example, that of *Letters from a Lady of Quality to a Chevalier,* by Eliza Haywood, published in 1721 with 309 subscribers. Turner, 152–211; Robert Adams Day, *Told in Letters: Epistolary Fiction Before Richardson* (Ann Arbor: Univ. of Michigan Press, 1966), 73–74.

44. *The Northern Heiress*, 6.

45. See Susan Staves, "Fielding and the Comedy of Attempted Rape," *History, Gender and Eighteenth Century Literature*, ed. Beth Fowkes Tobin (Athens: Univ. of Georgia Press, 1994), 86–112.

46. See John Harold Wilson, *All the King's Ladies: Actresses of the Restoration* (Chicago: Univ. of Chicago Press), 73, for the comic uses of the stage dame.

47. Ragnhild Hatton, *George I: Elector and King* (Cambridge: Harvard Univ. Press, 1978), 132, 168.

48. Stefanson thinks that Davys is attempting to win the support of George II, but the compliments are obviously aimed at George I who was still very much alive, both in the teens when the book was written and in 1725 when it was published.

49. *Told in Letters*, 177. The other four are *The Perfidious P* (1702), *Lindamira* (1702), and *Olinda's Adventures* (1693 and later).

50. Ruth Perry, *Women, Letters, and the Novel*. AMS Studies in the Eighteenth Century, no. 4. (New York: AMS Press, 1980), 123.

51. In *Cutting Edges: Postmodern Critical Essays on Eighteenth-Century Satire*, ed. James E. Gill. Tennessee Studies in Literature, vol. 37 (Knoxville: Univ. of Tennessee Press. 1995), 206–21.

52. Pope's poem "Answer to the following question of Mrs Howe: WHAT is PRUD-ERY?" suggests that rejecting a prude's advice is not necessarily a radical subversion of societal norms. The prude is described as "Old and void of all good-nature; / Lean and fretful; would seem wise," and thus located in a group generally marginalized by society—the old and unattractive single women. Alexander Pope, *Poetical Works*, ed. Herbert Davis (London: Oxford Univ. Press, 1966, 1967), 638, lines 6–7.

53. Davys enters an ongoing controversy as to whether or not women were capable of friendship. That Richardson should put disparaging comments about female friendship into the mouth of Lovelace is not surprising; but Clarissa's cousin Morden, a much more positive character, expresses similar convictions (see my article, "Composing Herself: Music, Solitude, and St. Cecilia in *Clarissa*," in *1650–1850: Ideas, Aesthetics, and Inquiries in the Early Modern Era*, vol. 2, ed. Kevin L. Cope [New York: AMS Press, 1995], 185–201).

54. See below, p 242 n. 66.

55. Perry, *The Celebrated Mary Astell*, 126–27.

56. See Patricia Carr Brückmann, *A Manner of Correspondence: A Study of the Scriblerus Club* (Montreal and Kingston: McGill-Queen's Univ. Press, 1997) for a description of the way the relationship among the Scriblerians manifests itself in a pattern of shared allusion.

57. Catherine Craft-Fairchild, *Masquerade and Gender: Disguise and Female Identity in Eighteenth-Century Fictions by Women* (University Park: Pennsylvania State Univ. Press, 1993), 35.

58. See Susan Staves, "British Seduced Maidens," *Eighteenth Century Studies* 14 (1980–81): 109–34, for a discussion of the way in which the seduction of a daughter affects the whole family; Mr. Friendly's decline exactly fits the pattern.

59. Samuel Richardson, *Clarissa, or, the History of a Young Lady*, 4 vols. (London and New York: Dent, Dutton, 1932, 1962), 3:210–11.

CHRONOLOGY OF EVENTS IN THE LIFE OF MARY DAVYS

~

ca. 1674	Mary Davys born, in either Ireland or England; parentage and therefore birth name unknown.
ca. 1692–94	Mary marries the Reverend Peter Davys, in Dublin.
1694	Peter Davys becomes headmaster of St. Patrick's School, Dublin.
1695	Death of Davys's daughter Ann.
1698	Death of Peter Davys.
1699	Birth and death of Davys's daughter Mary.
1700	Davys leaves Ireland for England.
ca. 1700–1704	Davys lives in London; *The False Friend; or the Treacherous Portugueze* written but not published at this time.
1704	Davys publishes *The Amours of Alcippus and Lucippe,* later republished in *The Works of Mrs. Davys* as *The Lady's Tale*; she moves to York.
1705	Davys publishes *The Fugitive.*
1716	Davys's play *The Northern Heiress* performed at Lincoln's-Inn Fields and published; she moves to London.
1716–18	Davys lives in London; her poem, "Answer from the King of Sweden to the British Lady's Epistle," published (no copy has survived); *Familiar Letters Betwixt a Gentleman and a Lady* written but not published at this time; *The Self-Rival* written, but not published or performed.
1718	Davys moves to Cambridge and opens a coffeehouse.
1724	Davys publishes *The Reform'd Coquet, or Memoirs of Amoranda,* by subscription.
1725	The publication of *The Works of Mrs. Davys* in two volumes, by subscription. In these volumes Davys

presented most of her work up to this point, much of it revised. *The Fugitive* becomes *The Merry Wanderer; The False Friend, or the Treacherous Portugueze* becomes *The Cousins;* and *The Memoirs of Alcippus and Lucippe* becomes *The Lady's Tale. Familiar Letters Betwixt a Gentleman and a Lady, The Self Rival* (with annotation "As it should have been performed at Drury-Lane"), and "The Modern Poet" receive their only publication in her lifetime. *The Reform'd Coquet* and *The Northern Heiress* are also included.

1727   Publication of *The Accomplish'd Rake.*

1731   Davys is satirized in *The Grub-Street Journal* and responds.

1732   Davys publishes *The False Friend; or the Treacherous Portugueze*, probably an earlier version of *The Cousins*; the dedication to Lady Slingsby, and the preface (an abridgment of the preface to *The Works of Mrs. Davys*) are prepared for this edition.

Mary Davys dies in Cambridge and is buried on July 3 at the Church of the Holy Sepulchre, also known as the Round Church.

NOTE ON THE TEXTS

~

This present edition is built on the work of Mary Davys's previous twenti-eth-century editors, William H. McBurney, Robert Adams Day and Donald Hal Stefanson. Their pioneering scholarship, in both textual and back-ground information, has provided me with an invaluable foundation from which to begin my project.

Of the three novels in this edition, only *The Reform'd Coquet* received more than one printing in Davys's lifetime. I have chosen to use the first (1724) edition of *Coquet* as the copy text, following Stefanson's assertion that the printer regularized the spelling and punctuation when it was published in *The Works of Mrs. Davys* (1725). In all three novels I have silently corrected obvious typo-graphical errors (and I have incorporated corrections of the errata noted in *The Reform'd Coquet)*, but I have not modernized or regularized spelling, punctua-tion, or printer's conventions, since that would result in a text that is not an authentic representation of the works as they were published in Davys's lifetime. Thus the reader will note variants (my self, my-self, myself), apparently arbi-trary paragraph structure and capitalization, and comma use that does not con-form to our usage. Proper nouns are italicized, which requires that they be pre-sented in nonitalicized form in passages that are themselves in italics. Direct discourse was not indicated by quotation marks, and I have not added them; instead, I have left Davys's speech tags in all their variety. In *The Reform'd Coquet* the speech tags are generally distinguished from the rest of the text by italiciza-tion; in *The Accomplish'd Rake* they are either not distinguished at all or sur-rounded by square brackets. I have changed the square brackets to parentheses (one of the few modernizations I have made), because I felt that modern conven-tion would result in an instinctive reading of square brackets as editorial interven-tion. In this and every case in which I have made editorial changes, I have sought to clarify, not modernize. I have thus replaced the long "s" with the modern equiva-lent; I have not, however, emended the use of apostrophes in plurals.

THE REFORM'D COQUET[1]

To The

LADIES

OF

Great Britain

At a time when the Town is so full of Masquerades, Opera's, New Plays, Conjurers, Monsters, and feign'd Devils; how can I, Ladies, expect you to throw away an hour upon the less agreeable Amusements my Coquet can give you? But she who has assurance to write, has certainly the vanity to be read: All Authors see a Beauty in their own Compositions, which perhaps nobody else can find; as Mothers think their own Offspring amiable, how deficient soever Nature has been to them. But whatever my Faults may be, my Design is good, and hope you *British* Ladies will accordingly encourage it.

If I have here touch'd a young Lady's Vanity and Levity, it was to show her how amiable she is without those Blots, which certainly stain the Mind, and stamp Deformity where the greatest Beauties would shine, were they banish'd. I believe every body will join with my Opinion, that the *English* Ladies are the most accomplish'd in the World, that, generally speaking, their Behaviour is so exact, that even Envy itself cannot strike at their Conduct: but even you yourselves must own, there are some few among you of a different stamp, who change their Gold for Dross, and barter the highest Perfections for the Lowest Weaknesses. Would but this latter sort endeavour as much to act like Angels, as they do to look like them, the Men, instead of Reproaches, would heap them with praises, and their cold Indifference would be turn'd to Idolatry. But who can forsake a Fault, till they are convinc'd they are guilty? Vanity is a lurking subtile Thief, that works itself insensibly into our Bosoms, and while we declare our dislike to it, know not 'tis so near us; every body being (as a witty Gentleman has somewhere said) provided with a Racket to strike it from themselves.[2]

The Heroine of the following Sheets will tell you the Advantages of a kind friendly Admonition, and when the little Lightnesses of her Mind were removed, she became worthy of imitation. One little word of Advice, Ladies, and I have done: When you grow weary of Flattery, and begin to listen to matrimonial Addresses, chuse a Man with fine Sense, as well as a fine Wigg, and let him have some Merit, as well as much Embroidery: This will make

Coxcombs give ground, and Men of Sense will equally admire your Conduct with your Beauty. I am

> LADIES,
> > *Your most Devoted,*
> > *And most Obedient*
> > *Humble Servant,*
> > > MA: DAVYS

The

PREFACE

IDLENESS has so long been an Excuse for Writing, that I am almost ashamed
to tell the World it was that, and that only, which produced the following
Sheets. Few People are so inconsiderable in Life, but they may at some time do
good; and tho I must own my Purse is (by a thousand Misfortunes)³ grown
wholly useless to every body, my Pen is at the service of the Publick, and if it
can but make some impression upon the young unthinking Minds of some of
my own Sex, I shall bless my Labour, and reap an unspeakable Satisfaction:
but as I have address'd them in another place, I shall say no more of them here.

I come now to the worthy Gentlemen of *Cambridge,* from whom I have
received so many Marks of Favour on a thousand Occasions, that my Gratitude is highly concern'd how to make a due acknowledgment; and I own their
civil, generous, good-natur'd Behaviour towards me, is the only thing I have
now left worth boasting of. When I had written a Sheet or two of this Novel,
I communicated my Design to a couple of young Gentlemen, whom I knew
to be Men of Taste, and both my Friends; they approved of what I had done,
advised me to proceed, then print it by Subscription: into which Proposal
many of the Gentlemen enter'd, among whom were a good number of both
the grave and the young Clergy, who the World will easily believe had a greater
view to Charity than Novelty; and it was not to the Book, but the Author,
they subscribed. They knew her to be a Relict of one of their Brotherhood,⁴
and one, who (unless Poverty be a Sin) never did anything to disgrace the
Gown; and for those Reasons encouraged all her Undertakings.

But as this Book was writ at *Cambridge,* I am a little apprehensive some
may imagine the Gentlemen had a hand in it. It would be very hard, if their
Humanity to me, should bring an imputation upon themselves so greatly below
their Merit, which I can by no means consent to; and do therefore assure the
World, I am not acquainted with one Member of that worthy and learned Society of Men, whose Pens are not employ'd in things infinitely above any thing I
can pretend to be the Author of; So that I only am accountable for every Fault of

my Book; and if it has any Beauties, I claim the Merit of them too. Tho I cannot but say, I did once apply myself to a young Genius for a Preface, which he seem'd to decline, and I soon consider'd the Brightness of his Pen would only eclipse the glimmering Light of my own; so call'd back my Request, and resolv'd to entertain my Readers with a Pattern, in the Preface, of the same *Stuff* the following Sheets are made of; which will, I hope, give them an hour or two of agreeable Amusement. And if they will but be as kind to me, as they have been to many before, they will over-look one little Improbability, because such are to be met with in most Novels, many Plays, and even in Travels themselves. There is a little Story in the beginning of the Book, of the Courtship of a Boy, which the Reader may perhaps think very trifling: but as it is not two Pages long, I beg he will pass it by; and my Excuse for it, is, I could not so well show the early Coquetry of the Lady without it.

A

LIST

OF THE

SUBSCRIBERS NAMES

Her Grace the Dutchess of *Rutland.*
His Grace the Duke of *Richmond.*
Her Grace the Dutchess of *Richmond.*
The Right Honourable the Countess of *Albemarle.*
The Right Honourable the Lady *Betty Monkton.*
The Right Honourable the Lady *Katharine Mannors.*
The Right Honourable the Lady *Frances Mannors.*
The Honourable the Lady *Wentworth.*
Mrs. *Wentworth.*
The Honourable Colonel *Moyser.*
The Honourable Colonel *Gee.*
The Honourable Sir *George Saville* Bart.
The Honourable Lady *Saville.*
Mrs. *Pratt.*
Mrs. *Pendergrass.*
The Hon. *Sir William Ramsden* Bart.
The Honourable the Lady *Cedrington.*
Hugh Bethell of *Swinden* Esq;
Mrs. *Bridget Bethell.*
Mrs. *Staggins.*
The Reverend Dr. *Burnet.*[5]
The Reverend Mr. *Key.*
Hugh Bethell of *Rise* Esq;
Mich. Newton Esq;
Mrs. *Mar. Blount.*[6]
Mr. *Festing.*
Mr. *Carbonelli.*
Honourable Colonel Povey.
Alexander Pope Esq;

Mr. *Gay.*[7]
Mr. *Armstrong.*
John Green Esq;
John Wright Esq;
Henry Slingsby Esq;
Mrs. *Slingsby.*
Lady *Gere.*
Lady *Wright.*
Mrs. *Glover.*
Mrs. *Nutting.*
Mrs. *Buttler.*
Mrs. *Martin.*
Mrs. *Whithead.*
Mrs. *Warren.*
Mrs. *Grombold.*
Miss Grombold.
Mrs. *Taylor.*
Henry Husie Esq;
Richard Trevor Esq;

Edward Wills Esq;
Lady *Gore.*
Lady *Hepton.*
Mr. *Philips.*
John Needham, Esq;
Sir *John Stead.*
Mrs. *Ormsby.*
Mrs. *Neal.*
John Lethieullier Esq;
Mr. *Higgins.*
Mr. *Howard.*
Mr. *Tew.*
Mr. *Calton.*
Mr. *Hull.*
Mr. *Thirlby.*
Mr. *Whitaker.*
Mr. *Harrison.*
Mr. *Frohake.*
Mr. *Bell.*
Mr. *Crownfield.*
Mr. *Arnold.*
Mr. *Bradgate.*
Mr. *Forster.*
Mr. *Taylor.*
Mr. *Mildmay.*
Mr. *Clypwell.*
Mr. *Holms.*
Mr. *Wyke.*
Mr. *Basset.*
Mr. *Trollope.*
Mr. *Lacy.*
Mr. *Bowman.*
Mr. *Atherton.*
——————*Wheeler* Esq;
——————*Loraine* Esq;
Mr. *Charles Loraine.*
Mr. *Byam.*
Mr. *Barley.*

Mr. *Price.*
Mr. *Rawstrone.*
Mr. *Smith.*
Mr. *Dennit.*
Mr. *Taylor.*
Mr. *Key.*
Mr. *Gibbons.*
Mr. *Davis.*
Mr. *Newton.*
Mr. *Richardson.*
Mr. *Bott.*
Mr. *Clarke.*
Mr. *Sandys.*
The Honourable Sir *Jer. Sambruge* Bar.
Mr. *Fuller.*
Mr. *Percival.*
Mr. *Baker.*
Mr. *Fenton.*
Mr. *Mires.*
Mr. *Martin.*
Mr. *Holmes.*
Mr. *Snow.*
Mr. *Morgan.*
Mr. *Seward.*
Mr. *Hawkins.*
Dr. *Anonymous.*
Mr. *Key.*
Mr. *Stillingfleet.*
Mr. *Parne.*
Mr. *Bishop.*
Mr. *Malotte.*
Mr. *Heyrick.*
Dr. *Anonymous.*
Mr. *Ingliss.*
Mr. *King.*
Mr. *Farr.*
Mr. *Dobson.*
Mr. *Mompesson.*

Mr. *Pringle.*
Mr. *Jackson.*
Mr. *Smith.*
Mr. *Wells.*
Mr. *Humphreys.*
Mr. *Stevens.*
Mr. *Aylmore.*
Mr. *Turner.*
Mr. *Markland.*
Mr. *Lambert.*
Mr. *Clarkson.*
Mr. *Stevenson.*
Mr. *Atquins.*
Mr. *Tempest.*
Mr. *Bate.*
Mr. *Aspine.*
Mr. *Whalley.*
Mr. *Valavine.*
Mr. *Gee.*
Mr. *Barnes.*

Mr. *Anonymous.*
Mr. *Castle.*
Mr. *Addington.*
Mr. *Buttler.*
Mr. *Lucas.*
Mr. *Pelham.*
Mr. *Shottow.*
Mr. *Selly.*
Mr. *Henshaw.*
Mr. *Ray.*
Mr. *Bateman.*
Mr. *Dove.*
Mr. *Thoresby.*
Mr. *Haworth.*
Mr. *Rant.*
Mr. *Urlin.*
Mr. *Nutting.*
Mr. *Watson.*
Mr. *Beckwith.*
Mr. *Bathersby.*

Reform'd Coquet;

or, the

MEMOIRS

OF

AMORANDA

The most avaritious Scribbler that ever took Pen in hand, had doubtless a view to his Reputation, separate from his Interest. I confess myself a Lover of Money, and yet have the greatest Inclination to please my Readers; but how to do so, is a very critical Point, and what more correct Pens than mine have miss'd of. If we divide Mankind into several Classes, we shall meet with as many different Tempers as Faces, only we have the Art of disguising one better than t'other.

The Pedant despises the most elaborate Undertaking, unless it appears in the World with *Greek* and *Latin* Motto's; a Man that would please him, must pore an Age over musty Authors, till his Brains are as worm-eaten as the Books he reads, and his Conversation fit for nobody else: I have neither Inclination nor Learning enough to hope for his favour, so lay him aside.

The next I can never hope to please, is the Dogmatical Puppy, who, like a Hedgehog, is wrapt up in his own Opinions, and despises all who want Extravagancies to enter 'em; but a Man must have a superior share of Pride, who can expect his single Opinions should byass[8] the rest of the Creation: I leave him therefore to pine at his Disappointment, and call upon the busy part of our Species, who are so very intent upon getting Money, that they lose the pleasure of spending it. I confess, the *Royal-Exchange, South-sea*[9] with a P-x, the *Exchange-Alley*, and all Trade in general, are so foreign to my Understanding, that I leave them where I found them, and cast an oblique Glance at the Philosopher, who I take to be a good clever Fellow in his way. But as I am again forced to betray my Ignorance, I know so little of him, that I leave him to his, *No Pleasure, no Pain;*[10] and a thousand other Chimera's, while I face about to the Man of Gallantry. Love is a very common Topick, but 'tis withal a very copious one; and would the Poets, Printers and Booksellers but speak truth of it, they would own themselves more obliged to that one Subject for their Bread, than all the rest put together. 'Tis there I fix, and the following Sheets are to be fill'd with the Tale of a fine young Lady.

A certain Knight who lives pretty deep in the Country, had a Father whose vicious Inclinations led him into a thousand Extravagancies; whoring and drinking took up a great part of his time, and the rest was spent in gaming, which was his darling Diversion. We have had so many melancholy Influences of the sad Effects of this Vice, that I dare say the Reader will not be surprized if I tell him, this Gentleman in a little time died a Beggar by it, and left the young Baronet no more than his Honour to live upon. Some Years before the old Gentleman died, the young one married a Lady clandestinely,[11] whose Fortune was then all their Support, and by whom he had one Daughter, now seven Years of Age, and for whom I will borrow the name of Amoranda. Sir John S——d,[12] her Father, had a younger Brother bred an East-India Merchant; his Success abroad was so very great, that it qualified him for showing large Bounty at home; and as he thought nothing so despicable as Honour and Poverty join'd, he was resolved to set his elder Brother above Contempt, and make him shine like the Head of so ancient a Family: in order to which, he first redeem'd all the Land his Father had mortgaged for Money to fling away, then re-purchased all he had sold, till at last he had settled the Knight in a quiet possession of that Estate, which had for many Ages devolved from Father to Son; but, as he was exceeding fond of his young Niece, settled the whole upon her, in case her Father died without a Son, not making the least reserve in favour of himself. When he had, with the highest Satisfaction, done a Deed of so much Goodness and Generosity, he left the Family he had just made happy, and went again in pursuit of his Merchandize; in the mean time, Amoranda, who was a little Angel for Beauty, was extremely admir'd, no less for that, than for a sprightly Wit, which her younger Years promised. If we trace Human Nature thro all the Stages of Life, we shall find those Dawnings of the Passions in Children, which riper Years bring to the highest perfection; and a Child, rightly consider'd, may give us a very great guess at his Temper, when he comes to be a Man. An Instance of this we have in the young Creature already named, who had, 'tis true, all the Beauties of her Sex, but then she had the Seeds of their Pride and Vanity too. Amoranda was no sooner told she was pretty, than she believed it, and listned with pleasure to those who said her Eyes were Diamonds, her Cheeks Roses, her Skin Alabaster, her Lips Coral, and her Hair Cupid's Nets, which were to ensnare and catch all Mankind.

This made an early impression upon the Mind of young *Amoranda*, and she now began to think as much in favour of herself as it was possible for others to do. Her Babies[13] were thrown by with scorn, and the time that should have dress'd them, was spent at the Looking-Glass dressing herself, admiring all those Graces with which she was now sure she was surrounded; her Father's Visiters were no longer to use her with their wonted freedom, but she told them with an Air of growing Pride, she expected to be call'd Madam as well as her Mamma, and she was not so much a Child as they would make her. Whilst she was in the midst of her grand Airs, a little Boy came in, who used to call her Wife, and running to her, got his little Arms about her Neck to kiss her, as he used to do. But *Amoranda*, who was now resolved to be a Woman, thrust him from her with the utmost Contempt, and bid him see her no more. The poor Boy, not used to such Behaviour, stood staring at her, in great surprize at the occasion of all this; but being a Boy of some Spirit, tho not capable of a real Passion, he said, Madam, you need not be so proud, I have got a prettier Miss than you for my Wife, and I love her better than I do you by half, and I will never come near you again. Saying thus, away he went to make his Complaints at home. When *Amoranda* saw him gone, and with a design to go to another, the whole Woman gather'd in her Soul, and she fell into a violent Passion of Tears; the thoughts of having another prefer'd to her, was intolerable, and seeing the Boy go off with Insults, gave her a very sensible Mortification: Resentment flash'd in her Eyes, and her Breast heaved with such Agonies, as the whole Sex feel, when they meet with Contempt from a slighting Lover. Her Mother, who was as full of Mirth as she was of Grief upon this cutting occasion, said to her, Why, *Amoranda*, did you send away your Spouse, if you are angry now he is gone? My Spouse! *cry'd the young Incensed*, I scorn the little unmannerly Brat, he shall never be my Spouse: What, tell me to my face he liked another better! But I know who the saucy Jackanapes[14] meant, and if ever she comes here again, I'll send her to him: I hate them both, and so I'll tell them; who can bear such an Affront? I shall never be easy till I am revenged of them. Here was Pride, Jealousy, and Revenge, kindled in the Breast of a Child; and as Princes love the Treason, tho they hate the Traitor, so Women like the Love, tho they despise the Lover.

> *Poor* Amoranda, *what will be thy Fate?*
> *So soon to like the Love, the Lover hate.*[15]

Her Behaviour, however, gave good diversion to her Father and Mother; and under that mistaken Notion, of every thing looking well in a Child, she was encouraged in many things, which she herself would probably have been ashamed of, had there been time given for Reason to play its part, and help to guard her Actions: Most Mothers are fond of seeing their Children Women before their time, but forget it makes themselves look old.

Vanity, which is most Womens Foible, might be overloook'd, or wink'd at, would it live alone; but alack! it loves a long Train of Attendants, and calls in Pride, Affectation, Ill-nature, and often Ill-manners too for its Companions. A Woman thus surrounded, should be avoided with the same care a Man would shun his evil Genius; 'tis marrying a Complication of the worst Diseases.

I remember when I was a Child, a Gentleman came to make love to a Sister[16] I had, who was a good clever Girl both in Sense and Person; but as Women are never perfect, she had her Failings among the rest, and mightily affected a scornful Toss with her head, which was so disagreeable, after a few Visits, to her Lover, that he came no more. My Father, a little surprized at his going so abruptly off, and being loth to lose so advantageous a Match for his Daughter, went to enquire after his Reasons, which, when he heard, he told the Gentleman he thought them very trifling. No, Sir, *said he*, a Woman who will throw up her Head at me before Marriage will (ten to one) break mine after it. I know, *continued he*, if a Woman be dishonourably attack'd, her Scorn is needful, her Pride requisite; but a Man of equal or superior Fortune, who has no Views but her's and his own Happiness, ought to be received with another Air; and if ever I marry, I will have at least a prospect of good usage. Thus the foolish Girl lost a much better Husband than she got, by thinking her Pride added to her Charms, and gave new Graces to her Behaviour.

Amoranda was now in the ninth Year of her Age, six more I leap over, and take her again in her fifteenth; during which time her Father died, and left her a finish'd Beauty and Coquet; I might here have said Fortune too, being sole Heiress to three thousand Pounds a Year: her Mother and Uncle were left her Guardians; but the former being a Lady of an infirm Constitution, the Grief of losing a tender good Husband made such considerable additions to her former weakness, that in less than half a Year, she died too, and left poor *Amoranda* open to all the Temptations that Youth, Beauty, Fortune, and flashy Wit could expose her to. Her Uncle but just come from the *Indies*, and whose Business would not admit of his going into the Country, had once a mind to send for her up to Town, but he consider'd *London* a place of too many Temptations; and since she was willing to stay in the Country, he was resolv'd she should, but desir'd she would let him send down one to supply his place, and take care of her in his stead. During this Interregnum,[17] *Amoranda* was address'd by all the Country round, from the old Justice to the young Rake; and, I dare say, my Reader will believe she was a Toast in every House for ten Parishes round. The very Excrescencies of her Temper, were now become Graces, and it was not possible for one single Fault to be joined to three thousand Pounds a Year; her Levee was daily crowded with almost all sorts, and (she pleased to be admir'd) tho' she lov'd none, was complaisant to all. Among a considerable number of Admirers, Lord *Lofty* was one, who had so great a value for his dear self, that he could hardly be persuaded any Woman had Merit enough to deserve the smallest of his Favours, much less the great one of being his Partner for life; however, he thought *Amoranda* a pretty Play-thing, a young unthinking Girl, left at present to her own Conduct, and if he could draw her in, to give him an hour's Diversion now and then, he should meet her with some Pleasure; if not (tho' he did not despair) he was her humble Servant, and had no farther design upon her. One day he came to see her so early in the Morning, that she was hardly up when he came; but sent down word, as soon as she could get herself into a dress fit to appear before his Lordship, she would wait upon him. While *Amoranda* was dressing, my Lord took a walk into the Garden, either to amuse himself with variety of pleasing Objects, or to meditate afresh upon his present Undertaking. He walk'd with the utmost Pleasure among the Jessamine[18] and Orange-Trees; at the end of the walk was a Seat, over which was a fine painted Roof representing the Rape of *Helen*, on which he gaz'd with some Admiration, and could not forbear comparing *Amoranda* to her, nor thinking the whole Scene unlike his own design.[19] After he had view'd this fine Piece, he happen'd to cast his Eye a little forward, and saw a Paper lie upon the Ground, which he went and took up, finding it directed to *Amoranda* in a Woman's hand: he was not long persuading himself to open it, by which you will believe my Lord a Man of none of the strictest Honour; however, he read it and found it thus:

> *If the advice of a Stranger can be of any import, I beg of you, good Madam, to take care of Lord* Lofty, *who carries nothing but Ruin to our whole Sex: believe me, who have too fatally experienced him, his whole Design upon you is to make you miserable; and if you fall into his Snare after so fair a Warning, nobody but yourself deserves the blame.*

This Letter put my Lord into a very thoughtful posture, and he now began to fear his hopes of *Amoranda* were at an end; the Hand he knew, and acknowledged the Person who writ it a much better Painter than him he had been so lately admiring, since she had drawn him so much to the life. My Lord was a Man of the best assurance in *England*, yet he began to fear his Courage would not hold out to face *Amoranda* any more, and was just resolving to leave the Garden, and go home, when he saw her coming towards him; he shuffled the Letter into his Pocket, and with a Countenance half confounded, went to meet her. Good-morrow, my Lord, (*said* Amoranda, *with the gayest Air;*) how are we to construe those early Sallies of yours? Not to Love, I suppose; because Mr. *Congreve* tells us, *A contemplative Lover can no more leave his Bed in a morning, than he can sleep in it.*[20]

Madam, *said my Lord*, (*who began to gather Courage from her Behaviour*) a contemplative Lover has some respite from his Pain, but a restless one has none; I hope you will believe I am one of this last sort, and am come to look for my Repose where I lost it. Fye! Fye! My Lord, how you talk, *said* Amoranda, you're a Man of so much Gallantry, there's no dealing with you. Come, *said she*, take my Hand, and let us go to the Fish-Ponds, I have order'd the Tackling to be carry'd down before us, we will try if we can find any Sport this Morning. Madam, *said my Lord*, every thing is Diversion in your Company, and if you can captivate your own Species, your Ponds will be in a little time quite ruin'd.

O! my Lord, *said* Amoranda, if I catch too many of either sort, I have a very good way of disposing of them.

After what manner, *said my Lord*. Why, *said she*, one I throw into the water again, and t'other may consume in his own Flames. Madam, *said my Lord*, he's a cruel Deity, who is pleas'd with nothing but the Life of his Worshippers.

N—ay, *said* Amoranda, so he is; I own I pity the poor Fellows sometimes: but you know, my Lord, we can't love every body, they should e'en keep out of harm's way.

By this time they were come to the Pond, and the Anglers fell to work; but before they had catch'd anything to speak of, a Footman came to tell his Lady, Mr. *Pert* was come to wait upon her. Fly, *said* Amoranda, and tell him I come. My Lord, *said she*, you will please to pardon me a moment, I'll go and try if I can engage Mr. *Pert* in our Diversion, and bring him with me. Without staying for my Lord's Answer, she ran towards the House, and left him with the Angle in his hand: he had now a little time to consider the Lady, but what to make of her, he knew not; he took the Letter out of his Pocket, and read it over again, then said to himself,—'Twas lost Labor in the Lady who writ it, for *Amoranda* takes no notice of it, her Behaviour is open and free as ever, I shall certainly meet with a critical Minute, and then adieu to Gallantry on this side the Country. Before he had ended his Soliloquies, he saw the Lady coming back alone, and went to meet her; What, Madam, *said he*, are you without an Attendant? Yes, my Lord, *said* Amoranda, I could not persuade Mr. *Pert* to venture this way, he said the Sun always put out the Stars, and he should give but a glimmering Light where there was such a superior Brightness.

Madam, *said my Lord,* I once thought Mr. *Pert* so full of himself, that he scorn'd Improvement; but I find your Ladyship's Conversation has made a considerable Alteration.

Pray, my Lord, have done, *said* Amoranda, for I freely own I am not proof against Flattery, there is something so inexpressibly pleasing in it——— Lard![21] you Men———Come, let us catch some Fish, and divert the Subject. Hang the Fish, *said my Lord*. Aye, *said* Amoranda, for we shall never drown them: But how comes it, my Lord, *said she*, you are so indifferent to such a fine Diversion? Because, Madam, *said he,* I have a much finer in view; 'tis to affront the Heart I am so eager in pursuit of, to give way to any other Diversion. Come, Madam, *said he*, let us leave this Drudgery to your Servants, and take a Walk in yonder pleasant Grove, where I may have an Opportunity of laying open to you a Heart ready to burst with Love. Here he took her Hand, and led her towards the Garden, when *Jenny, Amoranda's* Maid, met them, and told my Lord, a Servant was just come to tell his Lordship his Brother was newly alighted. Never any News was more unwelcome than this was to my Lord, who made himself now sure of *Amoranda's* consent to anything he should request of her, and he thought a very few Minutes would have compleated his Happiness. He stamped and cursed his Disappointment, and, with Vexation and Madness in his Looks, took his leave for that time. He was no sooner gone than *Jenny* (who was all poor *Amoranda* had now to advise her) began to talk to her Lady about Lord *Lofty*. I am no less concerned than surprized, Madam, *said she*, to see you so free in this Gentleman's Company, after the Account you have had of his Temper in general, and his particular Behaviour to the poor Lady who writ to you. I wish it were in my power, *said she*, to prevail with you to see him no more; I read his Designs in his Looks, and am satisfy'd his Intentions are dishonourable. At this, *Amoranda* burst out a laughing. The poor Lady that writ to me, *said she, in a jeering Tone*, one of his Tenant's Daughters, I suppose, who he, for a Night's Lodging, promised Marriage, perhaps, and the Creature thinks, because he made a Fool of her, he has and must do so by all the Sex: no, no, *Jenny*, some People, when they are gauled themselves, would feign make other Folks smart too; but I love to disappoint their Spite, and will, for that reason, take no notice on't.

Madam, *said* Jenny, that Letter looks as if it came from a finer hand than you seem to think it does; look it over once more, and— Aye, *said* Amoranda, *feeling in her Pocket*, but where is it? I had it last Night in the Orange-Walk, and have certainly dropt it there, let us go and look for it. No, Madam, *said* Jenny, we need not, if you dropt it there, my Lord has found it, for there he walked all the while you were dressing. That can never be, *said* Amoranda, he is a Man of too much Honour to open a Letter directed to me; I am sure, *said she*, had he found it, I should have had it again, therefore go and look for't. While *Jenny* was gone in quest of the Letter, *Amoranda* began to recollect herself, and remembered she saw my Lord at a distance putting a Paper into his Pocket, and when she came nearer to him, look'd confus'd; however, she had said so much already in vindication of his Honour, that she was resolved to conceal her own thoughts, and *Jenny* returning without it, they both went in.

As soon as Dinner was over, *Amoranda's* Visiters began to flock about her, while she, pleas'd with a Croud of Admirers, receiv'd them all with equal Complacency, and Singing, Dancing, Music and Flattery took up her whole time. Her Heart was like a great Inn, which finds room for all that come, and she could not but think it very foolish to be beloved by five hundred, and return it only to one; she found herself inclin'd to please them all, and took no small pains to do so: yet had she been brought to the Test, and forced to chuse a Husband among them, her particular Inclinations were so very weak that she would have been at the greatest loss where to fix, tho' her general Favours gave every Man hopes, because she artfully hid from one what she bestow'd upon another. Among the rest, she had two Lovers, who would very fain have brought her to a Conclusion; I shall call one *Froth*, and t'other *Callid*. The latter, tho' he had no cause to despair, grew very weary of Expectation, and was resolved to have recourse to other measures: but *Froth* push'd his Fortune forward, and, from an inward Opinion of his own Merit, did not doubt but he should bring *Amoranda* to crown his wishes, and in a few days bestow herself upon him for Life. One day *Amoranda* and *Froth* were set in a beautiful Summer-house in the Garden, which had Sashes to the High-way, and here they sat when *Froth* thus accosted her. Madam, *said he,* it is now six weeks since I first broke my Mind to you; and if I am six more in suspence it will break my Heart too. I am not unsensible of, or unthankful for the Favours you have shown me, I know I am the happy Man who stands fairest in your Esteem, and since your Eyes declare your Heart is won, why do you retard my Joys? You're a very pretty Fellow, *said* Amoranda *laughing*, to make yourself so sure of a Body! How can you believe I shall be so silly, as to think of marrying while I have so fresh a Bloom upon my Cheeks? No, Mr. *Froth, said she,* it will be time enough for me to be a Wife, when that dreadful thing Decay gets hold of me; but if it will be any satisfaction to you, I don't care if I tell you, I have not a less Value for you than for the rest of my Lovers. Madam, *said he*, my Extasy would have been more compleat, had you said a greater. Oh, *said she*, that's enough for once, but I don't bid you despair. As she spoke these words, she turn'd her Head, and saw *Callid* coming, and having a mind for a little variety of Courtship, desired *Froth* to go and pull a few Nectarines; which he readily did, laughing in his sleeve at poor *Callid*, who he was very sure wou'd meet with a cold Reception. As soon as *Callid* had reach'd *Amoranda*, he began with a very submissive Air, and said, Madam, I am now so far from coming to repeat my presumptive Love, that I come in the highest Despair to resign it; I am too sensible how little I have deserv'd a return from you, and since my Estate is too small for you— Your Estate, *said* Amoranda, *interrupting him*, I wonder, Mr. *Callid*, you shou'd name it; 'tis trifling indeed compared to your Merit: I wou'd have you believe I have so good a taste, as to set the highest Value upon the richest Gem, and I am sorry my Behaviour has given you any despairing Thoughts. Madam, *said he*, I have no cause to complain of your Behaviour, but Hope is a most tiresome thing when it hangs too long upon our hands; but here comes one, to whom I must give place.

Believe me, *said* Amoranda, you mistake, and I will comply so far with your satisfaction, as to say, you stand as fair in my Esteem as he does. By this time, *Froth* came to 'em, and complaining of Heat, threw up the Sash. Some little time after a Gentleman rid by, and threw in a Glove at the Window; *Amoranda*, at whose foot it fell, took it up, and found there was something in it, which she conceal'd, but was much surpriz'd at the Action. As she was putting it into her Pocket, she saw Lord *Lofty* coming, and leaving *Froth* and *Callid* in the Summer-house, went to meet him. What an age, *said he*, have I been detain'd from my charming *Amoranda*? Oh! come down this Walk, and let me tell you how Absence has tortur'd me ever since I left you.

While my Lord and *Amoranda* were walking in the other part of the Garden, *Froth* and *Callid* began to compare Notes, and talk of the weighty Affair in which they were both concern'd. Mr. *Callid, said Froth*, you and I come here upon the same Errand, and in regard to our former Friendship I must tell you, *Amoranda* is partly dispos'd of, and for that reason I wou'd advise you to desist; a Man's Discretion is greatly to be call'd in question, who, after so many repulses as doubtless you have met with, will still go on in a fruitless attempt. 'Tis true, we are both Men of Merit, but Love you know is blind, and if she finds just difference enough to turn the Scale to my advantage, I think you ought to drop your Amour, and leave the Lady and I to our own happy Inclinations. Hum— *said Callid*, you are, I must own, a Man of a sanguine Complexion, but a little too much upon the Volatile; your Understanding evaporates, and you never had a solid Thought in your Life, otherwise you wou'd tell yourself, this Woman has no more regard to you than to all Mankind in general. Perhaps she has given you some Cause to hope; why, she has done the same by me, and is this minute doing the same by yon Nobleman, and to-morrow, five hundred more shall meet with the same encouragement, if they attack her. No, *Froth, said he*, this way will never do; but if you will give into my Measures, we may find out one that will. You and I have been long Friends, and old Acquaintance, our Estates are sunk to a low ebb, tho' we have hitherto made that a Secret to the World; *Amoranda* is not the Prize we seek after, it is her Fortune we want, and part of it, at least, we will have, if you will close with my Design. Well, *said* Froth, I never sign blank Bonds, let me know what your Design is, and as I like it, I will comply with it; but why the Devil, *said he*, shou'd I lose the Substance for the Shadow? I am sure she bid me not despair an hour ago, and who wou'd desire more Encouragement?

I find, *said* Callid, you are running away with the old Bait, that has catch'd so many Fools already; for my part, I nibbled at it too, but it smelt so stale, I did not like it: and if you'll be advised by a Friend, who can see as far into a Millstone as you can do, you'll shun the Trap as well as I. Come then, *said* Froth, let us hear this Scheme of yours. I know, *said* Callid, it will at the first hearing seem a little impracticable, but I don't doubt of convincing you in a small time of its Possibility. I have often heard *Amoranda* say, she pass'd her whole Evenings in this Summer-house when the Weather is hot; now where would be the difficulty of whipping her out of this low Window into a Coach provided ready, and carry her to a House which I have taken care of, keeping her with the utmost privacy, till she resolves to marry one of us, and t'other shall share the Estate.

Aye, *said* Froth, if this were but as soon done as said, I should like the Contrivance well enough; but pray, *said he*, don't you think her Maid and she wou'd make a damn'd noise when they were carry'd off? Yes, *said t'other*, I believe they wou'd, but we might easily prevent it, by a pretty little Gagg for a minute or two, till we got them into the Coach. Well, *said* Froth, but when we have taken all these Pains, what if she will marry neither of us, and the Hue and Cry[22] catch us, as to be sure it will soon be after us; then, instead of a fine Lady, with a fine Estate, we shall each of us get a fine Halter.[23] Thou art a cowardly Puppy, *said* Callid, and I am sorry I have laid my self so open to you;

do you think I do my Business by halves? or that an Affair of such Consequence is to be neglected in any part? No, the Devil himself can't find her
where I intend to carry her; and if she will not immediately comply to marry
one of us, she will at least come to terms for her liberty; you know we cannot
stay long in *England* unless we have a mind to rot in a Jayl, and if we can but
screw out each of us a thousand Pound, we will away to the Czar, and let the
Law hang us when it can catch us.

Why Faith, *said* Froth, I believe such a Project might be brought to bear,
but how shou'd we get the Money brought to us? She shall draw a Bill upon
her Banker, *said Callid*, for as much as we can get out of her, then we'll ride
post to *London* and receive it. And when, *said Froth*, are we to go about this
Work? for methinks I wou'd fain have it over; I have still a fancy *Amoranda*
will be mine, and if she be willing to marry me, will you promise not to
oppose it? Nay, *said* Callid, if she will marry either of us, I do not see why it
may not be me as well as you; I will not make a Deed of Gift of the Lady
neither, but if it comes to that, she shall e'en draw cuts[24] for us, and the lucky
Loon take her.

What an unhappy Creature is a beautiful young Girl left to her own
Management, who is so fond of Adoration, that Reason and Prudence are
thrust out to make way for it; 'till she becomes a prey to every designing Rascal, and her own ridiculous Qualities, are her greatest Enemies. Thus it might
have fared with poor *Amoranda*, had not a lucky hit prevented it, which the
Reader shall know by and by. While this Contrivance was carrying on in the
Summer-House, my Lord was employ'd in another of a different kind; he thought
his Quality sufficient to justify all his Actions, and never feared a Conquest,
where-ever he vouchsafed an Attempt. Madam, *said he*, why are we to spend
our time in this Garden, where so many Interruptions may break in upon our
Privacies? I desire an Audience where none but Love may be admitted.

My Lord, *said* Amoranda, did you ever see a finer Goldfinch in your Life
than that Cock in the Pear-Tree? That very Cock, my Lord, is Grand-sire to all
my little warbling Company within doors, I remember him, and know him
by a little uncommon Spot over his Eye: Oh 'tis a charming Bird, I have set a
Trap-Cage for him a thousand times, but the dear Creature is so cunning—
Well, everything loves Liberty, and so do I; don't you, my Lord? Yes, Madam,
said he, I lov'd it, and always had it, 'till I knew you; but I am so intangled now
in your Charms, I never expect to disengage my self again.

Well, I'll swear, my Lord, *said* Amoranda, that's a pity; methinks a Man
of your Gallantry should never marry. Marry! *said my Lord in great Surprize,*

no, I hope I shall never have so little love for any Lady as to marry her: Oons! the very Word has put me into a Sweat, the Marriage-Bed is to Love, what a cold Bed is to a Melon-Seed, it starves it to death infallibly.[25] Aye, I believe it does, my Lord, *said* Amoranda; however, one thing I have often observ'd, when once a Woman's married, nobody cares for her but her Husband; and if your Lordship's Remarks be true, not he neither: so that, my Lord, I think we must live single in our own defence. But, my Lord, *said she*——————— what was I going to say—— Oh pray give me a pinch of Snuff. But Madam, *said my Lord*, this is trifling with my Passion, I cannot live upon such Usage; either ease my Sufferings, or take my Life. I'll swear, my Lord, *said* Amoranda, you are a bewitching Man; what a Breach have I made in good Manners by your agreeable Conversation! I left poor Mr. *Froth*, and Mr. *Callid*, in the Summer-House two hours ago, and had quite forgot they were there: sure the poor Toads are not there still. Damn the Toads, *said Lord* Lofty, are they a Subject fit for your Thoughts? No, my Lord, *said she*, you see I forgot 'em, but pray let us go in, we shall have the Owls about our Ears, if we stay here any longer, 'tis just dark. Lord *Lofty* was strangely ruffled at this Behaviour; and tho' he still hoped for a pleasing end of his Amour, he plainly saw it would not be so easily attained as he at first vainly imagined: he therefore took his leave for that Night, and hoped the next Interview would prove more favourable. *Amoranda* was very glad when she found herself alone, that she might have time to examine the Glove which came so oddly into the Summer-House Window. *Jenny, said she,* call for Candles, and come here. When she was set, and had got Lights, she took out the Glove; Oh *Jenny, said she,* what a sad afternoon has my Curiosity had, and how much have I longed to see what I have got here? She opened the top of it, and found a letter: So, *said she,* here is some new Conquest, but the strangest way of letting me know it that was ever invented. She opened it, and found these Words:

> *This Letter, Madam, does not come to tell you I love you, since that would only increase the surfeit you must have taken with so many hundred Declarations of that kind already; but if I tell you I am in pain for your Conduct, and spend some Hours in pitying your present Condition, it will, I dare say, be intirely new to you; since (tho' many have the same opinion of your Behaviour) none have Courage, or Honesty enough to tell you so. Consider, Madam, how unhappy that Woman is, who finds herself daily hedg'd in with self-ended Flatterers, who make it their business to keep up a Vanity in you, which may one day prove your Ruin. Is it possible for any Fop to tell you more than you know already? Or does*

not your Looking-Glass display every one of your fine Features with much more exactness, than the base, the fawning Rascal who pretends to die at your feet? Spurn him from you, Amoranda, as you would the worst Infection, and believe me rather than him, when I tell you, you are neither Angel, nor Goddess, but a Woman, a fine Woman, and there are in this Nation ten thousand such. If this little Admonition meets with a favourable Reception, you will, upon the first reading of it, discard three Fourths of your daily Attendants, who like so many Locusts are striving to devour you.

Why *Jenny*, *said* Amoranda, did you ever hear any thing so impudent in your Life? Oh Lud,[26] I have not patience with the familiar Brute, I would give a thousand Pounds to know the Author; what shall I do to be revenged? Truly Madam, *said* Jenny, I must own if this be a Conquest, 'tis made upon a very insulting saucy Lover; and yet I believe he means well too.

Mean well, said Amoranda; what good meaning can he have, who persuades me to banish the Bees, and live in the Hive by my self? No Madam, *said* Jenny, your Ladyship mistakes him, 'tis the Wasps he would have you discard, who come to sting and steal from those who have a better Title to the Sweets of your Favours: but Madam, *continued she*, do you think you should know him again, if you see him?

Not I, *said* Amoranda, I never saw his Face, he flung in the Glove before I knew any body was near; and had he not rid away in a Cloud of Dust, I should have thought it had been a Challenge to some of the Gentlemen in the Summer-House; but what vexes me most, *said she*, is his Pity; I always thought a Woman of Youth, Beauty, and such a Fortune as mine is, might raise Envy in many, but Pity in none.

Here the House-keeper came in to speak with her Lady, and put a stop to their present Discourse, by making way for something of greater moment. Madam, *said she*, if your Ladyship be at Leisure, I have a Secret of great Importance to communicate with you. Prithee then, *said* Amoranda, let us have it, perhaps it may put something else out of my head. Madam, *said she*, I went this Afternoon into my little Room over the Summer-house, where you know I dry my Winter-Herbs, and while I was turning them, your Ladyship came in with Mr. *Froth*, and *Callid* came to you. You may please to remember, Lord *Lofty* gave you an opportunity of leaving them, which you had no sooner done, than they began to lay a most dangerous Plot against you;— (so told her Lady what the Reader has heard already) but *continu'd she*, as soon as they had laid their Scheme, Mr. *Callid* said he would go and provide a Coach, and two or three Villains (like himself) to assist. As soon as he was gone, Mr. *Froth* began to consider with himself what was best to do, stick to the first Design, or discover all to your Ladyship. Now, *said he*, I have a fair Opportunity of turning *Callid's* Knavery to my own advantage, by discovering all to *Amoranda*; so signal a Service can be attended with nothing less than her dear self, and then I have her without any Hazard or Partner. But then, *said he again*, as my Friend has well observ'd, the Devil can't fix a Woman of her Levity; perhaps when I have ruined his Design, by telling her the Danger she is in, my Reward may be a Curt'sy, and I thank you Mr. *Froth*, and when it lies in my power I'll serve you again: there's an end of his hopes and my own too. No, *said he*, without I were sure of making Sport, I am resolv'd I will spoil none, and good Luck assist our Undertaking; while yonder Lord is so much at her Service, we need expect no Favours but what we force, so *Callid* I follow thee to provide for them. Saying thus, he went out of the Garden thro' the Back-Door. Oh the impudent Rogues! *said* Amoranda: Well, and when, *Brown*, (for that was the House-keeper's Name) is this fine Project to be put in execution? To morrow-night, Madam, *said she*. What, *said* Amoranda: whether I am there or no? Tho' I spend a good deal of time there, I am not always there. No, Madam, *said Brown*, I forgot to tell your Ladyship that part of the Contrivance; you are to be entertain'd with a Dance of Shepherds and Shepherdesses in the Highway by Moon-light, just at the Summer-house Window, and if you happen to have any Company, 'tis to be put off till next Night, under pretence of one of the Dancers being not well. Very fine, said *Amoranda*, well since the worthy Gentlemen have begun a Scheme, I'll throw in my Counter-plot among them, and see who will come best off.

Amoranda made her House-keeper a Present of some Guineas, and dismiss'd her. As she went out, a Footman came in, and told his Lady, an old Gentleman was just alighted at the Gate, who brought her a Letter, but must deliver it into her own hand. An old Gentleman! *said* Amoranda; wait upon him in however. The Stranger enter'd, and gave the young Lady a Letter from her Uncle, in which, when she had open'd it, she found the following words:

I have at last, my dearest Amoranda! fixed upon such a Person as I think fit to entrust you with; he is one for whom I have the greatest value, or, to sum up all in one word, he is my Friend, and as such I desire you'll use him; let him in my stead interest himself in all your Affairs. I have so good an opinion of your Prudence, as to believe you will not often want his Advice; neither will he offer it, unless he finds it necessary: for tho' he is an old Man, he is neither impertinent, positive,[27] or sour. You will, I hope, from my past Behaviour towards you, believe you are very dear to me; and I have no better way of shewing it for the future, than by putting you into such hands as Formator's, which is the name of the Bearer; and if you would oblige me, show it by your Esteem to him, which will confirm me

Your most Affectionate Uncle,
E. TRAFFICK.

When Amoranda had read her Letter, she look'd a little earnestly at Formator, possibly not very well pleas'd with a Guardian of such an Age; but she consider'd she had a Father and Mother to please in the Person of her Uncle, and he such a one as made up the Loss of both to her: for which Reasons she resolved to use him as directed in that Letter, and said to him, with a Smile, I find, Sir, I am no longer my own Mistress, but am now to live under your Restrictions; I promise you I will always listen to your Advice, and take it as often as I can; but I hope, Sir, you will remember I am gay and young, you grave and old, and that the Disparity in our Years may make as great a one in our Tempers: I'll therefore make a bargain with you, if you will bear with a little of my youthful Folly, I will bear with a great deal of your aged Sagacity, and we will be as agreeable to one another, as 'tis possible for Age and Youth to be.

Madam, *said* Formator, I agree to all your Proposals, and shall be very cautious how I presume to advise; and if I ever do so, it shall be when your own Reason must side with me, and I see already you have too much Sense to act against that, unless by Inadvertency. All young People, Madam, are fond of Pleasure, and every Thought that opposes it, is thrust out with disgrace; but —— O Lud! *said Amoranda,* I believe you are to be the Chaplain too, if you talk thus much longer, you'll argue me out of my Senses; I told you I could not come into your grave Measures of a sudden. Come, Sir, there's nothing in't, an innocent Chearfulness is much more acceptable both to God and Man, than a crabbed sour Temper, that gives every body the Gripes[28] to look at it. Madam, said *Formator,* you quite mistake me: I am not of that disagreeable Temper you have described; I would have both Young and Old act with that very innocent Freedom you speak of: but what I inveigh against, is an immoderate Love of Pleasure, which generally follows the Young, and too often leads them to Destruction.

Pray, *said* Amoranda, what is it you call Pleasure?

Madam, *said he,* I call every thing Pleasure that pleases us, and I dare say you will own a great many things may and do please us, which are in them-selves very faulty: as for example, suppose a fine young Lady of a superiour Beauty should spread her Purlieus[29] to catch all Mankind, I doubt not but it would give such a one exquisite Pleasure; but it is at the same time a great fault to give other People exquisite Pain, as the rest of the Sex must certainly feel, when they see one Monopolizer engross the whole Male World to herself. Nay, *said* Amoranda, there never was any such thing in nature, as one Woman engrossing the whole contrary Sex; believe me, Sir, you all love Variety too well for that, and your Affections, like your Money, circulates all the Nation over; so that it is only who can keep their Lovers longest we strive for, not who can keep them always, for that we none of us expect. But come *Formator, said she*, I must own you are come at a very critical Juncture, and since my Uncle has enjoin'd me to use you as I would him, after Supper I will give you an early Proof of my Duty to him, and my Confidence in you.

Supper ended, *Amoranda* told *Formator* the whole Story of *Froth* and *Callid*, their base Designs, as well as beggarly Circumstances. *Formator*'s Cheeks glow'd with Anger, and, in the highest Transport of Rage, cry'd out, How can such a Woman, such a lovely Woman as you are, subject yourself to such Company? Is it possible that fine Sense, which breaks from those lovely Lips with every word you speak, can find agreeable Returns from such Vermine? Can a Man mingle his Wine with Mud, then drink it with pleasure?

Pardon me, dear Madam, *continu'd he*, if my Zeal for so good an Uncle to you, and so good a Friend to me, hurries me a little too far; 'tis not possible for me to see any thing, so deservedly beloved by him, run into the least Weak-ness; beside, you seem to have too true a Notion of our Sex to be grossly imposed upon by them. Say no more, good *Formator, said* Amoranda, I now promise to be governed in a great measure by you; and since my Uncle has sent you to supply his Place, I will use you with deference, and bring myself to comply with your Desires as far as possible. This promise gave the old Gentle-man ten thousand Joys, which sat triumphant on his pleased Countenance; and *Amoranda* could not forbear being pleased herself, to see how much he was so. But, Madam, *said* Formator, methinks I long to know how you intend to use those Villains. That, *said she*, you shall do presently. When the hour is come for the execution of their intended Project, I design to place two sturdy Footmen, dress'd in mine and *Jenny's* Clothes, in the Summer-house; the hour they have appointed, will favour my design as well as theirs, for ten-a-clock's the time, and the Moon to be our Light: so that they will not easily distinguish betwixt the Fellows and us, till their sense of feeling lets them into the secret;

for the Footmen don't want Courage, and I hope my design'd Injuries will give them resentment to it: I dare say they will give them love for love, and pay them in their own coin. What do you think, *Formator, said she,* will not my Contrivance do better than theirs? I hope so Madam, *said he*; but I have one earnest request to make to you, and as it is the first, I hope you will not deny me. No, *said* Amoranda, I am sure you will ask nothing I ought to refuse, and therefore I promise. Then Madam, *said he*, give me leave to personate you in the Summer-house to-morrow night.

Alas! *said she,* what can your feeble Arm do with such robust Rascals? They will make no more of you than they would of me myself, and methinks I would not have 'em go off without a good drubbing.[30] Fear not, Madam, *said* Formator, this Arm can still do wonders in so good a Cause; a Vindication of *Amoranda's* Honour fills my Veins with young Blood, that glows to revenge her Wrongs. Well, *said* Amoranda, I find I have the Remains of a brave Man to take my part; and since you have so great a mind to show your Prowess, pray do: if you happen to be worsted, we'll invert the Custom, and instead of your delivering the distress'd Damsel, she shall come and rescue you. This made *Formator* very merry, in spite of all his Gravity: but it was now Bed-time, and he was conducted to his Chamber by the Servants, who were order'd to use him with great respect. The next morning *Jenny* came to her Lady's Bed-side, and told her she had been in the Garden, and had found a silver Box; I fancy, by the bigness of it, 'tis Lord *Lofty's* Snuff-box, *said she*, but there is nothing in it but a Paper. Draw the Curtains, *said* Amoranda, and let me see it; *Jenny* gave her the Box, and when she had open'd the Paper, she found it was a Contract betwixt Lord *Lofty* and a Lady, of whom she had often heard, but never saw her; and if Lord *Lofty* receded from his Promise of marrying the Lady, he should then forfeit Ten Thousand Pounds, as an Addition to her Fortune. This Contract nettled *Amoranda* to the very heart: How! *said she*, does my Lord come here to affront me with his Declarations against Marriage, and at the same time is going to engage himself so firmly to another? Base as he is, *said she,* am I a Person fit only to divert those Hours, in which he cannot gain admittance to one he likes better? Give me my Clothes, *said she*, I'll be revenged of him, or lose my Life in the Attempt.

Poor *Jenny*, who never saw her Lady angry in her life before, began to repent she had said any thing of the Box, and was now afraid her Lady loved Lord *Lofty*. Madam, *said she*, I would not have your Ladyship in such a passion, for by the Date of this Contract, one would believe my Lord never intended to give it the Lady at all; it has been sign'd and seal'd above a month, if it was dated at the same time. *Jenny, said* Amoranda, *recovering her self, and smiling*; I fancy by your Looks, you are afraid I have an inward private Inclination for this worthless Peer; but as thou hast always been a faithful, honest Servant, I will contribute so far towards thy ease, as to assure thee he is upon the same foot with the rest of his Sex, and I know none upon earth I have a superior value for; but I own I have so just a resentment against his behaviour to me, that if the Lady this Paper was design'd for, will accept of it, I will certainly make her a present of it to-morrow. But, Madam, *said* Jenny, maybe my Lord may come and enquire for it. If he comes today, said *Amoranda*, tell him I see no Company, and to-morrow I will put it out of his reach—— if my mind does not alter, *Jenny*, as I believe it will; for upon second thoughts, 'tis a matter of very great consequence, and I would not contribute to a Man's continual Uneasiness neither; however, I am resolved to see no Company to-day, except *Callid* and *Froth*, so pray give orders accordingly below stairs.

Jenny was very glad to see her Lady recover her Temper so soon, and when she had obey'd her Commands, she return'd to dress her, and then *Amoranda* went down to *Formator*; they paid each other the common Compliment of a Good-morrow and then went to breakfast in *Amoranda's* Closet,[31] for fear of a visit from Lord *Lofty*, who came before they had well begun. But his Errand was different from what they expected, for he neither enquired for, nor had miss'd his Box: but when they told him, *Amoranda* saw no Company that day; I know it, Child, *said he*, she told me yesterday she would see nobody but me; Where is she? Then without staying for an Answer, he ran from Room to Room till he found her. *Amoranda* thought his ill-manner'd Freedom proceeded from his Concern for his Box, and was once going to return it, in order to get rid of him, but a better Genius twitch'd her by the ear, and bid her keep it. Madam, *said he, with his wonted Assurance,* how will you answer this Behaviour to Good-nature? And what have I done to deserve Banishment?

My Lord, *said* Amoranda, I retire sometimes from Company, to make it more acceptable to me when I come into it again; and this, I think, I may do as often as I please, without a Breach in either Good-nature or Good-manners. True, Madam, *said my Lord*, but I would fain be acceptable always. Amoranda found by this Answer he had not miss'd his Box, or at least did not suspect she had it, and therefore told him, she was surprized to hear him say he would be always acceptable, after having declared so heartily against Matrimony. I fancy, my Lord, *said she*, you will find a Mistress a little given to Variety, and will hardly like you always as much as you may think you deserve. *Formator*, who colour'd at this Discourse, began to take up the Cudgels.[32] My

Lord, *said he*, I am sent here by very good Authority, and have a Commission to enquire every Man's Business that comes into this House; I therefore desire to know, if, as the Lady says, you declare against Matrimony, what your designs are in coming here? Prithee, Child, *said my Lord to* Amoranda, what queer old Prig is this? Hark-ye, Friend, *said he to* Formator, your Business is now in the other World, and you would do well to go and prepare for't, without envying us the Pleasures you are past your self. My Lord, *said* Formator, I am still very capable of Pleasure, and the greatest I can possibly have, is to preserve the lovely Charge committed to my Care, which I will do to the utmost extremity of my power; and do here promise you, till you give a better account of your Intentions, you shall never see her more. *Amoranda* was not very well pleased with what *Formator* said; for tho she was perfectly insensible of any Passion for my Lord, and knew his dishonourable Designs, she could not think of losing a Lover of his Title and Figure without some Emotion: and said to *Formator*, with a little warmth, I think, Sir, you assume a Power too great for so short a time, and I should take it kindly if you would give me leave to dismiss my Visiters myself. This gave my lord a new Supply of Hope, and he asked *Amoranda* leave to pull him by the Nose.[33] No, my Lord, *said she*, whoever lays a finger upon him, has seen his last of me. Madam *said* Formator, if I have been so unhappy as to say anything to disoblige you, I do here in the humblest manner ask you pardon; but if I am not to take notice of such Behaviour as Lord *Lofty's*, I have no business here, but may forthwith return to him that sent me: for your part, my Lord, you *dare* not pull me by the Nose. Saying thus, he left the Closet, but sent Jenny directly up to her Lady, with a charge to stay with her till my Lord was gone, unless she commanded otherwise, and then he knew what he had to fear.

Amoranda, on the other hand, found she had vext *Formator*, which she began to be sorry for, because she knew it wou'd highly disoblige one of the best Uncles in the world, and therefore begg'd my Lord to leave her for that time. He told her he wou'd do ten thousand Things to oblige her, and desired but one in return of all. When I understand you, my Lord, *said she*, I shall know what Answer to make; in the mean time, I repeat the Request I have already made you, to leave me now. My Lord, with a little too much freedom, snatch'd her to his arms, took a Kiss, and vanish'd. As soon as he was gone, she went down to *Formator*, and found him in the Parlor, in a very thoughtful, melancholy Posture; Formator, *said she*, I am come to tell you, I am under some Concern for what has happen'd today: I have, to oblige you, sent my Lord away, and do here faithfully promise you, I will never come into his

Company more, without your Approbation. I own I have the greatest Inclination in the world to please you, and as I believe you sincerely my Friend, as such I will always use you, and let this little early quarrel rivet our future Amity. *Formator* was so transported at her good-natur'd Condescension, that he cou'd hardly forbear throwing himself at her Feet; but he consider'd, Raptures were unsuitable to his Age, so contented himself with saying, Madam, of what use is our Reason, if we chain it up when we most want it? Had your's had its liberty, it wou'd have shown you the villainous Designs of your *Noble* Lover, it wou'd have told you how much he desires your Ruin, that all the Love he has for you, is to satisfy his own beastial Desires, rob you of your Innocence and Honour, then leave you to the World, to finish the Misery he begun, by being pity'd and despis'd as long as you live; 'Tis true, Madam, *continued he*, you have a Fortune that sets you above the World, but when I was a young Fellow, we used to value a Lady for Virtue, Modesty, and an innate Love to Honour. I confess, Madam, *said he*, those are unfashionable qualities, but they are still the chief Ornaments of your sex, and ours never think a Woman compleat without 'em.

Give me leave, Madam, *said he*, to go a little farther, and tell you how great your misfortune has been, in being left so long to the Choice of your own Company; your Good-nature, and want of Experience, together with a greedy Desire of Flattery, which, (pardon me, Madam) is a Weakness attending the whole Sex, has encourag'd such a heap of vermin about you, as Providence wou'd not suffer to live, were it not to give us a better taste for the brave, the just, the honourable and the honest Man. *Amoranda* was so touch'd with what *Formator* said, that the Tears stood in her Eyes, and she was just going to beg he wou'd have done, when the Bell rung for Dinner, and put a stop to what remain'd; she was never so lectur'd in her Life before, however, she told herself in her own Breast, that every Word he said was true. As soon as Dinner was over, my Friend *Froth* came in, with a design to sift *Amoranda's* Inclinations once more; and if he found her leaning to his Side, as much as he desir'd, then to discover all; if not, to stay till *Callid* came, and join with him, in the Invitation to the Entertainment at night. *Formator*, who was told before he came in who he was, left *Amoranda* and him together, and having a fair Opportunity of trying his Fortune once more, he thus began: Madam, I have often look'd with envious Eyes on the Favours you confer on Mr. *Callid*, but, Madam, as you cannot have us both, I wish you wou'd (for the ease of one of us at least) declare in favour of him you like, and let the other travel. Mr. Froth, *said she*, your Friend and you, are endow'd with such equal Merrit, 'tis hardly possible to say which I like best; beside, if I shou'd declare in favour of you, Mr. *Callid* wou'd not believe I was in earnest; and if I shou'd say I like him best, you are too conscious of your own Worth, to think I speak from my Heart. In short, every thing we do, you construe to your own advantage: if we look easy and pleas'd in your Company, we are certainly in Love; if grave and reserv'd, 'tis to hide our Love; thus you all imagine we are fond of gaining a Conquest over a Heart, which when we have got it, is perhaps so very trifling, that we dispose of it at last, as we do of our old Gowns, give it away to our Chamber-Maid. But, Madam, *said Froth*, if you please we will lay by general Comparisons, and come to particulars betwixt *Callid* and my self; and if I, from undeniable Reasons, prove I deserve best from you, will you promise accordingly to reward me?

I faithfully promise, *said* Amoranda, to reward you both as you deserve; but here's Mr. Callid coming, I'll warrant he has as much to say for himself as you have. (*Mr.* Callid *came to 'em, and said to* Amoranda) I have provided a little Country Entertainment for you, Madam, if you will do me the honour to see it anon. You are always so very obliging, *said* Amoranda,— but you know, Mr. *Callid,* I never go far from home. No farther than your own Summer-House, Madam, said he; I have engag'd a few of my Tenants to appear in a rural Dress, and give you a Shepherds Dance, they have been practising this Fortnight, and I am in hopes they may prove perfect enough to give you some diversion; I have order'd them to be there exactly at Ten o'clock, by which time the Road will be quiet, and the Moon up; and Madam, *said* Froth, a Dance of Shepherds and Shepherdesses, looks so *Natural* by Moon-light.— Yes, *said* Amoranda, so it does, and I promise my self already a great deal of Pleasure from the Hour you speak of; but I wish I had known in the Morning, I wou'd have engag'd Lord *Lofty* to come himself, and have brought some Ladies with him: no matter, *said she*, we'll have it to our selves, and Gentlemen, I desire you will not sup before you come, for I will take care of a small repast for you, and we will sup in the Summer-House, that we may be near our Diversion. Come then, Froth, *said* Callid, we will go and see them do it once more before they perform in the Lady's View, for nothing cou'd be so great a Baulk to me, as to have any thing wrong where she is to be a Spectator. As soon as they were gone, *Amoranda* called *Formator*, and bid him chuse a Companion for the Exploit in hand, for she told him, she had promis'd the two Gentlemen a Supper in the Summer-House, and she wou'd fain have them have a Bellyfull.

Formator took the young Lady's advice, and went to chuse a good sturdy

Fellow, to personate *Jenny*, while he did as much by *Amoranda*; and when the appointed time was come, they took their Places in the Summer-House, with each a good Crab-tree Cudgel by him, and after a little expectation, the two impudent varlets came, ask'd for *Amoranda* with their wonted sauciness, and being told she was in the Garden, flew to their hop'd-for Prize. *Callid* ran as he thought to *Amoranda*, and catching her in his Arms, cry'd, No Resistance, Madam, by *Jove*, you must along with me. *Froth* did the same by the suppos'd *Jenny*, and just as they were a going to gag 'em, and call their Associates, who waited in the Lane for the Sign, to their assistance, the two Ladies began to handle their Cudgels, and laid about them with such dexterity, that the Ravishers were almost knock'd on the head, before they cou'd believe they were beaten; so great was their surprize, and so little did they expect to meet with such resistance: but when they found the blows come faster on, without regard to either Sex or Quality, they began to draw their Swords; *Formator* struck *Callid's* out of his hand, and the Foot-Man trip'd up *Froth's* heels, before he cou'd get his out of the Scabbard, which he wou'd not have attempted to do, but that he thought his Antagonist a Woman. All this while the two Ladies laid on so unmercifully, that they began to cry Quarter and beg for Mercy, when the Noise reach'd the House, and they saw *Amoranda*, with Lights before her, coming in a great surprize, to see what the matter was. *Callid*, when he saw her, and *Jenny*, cou'd hardly believe his half beaten-out Eyes, but stood staring, first at the real Lady, and then at the feign'd one; but when he found out how Matters went, he cry'd, *Froth*, thou Villain, thou hast betray'd me. If I have, said *Froth*, I am ill rewarded for't, and believe I shall never stir either hand or foot again. Well, Gentlemen, *said* Amoranda, are the Shepherds come? When does the Dance begin? 'Tis over, Madam, said *Formator*, these Gentlemen have been cutting capers this half-hour, to a sorrowful new Tune. Why what is the matter said she? I hope you have not hurt 'em.

Nothing, Madam, *said* Formator, but *Harry* and I took a frolick to sit here this Evening in Masquerade, and those two Beaus had a mind to ravish us, I think, for they were going to gag us. I am sorry, Sir, (said he to *Callid*,) That I was forc'd to exercise my Cudgel upon you, I hope you will excuse it; had I been in another dress, I would have us'd another Weapon. I think, *said* Amoranda, he did not stand upon so much ceremony with *you*, for I see he has drawn his Sword, tho' he took you for a Woman. Yes, said *Callid*, ready to choke with rage, despair, and disappointment, I took him for you, on whom I wou'd have had a glorious revenge, had it prov'd so. Oh Death and Fury, *said he*, what malicious Devil interpos'd? But it is some Satisfaction to tell you how

I wou'd have us'd you, had Fortune been so kind as to have put you in my power; know then, proud Beauty, I wou'd―― I know already (*said* Amoranda, *interrupting him*) as much of you designs, as you can tell me; but Gentlemen, *said she*, if the *Czar* shou'd not take you into his Service, when you have receiv'd the Money from my Banker, pray let me know, and I'll make a better Provision for you. I have an Uncle going to the *Indies* who wants Slaves, and I believe at my request, he wou'd take you into his Service: in the mean time, do me the favour to leave this Place, for I have had just as much of your Company as I can dispense with. I hope, Madam, *said* Froth *(whose Tongue was the only Part about him, he cou'd stir without Pain)* you have more Hospitality in you, than to turn us out of your House in this Condition; you had more need send for a Surgeon, to set our dislocated Joints in order, and wrap us up in Seer-Cloth,[34] I don't believe I shall live a Week. That, *said* Amoranda, wou'd be a great pity, the world wou'd have a sad loss of so worthy a Man; but I hear you have a Coach hard by, I shall order two of my Servants to load each of them with a Knave, and convey you both to it. I hope you will own I have been as good as my Word, I promis'd you a Supper and *Desert*,[35] and believe you have had both. Upon which, she and her retinue went away, leaving the two batter'd Beaus in the Summer-House, till a couple of lusty Fellows came, to take them up and shoot the rubbish into the Coach. The Servants who carry'd them away, left them, and return'd home; and as soon as they were gone, *Callid* accus'd *Froth* of treachery, and laid the whole discovery to his charge. *Froth* declar'd his Innocence, and urg'd his own share of the Suffering as a proof he was so; but *Callid*'s disappointment had sour'd his temper, as well as made him desperate, and he was resolv'd to be deaf to all *Froth* cou'd say in his own Vindication: and tho' they were both so bruis'd they cou'd hardly stand, he made t'other draw, who was innocent in Fact, tho' not in Intention; and tho' they liv'd like Scoundrels, they went off like Gentlemen, and the first Pass they made, took each other's Life.

This News soon reach'd *Amoranda's* ear, whose tender Heart felt a great deal of pity for the tragical Catastrophe. But *Formator* told her, he thought she ought rather to rejoice, if she had a true sense of a Fellow-Creature's Sufferings; for, *said he*, when once a Man has out-lived his Fortune, and his Friends, his next Relief is the Grave. He had now pretty well cleared the House of the Catterpillars[36] that infested in it, and began to take the greatest Delight in his Charge; his constant Care was to divert her from all the Follies of Life, and as she had a Soul capable of Improvement, and a flexible good Temper to be dealt with, he made no doubt but one day he should see her the most accomplish'd of her Sex: in order to which, he provided a choice Collection of Books for her, spent most of his time with her, diverted her with a thousand pleasant Stories, possibly of his own making, and every moment was lost to *Formator*, that was not spent with *Amoranda*.

Lord *Lofty* had made two Visits during this time, but *Formator* would not admit him, and by *Amoranda's* Consent told him she was engaged; which nettled the Peer so much, that he writ to her in the bitterness of his Soul, the following words:

MADAM

If it were possible for me to unriddle a Woman's Behaviour, I should immediately try my Skill upon your's; but as I believe Men of deeper Penetration than I, have been baffled, I must e'en (with the rest) leave you to your own wild Mazes: One day caress'd, the next cashier'd, a third receiv'd again, and a fourth quite banish'd. However, tho this be a common Treatment from most of your Sex, I never had cause to mind it so much in you, till this old whimsical Fellow came, to give you ridiculous Advice, and your Adorers endless Torment: What the Devil have our Years to do with his? Or why must his pernicious Counsel disturb our Pleasures? If you have that value for me still, which you once gave me reason to hope you had, you will meet me in the little Grove at the end of your own Garden, about nine a-clock, where I will acquaint you with some Secrets you never knew before: I have contrived a way to it without coming near the House, and your old Argus[37] will never suspect you, if you come alone to the Arms of

Your Faithful Admirer,
LOFTY

Before *Amoranda* had done reading this Letter, a Servant came and told her, a Gentleman on horseback at the Gate desired to know if he might be admitted to her Presence for a quarter of an hour; his Business was a little urgent, but it would be soon over. Poor *Amoranda* had been so lately in jeopardy, that she was now afraid of every body, and durst do nothing without *Formator*, who went to know the Gentleman's Name; but when he came to the Gate, he saw a poor, thin, pale, meagre young Creature, hardly able to sit his Horse, who look'd as if he wanted a Doctor more than a Mistress: when he had view'd him well, he was ashamed to ask him any questions, thinking he might as well be afraid of a Shadow as such a Skeleton as he was, and therefore desired him to alight, which, with the help of two Servants he had with him, he did. *Formator* conducted him in, and left him with *Amoranda*; when the

Stranger was set (for he was very ill able to stand) he first begg'd *Amoranda* to shut the Door, that none might be witness to his wretched Tale but herself, and then with a flood of Tears began thus:

It is the way of the Damn'd, Madam, to desire all Mankind should be in their own miserable State; but tho I am as wretched as they, I am not so envious: and it is to prevent your Fate, and receive your Pity, that I am come at this time to you. Sir, *said* Amoranda, your Looks, without your Tale, call for Pity; and I intreat you to drink a Glass of something to comfort you, before you spend the few remaining Spirits you have left, in a Story which, I foresee, will give you pain in the repeating. Alas! Madam, *said he,* Food and I are become Strangers to each other; but 'tis all the pleasure I have to repeat my Wrongs, and my tortured Heart is never capable of a moment's ease, but when I am complaining. *Amoranda* was in the utmost perplexity to find out what whining romantick Lover she had got, and could not imagine where the Adventure would end, or how her Fate came to be concern'd in the matter; but the poor Afflicted soon let her into a Secret, which she began to be impatient to know. Madam, *said the Stranger,* I am now going to tell you a Story, which will melt you into the greatest pity; but before I proceed, intreat you will not be too severe upon my Conduct, or say, when I have done, I have reaped the Desert of my own Folly. *Amoranda* promised her best Attention, without any Reflection at all; and the Stranger thus began:

The first thing I am to inform you of, Madam, is my Sex, which is not what it appears to be; I am a Woman, a wretched, miserable, unhappy Woman: my Father was the eldest Son of an antient Family, born to a very plentiful Estate, and when he died, left only one Son and myself; my Mother died soon after I was born, and my Father left me wholly to the care of my Brother, who was at Age when he died, and my Fortune, which was five thousand Pounds, was to be paid me when I married, or was at age, and to be kept in my Brother's hands till then. I was then about fourteen Years old, and my Brother, who was Father too, used me with all the Tenderness that could be expected from so near a Relation; and had he kept within Bounds of Honour, and loved me only as a Sister, I might have reckon'd myself in the number of the Happy. A whole Year past over with the greatest Innocence, and my Brother's love seem'd faultless and natural; but when I was turn'd of fifteen, in the height of my Bloom and Pride of Beauty, I was one day dress'd to the most advantage for a Ball in the neighbourhood, when my Brother came in, and looking stedfastly at me, *Altemira, said he,* Oh *Altemira!* You are too lovely. Then snatching me to his Bosom, press'd me with a Warmth which a little surprized me. I broke loose from his Embraces, and ask'd him what he meant; he seem'd a little confounded, and left the Room. I confess I was under some apprehension of an approaching Misfortune, but was loth to harbour any Thought to the disadvantage of so dear a Brother, and therefore imputed the Action rather to Chance than Design. He came to the Ball, but would neither dance nor speak, nay, nor so much as look at any thing but me, which only I took notice of. When the Company broke up, he convey'd me home, and as we were going, he sigh'd, and said, I had made him very wretched. How, Brother, *said I, not willing to understand him,* by what Behaviour am I so wretched to make you so? Oh *Altemira! said he*, cease to talk, your Actions had been better, had they been worse; for who can see so much Perfection without Love, without Adoration? Oh *Altemira!* I must, I will enjoy you. It is not possible for me to tell you, Madam, how shocking this was to me, I could hardly keep from swooning in the Coach; but my Passion found vent at my Eyes, and with ten thousand Tears I begg'd him to recall his scatter'd Senses, to arm his Reason for his own Defence, to consider I was a Sister, nay, a Sister who was left wholly to his Care, and one who had none to fly to for redress of Injuries but him; and am I so entirely miserable as to find my ruin where I seek a Sanctuary? *said I.* Oh! by the Ashes of our dead Father and Mother, by all the Ties of natural Affection, of Honour, Virtue, and every thing we hold dear in this Life, if you have any regard to my Welfare or your own, stifle this guilty Flame, and let me quench it with my Tears.

I wish, *Altemira, said he*, I could quench it with my own; but 'tis grown too fierce to be extinguish'd; I have kept it under a great while, and with my utmost Care endeavour'd to suppress it: but alas! my Attempts were vain, it was too powerful for me, and is now broken out with such violence, that unless you stop its force, I must consume to Ashes in the midst on't. My Heart at those words sunk, both with Horrour and Pity; I saw an only Brother, whom I dearly and tenderly loved, a black Criminal entangled in a guilty lawless Love, while I, who only had the power of relieving him, lay under an indispensible Duty of refusing to do so. As soon as we alighted out of the Coach, we went to our different Apartments; how my poor Brother spent his Night, I know not, but mine went on with a heavy Pace, I counted every dull Hour as it came, and bathed in Tears, lay thinking how to extricate my self from the miserable Condition I was in. I found my unfortunate Brother was too far gone, to be brought to reason, and had often heard, a desperate Disease must have a desperate Cure,[38] I therefore resolv'd to end his pain, by absence, and go where he should never see me, till I was satisfy'd he had got the better of his own Folly.

In order to this, I got up when the Clock struck four, and calling up my Maid, who lay in a Closet just by me, I made her pack up some Clothes for me and her self, and taking all my Mother's Jewels, which were now mine, and what ready Money I had, we went down unheard or observ'd by any body, and took the road to a Wood hard by: I knew as soon as my Brother was up, he wou'd, as usual, come to enquire after my health, and when he mist me, make strict enquiry after me; I therefore thought it most advisable to stay a day or two where we were, till the search was a little over, and then pursue my intended Journey. My Maid favour'd my design, tho' she knew it not, by stepping into the Buttery[39] before she came out, and filling her Pocket with something for her Breakfast, which we liv'd upon two days. In a thicket in the Wood we found a Shepherd's Hut, deserted by the owner, where we lay that night; and the next day towards evening, we ventur'd to a Farmer's House, where for a Guinea to the Man, who was newly come, and knew neither of us, he undertook to carry us both where I directed him. When I was about Eleven years of Age, we had a Female Servant, who was Cook, and had liv'd in the Family many Years. She just then married away, and to her I went: she was exceedingly surpris'd to see me at such an early hour, (for we rid all night) and no better attended. Here, said I to the Man who brought us, there's your Hire, and a Crown to drink, make the best of your way home again. I now thought my self the happiest Creature upon earth, for I saw my self safe, and had one to whom I durst intrust my Secret, which I never did to my Maid *Kitty*, because I wou'd not expose my Brother, and for which she owed me, and paid me a Grudge. The Woman, to whose House we were come, was always call'd when she liv'd with my Father by the name of her Place, *Cook*; and so I shall call her for the future. She married a Gardiner, who liv'd some time, with Lord *Lofty*: I presume, Madam, said she, you know the Man, and so do I too well. It was, no doubt, decreed, that I should never have rest, otherwise I shou'd have miss'd his fatal acquaintance. Pray, Madam, *said* Amoranda, give me leave to interrupt you so long, as while I ask you whether you ever favour'd me with a Letter in your Life? That Madam, *said* Altemira, you shall know presently. I had not been three days at *Cook's*, before my Lord came that way a hunting, and just at dinner-time, being very hungry, he popp'd in upon us, before we were aware of him. 'Tis possible you will not readily believe I ever had a Face worth looking at, while you see no remains of a good one; but—— There I interrupt you again, *said* Amoranda; for tho' you have now, a livid, pale Complexion, your Features are still fine, and a little quiet of mind, wou'd raise those fallen Cheeks to their usual plumpness. Be that as it will, *said* Altemira, Lord *Lofty* saw something in it, which he thought worth his notice, and he no sooner cast an eye upon me, than he vow'd an everlasting Love: he took *Cook* aside, and found out who I was, but not the occasion which brought me there. He spent the remaining part of the day with us, and most of the night, before he cou'd be persuaded to leave us; and next day he came again, and said ten thousand things to win a foolish Heart, and I must own, I began to be too well pleas'd with every Word which fell from his bewitching Tongue; he soon perceiv'd it, and as soon took the advantage of my Weakness. One day as we were alone, he began to take some Liberties which I was not very well pleas'd with, and said; My Lord, you abuse the freedom I have given you, I have hitherto believ'd your intentions honourable, you know best whether they are so or no; if they are not, be assur'd your Quality will stand for very little in my esteem, and till I am better satisfy'd in that point, your Lordship must excuse me if I see you no more. Saying thus, I left the room and went to my own, where I lock'd my self up, and came no more out while my Lord stay'd, which was some hours. The next Morning before my Eyes were well open'd to read it, a Letter came from him, fill'd with ten thousand protestations of his sincerity, and if I wou'd but give him leave once more to throw himself at my feet, he wou'd soon convince me of his reality. I have already own'd his oily Tongue had made an impression on my Heart, and I took a secret pleasure in hoping all he said was true; I sent no answer back by the Messenger, which was giving a tacit Consent to another interview, and I saw him at my feet before I thought the Messenger cou'd have return'd. Oh! what an assiduous Creature is Man, before enjoyment, and what a careless, negligent wretch after it. Dear *Altemira, said my Lord*, why do you use me with such contempt? What shall I do to convince you of the real value I have for you? is there one Oath left, which I have not sworn to confirm my Love to you? or can my actions display themselves with greater ardency than I have already shown? Yes, my Lord, *said I*, there is one action yet remains, which must authorise all the rest; that once done, I am yours for ever, but till then, you know what you have to trust to. I understand you, Madam, said the base deceiver, and I greatly approve your cautious Proceedings, you shall soon be satisfy'd in every point, and I will break through all my own measures to make you easy; to-morrow's Sun shall see us one. After this promise he staid not long, but left me in the greatest, the highest tranquillity I ever knew. When my Lord was gone, *Cook* came to me, and told me she was afraid there was some juggle betwixt my Lord and *Kitty*; for I have seen him whispering with her twice, *said she*, and beg you will have a care what you do, and how you trust her; she is very sullen at something, and has been out of humour ever since she came here.

I know it, *said I*, and the reason is, because I have not let her into the Secret of leaving my Brother's House. I wish, *said Cook*, you wou'd part with her; I do not like her, I can recommend one to you just now, who will, I am sure, be very just to you.

No, *said I*, I will first be convinc'd of her behaviour, I hate a strange face. Well, Madam, *said* Cook, I wish you may not repent it. For my part, I was so full of satisfaction at the Promise my Lord had made me, that I cou'd find room for no other thought, and went to Bed that night two hours sooner than usual, that I might indulge it without interruption. As soon as day appear'd, my poor unwary Heart gave a fresh alarm to Love and Joy, and when I heard the Family stirring, I got up and dres'd me to the best advantage, expecting every hour to see my Lord attended by his Chaplain. At last I saw my Lord enter, but no Chaplain, he came to me and said, My *Altemira*, I am now come to remove all your doubts, take this, *said he*, (pulling out a Paper) and let it convince you how much I love. I open'd the Paper, and found it a promise to marry me, with a Bond of ten thousand Pound, if ever he receded from his Word. I own I was pleas'd with the Paper which he gave me in great form, as his Act and deed, before *Cook* and her Husband, who were both Witnesses to it: But I cou'd not find out the meaning of it, and said, My Lord, if you design to marry me, what occasion is there for all this formality and stuff? I presume you are your own Master; what then retards your design? I'll tell you, my dearest *Altemira, said he*, when you and I are alone. Well, *said I*, let me go and lay by this Paper, and I'll wait upon you again: I went up to my Chamber, and lock'd it up in a Scrutore[40] which stood in the room, of which I had the Key, and then return'd to my Lord, whom I found all alone; Well my Lord, *said I*, with a much freer air than usual, now we are alone, pray let me hear this Secret.

Altemira, (said this base Impostor) I now look upon you with a Husband's Eyes, you are in *Foro Conscientiae*[41] my Wife, and as such I will entrust you with all I know: About nine Months ago, I saw a Lady whom I admir'd then, as I do you now, and after I had made my addresses to her some time, she consented to crown my wishes, and we were to be married in a Month's time; but before it was expir'd (with the true Spirit of inconstancy which reigns in most of your Sex) she jilted me, and admitted another, to whom she is to be married next Week. Now, my Dear, *said he*, shou'd I marry first, she will fling all her own Levity at my door, and say the Falsehood was mine, for which reason, since she is so near marriage, I will deny myself the pleasure of thy dear Arms a few days, rather than undergo the Scandal of doing an ill Action to a fine Woman. Here was a gloss set upon as base a design as ever Villain invented; and I, who look'd upon all he said as from an Oracle, gave a pleasing ear to it. He stay'd not late that Night, but came again early next day, for he liv'd within three little Miles of *Cook's* House, and every time he came, grew more familiar with me: I must confess to you, good Madam, I lov'd this Ingrate to distraction, and after such a firm substantial proof of his, as I had lock'd up, I thought myself exceedingly secure; my fear and caution which us'd to attend me constantly, now left me, and I had no other desires than to please my undoer. Three or four days after he had given me the above-mention'd Paper, he came, and said, My *Altemira*, you have never seen my House, I desire you will go with me to-day, and dine there; I hope I have given you too many demonstrations of my Love, to leave you any room for fear. My Lord, *said I*, it is now my Interest to believe every thing that's good of you, and I have no fear of anything, but a want of Power to please you always. After some other discourse I went up to dress, and you may be sure I left no charm behind me, which I cou'd possibly take with me. *Cook* was not willing I shou'd go, but durst not be known to persuade me from it, because my Lord was a good friend[42] to her Husband; however I ventur'd to go, and met with all the civil treatment in the World. I now thought my self at home, and was pleas'd to think how soon I shou'd give my Brother an account of my good Fortune from thence: but alas! my Doom was near, my eternal Destruction just at hand. When we were at dinner, a Letter came for my Lord, which he read, and gave it to me, it was an account of the Lady being married, whom he had some days before told me of. Now *Altemira, said he,* 'tis our turn, to-morrow you and I will join our hands. When dinner was over, he sent his Chaplain for a Licence, who accordingly brought one which he shew'd me; the afternoon we spent in different Diversions, and at Night when I wou'd have gone to *Cook's*, my Lord said I should never leave the House till it was my own, and begg'd I wou'd be satisfy'd to stay all Night: he told me I shou'd have a room to my self and Maid, and in the Morning *Hymen*[43] shou'd crown our wishes. I own I was not long persuading to comply; but soon consented to my own undoing, for about One a-Clock, when all the House was gone to Bed, I heard a little knocking at my Chamber door; *Kitty*, immediately rose, without saying anything to me, and open'd the Door, my Lord enter'd, and came to my Bed-side. *Kitty*, the treacherous *Kitty*, put on her Clothes and left the Room, as she had been instructed. My dearest *Altemira, said my Lord,* it is impossible for me to rest, while you are so near me; give me a Bridegroom's privilege, and let me lie down by you. I found myself under some concern at his Proposal, but consider'd, a few hours wou'd give him a just title to all I had in my possession;

I call'd every circumstance to my memory; the firm engagement I had under his hand; the Letter from *London* of the Lady's Marriage; the Licence and Preparations, which were made; and the Millions of Oaths and Vows which I had receiv'd from a perjur'd tongue, of an eternal Love; all those, in conjunction with an unguarded hour, made me a prey to the basest of Men. In short, Madam, he gain'd his ends, and after some hours Enjoyment, got up and left me. *Kitty*, when he went out, came in again, but I was so little apprehensive of my own Fate, that I said not much to her, but got up and re-assum'd all my Charms. When we were at Breakfast, my Lord said with a sort of raillery; It shall never be said, Madam, that you come to me to be marry'd; if you think fit, we'll confirm our Vows at *Cook*'s, as you call her. With all my heart, my Lord, *said I*, she is Witness to our Contract, let her also see our Nuptials. When we had done, the Coach was order'd to the door, and Lord *Lofty* put me into it, and accompany'd me to *Cook*'s; Now, Madam, *said he*, I will leave you for an hour, and then return with my Chaplain: In the mean time, *said he to Cook*, send for what Provisions you think fit, for dinner to my House, and do you dress it well, and I will help to eat it. This was no sooner said, than my Lord whipt into the Coach and drove away. As soon as he was gone, my Maid came to me and said, Madam, I have heard by chance my Mother is not well; I beg you will give me leave to go and see her: If she recovers, I will return; if not, you may be pleas'd to provide your self of another, I shall give you an early account. *Kitty, said I*, it falls out unluckily for you, but who can help misfortune? I am not willing to part with you, and if you can return in a month's time, so long I will stay for you. The Jade thank'd me, and went away.

I was now left alone with honest *Cook*, then she asked me if I was married? I told her, No, but very near it. She shaked her head and said, she hoped I had brought the same Treasure back with me which I took to my Lord's, for he was going this Morning to *London*. How do you know? *said I, in a distracted Tone*. I went, *said she*, to enquire for you last night, but was not admitted to see you; and I then heard orders given for the best Horses to be gotten ready for *London* in the morning. Good Heaven! *said I*, can this be true? Is there no such thing as Justice in Man? No Faith in their Oaths and Vows? Oh *Cook*! *said I*, if you are still my friend, as I hope you are, send there this minute to know the truth of what you tell me: But I fear, *continued I*, there is too much in't, and by *Kitty*'s going away, that Wench has certainly sold me to him, and I am undone; for Oh! *said I*, all is gone. While *Cook* was preparing to send to my Lord's, a Footman came with a Letter for me; he just deliver'd it and went off, which I open'd, and read, as follows:

MADAM,

AN unlucky Accident has forced me away to London; it is so very sud-
den, that I have not time to excuse my going. I hope, at my return, I shall
find you where I leave you; and you shall find me

Your most Obedient,
LOFTY

As soon as I had read this Letter, my Spirits sunk, and I remain'd breath-
less in my Chair; when *Cook* came in to know what News, she saw the Paper
dropt at my foot, and guess'd something of the Contents. I was convey'd to my
Bed, where I lay for some days in a most miserable Condition; tho in the
midst of all my cruel Reflections, I found my Conscience clear'd myself, and I
was in hopes my Lord's Bond would in some measure justify my Actions to
the World. With this little Satisfaction I got up, and went to the Scrutore to take
out, and look at all the hopes I had left; I fully design'd, if he refused to marry me
at his return, to sue his Bond, recover the ten thousand Pound, and chuse a quiet
Retirement from the World, where I might end my days in peace; but Oh! what
Tongue can tell my Surprize, Confusion and Despair, when I miss'd the Paper
which I had put into a silver Box, and both were gone together.

I call'd *Cook* with a feeble Voice, who came to me, to hear my new Complaints. Oh *Cook*! *said I*, my Misery is now compleat, I have lost my Lord's
Bond and Promise of Marriage; it was in a silver Box in this Scrutore. A silver
Box, *said Cook*; I saw *Kitty* put one in her Pocket the fatal Day you went to my
Lord's, and ask'd her what was in it: she said, her Lady's Patches[44]: You would
trust that wicked Quean,[45] *said she*, whom I always disliked, and now—— Ay,
said I, and now she has undone me for ever; may her Perfidy to me meet with
a just Reward. Nature was so far spent in me by my previous Trouble, that I
sunk under this new Addition, past all hope of ever rising more; I was some
Weeks before I had the use of my Reason, but lay like a stupid Log, taking
what Sustenance they gave me, because I knew not what I did. At last, by
degrees I recover'd my Senses, but was infinitely less happy, than when I had
none, because I was then free from Reflection; my cruel Disquiet of Mind
made so great an alteration in my Face, that when I came to look at it, I could
not believe I was *Altemira*. After I had been in this condition four Months, I
heard Lord *Lofty* was returned from *London*; I immediately writ to him in the
most supplicating Terms, but he would not vouchsafe me an Answer: I writ
again, and he sent it back unopen'd. I had once a mind to go to him, but I
thought his Behaviour to myself would be of a piece with that to my Letters,
and I should only expose myself to his Servants, and pick up new matter for

fresh Grief: but I soon found why I was used with so much Contempt, and heard he made his Addresses to the rich, young, beauteous *Amoranda*. I own, Madam, your Person and Fortune has an infinite advantage over mine; but a Man, who is resolved to be a Libertine, has no true value for a Woman's good Qualities; the best she can show to please him, is to give into all his brutal Pleasures: and as I was sure you would shun such a Lover, I own I did write a Line to let you into the Temper of the Man. But now, Madam, that I have told you my Wrongs, I hope I have engaged your Justice, Goodness, and Pity, and you will no longer encourage his Addresses, but look upon them with the same Contempt, as from a married Man. Madam, *said* Amoranda, your Case I own is very deplorable, and what would give me a sensible Affliction, were it not in my power to do you some service; but I believe I can make you a very acceptable Present, and will contrive a way of serving you beside. At those words, *Amoranda* left *Altemira*, and return'd with the Box and Bond; This, Madam, *said she*, is, I presume, the Loss you have so much lamented, and I do assure you, Lord *Lofty* has not been at *London* since his Injuries to you, but at a Seat he has just by this House, and there he is now: that Box which I have now given you, he accidentally dropt in my Garden, nor does he know I have it; and till I see you as firmly his, as he has promised you should be, I will never leave contriving.

The sight of Lord *Lofty's* Bond, gave poor *Altemira* a satisfaction not to be expres'd; the Blood which had so long forsaken her Cheeks, began to run again in its Channels, and Joy diffus'd itself in every Feature of her Face: Is it possible, *said she*, that I am so happy as to recover this testimony of his Villany? 'tis some little satisfaction for my lost honour, that I have this small justification of my self. 'Tis a very great one to me, *said* Amoranda, that I can contribute towards it, and if I can but gain one point I have in my head, I hope I shall see you perfectly easy; but I have an old Gentleman in the House, who must be let into the Secret, or nothing can be done.

Madam, *said* Altemira, my Secrets are too well known to the World; engage who you please in the Scheme, but spare me the confusion of hearing it. Then, *said* Amoranda, I will leave you employ'd while I go to my Guardian, and desire you will write a Letter to Lord *Lofty*, to let him know you have recover'd the Bond and Contract which your perfidious Servant return'd to him, and that you expect all the satisfaction the Law can give you; then leave the rest to me. Here she left *Altemira*, and sent *Jenny* with Pen and Ink to her, while she told *Formator* the whole Story; he needed no Addition to Lord *Lofty's* Character to confirm him 'twas a very bad one: however, his Indignation was ready to boil over, and he express'd himself as every Man of Honour would do upon such an occasion. *Formator, said* Amoranda, I have this poor Creature's Wrongs so much at heart, that I shall never rest till I recover her Quiet; but you must give me leave, because I have promised never to see Lord *Lofty* more, unless I have your Consent for it, and without seeing him, nothing can be done.

Madam, *said* Formator, I applaud your just and generous Design, and am so far from desiring to hinder it, that I will be your Assistant to the utmost of my power. Then, *said* Amoranda, give me leave to send for my Lord this minute, and do you abscond. *Formator* consented to her Proposal; and she writ the following Lines to my Lord, and sent them by a Footman just then.

> *My LORD,*
> *I Do not want Inclination to meet you where you desired at Nine; but my Argus, as you have sometime call'd him, is gone abroad for this Night, so that we may have an Interview within doors. You know the Hand so well, that this Paper needs no other Subscription, but that*
>
> > *I am Yours.*

As soon as she had dispatched this Letter, she went to see how *Altemira* went on with hers, and found she had just finish'd it. I am before-hand with you, *said* Amoranda, for I have writ to my Lord, since I saw you, and sent it. 'Tis an invitation to a Man, I now hate, and if I can but gain my ends upon him—— Come, let me see what you have writ. She took the Letter from her trembling hand, and read:

> *If Prayers and Tears could mollify an unrelenting obdurate Heart, yours had long ago been soften'd into Justice and Pity: but as they have failed me so often, I think it needless to try them any more. To tell you, my Lord, of Heaven and Conscience, would only serve to make you sport; but methinks you should have some little regard to your bleeding Honour, which lies stabb'd and mangled in a thousand places by your own Barbarities.*
>
> *However, my Lord, I am now to tell you, a fortunate hit has put you into my power, and the Contract you gave me, and corrupted my Servant to steal from me, is once more fallen into my hands. I dare say you will easily believe I intend to carry it as far as the Law will bear, but am still forced to wish you would do a voluntary piece of Justice to*
>
> > *Your Injured*
> > *ALTEMIRA.*

This Letter was sealed, and directed for Lord *Lofty*; and the Summons *Amoranda* had sent him, soon brought him to receive her Commands. In the mean time, neither *Altemira* or *Formator* knew anything of her Design; but as she hoped it would be attended with good Success, she was resolved to have the Merit of it wholly to herself.

Altemira's Letter she gave to one of her Footmen, with an order to bring it in when she call'd for Tea; and to say (if any questions were asked) a Man on horseback enquired for my Lord, desired that it might be deliver'd to him, and rode away.

Amoranda, desir'd *Formator* and *Altemira* to go up into the Room over the Summer-House, where *Brown* heard all *Callid's* and *Froth's* Contrivance, and where they might hear what she said to my Lord; for in the Summer-house she intended to entertain him. They were no sooner plac'd in their different Posts, than they heard the Visiting-knock, and my Lord enter'd, and enquir'd for *Amoranda*, whom he found in the Summer-House: he ran to her with eager transport, and finding her alone, thought opportunity had join'd it-self to his Desires, and he had nothing to do but reap a Crop he never intended to make a title to. My dearest *Amoranda, said he,* how shall I return this favour? With what joy did I receive your obliging Letter, and with what delight am I come to die at your Feet? My Lord, *said* Amoranda, you seem'd so very earnest in your Letter for an interview, I was resolv'd to give you an op-portunity, and shall now be glad to hear what you have to say. To say, my Angel! *said he,* can any Man want, a Theme that has so glorious a Subject as *Amoranda*? Come to my arms, my lovely Charmer, and let me whisper out my very Soul upon thy lovely Bosom. Hold, my Lord, *said she,* before you run into those violent raptures, let me know your designs a little; I confess you have often rally'd a married State, but that I rather take to be a sort of a Com-pliance to a debauch'd, wicked age, than any real inclination of your own; come, my Lord, confess you have a mind to marry. To tell you, Madam, I have a mind to marry, is, to tell you I have not a mind to love you; why shou'd you desire to subject your-self to one, whom you may for ever make your Slave? The very thoughts of being bound to love, wou'd make me hate; and take it from me, as a very great truth, Every Man breathing, makes a better Lover than Husband. Pray, my Lord, *said she,* from whence do you prove your Asser-tion? I must own my experience and observations are but young, and yet I know several marry'd People, who in all appearance love one-another exceed-ingly well.

Yes, Madam, *said he,* in all appearance, I grant you; but appearances are often false. Why then, said *Amoranda*, by the same rule, we may believe the love of one of you to your Mistress, as forc'd and empty, as that of a marry'd Man to his Wife; we have no way to know either, but by their words and actions, and those that think contrary to both, we look upon with so much contempt, that we shun their Conversation, and think it a fault to be seen in their Company.

What a pity 'tis, *said my Lord*, so many good things should be said upon so bad a Subject. I wonder, *said Amoranda*, your Lordship does not get the House of Lords to endeavour to repeal the Law of Marriage: Why shou'd you Lawgivers impose upon other People, what you think improper to follow your-selves? Oh! Madam, *said the Peer*, there are politick reasons for what we do; but if you wou'd ever oblige me in any thing, let us have no more of Marriage. Why really, my Lord, *said Amoranda*, I am not yet at my last Prayers, so that I hope you will not think Despair has any hand in what I have said; and to divert the discourse, we will have a dish of Tea. Here she rung a Bell, and call'd for the Tea-table, which was immediately brought, and follow'd by a Servant, with a letter for Lord *Lofty*; who no sooner cast an eye upon the Superscrip-tion, than he knew the hand to be *Altemira's*. The effect of a conscious Guilt immediately seiz'd the whole Man, his tongue faulter'd, his cheeks glow'd, his hand trembled, and his eyes darted a wild horror; when striving to recover himself, he put the Letter into his pocket, and with a forc'd smile, said, A Man had better have a Wife it-self, than a troublesome Mistress. Nay, my Lord, *said* Amoranda, if that Letter be from a Mistress, I am sure you are impatient to read it, I will readily dispense with all Ceremony, and beg you will do so. Madam, *said he*, the foolish Girl from whom this comes, I own, I once had an intrigue with, but ——— I don't know how it was, she had a better knack at getting a Heart, than keeping it; besides, she gave me such a consumed deal of trouble, that I was almost weary of her, before I had her: No, my Charmer, *said he, Amoranda*, and only *Amoranda* commands my heart; I own no Mis-tress but her, nor will I ever wear any other Fetters, than those she puts me on. Now do I most steadfastly believe, *said she*, that you have said as much, a thousand times, to the very Lady, whose Letter you have in your Pocket; Come my lord, *said she*, either read it while I am by, or I will go away to give you an Opportunity.

Madam, *said he*, rather than lose one Minute of your Company, I will do Penance for three or four; but be assur'd, I intended to have return'd it unopen'd, as I have done several from the same hand: but to oblige you, I'll read it. While he was doing so, *Amoranda* watch'd his Looks, and found a fresh alteration in his Face at every line he read; but when he came to that part which told him, *Altemira* had recover'd his Contract, he turn'd pale as Death, stamp'd, and cry'd—— Zounds[46]——Bless me, *said* Amoranda, what's the matter my Lord? is the Lady not well? My Lord, after he had paus'd a while, said, he was mistaken in the Hand, that Letter came from his Steward, with an account of a very considerable loss he had had.

Pugh! *said* Amoranda, is that all? you know, my Lord, there are Misfortunes in all Families, as Sir *Roger de Coverly*[47] says; come, come, drink a Dish of Tea, and wash away Sorrow. My Lord sat very moody for some time, considering that since *Altemira* had recover'd his Bond and Contract, she would, if only to revenge his Ill-usage of her, be very troublesome: and again, he thought if once the World should come to see them, every body would say he was a Villain if he did not marry her. He therefore resolved to put a stop to her Expectations, by marrying of *Amoranda*, and then she would be glad to come to his Terms, and for her own Credit smother the matter. This was just as *Amoranda* expected, and hoped for; she wisely imagined that if my Lord once saw himself under a sort of necessity of marrying, he would be chusing the least Evil (as he thought all wives were) and rather marry a Woman he had not enjoy'd with as fine an Estate as he could expect, than take one with an inferior Fortune, and of whom he could expect no more than what he had had already. *Amoranda* saw the Struggles of his Soul in his Looks, how unwilling he was to come to a Resolution so much against his Inclinations; but he had just promised her, he would wear no Fetters but what she put him on, and she was as firmly resolved to fit him with a Pair.

My Lord, *said* Amoranda, your Tea will be cold; I wish I were worthy to know what weighty Affair imploys your Thoughts?

A weighty Affair indeed, Madam! *said he*; for I am now bringing my-self to a resolution of doing what I have often thought no Woman on Earth cou'd have had the power of persuading me to: But your Charms have dissolv'd every design, and I now offer you a Heart for Life. My Lord, (said *Amoranda*) a Man of your Estate and Quality, leaves a Woman no room for Objection; but if I shou'd comply too soon, you'll think I am too cheaply won, and value me accordingly. Madam, *said he*, I am one of those who hate trouble, and the less you give me, infinitely the more you'll engage me to you: Come, my *Amoranda, said he,* your old, crabbed Guardian is now from home, and there is no time like that present; I will send just now for my Chaplain, and we will do in half an hour, what I hope we shall never repent of. But my Lord, *said she*, the Canonical Hour is past, and you have no Licence. The Canonical Hours,

Madam, *said he*, are betwixt eight and twelve, and not a farthing matter whether Morning or Night;[48] and for a License,[49] I'll step home my-self, and take care of one. My Lord just remember'd he had one by him, which he had purchas'd to bamboozle poor *Altemira*, and since he was in such haste, 'twas no more than scratching out one name, and interlining another; whip'd into his Coach, bid his Coachman be at home in half an hour, and told the Lady, in another he wou'd be back. *Amoranda* call'd down her two Prisoners, who had been within hearing all this while, and leaving them in the Summer-House, she ran in, call'd for a Pen and Ink, and wrote thus to my Lord:

> *I Am, my Lord, in such Confusion, I have hardly time to write to you:*
> *Formator is just come home; I know he hates you, and will certainly*
> *prevent our designs, till he has writ to my Uncle. I therefore desire you*
> *will, with your Chaplain, come as you once propos'd, into the Grove your*
> *own way; and when it is dark, I will come to you: I doubt not but your*
> *Chaplain has the Matrimony by-heart; if not, pray let him con his lesson*
> *before he comes.*
>
>

Yours in great haste,
AMORANDA.

When she had sent this Letter whip and spur after my Lord, she return'd to the Summer-House, and desir'd *Altemira* to come in and dress her in the same Gown she had on; for tho' it was now past nine o'clock, it was light enough to distinguish colours. As soon as they had got ready, they went to the Grove, and *Amoranda* plac'd *Altemira* just where my Lord was to enter, and bid her whisper, under pretence of *Formator's* being in the Garden, as well to disguise her Voice, as to pronounce her own Name[50] without being fairly heard; and when you are married, (said *Amoranda*) tell my Lord you will go in, and go to Supper, and as soon as you can conveniently, get to Bed, and send *Jenny* to conduct him to you. She here told them, she had writ to retard his return till it was dark; and now *Altemira, said she,* I hope you are near that happiness you have so long wish'd for: I think I hear the Coach. *Formator* (who was all this while with 'em) and I, will place our-selves where we shall hear you if you speak never so low; but you shall see no more of us, till my Lord is in bed with you, and then we will come in and wish you Joy. As soon as *Amoranda* had done speaking, my Lord came, and found *Altemira* ready, whom he took for *Amoranda*; the Chaplain soon did the work, and made them one, to the un-speakable joy of the Bride. She observ'd all *Amoranda's* Orders, and whisper-ing, told him she wou'd go in, and send *Jenny* for him, as soon as she had an opportunity. My Lord sent away his Coach and Chaplain, and waited with the greatest impatience for *Jenny*, who came after some time, and convey'd him in the dark to *Altemira*. As soon as my Lord was gone out of the Grove, *Formator* and *Amoranda* came out too, who durst not stir till he was gone, for fear of being heard; when they thought he was in Bed, they went into the Chamber, with each of them a light in their hand, to wish the Bride and Bridegroom Joy. *Formator* went in first; and when my Lord saw him, he thought he was come to take away his Spouse, and cry'd out, Be gone, Sir, she's my Wife. Fear not, my Lord, (said *Amoranda*, behind) no body shall disturb you, only we are come to wish you Joy. How, Madam, (said my Lord, when he saw and heard *Amoranda*) are you there? To whom have you dispos'd of me, your Chamber-Maid? No my Lord, *said Amoranda*, I scorn so base an action, but I have given you to one, who has the best right to you; come, *Altemira, said she*, sit up and let's throw the Stocking:[51] besides, you are both gone supperless to Bed, and I have a Sack-Posset[52] coming up stairs.

When my Lord had look'd sufficiently round, and saw how matters went, he found it was a folly to complain, and was resolv'd to turn the Scale, and show himself a Man of Honour at last; in order to which, he turn'd to *Altemira*, and said, Can you forgive the Injuries I have done you, Madam? My Lord, *said Amoranda*, I dare answer for *Altemira's* pardon; but who must answer for yours? Madam, *said my Lord*, I am at age, and will answer for my self, and do upon honour declare, I am pleas'd with what you have done; there is certainly a secret pleasure in doing Justice, tho' we often evade in it, and a secret horror in doing ill, tho' we often comply with the temptation. I own my design was to wrong this innocent Lady, but I had an inward remorse, for what I was about, and I wou'd not part with the present quiet and satisfaction that fills my breast, to be Lord of the whole Creation. How great a truth is it, *said Formator*, that Virtue is its own reward; and who that knows the pleasure of a good Action, wou'd ever torment himself with doing an ill one? My Lord, *said he*, this happy turn of temper, has made you a Friend, which you may one day think worth your Notice: and now, Madam, (said he to *Amoranda*) let us leave the happy Pair, and *Altemira* to tell her Lord every Incident, that help'd to bring her wretched Circumstances to such a joyfull conclusion.

The next Morning, my Lord sent for his whole Equipage, and carry'd his Lady home, as became his Wife. *Formator* and *Amoranda* accompany'd them to the House, where my Lord had first decoy'd his *Altemira*; and as they went by, call'd at *Cook's*, who was soon inform'd of all the good fortune that attended her young Lady, and told her she had a Letter for her, from her Brother, which she gave her. *Amoranda* told her Ladyship, there was no body in Company, but who knew the story of her Brother; and desir'd she would read it, . which she did thus:

> *IF I burnt in an unlawful Flame for my dearest Sister, I have quench'd it with my Blood, I no sooner miss'd you, than ten thousand torments seiz'd my guilty Mind; I spent three days in search of you, but every Messenger return'd without any News: I fear'd the worst, and fell into the highest Despair. What have I done! said I, ruin'd an only Sister, left to my Care, who is now, if alive, destitute and a wanderer, and all this by an unlawful Love! Those thoughts distracted me so, that I took up a Sword which lay by me, and struck it into my Breast; my Wound prov'd not mortal, and a few days brought me a healing Balsam, for I was told where you were: I was resolv'd to drive out one extream by another, and see you no more, till I had try'd my Success on a Creature, superior in every Charm to her whole Sex; she listned to my Love, and I pursu'd it, till I made the Fair-one mine. And if Altemira will but forgive what is past, I may call my self the happiest Man in the World. You will, doubtless, be desirous to know my Choice; and to let you see I have not lessen'd my Family by it, know the Lady is Sister to Lord Lofty, who lives so near Cook, that you must have heard of him. I hope you will now return to the arms of your*
> *Repenting Happy Brother.*

Here was a new occasion of Joy for Lady *Lofty*, and my Lord was very well satisfied: they went all together to his House, and spent a few days with them, till Colonel *Charge'em* came from *London* to visit his Lordship; who no sooner saw *Amoranda*, than he began to attack, nor she him, than she began to parly: which, when *Formator* saw (whose Eyes were always open to *Amoranda's* actions) he told her, if she pleas'd they wou'd go home in the morning. She consented because she thought it in vain to deny; otherways, she had no dislike to a Feather, nor did she think a lace'd Coat a disagreeable Dress, and she cou'd have dispens'd with a little more of the Man of War's Company; but her trusty Guardian put a stop to all farther Commerce betwixt them, by ordering the Coach to be ready early in the Morning, so that they were almost half-way home before the Colonel was up, who very probably wou'd have been for waiting upon the young Lady home. Lady *Lofty* and *Amoranda*, after a mutual promise of an everlasting Friendship, parted with much unwillingness, but with a design to see one another often. As they were going home, their way led between two steep hills, where they met a couple of Men mask'd. *Amoranda* was exceedingly frighted, and said, she was sure they shou'd be robb'd; but

Formator bid her have a good heart, and call'd to the Coachman to stop. He got out of the Coach, and taking a Pistol from one of the Footmen, stood at the Coach-door on one side, while two of the Servants, by his order, did the same at t'other, and waited till the two Masks came to 'em. But they soon found Money was not their Errand, it was the Lady they wanted, who had no other guard than *Formator*, her Coachman, and two Footmen. One of 'em rid up, and shot the poor Coachman, who fell out of the Coach-Box, wounded, but not dead; the same resolute Rogue rode up to the two Footmen on one side of the Coach, while the other engag'd *Formator*, who hid his Pistol, till he had his Enemy pretty near him, and then let fly a brace of Bullets at him, which kindly saluted his brain, and down he drop'd. The other, who had beat back the Footmen, seeing *Formator*, an old Man, rode round, to dispatch him, and then get into the Coach-Box, and away with the Lady; but he found the old Man pretty tough, for before the Servants cou'd come to him, who were both disarm'd, he had clos'd in with the Rogue, wrench'd an empty Pistol out of his hand, which he had discharg'd at one of the Servants, but mist him, and with it knock'd him down: he was only stunn'd with the blow, but *Formator* stay'd not for his recovery; he order'd the two Footmen, to get the wounded Coachman into the Coach, and one of 'em to get into the Coach-Box, and drive home with all speed. *Amoranda*, when the Coachman was shot, fell into a swoon, and continu'd in it, till *Formator* got into the Coach; he laid her head in his bosom, and chafed her temples, till he had recover'd her. Her Reason no sooner return'd, than she enquir'd after his safety: Do you live, *Formator? said she*, and have you no Wounds? No, my lovely Charge, *said he*, (transported beyond himself, that he had her safe) I have no Wounds, but what the fear of losing you gave me; the dreadful apprehension of such a misfortune, stab'd me in a thousand places. Well, *said she*, I am glad you are not hurt, but I wish we were at home.

That, Madam, *said he*, we shall be presently; we have not above three Miles to your own House. As soon as they got home, a Surgeon was sent for, to dress the Coachman's Wounds, who was shot thro' the arm; and *Amoranda*, was some days before she recover'd her Fright. Three Weeks were now past, since they left Lord *Lofty*'s, in which time, *Formator* had, by a daily application, endeavour'd to form *Amoranda*'s mind to his own liking; he try'd to bring her to a true taste of that Behaviour, which makes every Woman agreeable to every Man of Sense. A Man, *said he*, of true Judgement and a good Understanding, has the greatest contempt in the world, for one of those Creatures we commonly call a Coquet: Levity, and a light Carriage, is so very despicable in a Woman, that it is not possible for the rest of her qualities, tho' never so good, to atone for them; how much more does it raise a young Lady's Character, to have one Man of sense vindicate her Conduct, than to hear a thousand Coxcombs, cry, ———— Gad she's a fine Woman, she's a Woman of Fire and Spirit? The Commendations of such Men, Madam, *said he*, are like the compliment of a Dog just come out of the dirt, while he fawns upon you, he defiles your Clothes. Nature, when it form'd you, show'd its greatest skill, and sent you into the World so very complete, that even Envy it self cannot charge you with one single blemish; your beauteous Form is all Angelick, and your Understanding no way inferior to it; a temper mild and easy, and a Fortune great enough to satisfy the avarice of the greatest Miser: and why, lovely *Amoranda*, must all these fine accomplishments be eclips'd, by that Foible of your Sex, Vanity? Why have you such a greedy thirst after that Praise, which every Man that has his eyes and ears, must give you of course? For Heaven's sake, dear Madam, *said he*, disguise at least the pleasure you take in it, and receive it with a modest, careless indifference: a Man who once sees a Woman pleas'd with flattery, has gain'd more than half his point, and can never despair of success, while he has so good, so powerful an advocate about the heart he aims at. *Formator, said* Amoranda, were you never flatter'd when you were a young Man? I fancy you don't know the pleasure of it, but I am resolv'd I will never think it a pleasure again, because you dislike it in me; for it must be a disagreeable quality, or you would never argue so strenuously against it. Nay, and there's another thing which will make me leave it, and that is—— Hush, *said she*, I hear a Coach stop at the door, let's go and see who's come. She ran into the entry, and was most agreeably surpriz'd, to see two young Ladies alighting, one of whom was a particular Favourite, and had been her Companion when a Child; the other Lady was a perfect stranger, but she came with *Amoranda*'s Friend, and for that reason was equally welcome: they came in a little before Supper, and *Amoranda* was exceedingly pleas'd she had got a Female Companion or two. When they were at Supper, and saw *Formator* sit at Table; *Arentia*, (for that was the young Lady's name) ask'd if he was a Relation of *Amoranda*'s. She said he was better than a Relation, he was a Friend, and one to whose Care her Uncle had committed her. As soon as supper was over, *Formator* left the Ladies to themselves, and he was no sooner gone, than *Arentia* ask'd how long he had been in the Family. *Amoranda* said, about six Months; he is, *said she*, a very good sort of an old Man, if he were not so very wise; but the truth is, we foolish Girls are not to be trusted with our-selves, and he has taught me to believe we are the worst Guardians we can possibly have. Madam, (said the strange Lady, whom we must call *Berintha*) if we young People give into all the whims of the old, we shall be so too, before we have liv'd out half our days; I hope Madam, we shall not have much of his Company, for of all the things I hate an old Man. Oh! *said* Amoranda, you will like him and will find him a very agreeable Companion; for all his Age, *Formator* has a sprightliness in his Conversation, which Men of younger Years might be proud of. This Encomium of *Amoranda's*, raised a blush in *Berintha's* Cheeks, which she took notice of, and laughing said, If you had not just now, Madam, declar'd your aversion to old Men, I should be half afraid you had a mind to rob me of my Guardian. After some other discourse it grew late, and *Amoranda* ask'd the Ladies, if they wou'd lie together, or have separate Beds? *Berintha* said she always lay alone, which accordingly she did. Next Morning, after Breakfast, *Amoranda* took them into the Garden, and there entertain'd them with the Story of *Froth* and *Callid's* contrivance, with every thing else which she thought wou'd divert them; but while they were in the midst of mirth and gaiety, *Formator* came into the dining-room, and with discompos'd looks, walk'd a few turns about it, saying to himself: From whence proceeds this strange uneasiness? Why is my Heart and Spirits in such an agitation? I never was superstitious, and yet I cannot forbear thinking *Amoranda* in some new Danger; there must be something in it, and Heaven in pity to her, gives me warning: Then after a little pause—— I'll take it, *said he*, and watch the lovely Charmer: I know not why, but methinks I tremble at the thoughts of those two Women, and fancy I see her more expos'd to ruin now, than when she was surrounded with Fools and Fops. Saying thus, he went into the Garden, and walk'd at a distance from the Ladies, but kept his eye upon them; he perceiv'd the new-come *Berintha*, close to *Amoranda*, one hand lock'd in her's, and t'other round her waist: This sight increas'd his doubts, and rais'd his indignation. At dinner he watch'd her looks, and found her eyes always upon *Amoranda*: The sight was death to him, his Soul was rack'd and tortur'd, and while he flung dissatisfy'd looks at *Berintha*, she darted hostile glances at him; his suspicions grew every day stronger, yet, was he in such a state of uncertainty, that he thought it not convenient to say any thing to *Amoranda*, till one Morning she came down before the two Ladies were stirring, and saw *Formator* walking in the Hall. She was glad of so good an opportunity, for she had for several days, taken notice of an unusual melancholy in his Looks. *Formator, said she*, what is the matter with you? What new trouble has taken possession of your breast? I see a Cloud upon your brow, and cannot be easy till I know the occasion of it. Madam, *said he*, the source of my trouble, proceeds from the real concern I have for your Welfare, which I have so much at heart, that the least appearance of Danger, gives it a fresh alarm. I confess myself extremely uneasy, but fear you will think me a very whimsical old Fellow, if I tell you; I suspect *Berintha's* Sex, and cannot but fancy he is a Man.

I shall always, *said* Amoranda, acknowledge myself obliged to you for your great Care and Caution, but beg, my good *Formator*, that you will not carry it too far: What in the name of Wonder could put such a Thought into your Head?

Madam, *said he*, Observation puts a great many things into our heads; you may please to remember, first, she would lie alone. Pugh! *said* Amoranda, that's what I love myself, and so may ten thousand more. True, Madam, *said he*, and had my Reasons stopt there, that would have dropt of course; but why so many kind Glances? So many rapturous Embraces? Such loving Squeezes by the hand, an eager Desire to please you? Eyes ready to run over with Pleasure at every word you speak? Are these the common Marks of Respect betwixt one Lady and another?

Consider, Madam, you have Youth, Beauty, Sense, and Fortune enough to bring our Sex to you in as many Shapes as ever *Jove* himself assumed, and we are always soonest surprized, when we are least apprehensive of Danger.

Formator, said she, every thing you say pleases me, because I know it comes from an honest Heart; but you are too full of Fears, and your Zeal and Care for my Safety, makes you look at things in a false light: I cannot give into your opinion for several Reasons; first, I think it is highly improbable a Person of *Berintha's* Sense should undertake so ridiculous a Project; next, I can never believe *Arentia*, who must be privy to it, would be so base as to betray me. No, no, *Formator, said she*, there can be nothing in it, and I beg you will lay by your Fears. Saying thus, she left him, and went away to the Ladies, who, she heard, were both up. *Berintha* met her with an Air of Gallantry, and led her a Minuet; then catching her in her Arms, kiss'd her with some eagerness. Hold, *Berintha, said* Amoranda, Kisses from our own Sex, and other Womens Husbands, are the most insipid things in nature; I had rather see you dance, I fancy you do it very well, but can't be so good a Judge while I dance with you myself: you will oblige me if you take a turn or two about the Room. This she proposed on purpose to mind her step, which she found somewhat masculine, and began to fear *Formator* was in the right. Good Heaven! *said she to herself,* can this be true? Is it possible *Arentia* can be so treacherous? Is there no Justice, no Honour, no Friendship to be depended on in this vile World? Methinks I could almost hate it, and every thing in it, unless honest *Formator*. While she was thus musing, *Berintha* run to her, and taking her again in her Arms, said, My dear *Amoranda*, what are you thinking of? Her dear *Amoranda* began now to disrelish her Embraces, and breaking from her a little abruptly, said, Madam, I was thinking of Treachery, Falsehood, broken Friendship, and a thousand other things, which this bad World can furnish us with. This Answer made both the Ladies colour, and they look'd at one another with the utmost confusion, which *Amoranda* took notice of, and applying herself to *Arentia*, said, Why, Madam, do you blush? Your Youth and Innocence are doubtless Strangers to all those black things I accidentally named. *Arentia*, willing to extricate herself from her Confusion, said it was a Vapour. O! *said* Amoranda, is that all? Then here's my bottle of Salts for you; and yours, Madam, *said she to* Berintha, is a Vapour too I presume: I'll call for another for you, since your Distemper is the same, your Cure ought to be so too. But come, Ladies, *said she (being resolved to try them a little farther)* I will divert your Spleen with a sight I have not yet shown you. She then led them up two pair of Stairs, where there was a large old-fashioned wrought Bed. This Bed, Ladies, *said she*, was the Work of my Grand-mother, and I dare say you will believe there was no want of either Time or Stuff when it was made. No, *said* Arentia, they had doubtless plenty of both, or it had never got to such a size; I don't believe it wants much of the great Bed of Ware.[53] Methinks, *said* Amoranda, they should bring up this fashion again, now that Men and their Wives keep so great a distance, they might lie in such a one with so much Good-manners. I dare say, *continued she*, we three might lie in it, and never touch one another. What think you, Ladies, shall we try tonight? No, *said* Berintha, for my part, I never loved one Bedfellow, much less two; besides, I never sleep well in a strange Bed. The Proposal however took off some Apprehensions from the two Ladies, but confirmed the third in her Fears.

Madam, *said* Arentia, I ventured to promise my Friend here, before we came from home, a great deal of pleasure upon your fine River, here's a cool Day, and if it be consistent with your inclination, we'll take a turn upon the Water this afternoon, for to-morrow we must think of going home. *Amoranda* was not sorry to hear that, but told them she cou'd not answer them of a sudden, for she knew they did not care to have *Formator's* Company, and whether he wou'd consent she shou'd go without him, she knew not.

I confess to you, Madam, *said* Berintha, I had much rather want the pleasure of the Water than to have the Plague of the Man; but hope you will prevail with him to stay at home, and let us go without him. Come, Madam, *said* Arentia, 'tis our last request, gratify us in this small matter, and compleat the favours we have already receiv'd. Well, Ladies, *said* Amoranda, if you will excuse the rudeness of my leaving you a minute, I'll go and try my Guardian's good-nature. She conducted the Ladies down again, and went to *Formator*. I am come, *said she*, to tell you something, which will, I dare say, be very grateful to your ears; my two Ladies talk of going home to-morrow, but they have a great mind to take a little recreation this afternoon in the Barge, and I desire your Opinion of the matter. Madam, *said he*, I am strangely surpriz'd at your having an inclination to go abroad with a Person you are utterly a stranger to; you know the Water, for some Miles, runs by nothing on one side but Woods and Desarts,[54] and has on the other, but one small Town; suppose there shou'd be a trap laid for you, and you shou'd fall into it, what account can I give your Uncle, either of your Safety, or my own Care? I am sure, *Formator, said she*, you do not think so indifferently of me, as to believe I have a mind to be trapan'd,[55] or that I wou'd not carefully avoid all danger; but I cannot see how it is possible, for me to be in any at this time, because I shall have all my own Servants about me, and if a hundred baits were laid, they cou'd not reach me, unless I were to land; which I faithfully promise you, I will not do: and supposing the very worst you fear, to be true, and *Berintha* shou'd prove a Man, he is neither a Devil nor a Monster, to devour all before him, I wish you were to go with us yourself. No, Madam, *said he*, I perceive myself a perfect Bugbear to 'em both, and wou'd not make your Company uneasy: May Heaven have you always under its kind Protection; I shall be transported at Night, when I see you safe at home again. Fear not, *Formator, said she*, that Providence which knows my innocent Intentions, will I hope conduct me back again. Here she left *Formator*, and went to order the Barge to be got ready, and then return'd to the Ladies. Well, *said she*, I have order'd all things for our long Voyage, and as soon as we have dined we will embark. Nay, *said* Berintha, let us take a bit of any thing along with us, and not stay for dinner. We shall not have half pleasure enough before Night else. *Amoranda*, willing to gratify them this once, sent fresh Orders to the Barge-Men, who were ready in half an hour, and when *Jenny*, by her Lady's Command, had laid in Wine and cold Viands,[56] they sail'd down the Water with a pleasant gale. The three Ladies were set at one end of the Barge, and *Amoranda*'s Servants, six in number, at the other; she herself was set between *Berintha* and *Arentia*, when *Arentia* thus began. Madam, *said she*, Fortune did me an early piece of Service, in making me your acquaintance, when I was yet but a Child, I have ever since done my endeavour to keep up amity and a good understanding betwixt us, and it shall be wholly your fault if ever there be a break in our Friendship; but Madam, our time is short, and there is a story ripe for your ear, which I must beg you will listen to, and hope you will contribute so much to your own happiness, as to comply with the Proposals we are about to make to you; 'tis neither my Cousin's inclination nor mine to use force, but something must be resolv'd upon in a very short space: Nay, Madam, *continued she*, don't look surpriz'd, what I say is fact, and so you'll find it. *Amoranda* gave a scornful smile at what *Arentia* said, and ask'd her, if she thought her a Woman of so little Courage, as to be bullied into any Compliance in the midst of her own Servants. No, Madam, *said* Berintha, *Arentia* has gone a little too far, give me leave to tell the ungrateful tale, for so I fear it will prove. Why, then, *said* Amoranda, do you tell it? a fault committed by chance or mistake, ought to be forgiven; but a wilful one we cannot so easily overlook. The poor Lady began now, to wish she had taken *Formator's* advice, and had staid at home, for she saw nothing, either on her right hand or her left, but a resolute arrogance in both their Countenances; however they kept within the bounds of Civility, and *Arentia* once more began: Know, Madam, *said she*, I am not going to tell you any thing, but what you might be very well pleas'd to hear, I have a near Relation, who is a Man of the greatest merit, a Man of fortune and honour; he had the misfortune, (as I fear I may call it) of seeing you once at the *Bath*, and tho' it be more than a twelve-month since, he still struggles with a Passion that will master him, in spite of all Opposition; Oh! turn to your left shoulder, *Amoranda*, and behold the Wretch.

Amoranda, who guess'd where it would end, look'd very serene and unsurprized, saying, *Arentia*, if your Friend *Berintha* be a Man of Fortune and Honour, as you say he is, why has he used clandestine means to get into my Company? Do you think, Sir, *said she, turning to him,* I am so fond of my own Sex, that I can like nothing but what appears in Petticoats? Had you come like a Gentleman, as such I would have received you; but a disguised Lover is always conscious of some Demerit, and dares not trust to his right Form, till by a false appearance he tries the Lady: if he finds her weak and yielding, the day's his own, and he goes off in triumph; but if she has Courage to baffle the Fool, he sneaks away with his disappointment, and thinks nobody will know any thing of the matter. *Biranthus*, for that was his true Name, was stung to the very Soul to hear *Amoranda* so smart upon him, but was yet resolved to disguise his Mind as well as his Body, and said, You are very severe, Madam, upon a Slave who dies for you; but if I have done foolishly in this Action, *Arentia* should answer for it, the Frolick was hers, and it was design'd for nothing else. But, Madam, *said he*, Time flies away, and every Minute is precious to a Man, whose Life lies at stake; it is now time to know my Doom, shall I live or die? Believe me, Sir, *said* Amoranda, it is perfectly indifferent to me which you do; and if nothing will save your Life but my Ruin, you will not find me very ready to preserve it at so dear a Price. If, *said* Biranthus, you give me cause to accuse you of Ill-nature, you half justify my Design upon you. Pray, *said* Amoranda, what is your Design? To force a compliance with my Wishes, *said he*, if you refuse a voluntary one. How, *said* Amoranda, *with a scornful Laugh*, will you pretend to force, while I am in the midst of my own servants?

Biranthus, now grown desperate, told her she was too merry, and too secure; for know, Madam, *said he*, those Servants of whom you boast, are most of them my Creatures; the Slaves have sold that Duty to me, which they owed to you, and therefore Compliance will be your wisest Course. Nay then, *said* Amoranda, I am wretched indeed: Oh *Formator!*—— *Formator, said* Biranthus, is not so near you now, as he was when you were attack'd in your Coach some weeks ago; I owe the old Dog a Grudge for his Usage of me then, and would have paid him now, but I had try'd the Strength of his Arm, and found it too powerful for me, otherwise you had had his Company this once, in order to see him no more; but you have taken your leave of him, as it is. And are you, *said* Amoranda, one of the Villains that—— *(here she fainted away.)* *Biranthus* was glad of so good an opportunity of getting her ashore, and calling some of the Men to his assistance, they clap'd Pistols to the Breasts of the two Bargemen, who were all *Amoranda* had on her side, and made them row to Land, just at the side of a great thick Wood. *Biranthus* and one of the Men took *Amoranda* up betwixt them, and carried her into the Wood, which the Bargemen seeing, prepared to follow and bring her back, but were prevented by the rest of the Rogues, two of which they knock'd over-board with their Oars, and the other they tied neck and heels in the Barge, then went in search of their Lady: but *Biranthus* had carried her such intricate Ways, and so far up in the Wood, that the poor Bargemen thought there had been Horses ready for them in the Wood, and they had carried her quite away: however, they were resolved to stay till night, in hopes of her Return. In the mean time, the Devils that carried her off, had convey'd her into the most unfrequented part of the Wood, and laid her on the Grass to recover herself; but who can express the Rage, Despair, and Grief, which appear'd in her lovely Eyes, when they open'd to such a Scene of Sorrow, when she saw herself in the full power of a threatning Ravisher, her own Servants aiding and assisting him, in the midst of a wild Desart, where nothing but Air and Beasts could receive her Cries? Oh *Amoranda, said she,* wretched *Amoranda!* what sullen Star had power when thou wer't born? Why has Nature denied us Strength to revenge our own Wrongs? And why does Heaven abandon and forsake the Innocent? But Oh! it hears not my Complaints.————— Oh *Formator!* did you but know my Distress, you would come to my Relief, and once more chastise this odious impudent Ravisher. Oh wretched me! what shall I do? *Arentia,* who had been a long time silent, and confounded at her own Baseness, went to her, and said, Why *Amoranda,* do you think yourself wretched? It is in your own power to be very happy, if your will but hearken to your Friends, and be———Peace, Screech-Owl,[57] *said* Amoranda, thy Advice carries Poison and Infection in it; the very Sound of thy Words raises Blisters on me, so venomous is the Air of thy Breath. Oh Madam! *said* Arentia, we shall find a way to humble your Pride; and since you are resolved to make your Friends your Enemies, take the reward of your Folly. Saying thus, she went away, leaving *Biranthus* and her own Man with her, to execute their abominable Designs against her. When she was gone, the hated *Biranthus* came to her, and said, Madam, if you will yet hear my Proposals, I am now in a humour to make you very good ones; but if you refuse 'em, you may expect the worst usage that can fall to your share, and I shall please myself, without any manner of regard to your Quality or Complaints. 'Tis true, my Estate is not a great one, but your's join'd to it, will make it so; and you shall find me in every thing such a Husband——— As I, *said she,* no doubt, shall soon have reason to wish hang'd: No, base *Biranthus, said she,* if Providence had design'd me a Prey for such a Villain, I should have fallen into your first Snare, but I was delivered from you then, and so I shall be again. Before I would consent to be a Wife to such a Monster, I would tear out the Tongue by the roots that was willing to pronounce my Doom. I would suffer these Arms to be extended on a Rack, till every Sinew, every Vein and Nerve should crack, rather than embrace, or so much as touch a Viper like thyself. Then hear, *said he,* and tremble at thy approaching Fate. This minute, by the help of thy own Servant, I will enjoy thee; and then, by the assistance of my Arm, he shall do so too. Thou lyest, false Traitor, *said she,* Heaven will never suffer such Wickedness. Just as she spoke these last words, they heard a dreadful Shriek at a little distance; the Voice they knew to be *Arentia's,* and *Biranthus,* who had taken hold of *Amoranda,* let her go again, and run to find out his Partner in Iniquity, who he saw just expiring of a Sting from an Adder. He then cry'd out as loud as she had done, when the other Rogue ran to him, and left *Amoranda* to shift for herself. She was no sooner rid of them, than she heard the sound of Horses pretty near her, and began to run towards them. Good Heaven, *said she,* has at last seen my Wrongs, heard my Complaints, and pities my Distress: The Horses were now within sight of her, and she saw a graceful, fine, well-shaped Man upon one of them, attended by two servants; to whom she thus apply'd herself: Stranger, *said she*, for such you are to me, tho not to Humanity, I hope; take a poor forsaken Wretch into your kind Protection, and deliver her from the rude hands of a cruel Ravisher. The Stranger looking at her, said, I presume, Madam, you are some self-will'd, head-strong Lady, who, resolved to follow your own Inventions, have left the Care of a tender Father, to ramble with you know not who. Oh Sir! *said she*, some part of your guess is true; but Father I have none. Nor Mother? *said the Stranger*; nor a Guardian? Nor Mother, *said she*, but a Guardian, a good one too, I have; and were I but once again in his possession, I would never leave him while I live.

Well, Madam, *said the Gentleman*, I am sorry for you, but I am no Knight Errant, nor do I ride in quest of Adventures; I wish you a good Deliverance, and am your humble Servant. Saying thus, he and his Servants rode away. Poor *Amoranda* follow'd them as fast as she could, and still with Prayers and Tears implored their Pity; but they were soon out of sight, and the loathed *Biranthus* again appear'd, coming in full search of her, and designing to drag her to *Arentia's* Corps, there satisfy his beastly Appetite, and sacrifice her to her Ghost. He found the poor Forlorn half drown'd in her own Tears, pulling off her Hair, and wringing her lovely Hands, calling, *Formator,* Oh *Formator!* where are you? *Biranthus* rudely seized her on one side, and her own Man on the other, and was dragging her along, when her shrill Cries filled the Air, and reached the ears of the Gentleman, who had just left her, and now returned again. Villain, *said he to* Amoranda's *Man*, unhand the two Ladies. Sir, *said* Biranthus, there is no harm design'd against her; but the cause of this Lady's Cries proceeds from her Concern for the Death of her Sister, who is just now stung to death by an Adder.

Oh! gentle Stranger, *said* Amoranda, believe him not, this very Creature, who has now spoken to you, is a Man disguis'd, and is going to murder me: O, as you hope for Happiness, either here or hereafter, leave me not. Sir, *said* Biranthus, her trouble has distracted her, do but ride forty Paces farther, and you shall see the poor Lady lie dead. Lead on then, *said the Stranger*. When they came to the Places where *Arentia* lay dead, the Gentleman look'd at her and shaked his head, saying, how does Vice, as well as Virtue reward it self! But Madam, *said he to* Biranthus, if those two Ladies were Sisters, what Relation are you to 'em? None, none, *said* Amoranda, I have already told you he is a Man, a Monster, a Villain and a Murderer; this very Man, Sir, *said she*, set upon my Coach about a Month ago, shot my Coach-Man, and wou'd have carried me away then, but I had my Guardian with me, my Guardian Angel, I may call him, and he preserv'd me that time: the Rogue when he thought he had me sure, confess'd he was a Man, and therefore, for Heaven's dear sake take me from him, tho' you throw me into the River when you have done. No Madam, *said the Stranger*, you look as if you deserv'd a better Fate than that; here, *said he to his Servants*, light, and set this Lady behind me: but *Biranthus* stepp'd between, and pulling out a pocket Pistol, discharg'd it at the Stranger, but miss'd him; which exasperated his Men[58] so much, that one of them ran him quite thro' the Body. When *Amoranda's* Man saw him fall, he ran away as fast as he cou'd, but was soon overtaken and brought back. *Amoranda's* Good-nature, as well as Gratitude, put her upon making ten thousand acknowledgements to her kind deliverer, and begg'd of him to finish the Obligation, by conveying her safe to her Barge. Madam, *said he*, I will wait upon you wherever you please to command me, but how shall we find the way out of this Wood? Sir, *said one of his Men*, I know the way to the Water-side. Upon which, he and his Companion went before, with *Amoranda's* Man bound with a Saddle-girth, till they came to the Barge: as soon as the two Barge-Men saw their Lady come again, they set up a loud acclamation of joy, and she got in again with the Stranger, who gave his Horse to his Servants and they rid by the Barge till it was just at home. When *Amoranda* was set down, at her first coming into the Barge, she ask'd the Barge-Men what that was that lay in a lump at the other end. That Madam, *said the Men*, is one of our Rogues, who we have ty'd neck and heels; and where, *said she*, are t'other two? Why, Madam, *said they*, we cou'd not persuade 'em to be quiet, but they wou'd needs go and help to carry your Ladyship away, so we knock'd 'em down with our Oars, and they fell plum into the Water, and we ne'er thought 'em worth diving for, but e'en let 'em go down to the Bottom, they will serve to fatten the Salmon. Well, *said* Amoranda, take this other Rogue, and tie them back to back, but set his neck at liberty, that part will have enough of the Halter, when he comes to be hang'd. As they were going home, the Stranger ask'd *Amoranda* how she came into the Wood, and in such Company. She briefly told him the whole Story; and Sir, *said she*, if you will but land and go in with me, you shall receive ten thousand thanks, from as good an old Man, as you ever saw in your Life. Madam, *said the Stranger*, I have had your thanks, which is more than a double recompence for the small service I have done you; and after that, all other will be insipid. Pray, Sir, *said* Amoranda, will you satisfy me in one point? You seem now to be a very good-natur'd Man, why were you so cruel to me, when

I first made my application to you in the Wood? Madam, *said he*, there is a Mystery in that part of my Behaviour, which you may one day know, for I hope this will not be the last time I shall see you; however, to mend your opinion of me, I will tell you, I left you with a design to return, and went no farther than behind some Trees, from whence I saw you all the time. By this time, they drew near home, and after some other discourse, perceiv'd the House: When they were almost at the landing-stairs, the stranger desir'd *Amoranda*, to let her Men touch the shore, that he might again take Horse, his Servants being just by; but promis'd to do himself the Honour of seeing her in a little time. When the Barge-Men had landed him, he gave each of them five Guineas, for their Fidelity to their Lady, and standing on the shore, till he saw the Lady land, with a graceful bow to her at parting, he mounted his Horse; and she, to return his Compliment, stood and look'd after him, as far as her eye cou'd reach him: when he was quite out of sight, she went in, calling to *Formator*. But *Jenny* came to her Lady, and told her he went to walk in the fields, just when she went upon the Water, and they had not seen him since: But Madam, *said* Jenny, where are the Ladies? Oh *Jenny, said* Amoranda, my Spirits are too much worn out with Fatigue and Fear, to answer you any question; I must repose myself a little, and when *Formator* comes in, let me know, for I have a long tale to tell that good old Man; in the mean time bid the two Barge-Men, *Saunders* and *Robert*, take care of their Charge. Here she went to her Chamber, and with a grateful Heart thank'd Heaven for her deliverance; but the Agent it had employ'd, ran strangely in her head. From whence, *said she to herself*, cou'd he come? He is a perfect stranger here-about, and how he came into that Wood, which is no road, and at such a needful time, I can't imagine: sure, Providence dropt him down for my safety, and he is again return'd, for he is too God-like to be an Inhabitant of this World, something so very foreign, to what I have observ'd in the rest of his Sex, a *Je-ne-sçay-quoy*[59] in every word, every action he is master of. ———— But what did he mean when he said his Behaviour had a Mystery in't? — will he come again?—— he said he wou'd, and tell me this mighty Secret; I wish he may keep his Word, methinks I long to see him again;—— but then, *Formator?* —— what of *Formator?* He will not find a fault where there is none: *Formator* is very strict, but then he's just, and will not take away merit, where he sees there is a title to it.———— I wonder what Love is, and if ever I felt either its pleasure or its pain, 'tis now. Those Reflections, and her weary'd Spirits lull'd her to sleep, and her disturb'd Mind had an hour's Rest. When *Jenny* had laid her Lady down, and observ'd something very extraordinary in her Looks, she made all the haste she cou'd, to go to the Barge, for Information from thence; but as she was a going, she met *Saunders* and *Robert* at the back door, dragging in two more of her Fellow-Servants, pinion'd down with Cords. Mercy upon us, *said Jenny*, what's the matter?

Aye, *quoth* Robert, Mercy's a fine word, but an there be any shewn here, I think we deserve none our-selves. Why don't you tell me, *said* Jenny, what the matter is? Matter, *said* Saunders, aye, aye, if such Rogues must go unpunish'd, for my part I will never take five Guineas again for being honest. Why, what the Devil have they done, *said* Jenny? Done, *said* Robert, nay, nay, they have done, and had like to have undone; but the Man has his Mare again, and so there's nothing done to any purpose, thank Fortune. Pox take you both, *said* Jenny, if I don't fit[60] you for this, may I always long in vain, as I do now; you couple of amphibious Rats, I'll make you tipple in the Element you are best us'd to, till you burst your ugly guts, before you shall ever wet your Whistles with any thing under my Care. Say you so, Mrs. *Jane, said* Saunders, then you shall swim in a Dike of your own making, before you ever come into my Barge again: you think, forsooth, because the Butler's your Sweet-heart, no body must come within smell of the Ale-Cellar, without your leave; but I-cod[61] your flat Bottom[62] shall grow to the Cricket[63] in the Pantry, before it shall ever be set on a Cushion in my Barge again. You may go, *said* Jenny, and hang your-self in your Barge, 'tis as good there as any where else, you great Flounder-mouth'd Sea-Calf.[64] While they were in this warm discourse, *Formator* came in, and ask'd *Jenny* if the Ladies were yet return'd? My Lady, Sir, *said* Jenny, is return'd, but no body is come with her, but the two Barge-Men, and a couple of the Footmen, with Ropes about 'em, in the wrong place I suppose. Where, *said* Formator, is your Lady? Gone to bed, Sir, *said* Jenny, but order'd me to let her know when you came in; I hear her ring just now. *Amoranda*, was not long coming down, when she heard *Formator* was come in, but meeting him with the greatest pleasure, said —— Oh! *Formator*, I'm glad we are met again, I will always allow you a Man of deep Penetration, and a discerning Judgement; come, *said she* let us go and sit down in the Parlour, and I will tell you such a story—— you little think what a fiery tryal I have gone through since I saw you. When they were set, Madam, *said* Formator, I fear you have been frightened, you look very pale, and yet I think we had no high Winds today; but where, *continued he*, are the Ladies? Ladies, *said* Amoranda, the Monsters, the Fiends, you shou'd have said, but they have receiv'd the just reward of their Wickedness, and are now no more. What, *said* Formator, are they drown'd. No, *said she*, I'll tell you their Catastrophe; so she began, and told him the whole story, but when she came to that part, where the stranger was concern'd, she blush'd and sigh'd, saying, Oh *Formator*, had you seen the fine Man, how graceful, how charming, how handsom ———— Pugh, I think I'm mad, *said she*, I mean how genteel he was; I'll swear, *Formator*, *said she*, now I look at you again, I think the upper part of your Face like his, and there is some resemblance in your Voices too, but that you speak slower, and have a little Lisp.

Madam, *said* Formator, I prophesy, I shall not be lik'd worse for having a resemblance to this fine Man; but beg you will have a care, he is a stranger as well as *Biranthus* was, and for ought you know, may be as great a Villain. Oh! 'tis impossible, *said* Amoranda; if he be bad, the whole Race of Mankind are so: No, *Formator*, Probity, Justice, Honour and good Sense, sit triumphant on his fine Face.

Madam, *said* Formator, *smiling*, 'tis well if this Gentleman has not made a greater Conquest than that over your Ravisher; but how can you forgive his cruelty, in riding away from you when you were in such distress? I told him of it, *said she*, in the Barge, and he said it was a mysterious action, which I shou'd know more of another time. What, then, *said* Formator, he intends to visit you, I find. He said he wou'd, do you think he will keep his word, *Formator*? *said she*. No doubt on't, Madam, *said he*, a Man of so much Honour as you say he is, will never make a Forfeiture of it, by breach of promise to a fine Lady. I remember, *Formator, said she*, you told me some time ago, that a Woman's conduct, vindicated by one single Man of sense, was infinitely preferable to a thousand Elogiums,[65] from as many Coxcombs. I have now brought my self to an utter Contempt for all that part of our Species, and shall for the future, not only despise Flattery, but abhor the mouth it comes from.

I own, *Formator*, the ground-work of this Reformation in me, came from those wholesome Lectures you have so often read to me; but the finishing stroke is given by my own inclination. I believe it, Madam, *said he*, by your own inclination for the Stranger, who (that he may prove worthy of you) I wish may deserve as well in the eye of the World, as he seems to do in your own. Well, *Formator, said she*, I find you think I am in Love, and for ought I know, so I am, for I'm sure I feel something in my heart that was never there before; but this I here promise you, I will never marry any Man, who has not your approbation, as well as mine. Why then, Madam, *said he*, in return for your good nature, be assur'd, I will bring my Opinion as near to yours, as I can, and doubt not, but they will meet at last. But Madam, *said he*, what must be done with the two Rogues yonder? I know not, *said she*, I think 'tis best to pay 'em their Wages, and turn them off. Yes, *said* Formator, off a Ladder,[66] if you please; shou'd we take no more notice than that, of stealing our Heiresses, every Rascal who has twenty Guineas to bribe a Footman, may come when he pleases: No, Madam, they must swing for example. I own, *said* Amoranda, they deserve it, but I'm not willing to take their Lives, perhaps a little Clemency may reclaim them. Madam, *said he*, the Mercy you wou'd shew them, is highly becoming your Sex; but you forget 'tis doing the World, as well as your self a kindness, to rid both of a Villain; I therefore beg leave to send them tomorrow Morning to the County Jail. Then do what you will, *said she*, I leave it wholly to you. Next day at dinner, *Amoranda* look'd very grave, and *Formator* very gay; Madam, *said he*, I begin to fear you are really in Love; else, where are all those pleasant Airs? that Vivacity in your Eyes? the Smiles that us'd to sit upon that fine Mouth? and the sprightly diverting Conversation, so agreeable to all that heard it? I think, *said he*, we must send a Hue and Cry after your deliverer, in order to recover your Charms.

I believe, *Formator, said she*, what I have lost, you have found, methinks you rally with a very gay air; I am glad to see you grow so chearful: but why shou'd you impute my Gravity rather to Love, than the late Fright and Disorder I have been in? Do you think a danger like mine, is to be forgotten of a sudden? While they were in this discourse, a Servant came in with a Letter for his Lady, and said the Messenger stay'd for an answer. *Formator, said* Amoranda, you shall give me leave to read it, which she did as follows.

> MADAM
> THE Raptures I have been in ever since yesterday, at the thought of having serv'd you, has depriv'd me of a whole Night's sleep: What pleasure can this World give us, like that of obliging a fine Woman, unless it be that of her returning it! but as that is a blessing I do not deserve, it is likewise what I dare not hope for, because my wishes are superior to any Service I have, or can do you. Believe me, Madam, I aim at nothing less than your lovely Person, and wish for nothing more. Oblige me with one Line, to encourage a visit; and if I can but make my-self acceptable to you, Formator and I will talk about the Estate.
> Yours, ALANTHUS.

While *Amoranda* read this Letter, *Formator* watch'd her Eyes, in which he saw a pleasing Surprize. When she had read it, with a quite different Look from that she had all Dinner-time, she said, I have seen this Hand before, but cannot recollect where: Here *Formator, said she*, I find you are to be a Party concern'd, pray read it, and tell me whether I shall answer it. When he had read it, he return'd it, and said, I fear, Madam, my Advice will have but little force; however, since you condescend to ask it, 'tis but Good-manners to give it: and I think you ought to have a care how you converse with a Man, for whom you seem to have a tender Concern already, till you know something of his Circumstances.

Nay, *Formator, said she*, that's the part you are to look after, you know I have nothing to do with that; but I think there can be no harm in one Visit, and it would be a poor return for saving my Life and Honour, to deny him the satisfaction of a Line: but I will write but a little, and you shall see it when I have done. She went to her Closet, and writ the following words:

> *I CONFESS myself so greatly obliged by the generous Alanthus, that it is not possible for the little Instrument in my hand to make a suitable acknowledgment for what I have received; but beg you will accept in part, of what it can do, and expect the greatest addition from a verbal Thanks, which is in the power of*
>
> > AMORANDA.

As soon as she had done, she brought it to *Formator*, and when he had read it, she sealed it up, and called for the Messenger, whom she had a mind to pump a little. Friend, *said she*, I have writ a line to your Master, but you must tell me how to direct it.

Madam, *said he*, it can never lose its way, while I am its Convoy; I'll undertake to deliver it safe. How many Miles, *said she*, have you rid to-day? That, Madam, *said he*, I cannot readily tell; for I called at several places wide of the Road. Was your Master born on this side of the Country? *said she*. I am very unfortunate, *said the Fellow*, that I cannot answer any of your Ladyship's Questions directly; but really, Madam, he was born before I came to him. May be, *said* Amoranda, you don't know his Name neither. Yes, Madam, *said he*, mighty well, and so does your Ladyship doubtless, for my Master always writes his Name, when he sends a Billet to a fine Lady. I fancy, *said* Amoranda, your Master's a Papist, and you are his Chaplain in disguise, for you have all the Evasions of a Jesuit.[67] No, Madam, *said he*, I have only Religion enough for one, I want the cunning part; but, Madam, *said he*, my Master will be impatient for my return, so beg your Ladyship will dismiss me. Here then, *said she*, take that Letter for your Master, and there's something for yourself, and be gone as soon as you please.

Formator stood all this while at a Window, leering at them, and laughing to hear the Dialogue betwixt them. Well, Madam, *said he*, I am sure you are pleased, your Looks are so much mended. Pugh! *said she*, I think I have the foolishest Eyes that ever were, they can't keep a secret; but they can tell you no more than I have done already, I have own'd to you, I do like this Man, who calls himself *Alanthus*, much better than any I ever saw before, and am fully determin'd to die as I am, if his Circumstances will not admit of a Union between us. But I am now going to be very happy in a Female Confidant, to whom I can entrust all my Secrets. Not another *Arentia*, I hope, *said* Formator. No, no, *said she*, it is a grave Lady, the only Relation I have on my Mother's side: I expect her to-morrow; she will be a rare Companion for you, *Formator*, and I can assure you she is a Woman of good Sense, and a pretty Fortune: I know not but we may have a Match between you, and while I am contriving for a Companion for myself, I am perhaps getting you a Mistress. No, Madam, *said* Formator, I have as many Mistresses as I intend to have, already; but if she comes to-morrow, I think I'll go and meet her. I'll assure you, *said* Amoranda, I intend her for my Companion and Bedfellow all this ensuing Winter. Yes, *said* Formator, if *Alanthus* does not take her place. Say no more of that, *said she*, but I desire you will not go out to-morrow, because I fancy *Alanthus* will come, and I would fain have you see him. Madam, *said he*, I shall not want an opportunity of seeing him; his first Visit will not be his last; *Amoranda* cannot make a half Conquest.

I'll swear, *said she*, you are very courtly, and I begin to take a little merit to myself upon your account; for they say a brisk Girl makes a young old Man: but I'll go and undress me, and by that time Supper will be ready. While *Amoranda* was undressing, she pulled out the pleasing Letter; and while she was reading it over again, *Jenny*, with the prying Eyes of a Chamber-maid, look'd at it, and said, I wonder, Madam, what delight you can take in that rude, unmannerly Letter. What do you mean, *said* Amoranda, you never saw it in your life before? Why, Madam, *said* Jenny, is it not that you had thrown in at the Summer-house Window in the Glove? I will swear it is the same hand. Ay, *said* Amoranda, and so will I too, now you put me in mind on't; I knew I had seen the hand before, but could not remember where. No, *Jenny*, *said she*, that Letter which you call rude, I now see with other Eyes, and have reason to believe it came from a Friend. Nay, Madam, *said* Jenny, you know best how you can bear an Affront; had any Fellow sent me such a one, I would have spit in his face the first time I saw him: Tell me I was no Angel! An impudent Blockhead. I find, *said* Amoranda, your Lovers must be very obsequious, *Jenny*; prithee what sort of a Husband would you have? Madam, *said she,* I would have one that could keep me as well as you do, one that would rise to work in a morning, and let me lie in bed, keep me a Maid to do the business of the House, and a Nurse to bring up his Children; and then I believe I should make a pretty good Wife. That is to say, *Jenny, said* Amoranda, if you can get a Husband that will keep you in perfect Idleness, you will be so very good, as to be very quiet; but I find you intend to take less pains than I shall do, for if ever I have a Child, I will not think it a trouble to nurse it, 'tis a Work Nature requires of us.[68] Aye marry, Madam, *said* Jenny, if I had follow'd Nature,[69] I should have had Children long ago for somebody to nurse; but I hear the Bell for Supper, will your Ladyship please to walk down?

When they had done Supper, *Amoranda* show'd *Formator* the first Letter, and ask'd him if he did not think it was the same hand which came subscribed *Alanthus?* Yes, Madam, *said he,* I believe it is; and how will you excuse such Plain-dealing? O! *said* Amoranda, you have taught me to relish it, and I have no longer a taste for Flattery; I see 'tis nothing but Self-Interest in your Sex, and a Weakness in ours, to be pleased with it. Believe me, Madam, *said* Formator, you make my poor old Heart dance with Joy, to see this happy Reformation in you: and I shall give a speedy account of it to your Uncle, of the advantageous Change in your Behaviour: As for *Alanthus,* I find he has made a way to your good opinion of him; and if I find his Estate answers, as he seems to hint it will, I will further his Amour, and try to make you happy in the Man you like.

Formator, said the pleased Amoranda, do not you think I ought to have more than a common regard for the Man who snatch'd me from the Jaws of Death and Ruin? But what, *said she,* can be the reason of his concealing himself?

Madam, *said* Formator, Man is a rational Creature, and you say *Alanthus* has good Sense, he doubtless has his Reasons for what he does; but when I see him, I will give you my opinion of him more at large. It now grew late, and *Amoranda* went to bed, but *Alanthus* (whom she expected to see next day) had taken such possession of her Head and Heart, that poor Sleep was quite banished. The Sun no sooner got up, than *Amoranda* did so too; and leaving a restless Bed, went into the Garden, to try if variety of Objects would divert her Thoughts: after she had spent some time among the Birds and Flowers, she thought she heard the noise of Horses in the Highway, and somebody groan; she ran and call'd *Jenny,* who came, and they with the Gardener ran to the Summer-house, and having open'd the Shutters, they saw a fine young Lady on a Spanish Gennet,[70] in very rich Trappings, the Lady herself in a pale Wigg, with a laced Hat and Feather, a Habit of Brocade, faced with a silver

Stuff, and attended by three Servants in rich Liveries, and her Women, all well mounted; but just at the Summer-house Window, one of her Men fell down, and broke his Leg. *Amoranda* had a just compassion for the unfortunate Man, and saw his Lady's Journey retarded; but the late Attempts which had been made upon her, made her afraid to desire her to come in: however, Good-manners took place of her Fears, and she said, Madam, if you will honour me so far as to ride into the Court and alight, my Servants shall get you a Surgeon. The Lady accepted of the Invitation, and *Amoranda* met her at the Gate; when she had conducted her in with that respect which she thought due to her Quality, she order'd her Coach to be got ready, to carry the Servant to the next Market-Town, within three little Miles, and where there was a very good Surgeon. *Amoranda* then call'd for Breakfast, and while they were drinking Tea and eating Sweetmeats, she kept her eye so long upon the strange Lady, that she was almost ashamed, and thought she saw every feature of *Alanthus* in her, only hers had a more effeminate Turn.

Madam, *said she*, if I may hope for the honour of being better acquainted with you, and that you have not resolved to make your Journey a secret, I should be very proud of knowing your Family, and where you travel this way. Madam, *said the young Lady*, I never thought any thing so troublesome as a Secret, and for that reason I never keep any: I can assure you, there is not one Circumstance of my Life worth knowing; but if it will oblige you to answer directly to the Questions you have asked, I will briefly tell you: My Father, who has been some years dead, was Marquis of W——r; I left a tender Mother yesterday, to go in search of an only Brother, of whom I hope to hear at Lord B——s: he has been from us above this half year, and tho he writes to us often, we know not where he is. Lord B——s is my Mother's Brother, and lives so near you, I presume, I need not name the Town, but think it is not above twelve miles from hence. And pray, Madam, *said* Amoranda, is not the young Marquis, your Brother, call'd *Alanthus*? Yes, *said the Lady*; do you know him, Madam? I believe, *said* Amoranda, I saw him once on horseback, when I was from home one day; he is a fine Man, and I think your Ladyship like him. By this time the servants returned, who had carried their Companion to the Surgeon; and the young Lady again took horse, after a great many Invitations from *Amoranda* to stay a day or two with her, but obliged herself to call as she returned, and stay a week with her then.

As soon as she was gone, a thousand Thoughts crouded themselves into *Amoranda's* Breast, and as many pleasing Ideas danced in her Fancy; she well knew *Formator* would share her Joy, and therefore call'd for him, to communicate the whole Affair to him; but was told, he rid out in the morning before seven a-clock, and said he should not return till night. She despaired of seeing *Alanthus* that day, thinking his Sister would wholly engross him; however, she was resolved to put on all her Charms both that day, and every day till he came, and call'd *Jenny* to go up and dress her to the very best advantage. Dinner over, *Alanthus*, who had Love enough to leave all the world for *Amoranda*, came in a Chariot and two Horses, attended only by as many Footmen. She was resolved to take no notice she had seen his Sister, or knew any thing of his Quality, but leave him wholly to himself, and let him make his own discovery when he thought fit. She received him however with a modest delight in her Countenance, and he approach'd her with Love and Transport. Madam, *said he*, if my faultering Tongue does not well express the Sentiments of my Heart, you are to impute it to that Concern which, I believe, most Men have about them, when they first tell a Lady they love. But *Amoranda, said he*, if you have well consulted your own Charms, you may save me this Confusion, and believe I love you, tho I never tell you so; for nothing but Age or Stupidity can resist them. *Alanthus, said she*, you come upon me so very suddenly, that I am at a loss for an Answer; but I don't wonder you are out of countenance at the Declaration you have made: Love is a Subject every Man of Mode[71] is ashamed of. It has been so long exploded, that our modern Wits would no more be seen in *Cupid's* Toils than in a Church; and would as soon be persuaded to say their Prayers, as tell a Lady they love her.

Madam, *said* Alanthus, you speak of a Set of Men, who are best known to the World by the Names of Beaus and Cox-combs. I beg, Madam, you will not take me for one of that number, but believe me a Man of a regular Conduct, one that was never ashamed to own his Maker, or to keep his Laws; and for that reason, whenever I take a Woman to my Arms, she shall come there with the best Authority that Law we live under can give us. Believe me, *Amoranda*, you are very dear to me, and I know you much better than you think I do. I think, Sir, *said* Amoranda, your Words are as mysterious as part of your Behaviour in the Wood was; I can very safely tell myself, I never saw your face till then, and if you ever saw mine before, I should be obliged to you, if you would tell me where. Madam, *said he*, a very little time will draw up the Curtain, and lay all open to the naked Eye; in the mean time, if you dare give yourself up into my hands, you shall find I will strive to make you very happy.

I dare say, *said* Amoranda, you do not expect any hopes from me, till I know who I give them to; or think I would bestow a Heart on one, who may run away with it, and I not know where to call for't again. No, Madam, *said* Alanthus, I have a much better opinion of your good Sense, than to expect an indiscreet Action from you; but if I convince you, my Family and Estate are equal to your own, and can procure your Uncle's Consent, have you then any objection against me? Yes, *said* Amoranda, for all your plausible Pretences and Declarations of Love, I can produce a Letter under your own hand, in which you tell me you don't love me. Then, Madam, *said he*, I'll renounce my Pretensions. *Amoranda* then pulled out the Letter which came in the Glove, and asked him if that was his hand? he said it was, but hoped he had not express'd so much Ill-Manners in it.

Take it then, *said she*, and read it over. Which he did with some emotion; then said with a smile: I did not think, Madam, you would have thought this Letter worth keeping so long, but you have put a very wrong Construction upon it; and I design'd it as a very great Mark of my Esteem: I sent it to put you in mind of turning the right end of the Perspective to yourself, that you might with more ease behold your own danger. I own the Obligation, Sir, *said she*, but as you have that commanding Charm of good Sense, I desire you will employ it in considering how early an Excursion I made into the World, left by Father and Mother before I understood any thing but Flattery, I might have said, or loved any thing but it; and had not my Uncle sent me as good an old Man as ever undertook so troublesome a Task, I might have fallen into a thousand Inconveniencies: I wish he would come home while you are here, I am sure you would like his Conversation mightily. Madam, *said* Alanthus, every thing pleases me, which gives you satisfaction; and if I can but find the Art of pleasing you myself, I have no other Wishes. Just here a Footman came in with the Tea-Table, and turn'd the Discourse; *Alanthus* drank in Love faster than Tea, and *Amoranda's* Charms were his best Repast. She on her side had not so great a command of her Eyes, but they made sometimes a discovery of her Heart, to the unspeakable inward Content of *Alanthus*. The Afternoon was now pretty far spent, and our Lover began to think of taking his leave; but first he told *Amoranda*, he would not press her farther at that time for an Assurance of his Happiness, because it was the first time he had declared himself, but hoped a few Visits more would make her forget the Ceremony and Formality of a tedious Courtship, and give him a glimpse of the only Satisfaction he was capable of. He then went with unwilling steps to his chariot, and *Amoranda* return'd in with a pleased Countenance, and sat down to meditate upon what had past that afternoon; but her Soliloquies were interrupted, by hearing her Cousin *Maria* was come, whom she had been expecting some hours, and went to meet with that chearfulness and good-nature, which shew'd it self in all her actions.

My dearest *Maria*, *said she*, taking her in her arms, you have brought me what I have long wanted, a Female Friend; and now I have you, we will not part this Winter. Madam, *said Maria,* I don't want inclination to spend my whole Life with you, but I have a small Concern at home, which will hardly admit of so long an absence; however, 'tis time enough to talk of that a Month hence. Nay then, *said* Amoranda, there's a Lover in the Case. I never was in a young Girl's Company in my life, *said* Maria, but she brought in a Lover, some way or other; but Madam, I am neither young enough nor old enough to be in Love; that Passion generally takes place, when Women are in their first or second Spring, now I am past one, and not come to the other. Ah! *said Amoranda,* I fancy when the blind Boy shoots his random Arrows, wherever they hit they wound.

The best on't is, *(said* Maria, *laughing)* I have had the good Fortune of escaping him hitherto, and if I thought my self in any danger, wou'd wear a Breast-plate to repel his Force. But I have heard, *said* Amoranda, Love is such a suttle thief, it finds a way to the Heart, tho' never so strongly guarded; besides, it is a pain we all like, tho' we often complain on't. You speak, Madam, *said* Maria, as if there were a good understanding betwixt you, but desire you will never introduce me into his Company; for I wou'd always say with the old Song, *I am free, and will be so.*[72] Well, well, *said* Amoranda, I have seen as bold Champions for Liberty as you, led home at last in Chains, to grace the Victor's triumph: Cupid's an arbitrary Prince, and will allow none of his Subjects to pretend to Liberty and Property: But come, *said she,* we'll go up stairs, that you may pull off your Habit,[73] and look like one of the Family. After they had sat for a while, *Amoranda* heard *Formator's* Voice below stairs, and said to *Maria,* there's my honest Guardian come home, we'll go down to him, he is one of the best Men upon Earth. They found him in the Parlour, to whom *Amoranda* presented her Relation, and he, with his wonted good-manners, saluted and bid her welcome; then turning to *Amoranda,* said, Madam, you are dress'd exceeding gay to-night, I doubt you have had a visitor, and am sure if you have, he's gone away in fetters, for you look more than commonly engaging. Yes, *said* Amoranda, so I have, and wonder you wou'd go out, when I told you I expected him. I am sorry, *said* Formator, I was not here, but did not think he wou'd come so soon. That, *said* Amoranda, must be an affront either to him or me; for either you think my Charms are not attractive enough, or you think him an unmannerly fellow, who does not know a visit defer'd is as bad as none: He told me, *Formator,* he knew me better than I thought he did, and I could have told him, I knew him better than he thought I did; but I was resolv'd to give him his own way, and said not a word of the matter. Why, *said* Formator, what do you know of him? I know, *said she*, he is a Marquis; that his Father is dead, that he has no Brother, and but one Sister; that —— How, Madam! *said* Formator, *in the greatest surprize,* do you know all this? Did he tell you so? No, *Formator, said she,* he did not tell me so, but one did that knows as well as himself: his Sister rode by to-day, whom you might have seen, had you been at home; an accident happen'd just at our door almost, which oblig'd me to invite her in, and seeing her the very picture of *Alanthus,* I enquir'd into her Family; of which she gave me a full account without reserve, and told me she had but one Brother, and his name was *Alanthus.* I see, *said* Formator, this *Alanthus* has found the way to please you, and this discovery of his Family will countenance your Choice; but, Madam, as you have found out one Secret, I must now tell you another: Your Uncle, before I left him, had provided a Husband for you, a Man of Worth, of Wealth, of Quality, and my Business was, to take care you married nobody else: Now, Madam, if your Uncle's Choice be every way as good as your own, will you scruple to oblige him, when you cannot find one Objection against the Man? Why, *Formator, said she, trembling,* have you used me so cruelly, as not to tell me this sooner? Why did you let me see *Alanthus,* to whom I have given a Heart which is not in my power to recall: No *Formator, said she,* I will die to oblige my dearest Uncle, but I cannot cease to love *Alanthus.* You your self say, my Uncle's Choice is but as good as my own; and if there be an exact equality between the Men, why am not I to be pleased, who am to spend my Days with him; and why must I be forc'd into the arms of a Man I never saw?

It wou'd be cruel indeed, *said* Formator, to force you to marry a Man you never saw; but Madam, you have seen him a thousand times, nay, and what is more, you love him too.

Formator, said she, with tears in her eyes, I did not expect this usage from you, 'tis false, by all my Love 'tis false; I never cast an eye of affection towards any of your sex in my Life, till I saw *Alanthus,* and when I cease to love him, may I eternally lose him. And when I cease to encourage that Love, *said* Formator, may I lose your Esteem, which, Heaven knows, I value more than any earthly Good; and now, Madam, *said he,* prepare for Joy, *Alanthus* is your Uncle's Choice. *Amoranda* was so overwhelm'd with delight, at this happy discovery, that she sat for some time both speechless and motionless: At last, *Formator, said she,* you have given me the most sensible Satisfaction I am capable of, for I now find my self in a Condition to please a most indulgent, tender, kind generous Uncle, and can at the same time indulge my own inclinations: But still I am at a loss, for a meaning to some of your Words: Why do you say, if *Alanthus* be the Man, I have seen him a thousand times? Madam, *said* Formator, you know there has been all along, something mysterious in that Gentleman's Behaviour; but the next visit he makes you, will set all in a clear light, and you shall be satisfied in every particular.

Very well, *said* Maria; 'tis no wonder, Madam, you have been standing up for Love's Prerogative all this while, I see you are an excellent Subject, and will fight for your Master; they say Love's a catching Evil: I think instead of staying all the Winter, I had not best to stay all the Week. What say you Sir, *said she to* Formator, is it not infectious? Madam, *said he*, I believe Love often creates Sympathy, but I never heard it was infectious; Love is a Passion of the Mind, which most resembles Heaven, and that Heart which is not susceptible of love, is certainly fill'd with more inferiour Passions; but I am an old Fellow, and have now forgot both the Pleasure, Pain and Power of it. No Sir, *said* Maria, I am sure you have not quite forgot it, you speak with too much Energy in its behalf. I shou'd laugh, *said* Amoranda, to see you two talk your selves into the Passion you are so very busy about; you can't imagine, *Formator*, with what pleasure I shou'd see you both made one. Madam, *said* Formator, the honour of being allied to you, is a sufficient reason, for breaking any Resolution I have made against Matrimony; but I will certainly see your Nuptials over, before I think of my own: beside, I fear this Lady will think me too old for her.

No, no, *said* Amoranda, *Maria* is not very young her self, and you may have the pleasure of going together, and no mortal take the least notice of either of you. Aye, *said* Formator, there lies the burden, so heavy upon old shoulders; we do not only sink under the Infirmities of Age, but we are despis'd for being Old: Tho' the Young are very generous, and willing to give us our revenge, by being content to live till that despicable time themselves. I don't think, *said* Amoranda, any body despises a Person for having 60 Years on their backs; but because they then grow Sour, Morose, Censorious, and have so great a pique against the young, that they won't so much as remember they were ever so themselves: Tell me, *Formator, said she*, you that are free from the weakness of Age, is not my notion just? Madam, *said* Formator, your Judgement runs in too clear a Channel, to be stopt by any sediment: I have often thought old People take the most pains to make themselves disagreeable. For my part, *said* Maria, I sit and tremble, to hear all this, and shall do nothing to-night but study how to avoid it: I once heard of a great Person, who had one always by him, to put him in mind he was a Man,[74] and I think it wou'd be very convenient for us, to have somebody by us, to put us in mind we are growing old, that, as he avoided Pride by one, we may Folly by the other. Nay, *said* Amoranda, we live in a very good-natur'd World, that will tell us our Faults without being hir'd to it; I'll warrant, you may meet with ten thousand, that will tell you for nothing you are an old Maid. Supper, and some other Chat of this kind, put an end to the Evening, and two whole days were spent without seeing or hearing from *Alanthus*; during which time, *Amoranda* was very uneasy, and *Maria*, who shou'd have diverted her, had seen so much in *Formator*, that she grew very dull, and wanted a comforter her self; by which we may see there are Charms, even in Old Age, when it is dress'd in the Ornament of an agreeable Temper. *Formator, said* Amoranda, you that are privy to all, will you tell me, what new Mystery has introduced itself into the Behaviour of *Alanthus* now? Is there no end of his ambiguous Proceedings? And must I never see the Riddle more?

Madam, *said he*, if you never do, I am satisfied *Alanthus* will have the greatest disappointment; for I know he loves you with a Passion not to be match'd in Man: but if we hear nothing from him by to-morrow, I will go myself for Intelligence. The morrow came, but still no News, and *Formator*, who read a great deal of uneasiness in *Amoranda's* Looks, told her, he would go just then, and bring her News; but as he was drawing on his Boots, a Servant from *Alanthus* brought *Amoranda* a Letter. She took the welcome Paper, and found these words:

> *I Do not complain, dearest Amoranda, of an Indisposition which has confined me to my Bed; but that I am robb'd of all my Joy, of all my Comfort, by being kept from her I love, from her I adore.*
>
> *Oh that Amoranda had but Love enough herself to guess at mine, she would then have some notion of those Torments, which Absence, cruel Absence, creates in me: When I shall be able to throw myself at your feet, 'tis impossible for me to know; but if you would hasten my Recovery, it must be by a Line from your dear hand to*
>
> *Your Burning*
> ALANTHUS.

Amoranda's Eyes soon made a discovery of the Sentiments of her Heart, and *Formator*, who saw her Concern, told her he would go and see *Alanthus*, and bring her better news. She waited with some impatience for his Return, which was not till almost night; and then he told her, it was only a light Fever, which his Physician had assured him would go off in a few days, and in the mean time, he would write to her every day, till he was in a condition to come in Person; which accordingly he did, and every Letter gave fresh advice of his

Recovery. When *Amoranda* found her loved *Alanthus* out of danger, as all his letters assured her he was, she began to rally poor *Maria*. Madam, *said she*, you are grown strangely grave of late; I thought, for some time, it had been occasion'd by your Concern for me, but tho' my Gaiety be return'd, yours is quite fled, I think: Come, *Formator, said she*, I don't know how far you may be concern'd in this Metamorphose; I assure you, I expect a good account of this matter, and shall be very well pleased to say, Here comes my Cousin *Formator*. Well, Madam, *said* Formator, when I see you in the Arms of *Alanthus*, I faithfully promise, you shall dispose of *Formator* as you please. But, Madam, *said he*, have you any Commands to *Alanthus*, I left two of his servants at the Gate. No, no, *said she*, he's well again now; but I leave that to you, *Formator*, send what Message you please. *Formator* went to dismiss the Men, and then *Maria* found her tongue again. Madam, *said she*, how will you answer this Behaviour of yours to your Good-nature? To say so many shocking things to me, before the very Man you fancy I have an esteem for: I declare, if I were not one of the best-natur'd old Maids in Europe, I should resent it past forgiveness. Prithee child, *said* Amoranda, don't be so foolish, why I can't believe there's any difference betwixt an old Man and an old Woman; and I dare promise, in *Formator*'s name, if ever he marries, the Woman must speak first. I don't know how it is, *said* Maria, but *Formator*'s intellects seem to be perfectly sound; and for his Outside, there is nothing old belonging to it but his Beard, and that, I confess, is a very queer one, as ever I saw in my life: for I have been here above a Fortnight, and I am sure it has never been a pin's point longer or shorter since I came. Why really, *said* Amoranda, I have often minded his beard myself, and I sometimes fancy the Man was born with it; for he has never shaved it since he came here, and one would think it might in that time have grown very well down to his Waist: But I am glad to see you so chearful again, prithee what was the matter with you to be so sadly in the dumps? Why, *said* Maria, if I tell you the whole truth, it will amount to no more than you have guess'd already; and I shall make no great scruple to tell you, if I ever liked a Man in my life, 'tis *Formator*. I am glad, *said* Amoranda, it will be in my power to serve you then, for you know when I am married myself, I am to dispose of him as I please: But what think you of the God of Love now, Mrs. *Maria*? I think of him now, *said she*, as I did before, that the Distemper he flings among Men is catching; however, he has but wounded, I am not slain: and if it were not for staying to be your Bride-maid, I would fly for my life, and leave the Place where I saw myself in so much danger.

But the poor Lady found herself in a much greater before the next

Morning's Dawn; for one of the Careless Grooms had left a Candle in the Stables, which set the Hay on fire, consumed the Stables, and burnt all the Horses: and for want of a timely discovery, the Flames being very violent, they had catch'd hold of one end of the House; but the Family being alarm'd, it was soon put out.

Formator, as soon as he heard the dreadful Cry of Fire, jump'd out of Bed, slip'd on his Night-gown, and ran to Amoranda's Chamber; he found her up, and in a horrible fright, but hearing Formator come into her Chamber, she turn'd to go with him out of the House, and had no sooner look'd upon him, than her fear gave place to her surprize. My Lord Alanthus! said she, how, or when came you here? Formator was as much surpriz'd to hear her ask such a question, as she was to see him there, and clapp'd his hand to his mouth to feel for his Beard, which in the fright and hurry he had forgot. Madam, said he, I fly by Instinct when you are in danger; but let me convey you hence, and in a safer place I'll tell you more. As they were going down stairs, they met several of the servants coming to tell them the Fire was quite extinguished; upon which they return'd up stairs, and went into the Dining-Room. It being now fair Day-light, Maria, who had been all this while with them, and had had her share of the Terror which had attended the Night, seeing Alanthus and Amoranda look with some confusion in both their Faces; began to recall her scatter'd Senses, and compare the present with the past. This Alanthus, said she to herself, is Formator in every thing but the filthy Beard, on which we have so lately animadverted; but I confess, thought she, it made a very great alteration, and I'll try if I can find it out: she left the two Lovers, and went, as she pretended, to see the ruin'd Stables. When Amoranda found herself alone with Alanthus; What, Sir, said she, am I to think of your being here at such an hour, in perfect Health, and in Formator's Gown, when I thought you on a languishing Bed of Sickness, in your own House or Lodgings? Must I always be a Stranger to your Intentions? Sure you have a very low opinion of my Prudence, while you dare not trust me so much as with your Name or Family; and if I am acquainted with both, I owe my Intelligence to chance: your Lordship will pardon me if I resent it. Saying thus, she rose from her Seat, and was going, when Alanthus snatch'd her hand, and said, My adorable Amoranda, if I value myself for any Action of my Life, it is for carrying on so clean a Cheat for so long a time; I have been these eight Months under your Roof, and have never lain one Night abroad; have been daily conversant with you, and dined and supp'd at your Table, and yet you never saw me more than twice or thrice. While Amoranda was waiting for an Explication of what Alanthus had said, she saw Maria come laughing in with *Formator's* Beard dangling at her fingers ends: Here, Madam, *said she, Formator* has cast his Skin, and left it me for a Legacy; for I plainly see, 'tis all that will fall to my share of the Man. *Amoranda* look'd at the Beard, and then at *Alanthus*; What, *said she,* do I see? Or what am I to believe? not my Eyes, for they have deceived me already; not *Alanthus,* for he has deceived me too. I beg, my Lord, you will disentangle my Understanding, and let me know at once who in reality you are; while you were *Formator,* I had all the value and esteem for you, which was due to a good Adviser, and a careful Guardian: when I took you for Lord *Alanthus,* I look'd upon you as a Man of the highest Merit, as well as Quality; and the additional service you did me in the Wood, gave you a very good title to a Heart which I thought you greatly worthy of: But now that you are no longer *Formator,* I have done with you as a Guardian; and till I am better satisfied you are Lord *Alanthus,* I have done with you as a Lover too. *Alanthus* was very well pleased with her Caution, but resolved to try her a little farther, before he gave her that satisfaction she expected. Madam, *said he,* was not the Authority I brought to introduce me sufficient? Did I not give you a Letter from your Uncle's own hand, to receive me as a Friend?

Yes, *said* Amoranda, to receive you as a Guardian, not as a Lover; to receive you as *Formator,* not as *Alanthus*: and if you cou'd so dextrously deceive me, perhaps you have done the same by him. I fear, Madam, *said* Alanthus, you would be pleased to find me unworthy of you, and would be glad of a fair Pretence to make me a Stranger to your Favour. No, *said she,* Heaven knows, to find you any thing but Lord *Alanthus,* would be the greatest disappointment I am capable of knowing; and I have made too many declarations to *Formator,* of my Love for *Alanthus,* to grow Indifferent to him all of a sudden: but such a gross Imposition as this might prove, would not only ruin my Fortune, but call my sense in question too; tho, I confess, there is one Circumstance, which makes me hope you are the Man I wish: and that is, the account I had from your Sister, of your Family. Nay, I have still another, which will croud in to justify you; a Face I own you have, which says a thousand things in your behalf, and reproaches me as often for my weak suspicion of you.

Let all Disputes for ever cease betwixt us, *said* Alanthus, as I will this hour give you satisfaction. He went away to his own Apartment, and when he had dress'd him, return'd with a Paper in his hand: Here, my *Amoranda, said he,* let this convince you. She took the Paper from him, which she knew to be her Uncle's hand, and found these words:

THE Man, my dearest Niece, who some Months ago appear'd to you as the grave, the wise, the old Formator; is now turn'd into the gay, the young, the accomplish'd Lord Marquiss of W——; and whenever he thinks fit to discover himself, it is greatly my desire you use him as such. He has done me the honour to accept of me for a Friend, and promised to make you the Partner of his Bed, if he liked you when he saw you, and could find a means to win your Affections; if not, you will never know him for what he is.

When *Amoranda* had read the Paper over, she re-assumed her chearful Looks, and Pleasure diffused itself in every Muscle of her Face: But my Lord, *said she*, this discovery being made by chance, who can say you design'd it should ever be made at all? I can, *said* Maria; for I was so near running away with *Formator*, that my Lord *Alanthus*, would have been glad to have brought himself off at the low expence of a little Secret. Madam, *said* Alanthus, if I had design'd to have lived in masquerade, as long as I staid in your House, you should never have seen me as *Alanthus* at all, neither would I have staid so long with you: I came to you, disguised like an old Man, for two reasons: First, I thought the sage Advice you stood in need of, would sound more natural, and be better received from an old mouth, than a young one; next, I thought you would be more open and free, in declaring your real Sentiments of every thing to me, as I was, than as I am: How good an effect my Project has met with, you are not, I hope, insensible; and I beg you will give me leave to remind you of the vast difference there is betwixt your Behaviour then, and now. My Lord, *said* Amoranda, I am so far from derogating from your Merit, that I own, when you first took me under your Care, I was a giddy, thoughtless, inconsiderate Mortal, fit only for the Company of those Coxcombs I too frequently conversed with: but then, my Lord, you shall own in your turn, that I received all your Lectures and Admonitions with the Spirit of a willing Proselyte; that I was ready to give into all your Maxims, and took your Advice as fast, almost, as you gave it. But pray, my Lord, *said she, (taking the Beard)* let me once more see my good old *Formator*, let me once more behold you in that Dress, which so artfully deceived me: methinks I grieve when I tell myself, I have lost the good old Man. Aye, *said* Maria, 'tis pity so good a Character should be a fictitious one; but alas for me! the Loss is mine, and if my Lord assumes the Dress again, I shall certainly lay some claim to the Man. *Alanthus* took the Beard, and dress'd himself as when *Formator*. Now, my Lord, *said* Maria, you are in the height of all your Charms; the grave, sententious, grey-bearded

Formator, had certainly Attractives[75] which the gay, smooth-chin'd Lord *Alanthus* wants. In your Eyes, *said* Amoranda; remember the Fable, the Fox complain'd of Acids, when he could not reach at——[76] and yet I can't but love that Form myself, when I consider the Advantages that accrued to me under its Government, the just Rebukes, the friendly Persuasions, the kind Admonitions, the assiduous care, to turn *Amoranda* from Folly and Madness, to that Behaviour so ornamental to her sex. Then it chastised the insolent Designs of *Callid*, and repell'd the rapid Force of *Biranthus*, when he shot my Coachman, and would have run away with myself. Can those things die in Oblivion? Can they be forgotten in a generous grateful Heart? No! *Formator's* Name shall always be dear to *Amoranda*, and shall for ever find a resting-place in her Breast. Madam, *said* Maria, you'll spend so many Raptures upon my old *Formator*, that you will leave none for your own young *Alanthus*. Yes, *said* Amoranda, I have one acknowledgement to make *Alanthus*, which is equivalent to all the rest; and that is the great Deliverance he brought me in the Wood: But now I think on't, my Lord, you promised to tell me why you left me in such exquisite Distress, when I sued for your kind Assistance in that dreadful Place. Madam, *said he*, you may please to remember, when you suffer'd yourself to be drawn from your own House by those two Impostors, it was extremely against my liking; and I said as much as Modesty would admit of, to put a stop to your design; but when I found, by your excusing them, you were resolved to go, I went to my servants, who are three Miles off, got on horseback, and with two of them rid directly to the Wood, where I knew the Scene would be acted, if they had any ill designs against you: I was there an hour before I met you, and rang'd about every part of it, till I heard some voices, and when the base *Arentia* shriek'd for her Life, I heard the cry, and thought it had been yours: I then clap'd Spurs to my Horse, and was riding towards the Sound, when I met you. How full of Joy my Heart was when I saw you safe, I leave to every Heart, as full of Love, to judge; but I was resolved, if possible, to cure you at once of rambling with Strangers: in order to which, I put on an Air of Cruelty, which, Heaven knows! my Heart had no hand in, and rode from you; I knew it would give you double terror, to see a prospect of relief, then find your self abandon'd; and I likewise knew, the greater your fear was then, the greater your care wou'd be for the future, to avoid such enterprizes: but I had yet a view in favour of my self, and had reason to believe, the greater your deliverance was, the greater value wou'd you set upon your deliverer; and those considerations carry'd me behind a tuft of trees, where I absconded till I saw you environ'd in the utmost danger: Methinks, I yet behold my trembling Fair, with lift-up Hands, and watry Eyes, imploring help, and striving to convince me, *Biranthus* was a Man, tho' some hours before, I seem'd ridiculous to her for only suspecting of it.

I own, my Lord, *said* Amoranda, I owe a thousand Obligations to your generous care, and my whole Life will be too little to thank you for them, but—— No more, Madam, *said he, interrupting her*, I had a glorious return for all that Care, when at Night, as *Formator*, I heard the whole story over again, and so much in favour of the happy Stranger, as *Jove* himself would have listen'd to with envy; and if ever Vanity had an advantage over me, it was that pleasing Minute. This call'd a blush into *Amoranda's* Cheeks, who said she little thought, when she made a free confession to *Formator*, that *Alanthus* was within hearing. But I have another piece of cruelty to lay to your charge, my Lord: Since you had by your disguise found out my weakness, and knew I had a value for you, why did you send me word you were in a dangerous state of Health, when at the same time you had no indisposition, but what proceeded from your Mind, in giving me pain when you had none your self? My dearest *Amoranda, said he*, pardon that one tryal of your Love, it was not possible for me to deny my self the exquisite pleasure I knew your kind Concern wou'd give me; but good Heavens! how did my longing arms strive to snatch you to my bosom when you had read that Letter, that I might have suck'd in the pleasing tears which drop'd from your lovely Eyes. Pray, Madam, *said* Maria, will you order your Coach to carry me home again; I am resolv'd to go into my own Country, and pick up some sweet Swain, to say a few of those fine things to me. My Lord, *continued she*, will you be pleas'd to oblige me with that engaging Beard of yours, that if the Man, whom Interest persuades me to, shou'd want exteriour Charms, I may clap it on his face, and fancy him *Formator*. With all my heart, *said my Lord*, there it is, and may it contribute as much towards your Happiness, as it has done towards mine; but I believe you are the first Woman under Thirty that ever fell in love with a grey Beard. Aye, or over it either, *said* Amoranda; but pray my Lord, *said she*, now that we have set things in a little Order between our selves, give me leave to enquire after your beautiful Sister, she promis'd to honour me with a few days of her Company, as she return'd from Lord *B*——. Madam, *said* Alanthus, you saw her since I did, I have writ to her several times, since you told me she was on this side of the Country, but have not seen her yet, nor does she know where to write to me. While the words were yet in their mouths, *Jenny* came running in, and said the young Lady who had been here some time ago, was come again in Lord *B*——'s Coach, and was just alighting. Pray, my Lord, *said* Amoranda, put on your disguise once more, that I may have the pleasure of seeing your own Sister as much deceiv'd as I have been. My Lord clap'd on the Beard, and *Amoranda* went to meet Lady *Betty (for so was she called,)* and when she had conducted her in, and the common Compliments had pass'd, *Amoranda* told Lady *Betty*, she now claim'd her promise of staying a few days with her. Madam, *said Lady* Betty, it is that promise that has brought me here now; and had I never made it, you had seen no more of me, for I own it was always my Opinion, that a Person who is not in perfect good humour, shou'd never incumber other People with their Chagrin, of which I am at present so very full, that you must have an uncommon share of good-nature, if you can bear with my Company. Methinks, *said* Alanthus, *disguising his Voice as usual*, it is a pity so young a Lady shou'd have so early an acquaintance with any thing that cou'd ruffle her Temper; you have likely, Madam, left a Lover behind you. Pshaw, *said Lady* Betty, you old Gentlemen always think a young Girl's Mind so set upon Lovers, that they have room for no other thoughts: tho' he that gives me a present uneasiness, is a Lover I hope, but he's a Brother too. I remember, *said* Amoranda, *smiling*, your Ladyship spoke of an absent Brother last time I had the honour of seeing you; have you never seen him since? No, Madam, *said Lady* Betty, I fancy he's got into *Fairy-Land*, he lets me hear from him, but will not tell me how he may hear from me; 'tis a little odd, he should make his own Mother and Sister strangers to his abode. Madam, *said* Maria, has your Ladyship any Faith in *Astrology*? this old Gentleman here, is so well skill'd in the occult Sciences, that he can in a quarter of an hour tell you when and where you shall see your Brother; nay, I dare be bold to affirm, he can, without stirring out of the room, shew him to you in his full health and strength, without so much as raising the Devil to help him. Madam, *said Lady* Betty, I shou'd never have taken the Gentleman for a Conjurer, he does not look like one, nor do I believe any Man upon Earth has a power of doing what you have promis'd in his name, unless Lord *Alanthus* be in some Closet in this Room. No, Madam, *said* Alanthus, there is no Man in this Room, but my self, and yet I believe I cou'd make a shift to perform all those difficulties which the Lady has told you of. *Amoranda*, who sat next to a Window which look'd into the Court, saw a Coach and six come in, with Servants in her own Livery: Bless me, *Formator, said she*, who have we got here? *Alanthus* ran to the Window, and saw Mr. *Traffick* alighting. Oh! joyful Day, *said he*, Madam, here's your Uncle! They ran to meet him, and brought him in, to Lady *Betty* and *Maria*, so full of raptures and tender sentiments, at the sight of his beauteous Niece, that his eyes ran over with tears of joy; no less did the sight of his beloved *Alanthus* transport him: But how comes it my Lord, *said he* that you are still *Formator*? I thought by this time, I shou'd have met you, with the Respect due to the worthy Lord *Alanthus*. Lady *Betty*, at those words, stood like one aghast, and looking round her for interpretation, she cast her eyes on Lord *Alanthus*, who had pull'd off his Beard, and whom she saw in her brother's Form; but so far from running to him with the kind Caresses of a Sister, that she shriek'd out, and fell in a Swoon. For *Amoranda* being an accidental acquaintance, and *Maria* a perfect stranger, who had just been telling her the old Man was a Conjurer, and she not expecting to find her Brother there, and seeing him all of a sudden turn'd from an old Man, whom she had never seen before, to a brother whom she knew not where to find, she thought herself in some inchanted Castle, and all about her Fiends and Goblins. The whole Company quickly surrounded her, and brought her to herself again; when Lord *Alanthus* took her in his arms, and said, Why my dear Lady *Betty*, are you so extremely surpriz'd? Look round you, Madam, with chearfulness, and believe your self in the arms of your unfeigned Brother, and among your real Friends: This, my dear Sister, is the *Fairy-Land* where I have so long Liv'd Incognito; and there, there's the Inchantress, who by a natural Magick, has kept me all this while in Chains of Love. Poor frighted Lady *Betty*, who had always done *Amoranda* Justice, in thinking greatly in her favour, began to hear and believe all, and when she had perfectly recover'd her surprize, she turn'd to *Amoranda*, and said, From the first moment I saw you, lovely *Amoranda*, I had an inward impulse to love you, and how well I'm pleas'd with that Alliance I foresee will be betwixt us, my future Behaviour shall shew; in the meantime I beg I may be let into the whole Affair, and know why Lord *Alanthus* affected the frightful Air of an old Man, rather than his own faultless Form. Madam, *said* Amoranda, I hope I need not take much time to persuade your Ladyship to believe I am very proud of your promis'd Friendship, and shall always, with my utmost industry, strive to deserve it; but for the Scheme of the Beard, since I had no hand in it, I leave it to be explain'd by those that had; Lord *Alanthus*, and Mr. *Traffick*, are the fittest to give your Ladyship an account, which I leave them to do, while I beg leave to go and dress me. *Amoranda* and *Maria* went to their Dressing-rooms, while the two Gentlemen entertain'd Lady *Betty* with the Story she desir'd to hear. As soon as *Amoranda* and *Maria* return'd, Lord *Alanthus* went to the former, and taking her by the hand, said, I hope, my dearest *Amoranda*, you remember what a long time of Self-denial I have had, and that during *Formator's* Reign, I never durst so much as touch your Hand, tho' my Heart had ten thousand flutters and struggles to get to you; but as we are now bare-faced, and know one another, as we have determin'd to make each other happy, I beg you will no longer procrastinate my Joy, but let this Day, this very Day, clap us into *Hymen*'s fetters, there to remain, till Death do us part. The whole Company join'd in the request of *Alanthus*, and Mr. *Traffick* added a Command, which met with no opposition. Every thing was immediately prepared, and the Nuptials solemniz'd that afternoon, to the very great Satisfaction of all Parties, and after a Week more spent where they were, they all took Coach, and went to *London*; where the Reader, if he has any Business with them, may find them.

FINIS.

Familiar Letters Betwixt a Gentleman and a Lady

~

The Preface to

The Works of Mrs. Davys, 1725[1]

'Tis now for sometime, that those Sort of Writings call'd *Novels* have been a great deal out of Use and Fashion, and that the Ladies (for whose Service they were chiefly design'd) have been taken up with Amusements of more Use and Improvement; I mean History and Travels: with which the Relation of Probable Feign'd Stories can by no means stand in competition. However, these are not without their Advantages, and those considerable too; and it is very likely, the chief Reason that put them out of vogue, was the World's being surfeited with such as were either flat and insipid, or offensive to Modesty and Good-manners; or that they found them only a Circle or Repetition of the same Adventures.[2]

The *French*, who have dealt most in this kind, have, I think, chiefly contributed to put them out of countenance: who, tho' upon all Occasions, and where they pretend to write true History, give themselves the utmost Liberty of feigning, are too tedious and dry in their Matter, and so impertinent in their Harangues, that the Readers can hardly keep themselves awake over them. I have read a *French* Novel of four hundred Pages, without the least Variety of Events, or any Issue in the Conclusion, either to please or amuse the Reader, yet all Fiction and Romance; and the commonest Matters of Fact, truly told, would have been much more entertaining. Now this is to lose the only Advantage of Invention, which gives us room to order Accidents better than Fortune will be at the Pains to do; so to work upon the Reader's Passions, sometimes keep him in Suspence between Fear and Hope, and at last send him satisfy'd away. This I have endeavour'd to do in the following Sheets. I have in every Novel propos'd one entire Scheme or Plot, and the other Adventures are only incident or collateral to it; which is the great Rule prescribed by the Criticks, not only in Tragedy, and other Heroick Poems, but in Comedy too. The Adventures, as far as I could order them, are wonderful and probable; and I have with the utmost Justice rewarded Virtues, and punish'd Vice.[3] The *Lady's Tale* was writ in the Year 1700, and was the Effect of my first Flight to the Muses, it was sent about the World as naked as it came into it, having not so much as one Page of Preface to keep it in Countenance.[4] What Success it met with, I never knew; for as some unnatural Parents sell their Offspring to Beggars, in order to see them no more, I took three Guineas for the Brat of my Brain, and then went a hundred and fifty Miles *Northward,*[5] to which Place it was not very likely its Fame should follow: But meeting with it some time ago, I found it in a sad ragged Condition, and had so much Pity for it, as to take it home, and get it into Better Clothes, that when it made a second Sally, it might with more Assurance appear before its Betters.

My whole Design both in that and the *Cousins,* is to endeavour to restore the Purity and Empire of Love, and correct the vile Abuses of it; which, could I do, it would be an important Service to the Publick: for since Passions will ever have a Place in the Actions of Men, and Love a principal one, what cannot be removed or subdu'd, ought at least to be regulated; and if the Reformation would once begin from our Sex, the Men would follow it in spight of their Hearts; for it is we have given up our Empire, betray'd by Rebels among ourselves.

The two Plays I leave to fight their own Battles; and I shall say no more, than that I never was so vain, as to think they deserv'd a Place in the first Rank, or so humble, as to resign them to the last.

I have been so anxious for the Credit of my *Modern Poet,* that I shew'd it to several of my Friends, and earnestly begg'd their impartial Opinion of it. Every one separately told me his Objection, but not two among them agreed in any one Particular; so that I found, to remove all the Faults, would be to leave nothing behind, and I could not help thinking my case parallel with the Man in the Fable, whose two Wives disliking one his grey Hairs, and the other his black, pick'd both out, till they left him nothing but a bald Pate.

Perhaps it may be objected against me, by some more ready to give Reproach than Relief, that as I am the Relict of a Clergy-man, and in Years, I ought not to publish Plays, *&c.* But I beg of such to suspend their uncharitable Opinions, till they have read what I have writ, and if they find any thing there offensive either to God or Man, any thing either to shock their Morals or their Modesty, 'tis then time enough to blame. And let them farther consider, that a Woman left to her own Endeavours for Twenty-seven Years together, may well be allow'd to catch at any Opportunity for Bread, which they that condemn her would very probably deny to give her.

A

LIST

OF THE

SUBSCRIBERS

[Her Grace the Dutches of Norfolk]⁶
His Grace the Duke of Richmond
Her Grace the Dutchess of Richmond
His Grace the Duke of Rutland
His Grace the Duke of Newcastle
Her Grace the Dutchess of Newcastle
Her Grace the Dutchess of Grafton
Her Grace the Dutchess of Ormond
The Right Honourable the Marquis of Hartington
The Right Honourable the Marchioness of Hartington
The Right Honourable the Earl of Gainsborough
The Right Honourable the Earl of Sussex
The Right Honourable the Earl of Donnegal
The Right Honourable the Countess of Essex
The Right Honourable the Lady Betty Monkton
The Right Honourable the Lady Katherine Mannors
The Right Honourable the Lady Frances Mannors
The Right Honourable Lady E——— R——l
The Right Honourable Lady Frances Clifton
The Right Honourable Lady Betty Aislabie
The Right Honourable Lady —— ——
The Right Honourable the Countess of Donnegal
The Right Honourable the Countess of Barramore
The Right Honourable the Lady Emilia Butler
The Right Honourable the Lady Londonderry
The Honourable Lady Dolben
The Honourable Mrs. Pelham
The Honourable Mrs. Yelverton

The Honourable Mr. Lumley
The Honourable Sir Darcy Daws
Honourable Sir William Ramsden
The Honourable Sir Jer. Sambrooke
The Right Honourable Sir John Cotton
Lady Taylor
Alex. Pope *Esq;*
Henry Slingsby *Esq;*
Tho. Page *Esq;*
B—— Martyn *Esq;*
Ben. Martyn *Esq;*
Charles Bathurst *Esq;*
Edmond Field *Esq;*
Robert Chilton *Esq;*
John Marshall *Esq;*
—— Long *Esq;*
John Burrel *Esq;*
John Brown *Esq;*
John Green *Esq;*
—— Letheulier *Esq;*
Charles Wingate *Esq;*
William Mildmay *Esq;*
John Clenche *Esq;*
Soam Jennings *Esq;*
James Aude *Esq;*
Ed. Thompson *Esq;*
The Rev. Dr. Young
The Rev. Dr. Savage
The Rev. Dr. Hall
The Rev. Dr. Loyd
The Rev. Dr. White
Mrs. Mildmay
Mrs. Waller
Mrs. Thoroton
Mrs. Lambert
Mrs. Dealtry
Mrs. Watson
Mrs. Stanton[8]

The Rev. Mr. Key
Dr. Smith
Mrs. Cunningham
Mrs. Duncombe
Mrs. Slingsby
Mrs. Barbara Slingsby
Mrs. Affleck
Mrs. Savage
Mrs. Lucy Pelham
Mrs. Jane Des-Bouverie
Mrs. Hammond
Mrs. Horton
Mrs. Whetham
Mrs. Hitch
Mrs. Coney
Mrs. Smith
Mrs. Kelly
Mrs. Kay
Mrs. Spence
Mrs. Woodwill
Mrs. Johnson[7]
Mrs. Lovesay
Mrs. Green
Mrs. Jenkinson
Mrs. Eliza Jenkinson
Mr. Banyer
Mr. Forster
Mr. Hascord
Mr. Alleyne
Mr. Coulton
Mr. Stevens
Mr. Kerrage

Mrs. Gillford

Mrs. Harrison

Mrs. Peirce

Mrs. Whitehead

Mrs. Hancock

Mrs. Reeves

Mr. Hall

Mr. Holden

Mr. Gache

Alderman Barber

Mr. Osberton

Mr. Jacob

Mr. Atkins

Mr. Elcock

Mr. Williamson

Mr. Tew

Mr. Markland

Mr. Turner

Mr. Lambert

Mr. Clarkson

Mr. Aspin

Mr. Nash

Mr. Gee

Mr. Arnold

Mr. Castle

Mr. Raby

Mr. Gibbon

Mr. Westle

Mr. Clark

Mr. Hawkins

Mr. Harding

Mr. Dobson

Mr. Whitehead

Mr. Green

Mr. Davis

Mr. Swinborn

Mr. Shelton

Mr. Higgins

Mr. Hamilton

Mr. Jones

Mr. Napper

Mr. Morrice

Mr. Wellington

Mr. Smith

Mr. Howard

Mr. Wild

Mr. Jackson

Mr. Harper

FAMILIAR

LETTERS,

BETWIXT A

GENTLEMAN AND A LADY

To BERINA

It is now six whole Days since I left the pleasures of the Town, and the more agreeable Amusement of *Berina*'s Company, for a lonely Retreat into the dull Country where Solitude indulges Melancholy, and Time, that used to fly, goes only a Foot-pace. Thought is now my only Companion, and it often diverts me with the pleasing Remembrance of your Promise of an eternal Friendship; but, as human Nature is very frail, it may possibly want the Supports of Correspondence to keep it up: I therefore earnestly sue for a speedy Answer to every Letter I write; which will greatly alleviate my present Disorder, and take off the Edge of my Chagrin. I have often told myself, it is much better never to know a Satisfaction, than lose it as soon as acquainted; since nothing can give a Man a greater Damp than a Reflection upon past Pleasures, when he has no View to their return. How much this is my Case, *Berina* will easily guess, if she has Friendship enough herself to regret the Absence of a Friend. You will say, I am very spightful, when I have told you, the only Pleasure I have had since I left you, was in seeing one of your Sex mortify'd. Certainly the God of Pride himself has not a greater Share of that Quality than a young Lady with a superior Beauty: She thinks all Mankind born to do her Homage, and despises the tasteless Fool that can resist her Charms. One of this sort lives hard by me, who is a Lady of a good Family, but small Fortune, and has been address'd by a Gentleman of a very good Estate: He (contrary to the Advice of all his Friends) would have made her a Jointure[1] of the greatest part of it; and his Folly in every thing shew'd his Love. She, on the other hand, depending upon new Conquests, repuls'd him with Scorn, and (ungenerous as she was) made him a publick Jest where-ever she came; which at last, from many Hands, came to his Ears, and rais'd one Passion to subvert another. He from thence grew indifferent, and forbore his Visits, resolving to try whether Absence could not do what Discretion had attempted in vain. She finding him cool, thought it the greatest Slur upon her beauty to lose a Slave, and therefore, by a Female

Engineer,[2] sent him a little Encouragement; which he turn'd to the right Use, and made subservient to his Revenge. Have I (*said he*) offer'd my Heart and Estate to one, who has, in return, made me ridiculous; and instead of common Civility for my Love, used me with Revilings and Contempt? Believe me, Madam, (*said he*) you shall be a Sharer with me in something; and since you have refus'd what I would so honourably have given you, it is but reason I send back part of what you have forc'd upon me. While he was thus expostulating with himself, a Relation of hers came in, and told him, he had at last prevail'd with the Lady to comply; which our revolted Lover seem'd pleas'd at, and desir'd the next Day might end all Disputes. A speedy Preparation was accordingly made, and the whole Country, for two or three Miles round, invited to this Wedding: They obey'd the Summons, and were punctual to the Hour; where, after a little time waiting for the Bridegroom, he came booted and spurr'd, with a grave elderly Gentlewoman, whom he brought to the young Lady, saying, Madam, here is a Person come to teach you Good-nature and Manners; when I hear you are a Proficient in both, you may possibly hear farther from your humble Servant. In the mean time, be a good Girl, and mind your Lesson; I am going from home for some time, and shall be glad, at my return, to find you improv'd. Which said, he paid a Compliment to the Company, and took Horse at the very Door. How much this has mortify'd the Bride Elect, *Berina* will never guess, because she knows nothing of her Pride and Vanity; but had you seen the Consternation of the Company, and the Looks of the Lady, they wou'd, I dare say, have made the same comical Impression upon your Fancy which they did upon mine. How happy are you and I, who have made the strongest Resolves against the Follies of Love! Be sure, *Berina*, keep your Friendship inviolate, and you shall find I will keep my Promise, in never desiring more.

Yours,

Nov. 1   ARTANDER.

To ARTANDER.

Last Night I accidentally fell into the Company of one of those modern Creatures call'd a *Prude*, who seem'd extremely fond of the instructive Part of Conversation, and being the oldest Lady in the room, took upon her to read us Lectures of Behaviour: Among several Heads upon that Subject, she told us, writing to any Man, except a Husband, a Father, a Brother, or some very near Relation, was an unpardonable Crime, and cou'd not be answer'd to Modesty.

Upon which I was going to write *Artander* one excusive Letter, and desire him to expect no more. But I began to consider, a Friend is not worth calling so, who dares not run the risque of so trifling a Censure, to maintain so noble a Character: and, therefore, bravely scorning all dull Reflection, I have taken my Pen in hand with a design to fight my way thro' all Difficulties, and make good my Friendship in spight of all Opposition. I pity the poor disappointed Lady you writ about, tho' I think she deserv'd her Fate; and the Gentleman's Revenge was very sharp, tho' very innocent. I cou'd send you a Story something like it, but Jilting in our Sex, and Deceit in yours, is so very common, that I think it will want Novelty to make it diverting. The Town is at present taken up with loud Acclamations of Joy for the Birth of a young Prince,[3] and a Vein of Satisfaction seems to run thro' the whole Court and City; the very Grums[4] look pleas'd, and it is much to be hoped, the little Blessing will make another Union.[5] A Gentleman this Morning sent me ten Lines upon his Birth, which I here send *Artander*.

> *Come, grateful* Britons, *sing aloud your Praise,*
> *Trophys of Thanks let us to Heaven raise:*
> *That Providence divine, to still the Noise*
> *Of restless Rebels, and to drown the Voice*
> *Of those who vent their Spleen on Foreigner*
> *Has crown'd our Wishes with an* English[6] *Heir.*
> *Sure all must now, internal Transports feel;*
> *A Joy like this, shou'd animate our Zeal:*
> *Shou'd bare-fac'd Traytors to Obedience bring,*
> *And make 'em doubly loyal to their King.*

There is no danger, I hope, of your thinking those Lines sent to insult you, since by this time, the honest Air you are gotten into, must have work'd off all your poison'd Principles, and substituted a grateful Acknowledgment to Heaven in their room. With how much pleasure shou'd I receive your next Letter, wou'd it but prove a Recantation, and heartily renounce all your former Errors? Why shou'd a Man of *Artander's* Reason and Goodness, be byass'd by a parcel of Monsters? who have nothing in view, but the Subversion of their Religion and Laws, and the utter Ruin of their native Land. Common Prudence teaches us, if we meet with a Creature whose Out-side only we are acquainted with, to keep our fingers at a distance, till we have inform'd ourselves of the Nature of it; lest a gaudy Feather, or a shining Scale, shou'd draw us into the worst of Ills. No less pernicious can it be to Men of honest designs, to be drawn in by a parcel of Villains, who pretend to gloss over all their

Actions with Conscience, tho' it was, long since, sear'd with a hot Iron. Oh! *Artander*, fly from their infectious Breath, for, *the Poison of Asps is under their Tongues!*[7]

I have just received a Letter out of the Country, which gives me an Account of a Maiden Lady of sixty five, who has poison'd her self for Love: the Use we are to make of it, is to hug ourselves in the midst of Liberty, and thank those Stars that inclin'd us to Freedom. I hate a Yoke that galls for Life, but find the greatest pleasure in subscribing my self

Your real Friend,

Nov. 5. BERINA.

To BERINA.

I Always told *Berina*, her greatest, nay, her only Weakness, lay in being a *Whig*. Methinks the very Name, so hated and despis'd, should give your Inclinations a turn: then do but look back to our *English* Annals,[8] and see the Practice of those Men, from whom the Name first took its Rise:[9] look at the Block, the Ax, the sacred bleeding Head: see the best of Men, the best of Kings, made a sacrifice to the Malice of Knaves and Fools: behold your persecuted Clergy, your defac'd and demolish'd Churches, your whole Religion become abominable, and nothing but Canting and Hypocrisy left.[10] Then tell me, *Berina*, when we have consider'd those Things; whether it be not every true Churchman's Business, to dread and crush the like Proceedings?

I thank you for the Poetry you sent me, but had a Poem on the same Subject before, written by one who complains the World takes no notice of him, and to eternize his Name, has publish'd burlesque Tautology and false Grammar, upon an Occasion that call'd for the best Pen among you. Where are all your bright *Whig* Wits? Have they taken a Stock in Invectives against the *Tories*? For shame, *Berina*, rouse 'em up, tell 'em its down-right scandalous to leave so noble a Theme entirely to the hand of a Fool. Bid the Sot call in his Nonsense, and make the young Hero a Bonfire of 'em: tell him it will be a much better way of shewing his Loyalty, than to expose the Child in Doggerel Verse. Methinks I can't but pity poor Mr. *T—k—l*,[11] who, in a ridiculous Dedication, is persuaded to defend the Stuff, and, as Reward for his Service, is promis'd some more of the same kind. But this has amus'd my Pain so long, that I have almost forgot to tell you the Occasion of it. Last Night, going to pay my Devoirs[12] to a young Lady, who has been twenty Miles from home, and just return'd from travel, as she calls it; I being very ceremonious, and full of Compliment at the Stairs-head, with an unlucky turn of my Foot, struck it against her prodigious Hoop-petticoat, and threw both her and myself down stairs.[13] The Hoop, like Bladders ty'd under the Arms in swimming, kept her from danger, but I am nothing but Pain and Plaister.[14] You Ladies are very dangerous Company, for if you can't break a Man's Heart with your Eyes, you'll break His Neck with your Dress. I doubt it has spoil'd me for a Courtier, and will make me very negligent to the Fair. How long I am to lie in, I know not; but beg *Berina* will contribute towards my Cure by writing often: her Letters will amuse my Pain, and turn every thing into Pleasure. How great mine is at the thoughts of her Friendship, none knows, but her own,

Nov. 7. ARTANDER.

To ARTANDER.

YOU sent me to the *English* Annals for a Cure of *Whiggism*, and (as if Heaven had design'd me for what I am) I insensibly found myself in Queen *Mary's* Reign,[15] where I had so many Objects of Cruelty presented to my view, that I was ready to creep into my-self at the dreadful Reflection. How many brave Men, courageous Women, and innocent Children did I see butcher'd, to do God good Service? Our Bishops burning both with Fire and Zeal, to confirm the Reformation so happily begun; while its Enemies, set on by Hell's chief Engineer, depress'd its Growth, and trod it under foot. From thence, I went to the *Irish* Rebellion, where I saw more than three hundred Souls murder'd in cold Blood, the Clergy's Mouths cut from Ear to Ear, their Tongues pull'd out and thrown to the Dogs, then bid to go preach up Heresy; Mens Guts pull'd out and ty'd to each other's Waists, then whipp'd different ways; some stabb'd, burnt, drowned, impal'd and flea'd[16] alive; Children ripp'd out of their Mother's Womb, and thrown to the Dogs, or dash'd against the Stones; crying *Nits will become Lice, destroy Root and Branch*: with a thousand other Barbarities, too tedious as well as too dreadful to repeat, beside what has been transacted abroad. And now, *Artander*, if those things be true, as we have the same Authority for, that you have for your Martyr'd King, tell me, to use your own Words, *Whether it be not every true Churchman's Business, to dread and crush the like Proceedings?* How many of our *English* Kings (to say nothing of those abroad) have been depos'd, and in the cruellest manner murder'd by the Hands of Blood-thirsty Papists?[17] And are we grown so very partial to those Men, to forget or wink at all their Villainies, and only remember a Fault committed by those who acted by (at least) a show of Justice? Not that I approve the Fact, but on the contrary, renounce and detest it: but still, I think there is more Reason to bury one Fault in Oblivion, which was the Result of their Concern for the Reformation, that then lay bleeding with the *Irish* Protestants, than to keep it up with a Spirit of Malice, to foment and heighten those unhappy Feuds which are already begun, and with so much Industry carry'd on. Believe me, *Artander,* there are thousands in this Nation who decry the Martyrdom of King *Charles,* more out of opposition to their Dissenting Brethren, than any real value they have for the Memory of that unhappy Prince: 'tis your only Plea; you have no other handle for your Animosities; drop that once, and like a drowning Wretch, who has just let go the Plank that kept him up, you'll sink for want of something to support you. That good Man's Fate shou'd be remember'd with Sorrow, not with Spite; and we ought to pray to Heaven to forgive his Murderers, rather than call for Fire from thence to destroy those that are left. Oh! *Artander,* let us always implore the divine Goodness, to preserve us from those Men, whose Mercies are Cruelty, and who are now lurking in secret Places for an Opportunity to devour us. I once heard an impudent Papist say,[18] *Guy Faux* was a Presbyterian, and that it was by them the Gunpowder-Plot was set on foot: I dare say, it wou'd be no hard matter, to persuade half the *Tories* in the Nation to be of that Opinion. But now I come to condole with you, for your Misfortune, and shall expect your next Letter with some impatience, because I have Friendship enough to make me interest my self in your Welfare: such an Accident might have been of very ill Consequence, both to the Lady and you; and I am glad you were in a Condition to make some merry remarks upon it. I am just going to the Play, and to subscribe my self,

Yours,

Nov. 10.   BERINA.

To BERINA.

THAT there have been ill Men in all Ages, no Man in his Senses will deny; and the Cruelty you speak of, as far as we may trust to tradition, is equally certain: But, *Berina,* we have always look'd upon that Person's Principles to be very trifling, who accuses another of a Fault, and the very next minute commits it himself. Is it a sufficient Warrant for me to cut a Man's Throat, because I just saw the Fact committed? No, *Berina,* when we renounced *Rome's* Errors, we renounced her Cruelties too: but these impudent King-killers, with their legal Proceedings forsooth, plainly shew'd the World they had a mixture of both remaining. Either we believe the Bible to be the Word of God, or we do not? If we do not, we are then in a State of Atheism and Damnation, and we may act as we will; but if we do, why do we run contrary to the Rules there laid down, and refuse to give *Caesar his Due*?[19] When we took it for our Standard, we resolv'd to refer ourselves to it, and model our Actions by it. Now do but shew me one Text in either Old or New Testament, that tolerates Rebellion, and I'll recede from all my past Opinions, and become as strenuous a *Whig* as *Berina*. If Kings are such sacred Things, that no Hand, but that of Providence shou'd touch; how shall we answer taking their Lives, and banishing their whole Posterity? At this rate, we shall soon forbear to do one another common Justice; and shall neither love the Brotherhood, fear God, nor honour the King. For my part, I am for invading no Man's Right, but giving every body what they can lay a just claim to: how far you *Whigs* have stuck to that honest Principle, I leave the last eight and twenty Years to show;[20] but of that, no more at present. This Afternoon, being quite tir'd of my Chamber, and pretty well recover'd of my Fall, I went to see an old Lady, who had often bespoke a Visit, and began to think me rude for my neglect. The whole scene was so comical, that I can't forbear sending *Berina* the Particulars. When I first enter'd, I found the Lady in her Parlour, set in an easy Chair, with her Feet upon a Cricket,[21] which rais'd her Knees almost as high as her Mouth; she was dress'd in a black Cloth Gown, over which she had a dirty Night-rail, and a coarse Diaper Napkin[22] pinn'd from one Shoulder to the other; upon her Head two yellow *Scotch*-cloth Pinners,[23] and over them a black Gauze Hood, ty'd under her Chin, one Hand in her Pocket, and t'other scratching her Head. After I had paid my Compliment, receiv'd hers, and gaz'd a while at the Charms of her Dress and Person, I made bold to fancy she was a little craz'd; and turn'd to take a Survey of the Room and Furniture, which was no way inferiour to herself: Upon her Tea-Table, instead of a Set of China, stood a Pasteboard,[24] with a piece of fat Bacon upon it; and on the seat of the Sash-window, a red earthen Pan, half full of Pease-pudding, which I guess'd to be the Remains of her Dinner. Upon one of the Silk Cushions were three greasy Plates, and in the Chimney-Corner, a Black-Jack all dropp'd with Candle-grease; upon the Squab lay a great Dog gnawing a Bone, whom she commanded off, and desir'd I wou'd take his Place, but I had too much respect for my Clothes, to accept of her Offer. However, as I was walking to and fro, watching the Cobwebs that they did not fall into my Wig, I slid over a piece of Bacon-Swerd, which threw me directly into the Lady's Lap, and over-set her Cricket: She grew very merry at the Accident, and I very much out of Countenance.

I think your Sex is fatal to me, and had I been cut out for a Lover, shou'd have some dreadful Apprehensions at the Omens; but as I am always safe in *Berina*'s Company, it, and a continuation of her Friendship, is all that is desir'd by

Nov. 13.   ARTANDER.

To ARTANDER.

WHAT a prodigious long time has poor *England* been an Anarchy! For it seems we have never had a King or Queen since King *James* the Second, of dreadful Memory; nor never are to have one, till the conscientious *Tories* can find a hold for the Pretender to creep in at. You always lay a mighty stress upon the power of a King. Methinks it is a little strange that Heaven shou'd make them so very absolute, without any Reserve for the People at all. Suppose God Almighty, for a Punishment of our Sins, shou'd set your Darling upon the Throne, and he shou'd take it into his head to turn *Mahometan*,[25] and condemn all to Fire and Faggot, that wou'd not renounce Christ? Why, say the Non-resisting *Tories*, if he shou'd do so, 'tis the Command of our rightful King, and Kings must be obey'd. 'Tis true, the Supposition is not very likely to come to pass, but it is very possible; and how far I am oblig'd to stand neuter,[26] and see the establish'd Laws and Religion of my Country sacrific'd to the Caprice of a whimsical King, let Reason say. When we swear Allegiance to a King, 'tis conditional; as long as he keeps his Oath, we'll keep ours. When God Almighty commanded our Obedience, he commanded his Care and Love; which if not express'd, is understood: how much of either, King *James* shew'd the bleeding Laws, imprison'd Bishops and slighted Protestants can witness. And how much of both King *George* has shew'd, his mild Behaviour, his Views to the Nation's Interest, and his unfeign'd Care of the establish'd Church, can witness too. Has not his Clemency and Good-nature over-look'd a thousand Insults? And among so many bare-fac'd Rebels, not one in forty met with their deserv'd fate. Is he not daily nos'd with C——m?[27] As if it were a greater Crime in him, than in the whole City beside. Base as we are, he was a Prince before he was our King, tho' the impudent Mob has always used him, like one of themselves. How much does he study the Nation's Interest, by disbanding his Army, and leaving himself hardly any other Guard, than his own Innocence and Goodness? The Church he has always made his Care, has promis'd to protect her, and has most religiously kept that Promise. What Reason then have we to fear Presbytery under his Administration? Do but name one profess'd

Dissenter in any publick Trust, and I'll be as canker'd a *Tory* as the worst of you. If there be so much Duty and Allegiance due to Kings, why must not he have a share? Or will you not own him for your King, tho' both God and the Nation have made him so? How fain wou'd I snatch *Artander* from that obstinate dogmatical Crew; a parcel of Men, who stop their Ears to every thing, that does not suit with their own pernicious Principles; and who wou'd, if their Power were equal to their Wills, lay us in immediate Confusion. But thanks to Heaven for its timely Care of us, for snatching us as a Firebrand out of the Fire, for stopping the raging of the Sea, the noise of its Waves, and the madness of the People.

I design'd this Letter for another Subject, but my Zeal has carry'd me to the utmost confines of my Paper; and I have no more room left, than what will serve to tell you, I am, in all Sincerity,

Yours,

Nov. 18.   BERINA.

To BERINA

I Doubt, *Berina*, you and I shall do as the whole Nation has done, argue ourselves into some Misunderstanding, which may not easily be rectify'd; which Consideration, made me, in my last, try to divert the Subject. You cannot suppose, I want matter to furnish this Letter with an Answer of the same kind; but I think nothing a greater Enemy to Friendship, than Disputes: and mine is so firm for *Berina*, that I wou'd not give way to any thing that could shake it. If yours be so, as I have no reason to doubt; you will comply, when I beg of you to put a stop to this sort of Correspondence; and let your Letters for the future, be fill'd with the innocent Diversions of the Town: 'tis a pity *Berina's* Temper shou'd be ruffl'd with Politicks. I am now going to divert you with something of a different kind. Yesterday being in a very philosophick Strain, I was resolv'd to visit Nature in its most private Recesses, and enter the Hollow of an adjacent Rock, of which you have often heard me speak. Curiosity only makes the Vertuoso;[28] and if I go on a little longer, I shall grow a perfect Sir *Nicholas Gimcrack.*[29] I took two or three of my Servants with me, and enter'd the Vacuity; which made me fancy myself, something like *Quixote* going to the cave of *Montesinos.*[30] After a few Paces advance, I found the Hollow grow very spacious, and to my great surprize I heard a Dog bark; I immediately consider'd, that sociable Creature never lives alone, and how I shou'd like his Company, I knew not: upon which, my Resolution and Discretion fell together by the ears; one persuaded me to go back, and the other forward; but the latter got the better, and on I went; the nearer we approach'd, the louder the Dog yelp'd; the Sound of which led us to a melancholy Mansion, inhabited only by the aforesaid Animal, and a half-starv'd Female. She look'd wild and frighten'd, but seem'd very tractable, and answer'd us directly to every Question we ask'd her; the first was, how she came there? She said, her father brought her there when she was but two Years old. I then ask'd her, what and who her Father was? She said, he was a Highway-Man, who had once been condemn'd to die, but made his escape, and had ever since liv'd in that Rock, till about a Month ago, and then he died. And what have you done with his Body? *said I.* Two or three of his Companions, *said she,* who used to come often to see him, bury'd him in a Clift of this Rock. Are you not willing, *said I,* to leave this dismal Dwelling? Yes, *said she,* if I knew where to go, but I know no body, nor no body me; and I have often wish'd I had died with my Father. I bid her then follow me, which she gladly did, and I carry'd her to my Mother, who has taken her for one of her Servants. The rest have work enough to stare at her; and all look upon her as a Spectre, and dare not sleep without a Candle by them.

The poor Girl seems to have a better Notion of Virtue than cou'd be expected from her Education, which makes me conclude Virtue is an innate Qualification,[31] born with, and inseparable from some People. This, *Berina,* is the true Account of my Adventure into the Rock; which, I hope, will not only amuse you, but serve for innocent Chat over the Tea-Table, and be a Reprieve, one day, for the Faults of the Absent. For tho' I know you have a Soul above Scandal,[32] I will not answer for the rest of your Sex. I am now going to be very vain, and tell you, a Gentleman has been with me to bespeak me for his Daughter; how to bring myself off with good Manners, I hardly knew; but was at last forc'd to tell him, I found an inward Decay, which put a stop to all thoughts of that kind, and wish'd the Lady a more suitable Husband! And I have once more given it under my Hand, that Marriage shall never spoil my Friendship for *Berina:* when it does, may I cease to be

Nov. 21   ARTANDER.

To ARTANDER

IF *Artander's* Heart were not as hard as the Rock he has been scrutinizing into, he wou'd never have laid such strict Injunctions on my Pen, and robb'd me of my darling Pleasure; but to let you see how ready I am to relinquish every thing that gives you uneasiness, I have, in compliance with my Friendship, laid by the Subject you dislike, and will, for the future, entertain you with something else.

My Uncle has been extremely ill of a Quinsy,[33] and Dr....... has not stirr'd from him these three days; from which you will conclude, the Town is very healthy, or the Doctor has not many Patients. He favour'd me with the Relation of a Journey he had once into the Country, which I shall think well bestow'd upon *Artander*. I happen'd, *said he*, some time ago to be in the Country, within some Miles of the Seat of a Peer: He was indispos'd, and hearing of my being there, sent his tatter'd Coach, with a sleepy old Woman in it, to fetch me; but I disliking both the vehicle and the Messenger, made a Demur, which might have cost my Lord his Life, had not the double Diligence of the old Woman, added to the Advice of my Friends, set me forward. It is not much to be suppos'd, my Journey was very pleasant, because it was almost Night, the Weather extremely cold, and my Company not very agreeable; however, after many a long Wish, and some long Miles, I at last found myself at my Journey's End, and was conducted in by my old Guide; where my Sense of Seeing was quite useless, having not the least Light so much as to help me to a Seat to sit down on. The old Woman, as soon as she had convey'd me into the Kitchen, (if it may be call'd one, where no Victuals is stirring) went to tell my Lord I was come. In the mean time, I stretch'd my Eyes as wide open as I cou'd, and at last discover'd a sort of a glimmering Light, which made way for itself betwixt three or four Fellows who were sate upon a Log of Wood before a Hatfull of Fire. I (as is very natural for folks in a dark unknown Place) made up to it, and cou'd discern the Fellows to be extremely dirty. Bless me! thought I, where the Devil am I got! among a Company of the *Black Guard*?[34] or is this some inchanted Den? I ventur'd to ask the Men some Questions, but their Answers were so intricate, that they only serv'd to confirm me in my former Opinion; and I wou'd freely have given a Twelve-month's Fees to have been at home again. At last, after I had been brought to such a condition, that I wanted a Cordial more than my Patient, I saw the happy Approach of a Farthing-Candle,[35] stuck in a Wooden Candlestick, and held in the Hand of one, who did not look like an Inhabitant of the Sooty-Region I had been so long confin'd to; his Face being wash'd, his Coat whole, and a clean Neckcloth about his Neck. He told me, my Lord would see me; but when I came to the Stairs-foot, I did as School-Boys do, when they are going to slide upon Ice, persuade some of the rest to go on first, to try if it will bear; so I desir'd my Guide to go up first, for I did not like their rotten Aspect. When I came into my Lord's Chamber, I found him within a Suit of Moth-eaten red Serge Curtains, where he look'd more like one swinging in a Hammock than lying in a Bed: the ponderous Weight of his own Carcass having sunk the Cords even to the Boards; so that whoever wou'd have seen my Lord, must have peep'd under the Bed. For my part, I was so tir'd with walking and standing, that as soon as I had felt his Lordship's Pulse, I turn'd about to look for a Chair, of which there were four in the Room; one stood upon three Legs, another wanted its Back, a third had lost his Bottom, and the fourth was half cover'd with a red Rag, and the ————[36] upon it. But before I had determin'd which to sit upon, my Lord desir'd me to walk down again 'till he had consider'd of my Advice; which I did, and was forc'd to take up with my old Walk again, 'till one of the Gentlemen upon the Log got up, and kindly offer'd me his Seat, of which I as thankfully accepted. But after an Hour's waiting for my new Commands, and receiving none, I ask'd my black Companions what I was to have for Supper? They told me, they knew nothing of the matter, for they had none for themselves. Pray then, *said I*, will you do me the Favour to shew me my Lodging, that I may lie down a little? Which the Fellow, who wanted his Seat, did, and carry'd me into a Room much like an old Goal,[37] where there was a Bed, but no Curtains; Windows, but no Glass; and a Door, but neither Lock, Bolt, or any thing to make it fast with. I was still apprehensive of some Danger; so drew all the Lumber in the Room to the Door, and then wrapt myself up in my Cloak, and laid me down, with a design to sleep 'till the Moon got up, to light me home; but the Fleas, who wanted their Suppers as much as I did, surrounded me on all sides, and fed so heartily, that they sav'd me Half a Crown to a Surgeon for bleeding me, and that was my Fee. As soon as Dawn of Day appear'd, I left my wretched Bed, and posted home without either Coach or Company; and soon after heard my Lord was dead, which all that lov'd him rejoic'd at: He having gamed away his whole Estate, his very Clothes and Furniture of his House. And thus, Madam, *continu'd he*, I have given you a true Account of my Lordly Patient; which I have not done with a design to expose Quality, but to shew the miserable Effects of that bewitching Vice which ruin'd him.

> *You see,* Artander, *what the Gamester wins:*
> *From the first Hour of Play, his Woe begins.*

I stumbled over these two Lines by chance, but am resolv'd, since you will not let me be a Politician, to invoke the Muses, and turn Poetess. Bless me! what Rheams of Paper will you have laid at your feet, cringing for Protection! But the Tea-Kettle boils, which puts me in mind of a Conclusion.

Yours,

Nov. 26   BERINA.

To BERINA.

WHEN I am *Berina's* Patron, I intend to be her Champion too, and with Pen in Hand defend whate'er she writes. The Doctor's Story I had heard before from another good Hand. Nor is it at all unlikely that (tho' a Man of very good Quality) he shou'd, after a Life spent in Debauchery and Extravagance, go off the Stage in scandalous Circumstances; but let the Dead rest. This Morning, after two hours Study by Candle-light, which sunk and tir'd my Spirits, and made me unfit for that Exercise any longer, I took a Walk into the Fields, where I promis'd myself a quiet Retreat: But Solitude itself is not always a Fence against Impertinence; for as I was going into one of my own Closes, I heard somebody call me; and turning to see who it was, found a Gentleman who lives within a Mile of me, with a Paper in his Hand. He very concisely told me he was in Love, and had been writing a few Lines to a Friend of his, who wou'd fain persuade him against the Lady, of which he desir'd my Opinion. I wou'd fain have excus'd myself, by urging, Love was a thing entirely out of my way; but he still press'd me to see them, which I at last comply'd with, and abating for the Subject, found them better than I expected: They must needs be acceptable to you, because you are going to turn Chymer[38] yourself, and have therefore sent them.

> *All Men have Follies, which they blindly trace*
> *Thro' the dark Turnings of a dubious Maze:*
> *But few, my Friend, in spite of all their Care,*
> *Retreat betimes from Love's inviting Snare:*
> *The eldest Sons of Wisdom were not free*
> *From the same Failings you condemn in me;*
> *They lov'd, and by that glorious Passion led,*
> *Forgot what* Plato *and themselves had said:*
> *My faults, you too severely reprehend,*
> *More like a rigid Censor than a Friend.*
> *You own'd my* Delia *once divinely fair,*

When in the Bud her native Beauties were:
Your Praises did her early Charms confess,
Yet you'd persuade me now to love her less;
Since to her Height of Bloom the Fair is grown,
And every Charm in its full Vigour shown:
Her whole Composure's of so fine a Frame,
Pride cannot hope to mend, nor Envy blame.
My Delia's *Words still bear the Stamp of Wit,*
Impress'd too plainly to be counterfeit:
Which, with the Weight of massy Reason join'd,
Declare the Strength and Quickness of her Mind;
Her thoughts are noble, and her Sense refin'd.
Why then, Dear Thirsis*, wou'd you strive to move*
A Heart like mine from its Commander, Love?

The very last Word of this Poem, will, I dare say, give you a Disrelish for all the rest: I will not Byass your Opinion by giving mine, but leave it wholly to a Judgement which cannot err: Let me know in your next how you like it. And pray let me have a little *London* News: I mean, such as the Tea-Table affords, for the rest, I refer myself to the publick Prints,[39] and expect nothing from *Berina*, but what she can answer to Justice and Good-nature; and what I may, without a Breach in either, read.

After I had parted with my poetical Neighbour, and was returning home again, I met with a Matter of some Speculation; for casting my Eye towards the top of a Tree, from whence I heard a rustling Noise, I saw a Crow, with a living Fish in his Bill: Pray send the Phaenomenon to the *Royal-Society*,[40] for, methinks I wou'd fain know how those Creatures, (neither of an amphibious Breed) came together.

I intended, when I began, to have been very prolix, but I find my self just seiz'd with a Fit of Chagrin,[41] which makes me a very unfit Correspondent for one of *Berina's* bright Genius, and therefore make haste to say,

I am
Always yours

Dec. 1.   ARTANDER

To BERINA.

THREE Posts are gone, and a fourth come, without one satisfactory Line from *Berina*: I grow impatient to know the Cause of your Silence, and have sent this as an earnest Ambassador, to bring me a faithful Account. Have I used some unmannerly Expression in my last? Or has it lost its way? Is *Berina's* want of Health the Cause? Or is she grown weary of her Friendship and Correspondence? I wish you do not at last play the Woman more than the *Platonick*, and quit your Friendship for a Husband. It is true, I have very great Hopes of your Sincerity, and cannot easily persuade myself you wou'd lay it by, for any Consideration. But Women, they say, are so like Quick-silver,[42] a Man can never be sure of them, either as a Friend or a Mistress; but as *Berina* is an Original in every thing else, I will believe her so in Friendship too.

My Mother, and a Female Companion of hers, have been diverting themselves with a Tragi-Comedy, as it was acted at a neighbouring Village, where lives a Farmer of some Note, who marry'd a young Woman of the same Town; and for the first three Years made a very thrifty, frugal Husband: At the end of which, finding he had no Children, nor hopes of any, he on a sudden run into an extravagant way of living, and let all fly he had been so long a gathering. His Wife grew extremely uneasy at his Proceedings, and used her utmost Efforts to reclaim him, tho' to no purpose; for continual Drinking had stupify'd his Senses, and he stopp'd his Ears to all she said. At last she left off to persuade, and began to take a more noisy Method, which render'd both him and herself ridiculous. However, he persisted in his drunken Resolutions, and the Ale-house had more of his Company than either his Wife or his Business. But last Night, he coming home very drunk, she fell into a violent Rage, told him, she wou'd never endure that Life, but wou'd go that minute and drown herself, to get rid of him. He, good-natur'd Soul, freely gave her both his Assent and Consent, and threw himself cross the Bed, where he fell asleep. She left him to enjoy a quiet Nap of three or four Hours; at the end of which, being in his Clothes, and consequently not very easy, he wak'd, and finding himself in the dark, and alone, he call'd his Wife, but got no Answer. Upon which he began to recollect, and had a faint Remembrance of what had pass'd; he immediately rouz'd from the Bed, half frighten'd out of his Wits, and groping about for the Door, after having broke the Looking-Glass, and black'd his Hands and Face in the Chimney, he at last found his way out, and got into the Kitchen, where he lighted a Candle, and went up to a Gentleman, who had left your noisy Town for a quiet Retirement in the Country, and lodg'd there, to get him to go with him to the Water-side, and find his Wife, dead or alive. When (Oh unheard of Misfortune!) he soon found his Journey was at an end, and his Wife laid warm and asleep in the Arms of the *London* Lodger. How it will end I know not, but most People think it will cost him his Life; he being now in a raging Condition, which is the only News we are at present full of: As more grows, you may expect it; as I do a Letter by the next Post: of which, if I fail, I shall conclude you have not the least value for the repose of

Decem. 5.   ARTANDER.

To ARTANDER.

YOUR Guesses at the cause of my Silence are quite wrong; I still retain my Friendship for *Artander*, and am still proud of my Correspondence. But during the time of my Silence, I was at Sir *John* ———, from whence I return'd but this day; and during the whole time of my stay there, I may justly say, I was never Mistress of so much time as wou'd write a Letter. I declare I am quite tir'd with Pleasure, and the Fatigue of constant diversion is more insupportable, than an everlasting want of it; but the Pleasures of this World, lose both their Name and End by being constant: we see by Experience, nothing pleases a great while; those things of which we are extravagantly fond, if once forced upon us, beget first an Indifference, and then an Abhorrence. This Consideration, with some others equivalent, has put you and I upon the Resolve of living single, lest too much of a Husband or a Wife shou'd turn us into just such indifferent things to each other, as I am now to Dancing and Cards. But now, *Artander*, I am forc'd to call up all the good-nature I am Mistress of, to help me to over-look the cruel Suspicion you seem to have of me, and cou'd be glad to know in what Point I have fail'd, that has given you cause to encourage such a Thought. If I were Mistress of Words that cou'd convince you, I wou'd immediately dress up my Protestations in 'em; but I have already said all I can upon that Subject, and have nothing to add, but my earnest Request, that you will believe me. By this time, I fancy you begin to expect my Thanks for the Poetry you sent me, which I shou'd very readily have given, had it been upon any other Subject; but Love is a thing so much against my grain, that tho' it be dressed up in a disguise of Wit, I see it thro' the Mask, and hate the base Imposture. Yesterday at dinner, your dear Cousin *Milner* happen'd to be the Table-talk, and a Gentleman from that side of the Country gave us a very good Diversion at his cost. He has, it seems, for this Month past, had two Mistresses in chace of equal Fortunes, but very different Persons; one being a Woman of tolerable Sense, a good Face and Humour, the other a mere *Miss Hoiden,*[43] a thing fit for no Conversation above her Maid and Footman, with whom she spends her whole time. To the first of those he address'd himself, and was as well accepted as an old Batchelor cou'd expect, especially by the Father, who had the greatest mind to the Match. After some time spent in this weighty Affair, all things were adjusted, and the Morning come, in which the Knot was to be ty'd: her Fortune was paid down, which the wary Bridegroom told over with great circumspection, and at last (fie upon such Mischances) he found a Brass Half-Crown, which with some earnestness he return'd to her Father, and desir'd it might be chang'd. The old Gentleman seeing him so earnest about such a trifle, seem'd a little surpriz'd, and knew not of a sudden how to answer him; but at last told him, he took it for a good one, and hoped it wou'd break no squares if he oblig'd him to do so too. Sir, said the Bridegroom, your being impos'd upon is no rule for my being so; and you shall either change it, or take the rest again. Upon which, the old Gentleman gather'd up his Stick and Gloves, and t'other old Gentleman his Stick and Gloves, and so they parted. The latter, (to the shame of his whole Family) went directly to pretty Miss, and her Money proving all *Sterling*,[44] they were immediately link'd.

The Remarks I make upon this Wedding, is, that before the Honey-Moon be half over, she will fret him to Death, or he will beat her to Mummy;[45] for old Batchelors have generally more Ill- nature, than any other Ingredient in their Compound; and his choice is so very ill, that he is like to have extraordinary exercise for it. I am surpriz'd you shou'd expect Tea-table Chat, attended with Justice and Good-nature: you forget that we Women as naturally love Scandal, as you Men do Debauchery; and we can no more keep up Conversation without one, than you can live an Age without t'other. The Town goes on as it used to do, full of Party, Pamphlets, Libels, Lampoons, and scurrilous Ballads: but the King's Guards are in mighty Transports, that they have escaped the Reduction of Light Horse.[46]

Pardon me, *Artander*, I had almost forgot your Injunction, and had like to have transgress'd; but there can be no harm saying,

I am

Yours,

Decem. 10.   BERINA.

To BERINA.

YOU are so tir'd with Pleasure, that if I were sure my Letters were any to you, I wou'd forbear writing for a while; but they are so dull, that I rather fear they are a Mortification; so write to tire you that way, in order to make you fit for

Diversion again. I wish you cou'd have transmitted some of your superfluous Mirth to me, who am as much in the other Extreme, and want what you despise. I cannot say I was ever so glutted with Pleasure in my Life, as to be weary of it, nor properly speaking, can any body say so; because, when once a Man is tir'd of a thing, it is no longer a Pleasure, but retiring from it is; so that a Person who has power to follow his own Inclinations, is always in Pleasure: but you, it seems, had not that power, your time being none of your own. As much a *Tory* as I am, I here protest to *Berina*, I am extremely pleas'd that the King's *Corps du Guard* are *in statu quo*; and think, since we have made him our King, we ought to use him like his Predecessors, and give him the Honour due to the Kings of *England*.

And now I hope I have pleas'd *Berina*: I wonder you have never sent me an account of the threescore Witches[47] Mr. *Flamsteed* has found out in *Westminster*; I hear he intends to beg 'em of the King, and roast them by the Blazing-Star next *April*. I am just going to sink a Vault for a Retreat from its sulphurous Effects, and wou'd have you come and share the Advantage of it before the Conflagration begins. Those Men of Profundity in the Occult Sciences, divert themselves with other Peoples Fears, and laugh to see the intimidated World shock'd with Horror at their Prognostications. Last Winter, when I was at *London*, I remember the Lords of the Admiralty were very busy with a Gentleman who had for certain found out the Longitude;[48] but having heard nothing of it since, I doubt the Project is dropp'd, and our Ships must fail as formerly. I hear a troublesome Disturber coming up, which at present puts a period to all but my best Wishes for *Berina*, and concludes me eternally hers.

Decem. 14.   ARTANDER.

To ARTANDER.

I was never worse qualified for writing in my Life, than just now, being nothing but Vexation and Ill-nature; the cause of which, I am going to tell *Artander*. The minute I received your last Letter, I was going into the City to supper, where Sir *Harry Wildair*[49] (as you call him) and Mrs. *Ha—g—n*, were of the Company; you know her so well, I need not give you her Character. I have often heard you say, she is a Lady of good Sense, and for that reason I am still more vex'd at the Misfortune: but no body is infallible, tho' every body think themselves in the right. At Supper a Dispute arose betwixt her and I, which was in itself very foolish, tho' it admitted of something very sharp on both sides: it is not worth Repetition, neither will a Sheet of Paper spare room for it; but Sir *Harry* and the rest of Company were so cruel, as to think her in the wrong; which made her very angry, and me very uneasy. I have made her several Overtures of Peace, but find her refractory to all; and I think she is resolv'd to persist in a Coldness, or rather a downright Hatred, not to be remov'd. I declare, I had not the least thought of incroaching upon her Prerogative of Wit, when I shot my own Fool's Bolt; but an Argument is no Argument without an Opposite, and for talk's sake I took up the Cudgels, with which I got the better of my Adversary, but I broke my own Head into the bargain; since, by that means, I have lost the agreeable Conversation of one for whom I had always the greatest Esteem. But since I came home, I have heard another cause for her implacable Aversion: they say she loves *Artander*, and has often made violent signs that way, to an insensible ———— as you are. However, I bear all the Brunt, and am, it seems, thought the sole cause of your Indifference; which, if true, I shou'd be sorry for, because I wou'd not play the Dog in the Manger.[50] I cou'd be very glad, to know the Truth, but am sure you are too generous to confess. I intend to let her know I will be her Advocate, and use my Interest in her behalf: say, *Artander*, will you give her hopes, and send the welcome News by me? Or must she despair of your Love, to preserve your Friendship for

Decemb. 18.   BERINA.

To BERINA.

I Cou'd almost wish that Person an ill end, who first invented those little foolish Sheets of gilt Paper; a Man is forc'd to compound half the Subject for the shining Edges of what incloses it: and therefore for the future, I bespeak a large Sheet of home-spun Paper, that will wear out a Pen of the first rate, to get to the bottom of it; for nothing vexes me so much, as to lose any thing *Berina* can write.

I wonder you wou'd undertake a Dispute with Mrs. *Ha—g—n*, unless you had a mind to make an everlasting Separation; she being one that cannot bear a Contradiction. Besides, as Mr. *Congreve* says, *Who cares for any body that has more Wit than themselves?*[51] As for her Love, I am an absolute Stranger to it; and she can no way oblige me, but by keeping me in continual Ignorance. I can't but laugh at myself, to think what a sheepish Figure I shou'd make, if I were to tell a Lady I wou'd not have her: but I fancy you only tell me this to try my vanity, which is never much rais'd by female Favours. Pardon me, *Berina*, I had almost forgot I was writing to one of that Sex, but it is to one so unlike the rest, that nothing I say of 'em can possibly touch her. Last Night, the Gentleman, whose Poetry I sent you, made an Entertainment, where I was one of the Guests; and after Supper we danc'd till Breakfast, tho' to the ungrateful Scrape of a Country Fiddle: I there saw the lovely *Delia*, who, when she has given place to *Berina*, stands fairest for Esteem; and not one of those Encomiums given her by her transported Lover, but comes short of her Merit. When I had considered her whole Person, I was forc'd to join with him in two Lines of his Poem:

> *Her whole Composure's of so fine a Frame,*
> *Pride cannot hope to mend, nor Envy blame.*

Methought I pitied the rest of the Ladies, who were only so many Foils, and stood like Farthing-candles around a Wax-Taper; the glaring Light of one eclipsing the faint Glimmers of the other. One of the Ladies, seeing the Eyes and Admiration of the whole Company drawn by a magnetick force upon the Taper, fell into such a violent Fit of Vapours, that she fancy'd herself Fourscore, and began to tell us how handsome she was when she was young, and how many Men of Quality admir'd her: another, who had often refused and slighted a present Lover, was forced to put on all her complying Airs to make his take notice of her: a third began her Discourse upon good Manners, and said, where the Company were equal, Respect ought to be so too. All which gave me a secret Pleasure, and I thought to myself, such Women as *Berina* and *Delia* shou'd (for the Quiet and Repose of the rest of their Sex) be confin'd to one another's Company, where neither can boast a Superiority, because both Nature's Masterpieces. The Gentleman of the House seeing all the Ladies in disorder, and knowing nothing gives them greater pleasure than to hear a fine Woman is married, because then she is out of the way, and no longer taken notice of, told 'em, *Delia* was his Wife; which like the Sun on an *April* Day, dispers'd the preceding Cloud; every body assumed their Gaiety, the Ladies left off to envy, and the Gentlemen to admire. So great is a fine Lady's Misfortune, when once she has given herself away for Life! I cannot but own, I think my Neighbour happy, if it be possible for Matrimony to make him so, which I fancy *Berina* will hardly allow. *Pug*[52] gives her humble Service to you, and takes it very ill, you have never in any of your Letters enquir'd after her Health. She, with the rest of our Family, presents you with their best Wishes.

I am

Dear Madam

Extremely Yours

Decem. 26.   ARTANDER.

To ARTANDER

HAD I ever been a Disciple of *Artemedorus*,[53] I shou'd have been very uneasy at my last Night's Dream, which made so dreadful an Impression upon my Fancy, that I have hardly yet recovered it. I thought I saw *Artander* blind; and when I wou'd have led him, he pull'd out my Eyes too. Pray Heaven avert the fatality of it, if there be any depending. I had a young Relation came this Morning to breakfast with me, who is just at Age, but so deeply engag'd in an Amour, that poor Coz languish'd over his Tea, and sigh'd over his bread and Butter like a School-Boy going to face a whipping Master in a Morning without his Exercise. The Lady he dies for, is turn'd of Fourteen, and has left off her Bib and her Babies[54] a considerable time. Her Father is lately dead, and left her 8000 Pounds, which, with herself, is put into the hands of two Guardians, who have each a Son design'd for pretty Miss: they have made Proposals about the Matter to one another, and have offer'd each other a thousand Pounds for his Consent; but they are so much of a mind, that 'tis impossible they should agree, which you will call a Paradox. However, the careful young Lady, who neither lov'd to lose her own time, or see her Guardians fall out, is, to prevent both Misfortunes, just ran away with her Father's Butler; who is a very well bred Man, drinks, whores, and games, and has just as much Estate as will qualify him for a Vote.[55] Of all the Gods, either Heathens or Poets ever made, there is none so silly as this blinking God of Love: he makes mere Idiots of Mankind, and puts them upon such ridiculous Actions, that one wou'd think we were made for nothing but to laugh at one another.

How happy he, that loves not, lives!

Said the ingenious Sir *John Denham*,[56] who learn'd his Lesson from Experience, and paid the highest Price for't too. Deliver me from *Cupid's* random Shots, and make my firm Resolutions a Racket to repel 'em. I wou'd have all those soft-hearted Ladies that are impress'd like Wax, read *Quevedo's Vision of Loving-Fools*;[57] I dare say, some of 'em wou'd find their own Characters very fairly display'd: but then the dismal Effects of not loving, to be call'd Ill-natur'd, and an old Maid, who wou'd not rather chuse to be undone, than lie under such scandalous Epithets? I have dwelt a little longer upon this Subject than I shou'd have done, because I think and fear *Artander* seem'd in his last Letter to lean a little that way. When once we approve of a thing, we implicitly act it; and if you be brought to think a Man happy in a fine Wife, the next Work will be to get one yourself: which, if you do, poor *Berina* may say she had a Friend; for *Artander* is lost past Recovery. I desire, in your next, you will either make a generous Confession, or give me some Assurance my Thoughts are ill grounded. I own, I grow impatient to be satisfy'd; for as I make but few Friends, I wou'd not lose them I have. You seem not pleas'd I writ no more last time, but you forget Women always talk more than they write, as Men always write more than they think: Your Sex seldom complain for want of Impertinence from ours, it being one of your chiefest Plagues: However, I did design to have fill'd up the empty Space of this Paper, but am interrupted by two or three Ladies who are just come in, and my Correspondence must give place to the Tea-Table; tho' nothing shall ever interrupt the Friendship of

Dec. 29.   BERINA.

To BERINA

LOSE your Friends! *Berina*, that's impossible; you have Merit enough both to secure and gain: and if *Artander* shou'd chance to stumble out of the Road he has so long walk'd in, *Berina* will be so far from losing a Friend, that she will gain a Lover too. Has any thing but Miracle made me resist your Charms so long? And can any thing but a greater Miracle make me fond of less Deserts than yours? No, *Berina*, 'tis you alone have Power to break the strongest Resolutions; and let the Witchcraft of your own Eyes answer for the Faults I commit. I have often heard, and with some Impatience, that Love and Friendship, notwithstanding the nice Distinction betwixt them, were inseparable Companions, especially between different Sexes; and 'till I knew *Berina*, and some time after, I thought all Arguments offer'd upon that Subject weak and trifling; tho' it was not long before I began to feel an Inclination to the same Faith: Yet was forc'd to dissemble it, lest a Confession shou'd have brought a

Forfeiture of that happy Friendship along with it, which you had so often and so generously promis'd me. I protest, *Berina*, I send you this with more Concern than I ever thought I shou'd have had upon this Occasion; but if it be true, that Love and Friendship are not to be parted, as many wise Men aver, then may I hope your Thoughts are of a piece with mine; and if so, how great wou'd be my Folly, shou'd I lose my Happiness, rather than tell how much I desire it? Tho' so great has been my Dread they were not, that I have made the most vigorous Defences against my Fate, and set up Bulwarks to oppose the little Thief, tho' I took my Measures by a wrong Handle; and while I with force of Arms thought to repel him, he, by Wheedle and Insinuation, found an Entrance, when I thought myself the most secure: Though the Wound he has given me has such an agreeable Smart, I feel it with Pleasure, and wish for nothing more than an Increase of his Power, that may make *Berina* own it too. Methinks it fares with the God of Love as with us poor Mortals: Our Faults are laid in our way as mortifying Blocks; but the Good we do, lies bury'd in Oblivion;[58] and the kind-hearted World takes it as a Due, without either Notice or Thanks. So *Cupid*, when he sets an ill-match'd Pair together, has many Out-Cries against him; but no body praises him for the Millions of Happy-ones who owe their Bliss to his Management: May he touch *Berina*'s Heart, and add one more to the Number.

I have now, *Berina*, made that very generous Confession you desir'd in your last, tho' I very much dread your Answer; but hope nothing will have Power to remove that Friendship which you always promis'd

Jan. 1.   ARTANDER.

To ARTANDER

WHEN I receiv'd your last Letter, I took it with my wonted Satisfaction, and open'd it with the same Air of Delight I used to do, but found it like Pandora's Box, full of Poison and Infection. I read it with so much Astonishment, that before I got to the end, I forgot the beginning, and was forc'd to read the displeasing Paper twice, before I cou'd believe my own Opinion of it. However, I gave myself time to reflect a little, and now, that my Surprize is pretty well over, I find myself inclin'd to conclude in your favour, and am persuaded your whole Design was to try *Berina*'s Easiness: And tho' a bare Suspicion of me be more than you can answer to the Friendship you owe me, it is much more pardonable than the other, and I shall be extremely pleas'd to see you own it in your next. What a World of Uncertainty do we live in? and how hard a matter to secure one Satisfaction? Did I ever think I shou'd live to see *Artander* become an Advocate for a Deity he had so often despis'd? Or find him adulterating Friendship, by mixing it with Love? No, *Artander*, it cannot be, you only have a mind to let me see you can write upon any Subject; and, *Proteus* like,[59] turn yourself into every Shape. I confess you are a good Mimick, and act a Lover's Part much better than I desir'd. Methinks you write as if you had a mind to draw me in, as you pretend Love has done you, by Wheedle; and wou'd fain persuade me to be of your new Opinion, *viz.* That Love and Friendship are so united, they are but one Thing with two Names: I confess, you are better at Argument than I, and therefore, like a cowardly Soldier, I think it safer to fly than fight. But Time and *Berina's* Carriage, may convince you of your Mistake.

I have often heard Men's Promises are so fabulous, that there's no depending on 'em; but I little expected *Artander* wou'd have convinc'd me of what I only disbeliev'd for his sake: That you are guilty of Breach of Promise,[60] you will not sure deny, when I refer you to your own first Letter, which I wou'd have inclos'd, but that I have a mind to keep it for a Testimony against you; however, you may remember the Conclusion in those Words. Be sure, *Berina*, keep your Friendship inviolate, and you shall find I will keep my Promise, in never desiring more. He that breaks one Promise, may break a thousand; and if you have deceiv'd me as a Friend, I have little Reason to trust you as a Lover. But I hope your next will end my Doubts; and therefore once more subscribe myself your

Real Friend,

Jan. 3.   BERINA.

To BERINA.

ONCE more, *Berina*, sounds as if it were to be the last! Good Heaven, must I lose you because I love you? And is it a sufficient Reason to withdraw your Friendship, because mine grows stronger? Don't, *Berina*, give me Cause to think you lie upon the Catch for an Opportunity to throw *Artander* off: if you ever were that real Friend you pretended to, you will remember what the Word implies; then ask yourself, if it be possible for one true Friend to see another in Distress without releiving him, if in his power? If not, how many Convulsions of the Mind tear and rack his Heart-strings for want of that Power? How willingly wou'd he undergo any Hardship to extricate his Friend; and when he finds his Assistance can do him no Service, sits down to lessen his Pain, by sympathizing with him: Tells him he was his Partner in Prosperity, and Adversity shall never break the Union. This, *Berina*, is my Notion of a true Friend; and if it be in your power to make me easy, and you refuse to do it, you must either call Friendship an empty Name, or own you never had any for *Artander*. But then you tax me with a Breach of Promise: Alas! *Berina*, no Man lies under a Necessity of keeping a Promise any longer than he has it in his power; and so long I was very punctual. But when every Post brought fresh Alarms to Love, and every Line gave Wings to my Inclinations, I soon found it was impossible to secure any Tranquility of Mind without an eternal Possession of the dear Author: It is very natural to desire the Company of those whose Conversation we like, and no body ever stood in competition with *Berina*: I never so much as bestow'd an empty Wish upon any body else, nor will I ever have any other Companion. Beside, *Berina*, remember how often you have rais'd my Vanity, by owning yourself pleas'd in my Company. Why then must we spend our Time at such a distance? Wast[61] those Hours in trifling Disputes, which might make us both for ever happy. Can *Artander* be such an agreeable Friend, yet want the Qualities of a Husband? No, *Berina*, try me that way too, and you shall find I will out-do your own Wishes, by giving myself up so entirely to your Will, that your least Inclination shall be a Command. And now, *Berina*, either comply, or own you never had the least Friendship for

Jan. 7.   ARTANDER.

To ARTANDER

NO, *Artander*, I will neither deny my Friendship, nor withdraw it; but will stick so close to it, as to make you happy against your own Will, and keep you in a State of Life, where Freedom and Liberty may be enjoy'd. Marry'd! that were to be both blind indeed.

You said once, you took your Measures by the wrong Handle, and so you have done again. I do assure you, the Promise you make of inverting the God of Nature's Rules, and being all Obedience, is no Inducement to me to become a Wife: I shou'd despise a Husband as much as a King who wou'd give up his own Prerogative, or unman himself to make his Wife the Head: We Women are too weak to be trusted with Power, and don't know how to manage it without the Assistance of your Sex, tho' we oftenest shew that Weakness in the Choice of our Advisers. The notion I have always had of Happiness in Marriage, is, where Love causes Obedience on one side, and Compliance on the other, with a View to the Duty incumbent on both:[62] If any thing can sweeten the bitter Cup, 'tis that. But this I give as my Opinion of Marriage in general, without any design of coming to Particulars, and wou'd fain secure Artander's Friendship, by dissuading him from every Thought on't too. But when once the blind Archer with a random Shot has hit a Heart, the wounded Fool grows stupid, sighs and cries, prays, and begs for Help and Pity, but never offers to pull out the Dart, which causes all his Pain. Wou'd but every body keep their Ground, and stand boldly in their own Defence, how easily might they baffle the Attempts of a Boy? But instead of fighting for their own Liberty and Property, they tamely yield to an arbitrary Power; and, like a Dog used to a Collar, hold down their Heads to take the Yoke. For shame, Artander, shake off your Chains, throw by your Non-resisting Principles, and fight for yourself: Remember your Liberty lies at stake, which every wise Man loves. But if my Advice be thrown away upon you, and you are still resolv'd to bind yourself Prentice for Life, all I have to beg, is, that I may chuse a Wife for you, one who will not abuse Artander's Good-nature, but mix every Action with Love and Prudence, a Woman of an unlimited Goodness, and one who will make you happy, since nothing but a Wife can do it. I own, Artander, I cannot think of giving you so entirely away, as to see you in the Arms of a Stranger; but if you take my Friend, she will give you leave to retain a little of that Friendship which has been do so often promis'd entire to

Jan. 8. BERINA.

To BERINA.

I Hope, Madam, I may take your last Letter for a Compliance with my Wishes, and believe you are already mine; since no body, but *Berina*, can deserve the Character you give the Lady I am to expect from your Hand.

Oh! what foolish Things are we Mortals![63] resolving against our Fate, which only laughs at our weak Endeavours, and makes a Jest of our broken Resolutions. Just so have all those doating Lovers far'd, who came within the Verge of my Observation: I have often made myself merry at their Sufferings, and thought Affectation had a greater share in their Behaviour than Reality;

but now, *Berina*, I am qualify'd, not only for a pitying Looker-on, but as one who wants that Charity I have so often deny'd to my Fellow-Sufferers. You have promis'd me Freedom and Liberty, but is it possible to enjoy either, while I am a Slave in Fetters? Or can any thing release me from that Bondage, but an ever-lasting Union with *Berina?* Who that saw me some Months ago in the midst of Ease and Pleasure, wou'd ever have suppos'd I cou'd become a Votary at *Cupid's* Altar? Or who that sees *Berina's* Charms, wou'd not be struck with Amazement at the long Resistance I have made? For once, *Berina*, call up that Vanity so peculiar to your Sex; let it display the Magick Force of your Eyes, indulge the height of its Suggestions, and then forgive *Artander's* Adorations: Look upon him as one grown restless and ungovernable; lost to every Joy, to every Satisfaction; no Taste, no Relish left for any thing but Love. Oh! how I cou'd tear my false foolish Heart! as Mr. *Cowley*[64] calls his, for betraying me just when I had so firmly resolved to subdue every Emotion that tended towards my present Circumstances. Sot that I was, to think it possible for me to withstand such Force! Pardon me, dear *Berina*, for complaining of any thing you're the Cause of; but when I consider the slender Hopes I have of bringing you over to my Side, it makes me wish for a Power equal to yours, which might give me that Tranquility I must never expect, 'till I can say, *Berina* loves. I am now dispatching a Hurry of Business with great Precipitation, and often curse Delay, because it retards my Flight, and keeps me from the Centre of my Wishes. A few Days more will, I hope, put an end to it, and then *Berina* will find a verbal Suppliant at her Feet. Oh! how I long for the happy Minute! How eager are my Wishes to see myself once more bless'd with that Conversation which alone can give new Life, and put an End to all my present Pain. But then how much I dread to meet *Berina's* Eyes, lest one indifferent Look from them shou'd, with a Basilisk[65] Force, strike poor *Artander* dead: The very Dread of losing you, has seiz'd my vital Spirits, and all I am able to add, is, that you will call up that Good-nature (of which you have so great a Share) to help you to pity your dying

Jan. 9.   ARTANDER.

To ARTANDER.

I'LL swear, *Artander*, I was never so merry in my Life, as at the reading of your last Letter; I don't believe there's a Man in the World, that defies Love as you do, cou'd ever assume the Lover like you: why, you mimick it as naturally as if you had serv'd an Apprenticeship to its God: Methinks the very Paper whines, 'tis writ in such a beseeching Stile. I declare, I thought you had been in Earnest, and was going to contrive some Way to comfort you; but I consider'd, it was morally impossible for a Man of *Artander's* Resolution and Courage to be conquer'd by a Boy. But methinks you are like a half-bred Player; you over-act your Part: The next time you put on the Lover, do it with an easier Air; 'tis quite out of fashion to talk of Dying, and Sighing, and Killing Eyes, and such Stuff; you shou'd say, Damn it, Madam, you are a tolerable sort of a Woman, and, if you are willing, I don't much care if I do you the Honour to marry you. That's the modern Way of Courtship, you shou'd never let a Woman think she has any Merit, let that be always on your own side; and when you vouchsafe to bestow your Favours, let it look like Generosity or Charity, to give such a Heart to one of that worthless Sex, who can no way possibly deserve it. And now, *Artander*, you see I understand something of Love as well as you, tho' I have an easier way of describing it. But tell me how I shou'd have brought myself off, had I been a Woman, whose Heart was susceptible of Love? I might then have gorg'd the Bait, and seen the cunning Angler laughing at the credulous Fool. I am almost angry with you for trying me so far, because Love, like Edg'd-Tools, shou'd never be play'd with. You seem to hint, as if you were to be in Town soon. I confess I cou'd wish that part of your Letter true, and please myself with the Thoughts of sitting down with you, to laugh at all that's past: Whenever *Artander* comes, or in whatever Shape, he shall always find a kind Reception from his

Real Friend,

Jan. 12.   BERINA.

To BERINA.

CRUEL *Berina,* can you be a real Friend while you laugh at all my Pain, and ridicule my Complaints? Is *Artander* fallen so low in your Esteem, as to be thought a Banterer of his dearest Friend? How can you use me thus? Believe me, Madam, if you were merry over my last Letter, I have been the very Reverse on't over yours, and have scann'd every Line with more Concern than I dare tell *Berina*, lest it shou'd serve, to make me yet more ridiculous. However, it has brought me one unspeakable Pleasure, which I thank you for; a Promise of a kind Reception in any Shape. I have just given Orders for my Servants and Horses to be ready by to-morrow Morning, since I die with

Impatience for a Performance. I am forc'd to conclude a little abruptly, be-cause I have some Business of Moment to dispatch by the Time prefix'd; 'till when, and always,

I am,
Dearest Berina's

Faithful Adorer,

Jan. 25.   ARTANDER.

FINIS.[66]

THE ACCOMPLISH'D RAKE,
OR *MODERN FINE GENTLEMAN:*
BEING
AN EXACT DESCRIPTION
OF THE
CONDUCT AND BEHAVIOUR OF
A PERSON OF DISTINCTION

~

When Conqu'ring Vice Triumphant takes the Field,
Virtue Dethron'd must to its Pow'r yield;
And when Good Characters are all at stake,
The Best of Bad Ones is th' Accomplish'd Rake.[1]

TO THE

BEAUS²

OF

GREAT-BRITAIN

GENTLEMEN,

THERE is a certain Ingredient in the Compound of a *Dedication,* call'd Adu-
lation or Flattery, which is a Weed grown so rank by Age, that I am afraid it
may offend your Nice Noses; and for that Reason, am resolved to pull it up by
the Roots, tho' it is very possible some of ye may believe there is no such thing,
since to Men of so much Merit all is due that can be said: But as I am now in
a Vein of Writing new to please ye, I intend to throw in a Scruple³ to the
contrary Scale; and for once, let Truth and Justice hold the Balance. I know if
I should tell ye of a Thousand Fine Qualities, to which ye can never make a
Good Title, it would be no more than a Weak Imitation of my Predecessors:
But as I now set up for an Original, my Words and Thoughts are to be entirely
my own, and I alone accountable for them.

It is very likely ye may be a little surpris'd, that I should draw the Character of a *Rake,*⁴ then lay it under the Protection of a *Beau:* But I must tell ye,
I had a very Advantageous View, when I pitch'd upon ye for my Patrons; for I
thought ye were much more likely to stand by me, than the Worthy Gentlemen decypher'd in the following Sheets. There is certainly a good deal of Difference betwixt the Two Characters; for tho' the one may not altogether preserve the strictest Morals; yet in many Cases he is careful to avoid any Material
Reflection on his Honour: For Example, he may have Bravery enough to leave
his Country in Defence of it, whilst the other stays at Home to guard his own
dear Person and the Ladies: And I must own myself better pleas'd with the
Courage and Conduct of a Real Engagement with the *Spaniards,*⁵ than in any
Protestations of Stabbing your selves for Love.

But Gun-powder and Perfume is a very odd Mixture; and why should I
talk of Battles to such a Peaceable Part of the Species? No! I shall confine
myself entirely to your Nicer Qualities; and particularly, enlarge upon the
Elegance of drawing Gold Snuff-Boxes instead of Daggers, and writing Billet-
doux's⁶ instead of Challenges: And every one must give into this Way of Think-

ing, who compares the Prudence of the one with the Rashness of the other. I can repeat a Thousand Things, wherein our Pretty Fellows excell the Unpoliter Part of Mankind, and most will agree, it better to drink Barley-Water for a Smooth Complection, than *Burgundy* for a Red Face.[7] Oh! how preferrable is the Charming Nonsense of our *Gentilshomme des Amours*[8] to those Profane Oaths, which make so great a Part of the Conversation of Blustering *Britons*. It must be owing to the Bad Taste of the Age, that a great deal of Powder and White Hands should be call'd Foppery and Effeminacy; or, that the Gentle, Easy Study of Women and Dress, should be thought inferiour to that of Men and Letters; and sure they must mistake the Literal Sense of Beau, who dont call IT a *Fine Gentleman*.

To conclude, That your Fine Faces may receive no Freckles, your Embroideries no Tarnish; nor your Fortunes any Shock, are the Unfeigned Wishes of
GENTLEMEN
Yours,[9]

THE MODERN

Fine Gentleman

YOUNG *Galliard* who is to be the Subject of the following Leaves, will (with his own Inclinations, and a little of my additional Discipline) be a very exact Copy of the Title Page; for tho' I shall be very punctual in delivering nothing but plain Fact in the fundamental Part of his Story, it is not impossible but by way of Episode I may intermit now and then a pretty little Lye, and since it is to be both little and pretty, I hope my Reader will excuse me if he finds me out, and let him convict me if he can.

The above-named Gentleman was born in one of the largest Counties in *England*; his Mother a Woman of Distinction, and claim'd a Share in some of the Best Blood in the Nation; her Education, perhaps, not very regular, an airy, roving Temper, unconfin'd, and free, would know no Bounds, nor bear the least Restraint. Pleasure was her Idol, at whose Altar she became a constant Votary, but the veriest Trifle in Domestick Affairs gave her insupportable Pain; two days spent in the same Diversion was Abominable Pleasure, but fresh Delights were worth continued Notice. His Father was a Person of a very different Character, wise and prudent, yet had the utmost Tenderness for his Lady, and look'd on her weak Behaviour, as one would on a Sick Child; with Pity, not with Anger or Reproach. He had served his Country in many Reputable Capacities, and was just chosen Knight of the Shire,[10] when the Small-Pox too fatally seiz'd him, of which in ten Days he dy'd; during which time he seem'd exceeding anxious for his Children, having, beside his Son, one Daughter, and both too young to be left to the Care of a negligent unmindful Eye. An Affair of this Importance requir'd more Time than he had now to spare; and how to manage for their Good jointly, with the Satisfaction of his Lady, he knew not. To leave them to her Care and Management (her Temper consider'd) was throwing them into the Mouth of Ruin; and to substitute another, at least while they were so very young, was shewing those Faults too plainly to the World, which his good Nature would fain have hid even from himself. Many of his poor restless Hours were made infinitely more so, by those sad Reflections, yet the tender Regard he had for his Lady took place, and he at last determined to do nothing with his latest Breath that should give her the least Indifference for his Loss, he consider'd his Children were hers as well as his, and hoped when he was gone, she would then consider, there was none left either to indulge or wink at her Follies, would wisely remember her self a double Parent, and shew her true Concern for his Loss by a more than common Care of them. He therefore, 'ere his dying Moments came too near him, call'd her and his Children to his Bed-side, and thus addrest them: I have now before me all I hold dear on Earth, and it is no easie Task to go for ever from your Eyes; but I am now arrested by a cruel Hand which will take no Ransom, but insists upon a speedy Payment of that Debt I owe to Nature, nor will by any Means let go his Hold till my freed Soul shall take her Flight and Find a Rest on some unknown Shore. Since then I must go, all that remains for me is to recommend those tender Pledges of our Love to the utmost care of you, the dearest Partner of my Bed, and as a dying Request beg their Education may be such as may give them a true and early Notion of Vertue and Honour.

As for you my beloved Son, you are now turn'd of fourteen, you are blest with a promising Genius,[11] and though you are yet but young you may re-member the Words of a Father, whose last Request to you is, That while you travel through this Life, you will learn to keep your Footsteps steady, that so they may neither sink you on one Side to the heavy dull Pedant, or raise you on the other to the light flashy Coxcomb, let a strict Vertue regulate all your Actions, despise and shun those Libertines[12] who may strive to poison your Morals, be dutiful to your Mother, love your Sister, and marry a Woman of Vertue.

I leave you sole Heir to a very flourishing Estate, which has for two Centuries been in your Family, I beg you will never lessen your Ancestors by a Misapplication of those Talents Heaven has blest you with. I would say more but my Spirits grow faint, and I have now no more to do but die in Peace, and close my Eyes for ever. He had hardly done speaking when a Convulsion seized him, and catch'd his latest Breath, and in him died a worthy Patriot, a tender Husband, and a careful Father, in the thirty-sixth Year of his Age, and had his dying Words been of any Force with those he left behind, his Children might have made as good a Figure in Life as their Predecessors had done before them, but Lady *Galliard* was left tollerably young, a good Face and a better

Joynture,[13] and dried up her Tears so soon, that Decency ashamed of such light Proceedings, with a Blush cry'd fie, and left her.

Sure unjustly are we called the weaker Vessels, when we have Strength to subdue that which conquers the Lords of the Creation, for their Reason tyes them down to Rules, while we like *Sampson*[14] break the trifling Twine and laugh at every Obstacle that would oppose our Pleasure. Lady *Galliard* had too much Resolution and Courage to strugle with Grief, but like an expert Fencer gave it one home Thrust and silenced it for ever, hardly allowing so much as the common Decorum of a Month's Confinement to a dark Room,[15] though her wild Behaviour told the World she was but too well qualified for such an Apartment for ever. But I now give up my Observations to Time, who will probably alternately bury and raise her Shame, to him I leave her for a while, and call upon young *Galliard* her Son, who is now arrived at one Step of Honour, being the Third Baronet[16] successively of his Family, Sir *John* therefore for the future we call him, and if he behaves below his Manhood and Dignity, we must beg the Mother to answer for the Son, since the Father left no Example behind him, but what was worthy of the strictest Imitation, and had not the too hasty Hand of Death, snatch'd him hence so soon, his indefatigable Care had made his Son what he really was himself, a perfect *fine Gentlemen*. It is a common Saying, *That Manners makes the Man,*[17] but that Word, like Friendship, includes much more than is vulgarly understood by it, and a false Education like false Wit only serves to varnish over the Defects of our Scene and Behaviour, which when tried by a true Touchstone, lays us open and shows the Deformities of both. But if a wrong Discipline in Youth be so pernitious, what becomes of those who have none at all? How many young Gentlemen have we among the better Sort of Men, that are in a Manner wholly neglected and left to branch forth into numberless Follies, like a rich Field uncultivated, that abounds in nothing but tall Weeds and gaudy scentless Flowers. This is doubtless the Reason why the Town is so stock'd with Rakes and Coxcombs, who wisely imagine all Merit is wrapt up in fine Clothes and Blasphemy; a laced Coat, gold clock't Stockings, and a Tupee,[18] qualifies a Man for a *modern fine Gentleman,* and if he can but whore, swear, and renounce his Maker, he is a modern fine Gentleman indeed. Too much like this it fared with our young Baronet, who is now left to think and act as he pleases himself, and he that is his own Teacher has too often a Fool for his Schoolmaster, tho' young *Galliard* did not want Sense, but on the contrary had more than could be expected from one of his Years, and yet alass, for want of due Measures, it grew up rank, and sprouted out with nothing but Excrescences. He now saw himself with the Eyes of Vanity, which was daily increased by the Flattery of the Servants, a Thing he liked so well that his whole Time was spent among the Grooms in the Stables, or the Wenches in the House; and doubtless his natural good Sense and acquired good Manners met with all the Improvement that such refin'd Conversation could furnish him with. Two whole Years slipt away in a careless Lethergy, which lost Time was of much more value than the annual Rents of the Estate, considering one revolves, but the other is lost for ever. We generally expect a Man compleat at one and twenty, and two Years out of seven is too considerable to be trifled away, beside the sad Disadvantage of imbibing ill Customs, which like the King's Evil[19] is seldom or never removed. The Neglect of this young Gentleman alarm'd all that loved his Father, which was just as many as knew his Worth; but in a near Part of the Neighbourhood lived one Mr. *Friendly*, who was always conversant with, and loved by, the deceased; he in a very particular Manner lamented the Misfortune of the almost ruin'd Sir *John*, but knew not where to apply for a Remedy, the Knight was too young too thoughtless and too fond of his own Will to hearken to any Advice that did not concure with it. And for Lady *Galliard*, she was too positive, too proud, and too careless, either to be perswaded by her Friends, or to joyn in Concert with Reason for the Good of her Child. However, he had a Stratagem in his Head, which kind Chance furnished him with, and which he hoped might be of some service to his Design, in order to put it in Practice, he made an Invitation to some of his nearest Neighbours, among which Lady *Galliard* and her Son were bidden; while they were at dinner, among the rest of the Attendants was a very spruce, clean Footman, who had something in his Air that look'd as if he was not born one. Mr. *Friendly* seemed to use him with some Deference, and said, pray *Tom* do so and so, *Tom* seemed very diligent, but a little aukward, and some of the Company observed a Tear often starting into his Eyes, which gave them a Curiosity to inquire who he was, and that gave a good Lift to Mr. Friendly's Design. Dinner was no sooner over than he took the Opportunity and gave the Company the following Account:

This young Fellow whom you all seem to enquire after, and whom I received but three Days ago into my Family, was the Son of a private Gentleman, who had a very easy Fortune in Life, but by an ugly Accident broke his Leg, which threw him into a Fever and kill'd him. This poor young Man who was then about twelve Years of Age, is too sad an Example of the Want of Care in a Parent, for his Mother though a very modest and good Woman, was extremely covetous, which prevented all that Care which should have been taken towards making her Son a Man, she fancied Time and Nature would do as much for nothing, as if she should put her self to a deal of Charge, which perhaps at last would turn to no Account. *Tom* on the other Hand loved Play and Idleness, hated School and Learning, said he would never have any Thing to do with crabbed *Greek* that stuck in his Throat, and was ready to choak him, tho' now and then for Variety he vouchsafed to make his Master a Visit, and handle a Grammar, though he was never rightly acquainted with its Rules. Time however would not wait till Reason Thought fit to show him his Folly; so spur'd on by his boyish Inclinations, and no body to restrain them, he run on from one Diversion to another, grown perfectly headstrong and spoiled till he was twenty Years of Age, at which Time his Mother fell sick, some say broken hearted at his Proceedings, which she might thank herself for, but be that as it will, she then died, and he was left for the other Year to the care of an Uncle, who managed so well as to cheat him of Part of his Estate, and the rest as soon as he came to age he squandered away on Game-Cocks and Race-Horses so that for want of due Discipline while he was a Boy, he was utterly ruin'd as too many of his betters have been before him, and is now grown up to Man as you all see under the honourable Circumstances of a Footman.

In all Probability Lady *Galliard* and her Son took the Application as it was designed to themselves, for they both coloured at the End of it, which Mr. *Friendly* perceived and was resolved to go on. We have the Advice of a very wise Man,[20] proceeded he, to train up Youth as we would have them act when riper Years take place. Learning we all know is the first Step towards the Improvement of our Sense, as good Conversation is towards that of our Manners, and it is so hard a Matter to bring a Man to an exact Behaviour in Life that he ought not to loose one Minute in the pursuit of it. But Madam, continued he, addressing Lady *Galliard*, now we are upon this Topick, may I with the Freedom of a Friend ask your Ladyship how Sir *John* is to spend his Time till he writes Man, methinks I long to see him in the Road his worthy Father travelled, to draw whose character requires too many Master-strokes for my shallow Capacity, nor would I attempt to delineate a Picture where the Original was so well known, your Fancies can form a better Judgement of his Perfections than a dull Discription from an unable Tongue, in short he was worthy of the Name of Man; which all who stand erect cannot make a just Title to, it requires a pretty deal of Pains to distinguish our selves from Brutes, we must have a Share of Probity, Honour, Gratitude, Good Sense, and a Complacency for our Species in general, to render us worthy of that Name, so that all who are design'd for Men, are not rightly call'd so, till acquired Advantages confirm their Title. Sir, said a Gentleman present, methinks you arraign the Care of the Almighty, or his Judgement in making Man, if you say they are not born compleat, beside Mr. *Friendly*, good Sense is not an acquired Quality.[21] To say I arraign Providence, return'd Mr. *Friendly*, when I affirm Man is not born perfect, is the same as to say, when I have a Thousand a Year given me, it is no Present unless the kind Donor sits down every Day to tell me how to spend it. When the bountiful Hand of Heaven was opened to Man with the noble Gift of Reason, it left that very Reason to improve itself, and there it is we joyn with Beasts when we neglect to listen to it. I own good Sense is not an acquired Quality, but it is so very capable of the highest Improvement that with a small Latitude of Expression it may be called so, for he that takes it in its natural Simplicity and lets it lye fallow, may be justly said to bury his Talent, and it dwindles by degrees till it degenerates into down right Folly, and we may as well expect a Boy to speak *Greek* and *Hebrew* without being taught, as good Sense to keep its Ground without some Care to improve it. During this Discourse, Sir *John* sat very attentive, making his own private Reflexions upon the Design of it, he was very conscious he wanted Improvement rather than a Talent to improve, and soon guest[22] the Point of the darted Arrow was aimed at himself, or his Mother, which was equally Piercing, because she had thus far indulged his Negligence, but as he had suck'd in a careless indolent Way of Life, he was now resolved to persist in it, and made the following Answer: I am too much a Boy Mr. *Friendly* to enter into Dispute with one of your solid Judgment, nor is it in my Power to baffle your Assertions, but I think—— Stay Child, said Lady *Galliard*, interrupting Sir *John*, you are not the Person concern'd in the oblique Affront, it is at me the side-long Glance is cast, and the Reproach reaches my Conduct, which possibly I could clear if I thought it worth my Trouble; but as I am resolved to be always Mistress of my own Actions, I shall never think myself obliged to account for them to any body. Madam, return'd Mr. *Friendly*, I blush to think your Ladyship can have such an humble Opinion of my good Manners, as to imagine I could say any Thing to you in my own House with a Design to Affront you, I wish you would put a kinder Construction upon my Words, and believe they were spoke with a very different View, Sir *John Galliard* succeeds the Estate and Honour, of one of the finest Men in *England*, and can you Madam, who are a Party so near concerned, blame those who loved the Father, if they wish to see the Son inherit his Vertues too. I own Mr. *Friendly*, replied Sir *John*, you have gloss'd your Affront with the best sort of Vernish, because it has the shining Appearance of Friendship, and I must likewise own I believe it is real, but while you make my Father (whose Memory I revere) a shining Brilliant,[23] you seem to call his Son a worthless Pebble. I am not yet seventeen Years of Age and if I have lost a Year or two of Improvement, I may possibly make it up in my future Life, but if I never do, I shall not miss it, a Man of Fortune and a Fool may be highly content with what he has, but where there is the additional Blessing of a fine Genius to accompany that Estate, it will act like a prudent Merchant, who when he has acquir'd one Thousand Pounds goes on and improves till he has got another. Even you yourself not seventeen, would call that Persons Conduct in question, who having but a hundred Pounds should daily spend it, and starve when it is gone; every Thing ought to be improved, or else we do not carry on the System of Life, as it was by Providence designed we should, and if our Money ought to be increased, sure our Sense should be so, which is infinitely more preferable, but I find all I can say meets with an unkind Reception, so let us drown the ungrateful Subject in his Majesty's Health.[24] Which when ended the Ladies withdrew, and after Sir *John* had a little recovered his Temper, he ask'd Mr. *Friendly* if he had a Mind to part with his new Footman *Thomas*: To which Mr. *Friendly* answered with his wonted good Nature, he had a Mind to do any Thing that could oblige Sir *John Galliard*, and hoped, if he did part with him, he would believe that was the only Motive: Upon which *Tom* was called in, and Mr. *Friendly* asked him, if he had a Mind to change his new Master for a better? The young Man answered very hansomly, That he had no reason to believe there could be a better, but as he had a new Fortune to raise in Life, he thought himself obliged to do his best in order to it. Then said Mr. *Friendly*, wait upon Sir *John Galliard* to morrow Morning, and receive his Commands. But Sir *John*, continued he, if I resign my Footman to you, will you oblige me in another Point: There is a young Gentleman of my Acquaintance who would make an extraordinary Companion for you, he is a Man of Worth and Learning, and his Example and Instruction would, I am sure, be of use to you, if you are inclined to something in the Nature of a Tutor: Inform Lady *Galliard*, and let me know your Result, he is a Man of the best Sense, and if you go no farther than his good Conversation, it will help to keep up the Spirit of your own. Sir *John* told him, he desired nothing more than to oblige him, and what he proposed was very agreeable to him, and he was very sure Lady *Galliard* would not oppose it, so desired the young Gentleman, whose Name was *Teachwell*, might come to him the next Morning; which he did, attended by *Tom*. Things were immediately concluded, and he was fix'd in the Family under two Capacities, one as Chaplain to my Lady, and the other as Tutor to her Son. He was of a sober mild Behaviour, affable to all, but very industrious to bring his new Charge to a Sence of those Rudiments which Neglect had made him a Stranger to, and had so much good Fortune attended Sir *John* as to have sent Mr. *Teachwell* two or three Years sooner, it might have been of the first Consequence to him, but alass, he was now grown headstrong and past Advice. *Tom* behaved very well in the Family, and gained the Love of every body in it, but after he had lived two Years with Sir *John*, he came one Afternoon into the Dining-room, where his Master and Lady were set at the Tea-Table, and desired to be dismist, for he heard his Uncle was dead, and was impatient to know how Matters went in his Family, but said, if Sir *John* desired it, he would wait upon him again in a few Days. I do not see, replied Sir *John*, any Business you have to go at all, or what Expectations there can be from the Death of an Uncle who has left children of his own, you may be sure when he cheated you as fast as he could, it was not with a Design to do you Justice at his Death. No Sir, returned *Tom*, I never expected any from him either dead or alive, but he has left but two Daughters, and one of them I think myself pretty sure of, though Absence perhaps may have made some Alteration, and that is, what with your Leave Sir, I would be satisfied in. Your most humble Servant, cry'd Sir *John*, I find then you are going to compleat your happy Circumstances in that mighty Blessing call'd a Wife, I wish you Joy Sir, but hope you are not in such violent haste but you can stay till I have filled up your Vacancy. For that Matter Sir *John*, said Lady *Galliard*, you may take *Dick*, or *Will*, 'tis pitty to hinder the poor Man, for there is nothing like a close Application to keep a Woman's Inclinations steady; come Sir *John*, at my Request dismiss him for a while, and when he has secured his beloved *Dulcinea*,[25] he will wait upon you again, at least till you can provide your self to your liking. Sir *John* gave a consenting Nod, and *Tom* vanish'd. I always fancied, said Lady *Galliard*, that *Tom* grew weary of his Livery, and would have had you some Time ago to have found a better Place for him, it is not unlikely but that is the Reason why he is gone. When you urged it, Madam, return'd Sir *John*, your Reasons were all wrong, had he been born a Footman, Promotion might have made him thankful, because so much above his Expectation, but to turn him into a Gentleman again, would never do, for he would doubtless have thought all due to his own Merit, and have grown so cursed proud upon it, that I should only have spoiled a very good Footman to make a very ill Vallet. While they were thus discoursing Mr. *Teachwell* came to them, and after some little Introduction to what he was going to say, he thus went on: I am a little surprised Madam, that neither your Ladyship or Sir *John* seems inclined to his spending a Year or two at the

University, or making a Tour into *France* or *Italy*. I have been his daily Attendant these two Years, and have often lamented to see his Time elapse without that great Improvement his fine Genius is capable of. I intreat you Madam, to joyn your Commands to my Request, and let us prevail with him to see the World, and know something more than killing a Fox or Hare, than leaping a Gate or setting a Partridge. For Heavens sake Sir, rouse yourself from this careless Lethargy, which has so long benum'd your Senses, exert your Reason, and give it Leave to act for your own Advantage, I am ready and willing to wait upon you any where, and hope I have not behaved so ill as to make you weary of my Company. You are come, answered Lady *Galliard*, in a very critical Juncture for the very next Thing I intended to say to Sir *John*, was to persuade him to spend a little Time at *Cambridge*, where I know his Father designed he should go, and it is what I as earnestly desire, you are now in your Nineteenth Year and if you ever design to improve yourself, it is high Time to begin, I was never so earnest for your going before, though I fear you are but indifferently qualified for any Examination.

Sure Madam, replied Sir *John*, you do not imagine that Men of Fortune go there for Learning, or any Thing else but to amuse Time and spend it agreeably among the best Companions, it is turning Porter to carry a Load on our Backs, and Learning is certainly the worst sort of Luggage, under which we founder before we get half way on our Journey, let those tugg at Learning's Oar that are destined to live by it, for my Part I am well provided for, and will be no Beast of Burden, though to oblige you Madam, I do not care if I trifle away some Months there, and if I bring away no *Greek* or *Latin* I shall be sure to meet with the best Conversation in the World. Sir *John*, said Mr. *Teachwell*, whatever your Inducements are for going to *Cambridge*, I am very much rejoyced to hear you resolve upon it, and doubt not, but when you come there, you will think very differently from what you do now, and will see a great many worthy Gentlemen of the first Rank tugging with Pleasure at that very Oar you have so lately mentioned, though few of them are unprovided for. But Madam, continued he, addressing Lady *Galliard*, will your Ladyship be pleased to take Sir *John* in the Mind,[26] and forward his Departure with the utmost Expedition.

Lady *Galliard* accordingly gave order to have all Things got ready, and in a Weeks Time he was to go, but the Morning before he was to begin his Journey, whether it run in his Head a little more than ordinary, or that he had any other Disturbance, I know not, but he was up some Hours before his usual Time, and after a Walk in the Garden, he ran up to Mr. *Teachwell's*

Chamber, whom he found in a very thoughtful Posture. Sir *John*, after the morning Compliment, asked him if he was thinking of his next Days Journey. He said no, his Thoughts were imployed on a more important Affair: What, I warrant, returned Sir *John*, you were thinking on your last Journey, and after what Manner you shall get to Heaven. You are out again, Sir, said *Teachwell*, it was of less Importance than that too. But ask no farther I entreat you Sir, Knowledge is what we often seek after, but Ignorance gives us the most Ease. Then what the Devil are we going to *Cambridge* for, reply'd the Knight, I always told you Knowledge was a damn'd troublesome Thing, and yet methinks your last Words have raised my Curiosity, they seem to have something ambiguous in them, and sound as if I were a party concern'd; I am however, too well assured of your Veracity, to believe you would know and yet conceal any thing to my Disadvantage, I therefore insist on a clear Explanation of what you have said, and as you value my future Friendship, be brief without Reserve. Sir *John*, returned *Teachwell*, none breathes that Wishes your Happiness more than I do, and it is to preserve it, I would keep this secret to myself, but as we all lie under an indispensable Duty of preventing Evil if in our Power, I think it mine to acquaint you with this Affair, that you may endeavour to put a Stop to a very Pernitious one, which at present rages in your Family, know then (but arm yourself with Patience to hear it) your Mother is the Criminal.

My Mother, cry'd Sir *John*, with the utmost Surprize, my Mother a Criminal, how, when, where, what is her Crime? Who her Accuser, who dare accuse her? Speak, Distractor, or——— Be calm Sir *John*, interrupted the good Man, least your too furious Vindication of her Honour, should expose it more, the Family I believe is at present unapprised of the Matter, and unless her Woman be privy to it, as sure she must, I think myself the only Person who have found it out, which I by the greatest Accident did this very Night, when I came up to Bed I cast my Eye upon *Moliere*,[27] which lay upon my Table, and got so deeply engaged in it, that I read till almost two a-Clock: There is a little wooden Window yonder at my Bed's-head, which looks into the great Hall, and which I never opened in my Life till this Night, because I always took it for a Cupboard, which I had no Use for. Before I had a Mind to part with the Companion in my Hand the Candle burnt out, and when I had thrown the Snuff in the Chimney and was getting to Bed in the dark, I thought I saw a Gleam of Light in the Cupboard, as I took it to be. I went immediately to it, perhaps a little startled at a Thing so unexpected, and trying to open it, found it very ready to comply, not so willing were my Eyes to consent to the Sight they met with, which was Lady *Galliard* hanging upon the Arm of a Man, the Light shaded so that I could not command a full View of his Face, but fancied he resembled *Tom*, I ran immediately to my Chamber-Door, which I opened before they came within hearing, and flew to the end of the Gallery, which you know faces my Lady's Lodgings, and there I saw *Tom* so plain that I was soon convinced I was not at first mistaken, they both went in together and left me in a State so restless, that I have never either warm'd my Bed or closed my Eyes this Night: Oh Sir *John* I grieve for your Distress, nor am I less at a Loss how to advise you on this sad Occasion. Sir *John* who till now had never been touch'd to the quick, flung himself on Mr. *Teachwell's* Bed, where his Eyes gave vent to a heaving Passion, he indulged it for some Time and then got up crying out with transport, tell me Mr. *Teachwell*, for you know the World, tell me I say, are all Women such? O say they are, and give my Mind some ease. Hum, Sir *John*, said *Teachwell*, you may with the same Reason ask, when you see a Malefactor executed, whether all Men deserve the Gallows. No, Vertue forbid, one single Faulter should infect the whole Species. Women no doubt, are made of the very same Stuff that we are, and have the very same Passions and Inclinations, which when let loose without a Curb, grow wild and untameable, defy all Laws and Rules, and can be subdued by nothing but what they are seldom Mistresses of.

What shall I do, cry'd the enraged Sir *John*, shall I ever more behold the Face of her that gave me Being? Can I survive the Infamy she has brought upon her Family, or be so much an Accomplice in her lewd Proceedings as to suffer her Paramour to live? No! I'll first make that Dog a Victim to my just Resentment, and then leave the Kingdom where I must share the Scandal, though I am innocent of the Crime. Death, I now can penetrate into all, and fairly see the whole Design, first to secure the Gallant, and then to banish her Son, whom she would never hear of parting with, till now. Confusion seize him, how I long to drench a Poniard in his lustful Heart. Ah Sir *John*, return'd *Teachwell*, how Nature mixes it self with your Displeasure, I see you would fain lay a Mother's Crime to the Charge of one whose humble Thoughts were deprest too low for such aspiring Hopes, had not something more than bare Encouragement raised them, but as I have been the unhappy Discoverer of this Intrigue, I would by all Means divert you from a cruel and dangerous Revenge, Murder is certainly a greater Crime than Fornication, and while you would wash out your Mother's stain, you blot your own Character, without Success in your Endeavour, again, to kill the Man, would only serve to fill Fame's Trumpet,[28] and that which is but whisper'd now in your own House, would in a few Days be sounded all the Nation over, beside Women of a warm

Constitution, if they loose one Lover will soon provide themselves of another. So that what I would advise you to do is this, defer your intended Journey to Morrow, and find an Opportunity to catch them together, reproach her (as you justly may) with stigmatizing her Family, get her Promise of banishing the Fellow, and then persuade her to marry. As for my designed Journey, return'd the Knight, I have already lay'd it by and am resolved to leave the Kingdom, but first I must lay a Charge at a Mother's Door, and in such bitter Invectives as cannot fail to shock my very Soul, even while the Words are yet upon my Tongue. Yes, this Night I will surprise them together, which I can easily do, for last Week I found in my Father's Study a Key, which commands all the Doors in the House, Lady *Galliard*'s Chamber is within the little Dining-room,[29] the Door of which is always open for the Advantage of the Air, so that I can convey myself into her very Bed-chamber without the least Noise, and my Key will let me into the Dining-room: But how, dear *Teachwell*, tell me how to govern my exasperated Spirit, to chain up the wild Emotions of my just Resentments, say, is it possible for me to see that Dog in my Father's Bed with Temper? Can I behold a guilty Mother's Shame, and stand unmoved at such a vile Accomplice. O *Teachwell*, my Reason leaves me, and I grow distracted at the Thought; say then, if the bare Thought can rack my tortured Soul, what shocking Horror will attend the Sight? I know Sir *John*, replied Mr. *Teachwell*, your Anger, Pride, Shame and Confusion, are altogether up in Arms, hurrying you on to dire Revenge, but I have already said all I can to divert your Hand from Blood, and have no more to do than beg you will put it out of your own Power to do an Action which may bring you many Days of Repentance, as well as the Hazard of your own Life, by going arm'd with nothing but your Patience, that Weapon can do no Harm, and a very little Time will cool your Blood, and set your Reason in its proper Place. Come Sir, if you please, we will go down and try to dispel those angry Vapours which croud your Understanding and strive to eclipse your natural good Nature; I advise you to fein an Indisposition to retard your design'd Journey, and a little Time will too certainly convince you. Our young Knight had no Occasion to feign an Indisposition, the real Agitations of his Mind had made him exceedingly restless and disordered, which Lady *Galliard* at dinner took Notice of, and said, I fear Sir *John*, you are not well to day, for you neither eat nor talk as usual. I believe Mamma, said Miss *Dolly* his Sister (of whom we have hardly yet spoke) My Brother is in love with our *Jane*, for I saw him kiss her one Day when she was making my Bed, and she has been so proud ever since that I can never get my Tea in a Morning till she has done. This made a little Mirth quite round the

Table, and forced a Smile even from the disturb'd Sir *John*, to hear the young Tell-tale; but the rest of the day went off with the utmost Impatience for Night, and no transported Lover, who was to sink into the Arms of a yielding Mistress ever wish'd for it more; at eleven of the Clock Sir *John* proposed going to bed, as having not rested well the Night before. Lady *Galliard* seemed sleepy and was ready to comply; all disperst separately to their several Apartments, only Sir *John* got privately into *Teachwell's* Chamber, where he placed himself, in the dark, at the little Window, to watch whether *Tom* was conveyed the same way as the Night before: The House was now grown very still, when Sir *John* discovered a Light in the Hall, and in short every Thing contributed so much toward his Expectation that he was extreamly mortified with the cutting Sight. He gave them Time to get to Bed and then prepared with trembling Steps to visit them in their Retirement, he got by the Assistance of his Key in the Dining-Room, without any Noise, and coming to the Chamber-door, he heard his Mother in the Height of Passion,[30] say as follows: And is it thus you reward all the tender Sentiments I had had for you? Can it be possible that what you say is real? And can you barbarously snatch yourself from my Arms when I so fondly gave myself to Yours? Have I not sacrificed my Honour to the irresistable Love I had for you, and in a Manner banish'd my only Son, whom I could never think of parting with before, that so no Interruption might break in upon our happy hours, did I not invent a Way to disengage you from your Master's Service, because I could not bear the Thought of cruel Separation, and do you after all, tell me you must be gone, O Monster of Ingratitude, unsay that Word, and save a Heart that breaks when e'er you leave it. Madam, said *Tom,* I do acknowledge you have loaded me with unexpected Favours, but I entreat your Ladyship to remember, that when you first discover'd your Passion in a letter you gave me one Day, the first private Interview I had with you, I laid before you the Inconveniencies that must inevitably attend what you proposed, yet nevertheless I have been subservient to your Will, even to the Hazard of my Life, and the disturbing of a quiet Mind. Then replied Lady *Galliard,* to put you out of Danger and remove your inward Disorder, but above all to convince you of my utmost Esteem take one Promise more, and that a superior one to all I have ever yet made you, I'll marry you the Hour Sir *John* leaves me. O Madam, answered *Tom,* those Misfortunes which before hung loose upon my Shoulders are now, by so kind an Offer firmly riveted, and that Secret must come to Light which has so long been hid in Obscurity, know therefore to my eternal Uneasiness I am married already, and to the very Person my abused Master thinks I am gone to, this I had told you at first, but that I hoped your Passion would have worn out with a few Nights Enjoyment, and I found an inward Check when I first complied, but if we once consult with Flesh and Blood, they certainly get the better, and the most forcible Arguments are on their Side. The impatient Sir *John* no longer able to hear, enter'd at these last Words, and snatching up a Taper which stood upon the Table, he ran to the Bedside with as much Temper as he could possibly command, just when Lady *Galliard* was going to swound,[31] but one Surprize beat back another, and the fresh Concern of her Son being so near, recall'd her sinking Spirits, though poor Sir *John* lost his, for the blasting Sight had such an Effect upon him, that his Tongue faulter'd, his Hand trembled, and his Legs not able to support his Weight, lay'd him speechless on the Floor. The guilty Couple in Bed took the Advantage of his retired Reason, and e're he could recover it, had gotten on their Clothes and left the Room. *Tom* made the best of his Way, from a House he was now grown weary of, and consequently never desired to see again, but Lady *Galliard*, who had always been subservient to Nature, was now touch'd with it in behalf of her only Son, and no sooner saw her favourite Footman gone than she returned to her Chamber, where she found Sir *John* as she left him, in a happy State of Ignorance, she then call'd for help, which with the Assistance of Time brought him to himself, but the Return of his Senses were accompanied with such Reproaches as let Lady *Galliard* into the Secret of her own Character, but as she was a Woman of the most consummate Assurance, it gave her the least Disturbance in Nature. And is it thus, Madam, said the recovered Sir *John*, that you treat the Memory of the deceased, and the remaining Part of him, his Children, do you imagine while your Honour suffers Shipwreck, that ours can escape the Storm, or even his that is no more, do you not rake up his Ashes to Disgrace and Infamy, calling his Fondness Folly, that could doat of so much Ingratitude, and believe a Woman could be faithful, Good Heaven! Was there nothing in the Race of Mankind to please a depraved Appetite but a worthless Footman— Pardon me, Madam, continued the Knight, I now recollect you are my Mother, but beg you will likewise remember I am your Son, and you the first Aggressor, and if a criminal Behaviour should alienate the Duty and Affections of your Children from you, but say it softly, I deserve it all. While Sir *John* was going on with his just Invectives, Lady *Galliard* was studying an Evasion, and thought as the Fellow was gone clean off, and her Son had for some Time been senseless, it would be no hard Matter to persuade him all he saw and heard, was Delusion or a Dream, and answered as follows: I own Sir *John*, your Words are extremely shocking to me, because I plainly see your

Brain is turn'd, nor dare I so much as ask you the Meaning of them, lest it should throw you into a farther Delirium, but beg you will give me leave to call up some of the Servants again, that they may help me to convey you to your Bed, I was afraid of some growing Distemper, when I saw you indisposed at dinner Yesterday. I confess, return'd Sir *John*, such Proceedings where a Man is so nearly concern'd, may well be thought to turn his Brain, and my Confusion, Grief, and Shame is too great to bear many Witnesses. No! Madam, I can go to my Bed without Assistance, but remember you have destroyed the sweet Repose that should attend me there, and do you after all to excuse yourself, persuade me I am deaf and blind, would I could wipe away those Faults which busy Time is laying up in store, and will at last produce to your Confusion, O would I could blot them out, though even at the Expence of Eyes and Ears which at present are of no use to me, but to confirm the ill Opinion you have too justly given me of your Conduct, and I am now so far let into Women's Frailty, that the whole Race of Mankind should cease e're I would endeavour to increase my own Species. Heaven! That it were in my Power to believe my self deceived, but Madam you may be assured this unhappy Son of yours is not the only Witness to your Weakness. I will now leave you, though with much Concern, and hope you will make some home Reflections on your past Actions, how far my tottering Principles may suffer by such Examples I cannot yet determine, but if you never see me more, do not rack your Invention for the Cause.

At those Words Sir *John* with some Precipitation left the Room, where Lady *Galliard* continued in much Confusion, and spent the rest of the Night in Tears, perhaps more for the Loss of the Lover gone, than the Son going, but that which touch'd her most sensibly, was telling her, he was not the only Witness to her Faults, that nettled her exceedingly, and she would fain have been informed, who it was that shared the Secret with her Son, but fear'd to ask him any Questions, least they should be answered with new Reproaches; but being impatient of Spies about her, she resolved to rid herself of every Mortal in the House, except her Woman who was privy to all her Affairs. Sir *John* she thought would soon steer his Course towards *Cambridge*, and then she might make what Revolutions in the Family she had a Mind to: Accordingly in two Days he took his Leave, attended only by Mr. *Teachwell* and one Servant, the latter after three or four Miles riding, Sir *John* ordered to keep at some Distance, and then applied himself after the following Manner to his Tutor. I believe Mr. *Teachwell*, I shall a little surprize you when I tell you, I am absolutely bent against the Journey you think I am going to take. The Seat of

Learning is no Place for me, I now begin to have a Tast for Pleasure, and am resolved to spend my Days where I may glut myself at the Fountain-head, *London* therefore is the Way, the very Road which I intend to travel, leads to that glorious City so much extoll'd by all that have a Tast for true Delight, thither I mean to go, and try to wear away those disagreeable Thoughts which gnaw and interrupt my Ease and Peace, you will I doubt not, disapprove of my Design for double Reasons, I know you will be anxious for my Welfare, and perhaps a little dubious about your own, but I will certainly see you well provided for before we part, and for my own Actions I am fully determined to let them take their swing. Mr. *Teachwell* who had been forming many Schemes in his own Breast for the Advantage of his young Charge, listned to his Resolutions with the extreamest Concern, and told him, he very greatly fear'd the success of his unadvised Design, and pardon me Sir *John*, continued he, if I say you are in the Height of Danger, and may very possibly lift yourself under the Banner of Knaves and Fools, for know Sir *John*, to the great Discredit of Humanity, there is a superiour Number of that sort to those of a different Character. You are young, raw, and unpracticed in the Artifices of those Men, and when you have bought Experience at too high a Price, you will have more Time for Repentance than perhaps you will care to bestow upon it. I wish my Words were of any Force with you, I should then with Pleasure multiply them, but to my very great trouble I find you resolute and past all Advice, but what you give yourself. Would but that great Share of Reason which Heaven has bestow'd upon you, interpose betwixt you and Ruin, it would advise you to seek out some Improvement, and if you dislike Learning, spend a Year or two abroad, make a Tour into *France* and *Italy*, and since you love not Books, read Men, study your own Species through every Stage and Scene of Life, then try whether it be possible for one of your early Sence to give into the grosser Part of Mankind, and joyn their guilty Actions with Ease and Approbation. Mr. *Teachwell*, replied Sir *John*, I cannot but own the Justness of your Remarks, and will always acknowledge they are greatly worth my Notice, but I am young as you yourself observe, and Pleasure must be had whatever it cost.

Pleasure Sir *John*, said *Teachwell*, is in strictness no longer so, than while like an easy Meal it goes lightly of the Stomach, without loading or loathing, and what we vulgarly call Pleasure too often includes a great many criminal Actions, could I by strength of Argument be so happy as to instill an innocent Notion of Pleasure into your Breast, I should gain a very considerable Point, but you are now going to a Place where Religion, Vertue, Sobriety, and in short every Action worthy Praise is by the gay and young exploded. To carry you through the Course of the Town, you must learn the following Axioms: You are to kill your Man before you can be reckoned brave, you must destroy you Constitution with Diseases e're you are allow'd a Man of Gallantry, unman youself by immoderate drinking, to qualify you for a boon Companion; blaspheme your Maker by execrable Oaths and Curses to avoid all Shew of sneaking Religion; and if Fortune forgets to be your Friend, while the Dice are in your Hand, you must fling away your Estate to some wining Bully, lest you should pass for a Man of Prudence and Thought, which brings you to the last Degree of Misery, and you are a Beggar before you know your Danger. And thus Sir *John*, I have described the Modern Man of Honour, which in my Opinion is the most dishonourable Man upon Earth, from which Character as from the Plague may Heaven always keep you.

But why a Man of Honour, return'd Sir *John*, is Honour concern'd in any of the Crimes you have named? Yes, replied *Teachwell* in the major Part of them, as the World goes, for if you receive a Challenge and refuse to answer it, your Honour bleeds to save your Carcass; if you have an Intrigue with a fine Woman, though another Man's Wife, you will readily tell her you have too much Honour either to disappoint her, or tell again; When you have lost a Thousand Pounds at play, tho' you have not a Hundred to answer it with, you cry, 'tis a Debt of Honour, and though my Family at home should starve, it must and shall be paid. Indeed as to drinking and swearing, I think there is not much Pretence to Honour, nor did I ever hear any body lay a Claim to it on those Occasions, but alass, it is very falsely placed where it is lay'd, and Honour like a Virgin's Vertue is too nice to be finger'd by every dirty Hand that knows not the Value of what they sully; No! Sir *John*, a Man of true Honour will avoid every Action that cannot be answer'd for by it: Remember what your Favourite *Hudibras* has said upon that Topick,

> *Honour is like that glassy Bubble*
> *Which gives Phylosophers such trouble,*
> *Whose least Part crack'd the whole does fly,* &c.[32]

Now if a Breach in Honour be like one in the Commandments, how careful should we be to make a just Title to every Branch of it, believe me Sir, the Word Honour, is no more than a strict Observance of that Duty we owe to God and Nature, and when we fail in any Part, the smallest Breach extends itself till it becomes a dreadful Chasm, gaping with Pleasure to devour every Action that Vertue and Reason commends. It is commonly said Example goes beyond Precept, and we are certainly too apt to follow a Multitude in doing

Evil. Fashion (both in Dress and Action) is what we all imitate, though never so ridiculous, and when our Faults are once in vogue, it is then a Crime to think them such, because what every body does, no body thinks wrong, or at least no body will own they do.

How often, return'd the Knight, have I told Mr. *Teachwell* he is an excellent Preacher, and what a pitty 'tis he has not now a fuller Audience, tho' there are some Criticks that would have charged you with too hasty a Transition from Honour to Fashion, which I pass over because I know your Zeal. Come Mr. *Teachwell* I believe you are my Friend, and as such I will always use you, but I now beg we may have no more of this grave Stuff, it is Fortune only that divides our Opinions, she has confined your Notions of Pleasure by a scanty Pattern, while mine is dilated by a more affluent Turn of her precarious Wheel, and when we get to *London*, perhaps I may do better than you imagine.

I hope Sir, answered *Teachwell*, you do not take Heaven's Favours as a Toleration for misusing them, they were design'd for Blessings which they will never prove if, wrong applied, you are extreamly out when you imagine Plenty makes the Rake, because I have known many of that Character reduced to the lowest Ebb, who have yet pursued what you call Pleasure with as strong a Goust[33] as Sir *John Galliard*, can possibly do in the midst of a fine Estate: Again, I have seen a Man whose lavish Fortune has defied Extravagancy, yet reduced to the Want of Necessaries, because he wanted a Heart to enjoy his Wealth, so that it is here very plain, neither Poverty nor Riches make one Happy or Wretched, but the Want of a due Application has many Proselytes of the latter Sort, and it is Depravity of Inclination that must Answer for the Failure, but I find this Sort of Conversation is perfectly disagreeable, and though I know myself obliged to urge it farther, the Despair which attends my Hope of Success puts my good Designs to silence, yet I have one Question to ask, which I hope will be neither improper or impertinent: how do you expect to be supplied with Money at *London?* I doubt Lady *Galliard* will be so exasperated at your willful Journey, that she will be a little backward in answering your expensive Demands; for *London*, Sir *John*, is no Place of Pleasure if a Man pulls out an empty Purse in it. Those Mr. *Teachwell*, answered Sir *John*, who make false Steps themselves, will never be surprized to see another stumble, Lady *Galliard* will certainly give Liberty as well as take it, and while she considers her own Conduct will never be angry with mine, but if she should happen to like her own Faults better than other Peoples, (as I believe most Folks do) and should deny to answer a few extraordinary Expences, I have been told there are Scriveners in *London*, and it is but taking up upon the

Reversion at last, you know I am now pritty well advanced in my nineteenth Year, and shall e're long command what I am now forced to sue for.[34] Mr. *Teachwell* was just going to enter his Protest against that unhappy Project of taking up on the Reversion, when they were overtaken by a Coach and Four, which inclosed Mr. *Friendly*, his Lady and Daughter, going to *London*; he was full of Astonishment to see Sir *John Galliard* on that Road, because he thought him gone to *Cambridge*, and had accordingly taken leave of him a few Days before. Sir *John* was surprized as well as Mr. *Friendly*, and not in a very good condition to excuse himself, he knew some Questions would come from the Coach, which he could not very readily answer, but being resolved to pursue his own eager Desires after Pleasure, he thought it best to look easy, and seem pleased that Fortune had favoured him with such good Company; then turning his Horse's Head towards the Coach, he saluted the Ladies with an Air of profound Civility, and expressed the greatest Satisfaction at a Prospect of such entertaining Company to *London*, for thither I am going Mr. Friendly, and beg you will not lecture me, because Mr. Teachwell here, has done it already so very home, that if my Will, like the Laws of the *Medes* and *Persians*,[35] were not unalterable, I should e're now, by Dint of Argument, have been beaten out of this Road, but Resolution added another Spur to my Heel, and has kept my Horse's Head forward; I dare say Mr. *Friendly*, you can remember since you thought it hard Young Men should not indulge.

Sir *John*, (said the Modest Mr. *Friendly*) when the Beginning of our Days are called to Account by the Middle Part of them, we generally answer with a Blush. I must own, though I was never head-strong, or past Advice, I can call a great many inadvertent Actions to Mind, which I am now ashamed of. I know, Youth, like a Wild Horse, is ungovernable, and loves no Reins or Bit, till Years and Experience cure the Folly; but for your Part, Sir *John*, you are a Man of so much good Sense, that I shall leave you wholly to the Dictates of it, without the least Admonition, tho' never so kindly design'd or received. I fancy you have no Acquaintance at *London*, and wish, when you have, they may all prove *Sterling*. In the mean time, if you please to command a Bed at my House, both that and my Table are at your Service, as long as you will honour me with your Company.

Sir *John* seemed very sensible at so Kind an Offer, and when they got to *London* accepted of it, to which Place Three Days more conveyed them; where I shall for a While leave Sir *John*, and cast an Eye back to Lady *Galliard*, whose Story would end very abruptly, unless a little further pursued. I left her somewhat uneasy in her Mind, with a Design of turning away her whole Set of

Servants, because her Son had assured her, there was some in the Family privy to her Mismanagement; and since she knew not where to fix the Knowledge of her Failings, was resolved to turn out all at once (her Woman excepted, as I said before) not considering, that had any of them been in the Secret her Proceedings was the only Way to publish her faults all over the Country: But she consulted nothing further than getting rid of her Spies; and the poor innocent Servants who knew nothing of the Matter, were turned off with no Satisfaction but their Wages, full of Wonder at so sudden a Revolution. Miss *Dolly*, her Daughter, was now grown a great Romping Girl; and lest she should turn Observator too, was sent to a Boarding-School to confirm that Character; for, as the poor young Creature had always been left to her own Will, running about the House like a tame Rabbit, or rather a wild one: she had no Notion of any thing but Play and Impertinence, which turned her Instructions into the most Ridiculous Imitations; so that Mr. *Hop* her Dancing-Master only fixed the Hobble in her Pace, and Mr. *Quaver* made her squall worse than *Grey-Maulkin* making Love; all Musick in general was her Aversion, and every sort of Work she abhorr'd. The *French* Tongue she chew'd and mumbled, till it banished her *English*, without taking its Place, and she gabbled so many Incoherences, that her Master in a Passion left her, and said, he should teach her a new Language, till she knew none at all. However, there she was placed, if not to improve, at least to waste her Time; she was neither Ugly, or a Fool, but had a sprouting Pride, and a full-groan Ill-Nature, which blasted the Blossoms of her Wit and Beauty. In short, she had more of the Mother than the Father; and here I leave her for some Time to get a-head, then catch her again, when she thinks herself out of my Clutches. Lady *Galliard* having thus cleared her House of every inspecting Eye, entertained a New sett of Servants, but not so much to the Advantage of either Fortune or Credit as she expected; for *Tom* (the Occasion of the general Remove) was now to be recalled, though at the Expence of both, and the following Invitation was accordingly sent him from his Lady's own Hand.

> *IT is now but a few Days since I had some Reasons for parting with all my Servants. The Vacancies which the Steward and Housekeeper made are yet to be fill'd up; and if Your Wife and You think them worth Your Acceptance, they shall be Yours, with all Encouragement from*
>
> B. GALLIARD.

This Letter was wrote for the View of the Wife, tho' the first that was ever sent with that Design; which she no sooner read, than she seemed transported, because she knew nothing of the previous Intrigue betwixt the Lady and her Husband. But *Tom*, not quite so ignorant, was fill'd with very different Sentiments from those his Wife indulged upon such a happy Occasion (as she, poor Fool, thought it) he foreknew what Accounts would be expected from his Stewardship, and plainly saw, while his Wife kept the House, she must give up her Right to his Affections, which he thought within himself was a little hard: But the Offer being so very advantageous, and his Innocent Wife amazed at the full stop he made; after some Minutes Silence, he considered it was impossible to refuse it, without discovering the whole Affair, since no other Objection could be made; and therefore sent her Ladyship Word, they would both wait upon her as soon as they could put their own small Concerns into a little Order. This made Lady *Galliard* perfectly easy as to that Point; but then a dissatisfied Blast blew fresh upon her Hopes, when she considered what the Sentiments of her Inraged and Absent son would be, when he once came to see, or hear the Defiler of his Mother's Bed was again returned: But her sanguine Temper soon dispell'd the Mist that would have clouded her warm Imagination, and she was resolved to hope Sir *John* would like a College-life so well, that some Years would drop before he came again. But while she was pleasing her self with Thoughts of this kind, the Post-man knock'd with a Letter for her; the Hand she knew was Mr. *Teachwell's*, and making a Ready Passage to the Inside, she read these Words:

MADAM.

THE Concern which attends my Hand, while I send Your Ladyship this Account, makes me almost unable to Write at all. It proceeds from a double Cause, First, I dread the impending Ruin which may attend Sir John*, in this New World of* Temptation*; and next, I fear You will blame my Care and Conduct, that has not diverted his Design in Coming here: But may his Misfortunes be as far from him as my Endeavours and Persuasions were near at Hand when he first assured me he would go to* London*: Yet let this bring You some Consolation, he is now under Mr.* Friendly'*s Roof and Care, with whom I shall always join in giving the Best Advice I am able, as he does now with me, in sending*

Our most Profound Respects
To Your Ladyship.

London,
Oct. 20.

Lady *Galliard* read this Letter with a vast deal of Surprise, because she never knew Sir *John* seem to be the least desirous of going to *London*; and it was very likely such a Resolute Action would have given her a considerable share of Uneasiness, had not a Prospect of her own Satisfaction banish'd the present Concern. She was now unapprehensive of any Interruption in her own Faulty Pleasures, and with Reason believed those of the Town would so firmly engage her Son, that she might with the greatest Safety indulge her self in the Criminal Company she best liked. But whatever her private Sentiments were on this Occasion, she thought it very proper to shew some Resentment, which she did in a letter to her Son filled with Reproaches, both for his want of Respect and Duty to her, and for going to *London* with so much Obstinate Folly, before he had spent a Year or two at a Place more proper for him. However, she expressed her Satisfaction, that he was under Mr. *Friendly*'s Care, and begg'd him to continue with him, as he valued either his own Good, or her Favour. Sir *John* received the Epistle, read the Rebukes with perfect Indifference, and took the Advice as far as he thought fit; yet it must be own'd in his Favour, that while Mr. *Friendly* continued in Town he kept to pretty good Decorum, which was some Months; and since I have nothing to say of the Knight at present, rather than lose so much Time, I think fit to return into the Country, and see how Things are transacted at *Galliard-Hall*, where I no sooner entered, than I saw *Tom* and his Wife arrive, one to take Possession of a New Place, and the other of his Old one. To say much upon this Head would swell my Episode to a Bulk too large; but though I would avoid Irregularity, I cannot but fancy the Reader will be a little Curious to know how Lady *Galliard* goes on with her New Steward. The Wife indeed was a Woful Obstacle betwixt her and her proposed Enjoyment, and often stood in the Way, while as often wish'd out on't; but the Incumbrance was a Force upon Lady *Galliard*, because without the Wife the Husband was inaccessible. The Poor Man had certainly an Honest Value for her, and one faultless Moment spent with her was more preferr'd, than all those guilty Hours which ended with Remorse; but Interest is no single Devil, it is a *Legion*, attended with as many Ills: His Fortunes were now sunk too low to be raised again without a wretched disagreeable Compliance; and every other Day (under Pretence of being sent Abroad) confined him in his Old Apartment till Night. But the Wife, who had no Notion of those frequent Excursions from Home, and at Night too, began to ask herself the Meaning of those Nocturnal Sallies; for the Night succeeding those Days he always shared his Lady's Bed. She had had many Disputes with her own Thoughts about this Occasion, but had never opened the Grievance to her Husband, for fear he should think her jealous. But a little

While after, in the midst of one of his Absent Nights, she awoke out of a Frightful Dream, which told her she was in a great deal of Danger; that her Husband was in Bed with her Lady: and if she did not suddenly leave the House, she would never leave it alive. All this, though she believed it no more than the Effect of her Troubled Fancy, lay upon her spirits for some Hours; and Tears instead of Sleep now filled her Eyes; she heard the Clock strike Four, then left her Restless Bed, expostulating with herself in Favour of a Husband, whom she would feign believe she had wrong'd by an unjust suspicion of him. Her Roving Fancy carried her from the Chamber, tho' she knew not where she went, or why she left it; when, after a Wandering Half-Hour spent she knew not how, she cast her Eye towards a Window that looked into the Back-Yard where the Stables were; she heard a Door unlock, but could not see the Person that unlock'd it, Fear, Rage, Despair and Jealousy, had all taken their seats in her Breast; but a bare suspicion, without Certainty of her Fate, was more intolerable than all the rest; she therefore resolv'd, while she shudder'd with the Dread on't, to venture out, and see whether it was her Husband, as Fancy had suggested to her: And when she got into the Kitchen she saw a Dark-lanthorn[36] stand on one of the Dressers with a lighted Candle in it, which was, as she supposed, left there by the Person that had just entered the Stables. She was well pleased at so Ready a Provision for her Discovery, and taking it up, shaded the light till she heard a Horse come out; she then raised it to the Face of the Rider, which prov'd to be one she was pretty well acquainted with, but she concealed herself, and got in undiscover'd, tho' not unsuspected. *Tom* rode off as usual, and his Wife now satisfied of her Ill-Usage returning to her Bed, where no Interruption disturbed her Racking Thoughts, but Gloomy Despair gave an helping Hand, and added to the Pressures of a Wounded Heart. She lay till Day-light call'd her to her Business in the Family, but her swollen Eyes and dejected Countenance told the inward Troubles of her Mind; she was now but too sure that some Intrigue was privately carried on, but was still a Stranger to the sharer in her Husband's Iniquity, tho' she had little Room for Doubt, when she consider'd Lady *Galliard* the very individual Person who always sent her Husband on those pretended Errands. The usual Hour brought him home, and the Wife resolving upon a more compleat Discovery, received him with her wonted Cheerfulness, disguising her Chagrin with all the Art that True Dissimulation could assist her with. The Night came on, which carry'd *Tom* to the lawful Embraces of a Wife he loved; and tho' all her Art was summoned to conceal her cold Indifference, it was plain, from all her slight Embraces, that every one was forced. *Tom* perceived it, and as soon guessed at the Cause; he had all Day fancy'd his Wife was the Person that clapp'd the Dark-lanthorn to his Phyz[37] in the Morning; and if so, had good Reason to believe it would cost him some Pains to clear up the Matter: But, as he knew his Wife a Woman of some Penetration, he was very sure a Thousand Lies would never satisfy her Doubts; and being weary of the Engagement upon his hands, he e'en resolv'd, if she charged him with his Crime, to own it all, and join their Endeavours to extricate themselves as soon as possible. *Tom* then asked his Wife (and desired her Answer without Hesitation or Reserve) whether she had seen his Face any time that Day before Ten o'Clock. She told him with Tears she had, but hoped he had not known her: But since you are upon Enquiry (continued she) may I not ask in my Turn, where you were going at such an odd Hour, and where you had been all Night? I confess your dark Proceeding has given me a great deal of Pain, because I always made myself very sure of that Heart, which I now have cause to fear is lodged in another Breast; Heaven knows I always prised[38] it at too high a Rate to part with it while I had Power to keep it, but now that Power is gone, and it is mine no more. Think not so cruelly (replied *Tom*) my Heart is now as firmly yours as it was the first Moment I gave it to you; though I will briefly own, I have wrong'd your Bed; and it was to prevent those Wrongs, that I so unwillingly consented to my Lady's Proposals, which nothing but your own Eager Persuasions should have forced me to comply with; but I had no Objection to make against such an Advantageous Offer, unless I had confess'd my Fault to you, which I now wish I had done, since I am force to it at last, after many Repetitions of my Crime.

If I have been the Cause of my own Injuries (replied the Wife) it was because I was ignorant of your private Dealings; but now that I am let into the Secret, I will resolutely starve, rather than stay another Day within these cursed Walls: Oh! Infamy, Infamy, who can bear it! Nay, hold Cousin *Margaret* (as he often called her) replied *Tom*, and believe me when I tell you I am full as weary of those Walls as you can be; but since I have been a Rogue so long, I will have my Reward before I leave them, and beg you will stifle this rising Anger, which yet I do not blame you for, till a very short time has finished my Design; my Lady's Bed I will never more approach; but I'll be paid, and very roundly too for all the Guilty Time I have spent there. His Villany was rather persuasive than natural, and ill Advice from our Superiors is too often swallowed with Greediness; and it is almost impossible for a Man to see his Danger before he falls a Victim to the Temptation. This was at first *Tom*'s Case, he thought it a Fine Thing to be liked by a Fine Woman, and one so much above him too:

But what feasted him then glutted him soon after, and he is now resolved to put an End to all. In order to which, he told his Wife, he would acquaint his Lady, that she had found out the Intrigue, and bid her, if any Questions were asked her by Mrs. *Busy*, the Lady's Woman, to say she watched him more than once into her Lady's Apartment. The next Day *Tom* was to go from home, as usual, on his Sham-Errand, and was at the wonted Hour conveyed by *Busy* into her Lady's Bed-Chamber, where she left him, and went to her own. He no sooner saw himself alone with Lady *Galliard* than he affected a Melancholy silence, and waited to be asked the Cause; but instead of that, the Lady herself put on a Gloomy Air, and some Minutes succeeded one another before either spoke. This made *Tom* think his Lady understood *Mekachesa*,* and had like to have baulked his Design; but being fully determined to keep the Word he had given his Wife, of coming near his Lady's Bed no more, he thus began: I know not, Madam, nor can I so much as guess at the Reason of your Silence, unless you know the Cause of mine, which is easily justified when once it is ex-plained; but the Story is so ungrateful it hangs upon my faultering Tongue, nor can it force a passage hence, yet———— Peace, Dissembler (interrupted Lady *Galliard*) I know thy Base, thy Treacherous, thy Black and Mercenary Soul, better than thou dost thyself.

Believe me when I tell you, I am as weary of those Walls as you can be; but since I have been a Rogue for so long, I will have my Reward before I leave them. *Tom* was under some Astonishment, when he heard his own Words repeated, and was going to reply, when Lady *Galliard* thus went on——— Most justly hast thou stiled thyself a Rogue, and it is a Pity the Reward thou art gaping for is not answerable to thy Character——— But I will be paid, and very roundly too for all.——— Pray, Madam, (said *Tom* interrupting her) Do you think it an easy Matter to account for sending Spies to watch a Man's Words and Actions in private with his own Wife? No, Villain (returned Lady *Galliard*) I sent no Spies; it was I that left the Dark-lanthorn in the Kitchen, the errand to which Place was too kind for thy ungrateful Ears to hear, I perceived some-body coming, and Absconded till your Wife had taken it up, and went out with it. I then foresaw a Discovery, and my Curiosity carried me last Night to your Chamber-Door. Then Madam (returned *Tom*) that very Action has let you into my Design, and I may save myself all future Trouble. Very well Sir (replied Lady *Galliard*) and pray, may I know how high this Round Payment runs which you expect, it is Pity methinks, to baulk your Reasonable De-

---

* A Word in the Persian Tales for knowing Peoples thoughts. [Davys's footnote]

mands. Madam (answered *Tom* very pertly) my Demands run high in proportion to the lowness of my Fortunes, which you well know are below my Raising, Three Hundred Pounds will pay off a Mortgage of Part of my Estate, that Sum you can spare, and it is that only that can set me above Want, and you safe from Scandal. I understand you, Sir (said Lady *Galliard*) and if I can preserve my Credit at Three Hundred Pounds Expence, I shall think it no Dear Purchase, would you could give me up my Honour too for such another Sum. Not a Farthing more, Madam (replied *Tom*) I intend to throw in Your Ladyship'd Honour to the Bargain; and as I never desired the keeping of it, I can with less Regret give it up again. Lady *Galliard* was so provoked at this saucy Treatment, which joined itself to her own inward Accusations, that though her Pride forbade her Tears, her Passion with her irritated Blood burst out at her Nose.

Villain (said she) am I become thy Sport? leave me this Moment, and expose me the next to all Mankind; I had much rather write my Faults in my own Forehead, than stand obliged to thee for thy Concealment, though bought at a Price that should not be worth thy Thanks. Begone, and know thou art already wounded in a Part it seems I never had a share of. *Tom* found he had gone a little too far, and would feign have recalled his Words, but Lady *Galliard* too much incensed to listen to any Excuse, got up and left the Room, telling him he had liberty to go whenever he pleased; and as for his Reward, Part on't, he was like to take with him, though he knew it not, the rest she hoped Fortune at some Time or other would pay for her. When *Tom* saw himself alone, and his Bullying Project come to nothing, he returned to his Wife, and gave her an Account of his successless Proceedings. She told him she was not very well, and begg'd, whatever came of it, he would begone, for Poverty with Innocence was in her Breast of much more Value, than Affluence purchased by Guilt. He promised to give up his Accompts[39] the next Day, and desired she would be easy till then. What other Discourse they had I know not, because I was called away to lend an Ear to Lady *Galliard* and *Busy*. I see Madam, by your Eyes (said the latter) you have had some unpleasing Contest with *Tom*; I wish it were in your Power to withdraw your Affections from that Ungrateful Whelp, who has always returned your Love with Contempt, or at least, Indifference: Every Thing, Madam, partakes of its Origin; and the sordid Fool is better pleased with the Trifle his Wife, than with the shining Jewel you put into his Undeserving Hands: snatch it from him, Madam, and see the Brute no more.

Ah! *Busy!* (replied Lady *Galliard*) what friendly Advice would this have been, had it come when first I made you privy to the Reigning Folly in my Breast: Remember your own Faulty Words—— Why, Madam, are you uneasy, while you can redress your own Grievance; if Heaven has given us Appetites, can it be angry that we indulge them; and when we have a Choice of being either happy or wretched, who would not choose the former? If you like *Tom*, let *Tom* be the Man, I think it is now fit you should cater for yourself. This (base as thou art) was thy Pernitious Counsel, which I, Unhappy I, with a too voracious Appetite most greedily swallowed till the Poison infected my whole Mass of Blood, and has turned me from thy Mistress to thy Slave, obliged to buy your Secresy at the Expence of my own Liberty: And instead of Commanding, as usual, must now act the servile Part, and be subservient both to him and you. Why did I not consider this before I involved myself in a link of Faults, before I gave a loose to my own Desires, and e're I resigned my Virtue to its Cursed Opposite Vice. But what's to be done? Say what Measures I must take to disengage my self from this Labyrinth of Destruction, which on all sides surround me?— but alas thy Talent lies toward nought but Mischief; thou art dumb and Mute, where good Advice is wanting.

The Misfortune of Servitude, Madam (answered *Busy*) never shews itself in fuller Colours, than when our Chiefs humble themselves so low, as to ask the Advice of one they know dare give none but what they are satisfied will concur with the Inclination of those who ask it: And had my late Advice run counter to Your Ladyship's Wishes, the Consequence on my side would have been to lie under a lasting Grudge, and on yours to act as you thought fit without it. You may be assured Madam, when I first observed your Affections growing so fast towards a Man, in every Respect so unfit for you, I likewise saw the innumerable Inconveniences that would attend it: And as you have been pleased to remember my Words, give me leave to repeat a few of yours.— — I tell thee *Busy*, it is the hardest thing in Life to subdue our Passions; and I have one for *Tom* so very powerful, that all my Attempts are fruitless, and I can no Way bring it under; have him I must, nay will, though I Marry him.—— Now Madam, after such a Declaration, what could my weak Persuasions avail? Why then am I blamed for consenting to what I could no Way hinder or prevent.

It is now in vain (said Lady *Galliard*) to talk any more of what is past, I am now to consider of what is still to come; 300*l.* is *Tom's* Demand with which he would disengage his incumbered Estate. I do own, I have done him an Injury which a greater Sum cannot atone for, and which I now lament, but it is past, as many more of my Crimes are, and the remaining Part of my Life shall be spent in Contrition for them: Go you to him in the Morning, and carry what I shall then give you to his Wife, tell her I beg her Pardon for all I have done to her, and desire them to be gone immediately; her Wrongs indeed are great and so is my Concern for them: But no more, I will now to Bed, and try if Kindly Sleep will lull me to a Dream of Quiet; for waking I shall ne'r be so. The Morning no sooner appear'd than Lady *Galliard* rung for her Woman, by whose Assistance she got up, and going to her Closet fetched thence a Bag, and bid her give it to *Tom's* Wife, with her last Desire of going away as soon as possible. The poor Woman was no less transported with the Order to be gone than she was with the Present, sent her Thanks to her Lady, and a few Hours carried them away. *Tom* made a right Use of the Money, and Redeemed part of his Estate; but his poor Wife had a short Enjoyment of it, for in less than Three Months she died of a sweating Illness which wore her to nothing, not without violent suspicion of Foul Play. *Tom* was inconsolable for the loss of her, and looked upon her as a Martyr to his Villany and his Lady's Malice, whose Words he often called to Mind, when she told him, he was already wounded in a Part she never had a Share of; he knew his Wife a Woman of Virtue, and thought it hard she should be sacrificed to one of a different Character: Every new Minute filled his Mind with Tender sentiments succeeded by Grief, till at last Revenge took Place, of which more hereafter; for I am this Minute going to take Coach for *London* again, where I left my young Knight in the Careful Hands of Mr. *Friendly* and Mr. *Teachwell*; but at my Return, I heard the latter was fallen ill of a Consumption, and went to the *Bath*, where he died; and Mr. *Friendly*, after seven Months stay at *London*, was now preparing to go again into the Country, to which Place he would feign have persuaded Sir *John* to accompany him, but the Town was now grown dearer to him than any other Place, and not to be parted with on any Terms. In three Days Mr. *Friendly* and his Lady went home, leaving his Daughter, a lovely young Girl, to the Care of his own Sister. Sir *John* is now left at *London*, sole Master of his own Actions, and Mr. *Friendly* was no sooner gone than he took Lodgings at the Court-End[40] of the Town, and began to frequent all publick Places more than ever, by which Means he soon became acquainted with all sorts of People, but unluckily pitch'd upon a wrong sett for his constant Companions. He was a Man of very exact Form, and made as much for Admiration as any young Beau about the Town; he had a pleasing sweetness in his Looks, an easy regular shape, a gentile[41] rakish Air, but a Temper so very affable, that it Complied too readily with every Temptation. The first Progress he made in Modern Gallantry was to get into the unimproving Conversation of the Women of the Town, who often took Care to drink him up to a pitch of Stupidity, the better to qualify him for having his Pockets pick'd; and a frequent Repetition of this sort of Usage forced him to write home for more Money, as he had often done since Mr. *Friendly* left the City, whose Purse as well as House was always at Sir. *John's* Service. But Lady *Galliard*, whose Adventure with *Tom* was quite ended, and who now resolved to leave off Intriguing, had the greatest Desire in Life to get her Son home again; she knew feeding his growing Extravagances with more Money than a Minor ought to spend, would be no politick Scheme for getting him from those Pleasures he was now grown too fond of, and to bridle his Follies when they were grown headstrong, would only serve to give him an Opportunity of breaking the Reins, and hating the Hand that laid them on. She therefore thought it best to interlard her Letter with a layer of Wheedle and a layer of Severity. She first told him how agreeable his Company would be at *Galliard-Hall*; that she had now given up all Pleasures but those that centred in him: That if he valued the true Repose of a Mother, he would endeavour to contribute towards it by consenting to her Wishes: But if he wanted that Love and Duty he owed her, she was resolved to return it by retrenching his Allowance, and bringing it into a narrower Circumference. It is certain, good Words do not mollify so soon as Threats exasperate, and the latter Part of the Letter roused the Lion in the Knight, which provoked him to the following Answer.

MADAM,

SINCE the Reception of your last I have considered your Project, which I find is to starve my Pleasures, but as I love them too well to see them want, I am this Minute come from the Scriveners, where I have taken up a Brace of Hundreds on the Reversion of my Estate. I hope Madam you remembered last Thursday was my Birth Day, and that enter'd me into that Year, which ended, will give me a Power separate from that you now use with some Tyranny. As for Galliard-hall *it is a Country Seat, and till I am tired of* London *shall hardly see it, though my Respects and Duty are always there to attend you, and assure your Ladyship*

I will always be

Your most Obedient Son, and

Humble Servant,

J. Galliard.

How Lady *Galliard* digested this return from her Son, I never heard, because I never enquired, but my Knight went on in the beaten Road of modern Gallantry, and as he thought his own Stock of Wit sufficient for a whole Company, his Set of Companions were a disagreeable Mixture of Fool, Knave, and Coxcomb. The last was a full grown Baronet got to Years of Discretion, though he never had any, whom I shall call Sir *Combish Clutter*,[42] the first a Country Esquire, called *Clownish Cockahoop*,[43] an excellent Companion when a Man aims at nothing but sport, the other (and much the worst of the three) was a stooking Gamster,[44] who generally took Care of the loose Coins the pretty Ladies left in Sir *John's* Pockets, tho' sometimes he got the start of them, and left only the Gleanings. O Men of Merit say, what avails good Sence when left in the Hands of a careless Libertine, who had much rather tye it down with Links of Iron than listen to the Friendly Admonitions it kindly offers. Sir *John Galliard* had so good a Share of that fine Quality, that had he given it room to play, it would have made him a shining Companion for the finest Genius in the Nation, but Vanity, Pride, Folly, and every other opposite to it, were let loose in a wide Room, while it was confined to a narrow Closet, starving and rusting for want of Food and Exercise. A Night or two after carried Sir *John* (with a set of his choice Companions) to the Play, where he saw Miss *Friendly* conducted to a front Box, by a Gentleman he had never seen at her Father's. The Advantage of her Dress added to her natural Charms, and shew'd her much more amiable than he ever thought her before, that Minute created a criminal Admiration in him, and he made himself large and pleasing Promises of her Ruin, it is true his barbarous Design against her shock'd him a little, when he call'd to mind her Father's disinterested Friendship towards him, but Men of Pleasure find little Room for Reflection, at least till they have gratified their own unreasonable Desires. The Lady was young, brisk, airy, and something of the Coquet, which made her Aunt very watchful over her, and the Gentleman with whom she had intrusted her was her own Son, come just from *Italy*. Sir *John* paid a distant Respect to her, and ogled her the whole Time the Play lasted, he grew impatient for the ensuing Day, the Afternoon of which carried him to visit her, which was but the second Time since her Papa left her, he approached her with more Respect than usual: She on the other hand was not pleased he came so seldom, told him he was a very slow Visiter, gave her Fan a flurt[45] and said, she did not care, that, for him, but Sir *John,* continued she, I think I saw you at the Play last Night, how did you like the Scene betwixt—— Madam, interrupted Sir *John*, every Scene was alike to me, because I minded none, I had too lovely an Object from the Box you sat in, to admit of any inferiour Amusement. O lud, cry'd Miss, I think the Man is going to make Love to a body, or do I take a Compliment to myself that was not design'd for me, Aye, aye, I believe 'tis so, for now I remember there was two Ladies more in the same Box, tho' I think they were not very hansom neither; Come Sir *John*, if I am to be your Confidant, only tell me the Secret and I'll keep it— if I can. That (if) Madam, reply'd Sir *John*, was a very considerate Addition to your Promise, but if a Woman can keep a Secret at all, it is certainly her own, though sure it is none to tell you, I admire and adore Miss *Friendly*. Well, I'll swear now, said Miss, I believe I shall grow grave upon this Declaration, for I heard Papa say once, That Surprizes when they are a little over, set Folks a thinking, and you know Sir *John*, we can't think without being grave, hang Gravity it gives ones Face an oldish cast, which makes me mad at you for setting mine into such a disagreeable Form. Let not that give you Uneasiness, return'd the Knight, for there will be nothing displeasing in your Face these twenty Years, which I must tell you is a long Reign as Faces go now, but I have one Question to ask you Madam, Would you have me like your Face? Like it said Miss—— Well I'll take my Oath I don't know whether I would or no, but I think I would not, because I have often heard you say, you did not love Rivals, and my Face must have a very odd turn, or Sir *John Galliard* a very odd Fancy, if no Body likes it but himself.

I own Madam, return'd Sir *John*, your Remark is very just, and I should certainly be ashamed of a Fancy that no body jumpt with but myself, yet, though I would have a Mistress generally liked, I would have her pleased with no Adoration but mine.

This, said Miss, is just what my Aunt told me Yesterday, when I was romping a little with my Cousin *William*, Child she cry'd, leave off those girlish Airs, you are now almost fifteen Years of Age, Men love to take Freedom themselves, but don't care we should, they like to show their Fondness to a hundred Women, but expect we should only smile on one. Now I would fain ask, why we may not love Variety as well as you, yet your imperious saucy Customs has made me perfectly ashamed of my own Behaviour, for there's Mr. *Hatchet-face* a Mercer from *Covent-Garden*, and a rich one too, they say: Then there is Beau *Spangle* from the Horse-Guards, and a Trader from Exchange-Alley worth a Plumb, and a huge Limb of the Law, as big as one of an Ox, from the Temple, with a Man of Quality to bring up the Rear, which have all accosted me with equal Ardour and Complacency, and yet the Duce[46] take me if I dare be civil to any of them, because I don't know which I love best, so e'n let good Nature and good Manners shift for themselves, for I'll have nothing to do with either, where People are concern'd that will take all for their own shares, and leave nothing at all for me. Sir *John* could have told her, there was a vast Disparity betwixt a modest Woman and a Man that lived at large, but his present Business was to get into her favour, without disputing the Matter, and try (since she was perfectly disengaged) to make himself the happy Man, who might at last lay Claim to her Favour; He told her of his mighty Passion, swore himself the humblest of her Voteries, though if she had a previous Inclination, he saw no Reason why she should not indulge it, though even to his Undoing, for Confinement he own'd in any Capacity was a Thing intollerable to a free-born Agent, even the Beasts and Birds, continued he, prefer Hunger and Liberty, to Constraint and Plenty, and shall Man, that noble Creature Man, tye up his capacious Inclinations, and force them into the Circumference of a Mousetrap, while he has the Globe to furnish his Desires with new and many Joys, no Miss, went he on,

> *Liberty's the Soul of Living*
> *Every Hour new Joys receiving.*

That, cry'd Miss, is a Piece of an old song, but pray what follows———
neither *taking Hearts nor giving*[47]—— so then Sir *John*, you and I are just where we were, and may wander in Liberty till we loose one another. F—th[48] Madam, said the Knight, you are grown so very witty, I fear I shall loose you indeed for want of spirit to keep up with your Repartee, and yet methinks it would vex me a little to be baffled by a Woman, though I know you generally fight well at your own Weapons, which are what we do not greatly understand, come no more Disputes, shall I wait upon you to the Play to-morrow Night.

To-morrow Night, said Miss, laughing, nay then you are in love without Dispute, what would you go in to the Play on Sundays? But if you have a Mind to show your Gallantry to Perfection, you shall squire me to Church if you please.

Why f—th Child, replied the Baronet, if I were inclined to go to Church with any Body, it should be with you, but I have too great a Regard for the Drum of my Ears to come there among a Parcel of unmusical Baulers,[49] that fancy God Almighty is to be charm'd with Noise, beside it is not above three Months since I was there, and then was absolved by half the Parish, who no sooner heard the Parson begin the Absolution than they raised an audible Voice and pronounced it as loud as he did.[50] Nay, return'd Miss, I'll say something in behalf of our quiet Congregation in the Country, for they disturb no

Body, nor is it an easy Matter to disturb them, the Minister no sooner begins to pray, than they begin a comfortable Nap, which always lasts till he has done, and then they wake and foot it home to dinner, Papa was rallying our Parson one Day, and asked him why he did not speak loud enough to keep his Congregation awake, he told Papa, a natural Stupidity could not be roused tho' even by the Voice of Thunder, unless they thought the Lightning that attended it should set their Hay-stacks on fire: Alas Sir, continued he, Religion is in a very dangerous Condition, for Men of low Understanding have no Notion of it, and those of an exalted one are too apt to despise it. You have an excellent Memory, reply'd Sir *John*, but I doubt Madam, you have misplaced some of the good Gentleman's Words, because Lightning is a Forerunner of Thunder, not an Attendant on it. In the midst of this Dialogue Miss Friendly's Aunt came to them with a Letter in her hand, and told her Neice she had received a Command from her Papa to send her Home. This News was not very agreeable to the young Lady, whose hankering Inclinations after Gaiety and the Town, made her very unwilling to part with them, but to sooth her own Disturbance she softly told herself, every County in *England* was furnished with Admirers of a fine Woman, as she really was. Sir *John*, however began to ask himself how the remaining Time was to be imploy'd, have her he must, if all his Wealth or Wits could furnish him with a Scheme that would bear, his Brain was fertile enough and produced a thousand Plans, but every one was attended with a superior Objection, the Week after was the Time appointed for her Journey, and Sir *John* then took his Leave and went to his Lodgings, where again he began to contrive, his greatest Concern was to gain a few Days more for her stay in Town, the young one he believed might easily be persuaded, but the Cunning lay in catching the old one, he therefore resolved not to visit her again till Tuesday, that frequent Attendance might give no suspition, and when he did go, made his Application to the Aunt as follows: Mr. *Friendly*, Madam, has been gone from *London* some Months, and I ungrateful as I am have never made the least Return to the many Favours I received from him when here, I blush to think how Miss will accuse me when she tells her Papa I have not so much as waited upon her to a Play or any other Diversion since he left her, I beg you will stand my Friend, and put off her Journey home till next Week, that I may conduct you both to the Masquerade[51] on Thursday Night.

Sir *John*, reply'd the Lady, I shall leave your Request to be determined by my Neice, if she has a Mind to stay another Week, I will not oppose it because I know the value my Brother has for you, but hope you will pardon me if I refuse your Civility, for I have taken leave of the gay Part of Life ever since I was turn'd of Forty. I'll assure you Sir *John*, reply'd Miss, giving her Head a Toss of Contempt, if I had not a greater Regard to my own Pleasure than gratifying your Desires I would not stay, because you did not ask me First, but no Matter, I am now going to the dull Country, and may be Papa will never let me come here again, so for once I'll comply. And now let us consult about our Dresses, Miss *Wary* shall take the Ticket you design'd for my Aunt, and I dare say Sir *John Galliard* will change a Matron for a Girl at any Time, for my Part I intend to personate a Sea-Nymph and dress in Moss and Shells, you Sir *John* may appear like Neptune, because you know he is as much obliged to take Care of the Ladies of his own Dominions as you are to protect me, as for Miss *Wary* she has just finish'd a whimsical Dress, so all you have to do Sir *John*, is to go and bespeak ours. Sir *John* accordingly went and they were sent as order'd. The Night was no sooner gone than our young Lady sent for her favourite Companion, who was a near Neighbour, and the only Daughter of Mr. *Wary*, a Man of Worth and Substance; she had a Frolick in her Head, which was soon communicated to Miss *Wary*, and she asked her if she would joyn in it to cheat Sir *John Galliard*. The Scheme was for the two young Ladies to change Habits and go to the Masquerade before Sir *John* came. Miss *Wary* comply'd, and in the Evening they drest in their several Habits that they might not mistake one another when they came next Night to the common Rendevous. About half an Hour before the appointed Time of Sir *John*'s coming, Miss *Friendly* proposed going but desired her Companion, if the young Baronet should chance to make Love to her in her Likeness, she would use him well for her sake, but if (continued she) your Inclination should chance to stand to-wards a little satyrical Raillery never baulk your Fancy, it is no more than I should do myself, and he will never distinguish feign'd Voices. Chairs[52] were call'd and away the Ladies went. Sir *John* at the usual Time came, and was not a little nettled to find they were gone without him, he took it for a Slight, and resolved to mortify them accordingly, to compleat his Design he orders his Chair-men to carry him to Covent-Garden, where he changed his Dress, then followed the Ladies whom he soon distinguish'd from the rest, but took no Notice of them; they on the other Hand kept a watchful Eye towards the Door, and expected every Enterer would prove Sir *John* who was much nearer to them than they thought and follow'd them wherever they went, which at last Miss *Friendly* took notice of, and casting a-side look at him now and then, she observed his naked Hand going to convey a Pinch of Snuff to his Nose, and knew a Ring he had on his Finger, by which she found him out, and told the Secret to her Friend, but still behaved as before, and seem'd as indifferent as ever; Sir *John* at last came up to Miss *Wary*, whom by the Dress he took for Miss *Friendly*, and asked her in a Puppet's Tone— Do you know me? She reply'd in the same squeeke——Yes, better than you know me, and since we are deserted by our Guardian that should have followed us, we don't much care if we substitute you his Representative, and—— Hold Madam, interrupted Miss *Friendly*, still feigning her Voice, I will have nothing to say to him till he lets me into the Secret of the Ring on his Finger, which I am sure belongs to Sir *John Galliard*, and for ought I know you are some Ruffian that has murdered the Man and ran away with his Moveables, come, come Sir, off with your Mask or I'll send for a Constable. Sir *John* found by all this Raillery his Ring had discovered him, and then began to say a thousand tender Things to his Nymph in double Masquerade, who took all possible Care to prevent any farther Discovery. Some Hours were spent in the common Diversions of the Place where Wit and Humour flew about like Squibs,[53] and when they came to the Boufet[54] Sir *John* unmask'd, and would fain have had the Ladies do so too, but they were too full of the Project of cheating the Knight to end it so soon, and therefore refused to drink any Thing, only put a few dry'd Sweetmeats into their Pockets, which they eat as Opportunity offer'd: But while they were yet at the Boufet a little dapper Gentleman came to Sir *John*, and asked him if he would part with one of his Ladies, for he thought it hard he should have two and himself not one. Sir *John* told him he could not guess from his Looks that he wanted one, since they promised but very indifferently in his Favour, however if he could gain either of the Ladies Consent to run away with a Tom Thumb[55] he should pity their want of Judgment, but that was a Place of Freedom, and he could not use Force to keep them.

The Beau told him he wore a Sword and should find a Time— I know not Sir (replied Sir *John*) what Time you may find, but am sure mine would be lost if it were spent in killing a Pigmy, and for your Sword if it be no longer than yourself it will never make Work either for a Surgeon or an Undertaker, prithee keep it in its peaceable Scabbard, and go thy Ways for a little Fool as thou art. At this the Ladies laugh'd and the Bauble went muttering away. The Variety this Place afforded of new Diversions carried the Night insensibly off, and Day began to break before the Ladies were tired, at which Time they desired Sir *John* to provide Chairs. He went that Minute and provided three, but gave the Chair-men the following Directions, the two first was to go to the *Bagnio*,[56] and the third to Mr. Wary's the aforesaid Father of Miss *Friendly*'s Companion. He then return'd and conducted the Ladies out, putting Miss

Friendly (as he thought) into the second Chair, and Miss *Wary* into the third (who was immediately carried off) and Sir *John* got into the first himself, and was as by order conveigh'd to the *Bagnio*, as soon as they got to the Door the well designing Knight got out and handed the following Lady from her Chair, who seeing another behind her, (for one there was) thought it had been Miss *Friendly*, and that the Jest was now at an end, pull'd off her Mask and laughing cry'd, how do you like your Sea-Nymph now, God Neptune, that should have been? Then running to the other Chair, come Miss (said she) all is out: But what was her surprize when instead of Miss *Friendly* she saw the little Gentleman coming out, with whom Sir *John* had had a short Contest at the Masquerade. He was now so mad at his Disappointment, that he was glad to see one on whom he might revenge himself, and turning to Miss Wary said, here is some Mistake Madam, those Chairmen (who were then gone off) have brought us to the *Bagnio* I think, perhaps by a Bribe from this Gentleman, who I fancy has made a Quarrel of what past at the Masquerade, I therefore beg you will take his dismist Chair and go home, where you will find Miss *Friendly*, for I order'd them all to your House, I would very fain wait upon you, but you see my Honour is engaged and I know you Ladies hate Cowards, I will therefore conduct you to the Chair and I wish you a good Morning. The young Lady was soon at home, where she found Miss *Friendly* full of Wonder what was become of her and Sir *John*, I will now leave them a while to compare Notes together, and step back to the *Bagnio* to see what becomes of the two Antagonists, they were both got into the House before I came, and the little Gentleman began to bully, Sir Knight told him he had affronted him so far that his Spirit could not bear it, and his Design in following him was for Satisfaction. Sir *John* ashamed of such a Combat, urg'd the Folly of taking any Thing ill that was said in a Place where a little good Raillery was design'd for the best Part of the Diversion, and I farther know (continued he) my Sword and Arm will meet with nothing but Disgrace from so poor a Victory, yet if you insist upon Satisfaction, I will give you all I can, but I think it your Business to go and provide Weapons since the Place we come from admitting of none we are unluckily both without, another Thing I insist upon is uncaseing your Face, for I never love to fight with a false one, mine is bare and I expect yours should be so too. It will be of little Service to you, reply'd the Challenger, to show my Face since I am sure you never yet have seen it, but yet e're I unmask I have a secret to disclose to you, and yet I must keep it too, know then I am a Woman, a married Woman, and I once thought a Virtuous Woman, my Husband too is deserving of my Love, he is young, hansom, rich, and doats upon his Wife unworthy as she is, nay above the World I love him too, and all that's in it should never prevail with me to wrong his Bed, were it not entirely for his own ease. I own Madam (return'd Sir *John*) I have often hear'd that Women are Riddles and sure you are come to confirm the Assertion. No, replied the Lady, I shall soon clear up the Matter when I tell you I have been eight Years a Wife yet have nothing to shew for so much Time spent in Matrimony, but a great Estate without an Heir to it, and there lies the bitter Pill that takes away the sweets of Life, that is the cutting Blow, the smarting Wound my Husband always feels, 'tis that alass— and could I— but O spare a farther Declaration and guess the rest. No Madam, return'd Sir *John*, I can guess at nothing till I see your Face, and if that proves good, I'll guess just as you would have me; though I think you have spoke so very plain, that you have left no Room for any thing but Certainty.

The Lady unmasked, and shewed a Face both fair and young, which our Knight liked so well, that nothing could be denied, no Resistance is Force against so fine a Temptation, yet still he wanted to know the Tempter's Name; but that at first she was resolved to conceal, which proved no bar to his invited Desires, which were always too sharp set to want a Poynant Sauce.[57] She told him however, she was a Woman of Distinction; that she could not promise he should ever see her Face again: but by that Honour she was now going to sacrifice he should hear from her, and have a just Account of the Success that attended the present Undertaking. They retired, and I left them to go back to the Ladies, whom I found in much Disorder at what had happened so lately to them. Miss *Wary*, a cunning young Baggage, would have it that Sir *John Galliard* had certainly some Ill Design upon the Sea-Nymph, and was sure it was more than Chance that conducted them to the *Bagnio*. Miss *Friendly* could not be of her Mind for several Reasons, and first, she was sure Sir *John* had too great a Value for her Papa to offer any thing ill to his Daughter; beside, her Opinion in general was too good of him to believe he would do an ill Action to anybody: And it signified nothing to enumerate Reasons against a perfect Improbability, since, had his Inclinations been never so vicious, the *Bagnio* was a Place as improper for such an Undertaking as a Tavern, or any other Publick House. You are mistaken Madam, (said Miss *Wary*) those Places for a small Sum will find a Thousand Ways to avoid Discoveries, and prevent Disturbance. My Papa, when he was in Commission for the Peace, had several of those Things brought before him: And I once heard a Gentleman say, A *Bagnio* was no more than a Tolerated Baudy-House.

Say no more my Dear *Kitty* (replied Miss *Friendly*) I will hear no more of it till I see Sir *John*, and hear what he says for himself: But come (continued she) will you go with me, and let us go to Bed for an Hour or two, for fear we should fall asleep at the Play anon, where I am resolved to go at Night, because it will be the last I shall see while I stay in Town, for To-morrow you have engaged me, and on Monday I must set forward towards the West. They changed their Clothes, and went together, got their Breakfasts, and went to Bed. In the Afternoon Sir *John* came to see how they did after their last Night's Diversion. O Lud! Sir *John!* (cried Miss *Friendly*) I am glad to see you Alive, I expected To-morrow's *Journal* would have given some Dismal Account of your Proceedings with the little Gentleman, I hear he followed you for *Satisfaction*; but as I see your Arm is not confined to a Scarf, I hope you came off with Honour. Yes Madam (replied Sir *John*) pretty well; we had indeed a little Skirmish, but it was soon over, and we parted good Friends at last. But the Adventure of the *Bagnio*, Sir *John* (said Miss *Wary*) methinks I would feign be let into the Secret of that Scheme, which seems to have a sort of an unaccountable Odness in it that will not be presently answered for. L—d! Madam (replied Sir *John*) I am surprised that you that know the Town should take Notice of a few Blundering Chairmen; they heard the Gentleman, I suppose, that dog'd me, give Orders to the *Bagnio*, and thought they were to go there too. Miss *Wary* told him that would never hold, because it was plain he had given Orders to the Chairmen, before the Gentleman came out whose Design was to dog him; beside, if it was a Mistake, why did not Miss *Friendly*'s Chair go with the rest? Well, well, Sir *John* (interrupted Miss *Friendly*) suppose we leap over all those Difficulties, how will you excuse yourself, when you are charged with taking a Couple of Ladies to the Masquerade, and wanted both Good-Manners and Gallantry to see them safe home again? Nay, Ladies (said Sir *John*) if ye both fall foul upon me at once, I must strike my Flag and surrender; but be pleased to remember you denied me the Pleasure of waiting on you there, which will a little excuse my Behaviour afterwards, tho' I would not have lost the Honour of seeing you back, had not that little Trifler with his foolish Punctilio's[58] prevented me: And yet methinks it pleases me, when I remember how I revenged myself. But I now ask Ten Thousand Pardons for all the Faults you can charge me with, that so we may part Friends, for my errand now is to take my leave of you, having engaged myself to accompany a Friend who is going to take a Trip to *France*: This Afternoon we go on Ship-board, so Ladies, if ye have any Commands to that Nation, I am at your Service to convey them. O Lud! (cried Miss *Friendly*) here's Manners; Why, did you not make us promise to go with you to the Play to-Night? And now he is going to *France*. Pray go and tell the Creature you have a Pre-engagement upon your Hands, and you can't go till the next fair Wind. Sir *John* made some scurvy Apology for his Non-compliance, and took his leave. He was now resolved to try another Expedient to accomplish his Design upon Miss *Friendly*, and to lay it on so sure a Foundation, that even Fate itself should hardly have Power to baffle it. He went directly to his Lodgings, and sent for his Apothecary, telling him he had now a very urgent Occasion for his Assistance, tho' of a different Nature from any thing he had ever served him in yet;[59] told him in very plain Terms, he had a Mind to a certain young Lady, of whom he did not despair, though he should use no clandestine Means, but he had a reason for working with the Mole under-Ground,[60] and had rather have her unknown to herself than with her own Consent, in order to which, he desired him to make a private Conveyance of some Opiate into a few Mackroons[61] (which was what the Lady greatly loved) to cause a Lethargy for some Hours; and desired it might operate as soon as possible. This was no sooner proposed than complied with, because Sir *John* was an excellent Customer, and his Bribe pretty large. The prepared Mackroons were speedily brought, and in three Hours after eating they were to begin their Work. He no sooner saw himself Master of the soporiferous Dose than he resolved to try the Effects of it, which he did that Night on a Maid-servant in the House where he lodged; he found it answered his Expectations, and in the Morning he called for his Groom, order'd him to saddle his Horse, which he mounted, and unattended left *London*, and went to the Inn where he knew the Innocent Sacrifice must lye the first Night upon the Road, and thought it fit to be there two or three Days before his Victim, that he might have Time to corrupt one of the Servants, to assist him in his Base Design against Poor Innocent Miss *Friendly*. He well knew a Plebeian Mind was never Proof against the Persuasive Power of Tempting Gold; a Metal which insensibly diffuses itself into every Sense we have, and by Art Magick forces a liking, though Death and Ruin be its Attendants. Sir *John*, the Base, Ungenerous, Sir *John*, is now got to the Inn, where he soon singled out one of the Wenches for his Tool. He saw she thought her self handsome, and knew the only Way to get into her Favour was to make her believe he thought so too: In order to which, he praised her Beauty, and told her of much more than she ever had, which with a Kiss now and then, and Half a Crown sometimes, made him the Finest Gentleman that ever came that Road before: He soon saw he gained Ground, and at Night, after having sate up pretty late with a silly Landlord, whom he made very drunk, he ordered *Sarah* his chosen Accomplice to bring a Pint of Wine into his Chamber, and come up with it herself, which she readily did, Sir *John* had no Occasion to make use of his Opiate, the Wench was very complying, and he to strengthen his Interest in her gave her leave to take share of his Bed that Night. In the Morning he began to think of letting her into the Secret that brought him there. *Sarah* (said he) I am now going to trust you with a very Grand Concern; and after what has passed betwixt us I hope I may confide in you: This Night I expect a young Lady to come to this House, with whom I had once an Intrigue: but a little Misunderstanding happened betwixt us, and I would feign make my Peace with her again: Now *Sarah*, what I have to beg of you is to convey me privately into some Part of her Chamber, where I may lurk till she is in bed; and when you have done me this Piece of Service you shall have a very suitable Reward. *Sarah* who was too profuse of her own Chastity to endeavour the Preservation of that of another, not only complied with what was already proposed, but promised her farther Assistance, if any more was necessary. Sir *John* upon this Promise produced the Mackroons, and asked her, if she could by some clean Contrivance give one half to the Lady, and the other to her Maid? At which the Wench looked a little startled, and told Sir *John*, she hoped there was no Poison in them, for she did not much care to be hanged neither. No (replied the Knight) to cure your Suspicions, see here I eat one of them myself, which he did.

Sarah was satisfied, promised to assist, and then went to call up the Guests to be gone. O Man! how strong are thy Passions, how exorbitant thy Desires, and how impotent thy Virtues? Here have we a Person of Birth, of Fortune, of Sense before us, a Man, who might have been a Credit both to his Country and Species, had the early Rudiments of that Behaviour, which makes us value one another, been timely instilled while his tender Years were capable of Impression; but alas! the Want of Care in his Education made him a Perfect *Modern Fine Gentleman*; which, when we consider the sad Ingredients, they make a very Woful Compound: It is true, if we abstract bad Actions from Folly (which in my humble Opinion can hardly be done) Sir *John* was very free from the Imputation of a Fool, but then he had a double share of the Rake to make up his *Quantum*,[62] and finish a very bad Character. The Close of the Evening brought in the Stage- Coach, and in it the Pretty Lady expected. *Sarah* that B——[63] was ready at Hand, when she desired, as soon as she alighted to choose her Room; she conducted her to one which she knew fit for the Design in Hand, with two Beds in it (for Sir *John* had told her before, that the Lady's Maid always lay in her Room, but never in her Bed) she pitched upon the first she saw, and being a little weary with her Journey, and sadly tired of the Dull Company in the Coach, she threw herself upon one of the Beds, and dosed till Supper. Sir *John* saw her at some Distance, but kept *incog.*[64] himself, and felt a Remorse for what he was about, but it proved too weak to conquer. While Miss *Friendly* was with her Disagreeable Company at Supper, Sir *John* was conveyed into a Closet, which he lock'd with-in-side, and stayed till his Time came of coming out. Supper was no sooner over, than poor Miss *Friendly* returned to her Chamber with her Maid, who was just going to undress her Lady, when *Sarah* came into the Room with a little Salver of Sweet-meats in her Hand. Here Madam (said she) I have brought you a Present.

A Present (replied the Lady) from whom prithee? Oh! Madam (said *Sarah*) from a very Civil Gentleman I'll assure you, I am sure I have experienced his Kindness more than once; he saw you alight out of the Coach, and bid me pay his *Devoirs* (I think he call'd it) to you, and beg you would please to taste two or three of the finest Mackroons you ever tasted in your Life. I believe (said Miss *Friendly*) the Gentleman is a Witch, for I know nothing I love so well as a Mackroon. Here *Jenny* (continued she) I know you love them as well as I, take them three, and I'll eat the rest, for my Supper lies on my Stomach, and I can master no more; as for the rest, Sweetheart, you may either eat them your self, or return them, with my humble Service and Thanks to the Gentleman: And be sure you call me early, for I always take a deal of Time to persuade myself to leave my Bed in a Morning. The Jade dropp'd her Court'sy, promised Obedience, and away she went. While *Jenny* was undressing her Lady, I wonder Madam (said she) where Sir *John Galliard* is now; he can't be got to *France* yet, can he Madam? I do not know (returned Miss *Friendly*) where he is, nor what Time it takes to go such a Voyage, but I think he left the Kingdom very abruptly; And I dare say Lady *Galliard* will not be pleased with his Ramble, but what is that to me? Nay Madam (replied *Jenny*) I know your Indifference pretty well, and dare lay my Head to a Row of Pins, you do not value one Man upon Earth, or name any for whom you have a superior Esteem; if you could, you would certainly talk a little of young Mr. *Wary*; that's the Man for my Money: A Man, that has every thing good in him, sober, virtuous and rich, and—— Why, thy Tongue's upon Wheels I think (interrupted Miss) What dost thou tell me of his Virtue, and stuff, I'll think of nobody yet, but when I do, for all your Head to two or three Pins, I can tell you, I should value Sir *John Galliard* with all his Faults much more than young *Wary* with all his fine Qualities; such a deal of Reserve and Gravity becomes a Young Man as ill as Frolicks and Gaiety does an Old one; And he that gives himself such very exact Airs, will doubtless expect the same from his Wife:

And for my Part, I love an easy, open, free Behaviour, guarded by Innocence; and would not for the World be forced to sit primming and screwing my Face into a Prudish, Hypocritical look. Oh! *Jenny*, I always suspect those sort of Women, and believe, there are more Faults committed under a sanctified Phiz, than are commonly found among such Giddy Girls as I am. Lord, Madam (replied *Jenny*) you talk like any Angel to-night, I wish Sir *John* was a Mouse in some Hole, to hear the Declaration you have made in his Favour, he would hardly sleep a Wink all Night for Joy. You are mistaken (answered Miss) Sir *John* is not much transported with Womens Favours, he is too well used to 'em to set any Price upon them; neither are my Thoughts of him so free from Reflections as they were once: I cannot reconcile the Story of the *Bagnio* to Honour, and am sometimes forced to think my own Safety was owing to my Change of Dress. O Ingratitude (cried *Jenny*) if that be true, all Mankind are Monsters; but Madam, you forget you must be early up, will you please to think of going to Bed? Yes (said Miss *Friendly*) and to sleep too, for I begin to grow drousy. Sir *John* was all this While snug in the Closet, where he heard all, and sometimes wished it out of his Power to ruin the Lady, but his Scheme was laid, and all Things succeeded to his Wish. The Time came, the Lady asleep in one Bed, her Maid in another, and Sir *John* had all the Opportunity he expected. As soon as he heard the least stirring in the House he got up, called for his Horse, gave *Sarah* her Reward, and away he rode to *London* as fast as his Horse could carry him. The Guests at the Inn were now calling up to be gone, but Miss *Friendly* and her Maid could by no Means be awaked; the whole House was alarmed and surprised, a Doctor was sent for, who when he came said, they had taken some stupifying Dose, and all the Art of Man could not bring them to their Reason till it was slept off. *Sarah* was frighted out of her Wits, and feared they would die, but kept her own Counsel, as any-body else would have done. The Coach-man stood swearing, and would feign have gone without them, but not one of the Passengers would go into the Coach till they came. At last Miss *Friendly* came to herself, and in a quarter of an Hour more so did her Maid. They were both surprised at what had happened, but made Haste to get on their Clothes, and proceede on their Journey, but continued drousy, and out of Order all Day. At Night when they came to their Inn, Miss *Friendly* ordered her Supper to be brought up into her own Chamber, the better to procure an Opportunity of talking with her Maid. *Jenny* (said she) I am strangely embarassed about this sleepy Fit you and I have had, and am entirely of the Doctor's Opinion, that it was no Natural Repose; yet where to place either the Deceit or Design of it I know not, but my whole

Thoughts have been chained to that one single Subject all this Day: Prithee
what is thy Opinion of the Matter? Indeed Madam (replied *Jenny*) my Thoughts
had as little Variety as yours, nor am I less perplexed to find out what I am sure
has a Secret in the Bottom; but when it sprung, or what Drift they had is past
my Comprehension: I am only vexed I did not ask the Maid at the Inn, from
whom she had the Sweet-meats she brought; for, if there was any Design at all
against you, it was certainly lodged in the Mackroons, because Madam, you
may please to remember, neither you or I eat of any thing else. That (answered
Miss *Friendly*) is what increases my Astonishment, because they certainly came
from some-body that knows how fond I am of them. But are you sure, *Jenny*,
you locked the Door before you went to Bed, for there is a great deal in that
one single Article. Yes Madam (answered *Jenny*) I am very sure I lock'd it, but
I doubt it was open in the Morning, or how did every body get in. Perhaps
(replied the poor Lady in Tears) they broke it open when they could not awake
us; but be it how it will, I fear I am ruined past Redemption. *Jenny* seemed
confounded at what her Lady said, and was now sorry she had owned so much:
But while she was striving to remove her Lady's Fears, a Servant came up and
said, A Gentleman below enquired for one Mistress *Friendly*. But her late Disturbance gave her a new Concern, and she trembling, answered, she would see
no-body. Yes my Dear (said a Voice behind) You will see me I am sure. She
soon knew it was her Father's, who, with a Tenderness worthy of the Name,
was come to meet her; the sight of whom for some time banished all Concern,
and she recalled her own Pretty Temper to entertain him with Cheerfulness.
After she had enquired after her Mamma's Health, and such Things, Supper
came up; and as they eat, Mr. *Friendly* kindly enquired after Sir *John Galliard*.
Miss told him, he went to *France* about Three Days before she came from
London; but believed it was rather a *Frolick*, than any Desire he had to travel.
Methinks (replied Mr. *Friendly*) I feel Pain for the Mismanagement of that
young Gentleman, because, next to my own, I have a Tenderness for him, and
it would please me more to see him Old Sir *John* in Behaviour and Principles,
than to increase my Estate some Hundreds in a Year. Indeed Papa (said Miss)
my Brother and I have little Cause to thank you for that; but I hope there is a
great deal more Expectation of your doing one, than seeing the other. Why,
Child (answered Mr. *Friendly*) do you hope so? I have enough to make ye both
easy in Life: And should a Luxurious Superfluity take place against the Good
of our Neighbour? No! I am so far from retracting what I have said, that I
would freely give some Hundreds out of what I already enjoy, to see him what
I wish: It is a poor sordid spirit that is confined to itself only, a Generous Good

Man has an extensive Fund of Good Wishes for all Mankind in general; but in a particular Manner for his Friends, and those he loves. Truely Sir (replied the Pert Chamber-Maid) if Sir *John Galliard* goes on as he begins, for ought I know, he may come to thank you for all you can spare him. Forbid it Heaven! (said the Good Old Man) that he should ever want my Bounty; but if he does while I have Life and Six-pence he shall share the latter. Too Kind, too Generous a Declaration, in Favour of one whose Black Ingratitude made him the least deserving of such strict, such noble Friendship. The Worthy Gentleman and his Darling Daughter got safe home the next Day, and Sir *John* was now again at *London* entertaining his Five Senses with every Modish Delight: But though he had always indulged himself in Libertine Principles, and believed, that Man was made for nothing but to gratify his own sensual Desires; yet the secret Impulses of his mind (which he was very loth to call Conscience) often gave him the Lie, and told him, A Curb was sometimes necessary for Man as Beast: He could not reflect on the Base Action he had so lately done to an Innocent Virgin, the Only Daughter of a most Worthy Gentleman, who loved him, and had given him a Thousand Demonstrations that he did so; one whose seasonable Counsels had once made an Impression on his Mind, given with all the Sweetness, Candor and Affection in the World, though now worn off to make Way for every contrary Quality: He could not think on those Things without Remorse and short-liv'd Pangs, which he always suppress'd and stifled with some Faulty new Delight. Drinking has too often been used as an Amulet against Troublesome Thoughts, which for some time stuck pretty close to our Knight, and which he endeavoured to drown in *Burgundy* and *Shampain*:[65] But as Drinking was not his favourite Vice, he soon left that off, and struck into the *Groom-Porter's*,[66] where his Worst Luck pursued him close, and in one Hour he saw himself rook'd out of all his Money, Watch, Ring, and every Thing of Value he had about him. He now in a Rage flung out, and called a Coach to go home, though he had not a Shilling left to pay the Hire; and in Compliance with a Weak Resolution, swore he would never go there again: But in two Hours Time the Spirit of Revenge took Place of the Fretful Devil in his Breast, and he went for a new Recruit,[67] with which he pointed again towards the *Groom-Porter's*; and though he feared he should not meet with the proper Person on whom he would willingly vent his spleen; even he was the first Man he saw, to whom he immediately gave a Challenge to meet him, not with Sword and Pistol behind some Old House, but with Box and Dice at a Publick Gaming Table. The Brave Antagonist answered the Bold Challenger, and to it they went again. Sir *John* set high, and for some time seemed a Favourite of Madam *Fortune's*; but her Wheel turned of a sudden, and in half an Hour's time he lost an Hundred Guineas in Ready Money, and double the Sum to be paid *upon Honour* in Three Months. But all those Amusements did not answer their End, which should have driven the Injured Miss *Friendly* out of his Head; but, on the contrary, set him on Thinking more than ever: And in his Intervals, when Reason was admitted, and a serious Thought had Leave to thrust in, he fancied all his Ill-Luck was sent him upon her Account, but that he presently stifled, and cried to himself— Z——s,[68] Fool, there's nothing in't— Conscience! D—n the Bugbear! 'tis a Cursed Imposition forced upon Man, to keep his free-born Mind in subjection, and make him a Slave to the Caprices of a Whimsical Priest. No, *Galliard* (continued he) regard not what is past, but study to gratify the present, and to come; if our Lives are confined to a few Years, who would lose a Moment's Pleasure? We are sure of what we have, but what is to come is uncertain; Therefore, as an Industrious Tradesman takes daily Care to provide for his Family, so will I for my Delights: He that wants Courage to pursue his Pleasures has lost the Goust of Life; and, like a Tedder'd[69] Horse, sees his Confinement to a Fairy Circle of the same Food, without the least Prospect of Dear Variety.

This sensual Soliloquy set our Kinght upon searching after new Pleasures; he had heard very much of a Goodly Sett of Men, who distinguished themselves by the Name of the *HELL-FIRE-CLUB*;[70] and thought, if he could but make Friends to get himself initiated a Member of that Glorious Dare-Devil Society, he should be a Compleat *Modern Fine Gentleman*. But before they would admit him, they resolved to try his Courage, and a small Detachment from the whole Body was selected to make the Experiment. Sir *John* was order'd to meet them in St. *Martin's* Church-Yard[71] about One o'Clock in the Morning, where, on a Tomb-stone were set Wine and Glasses, with no Light but a Bundle of Brimstone-Matches set on Fire: And if Sir *John* could Devoutly Drink *A Health to the DEVIL*, without Hesitation, or being shock'd, he was from that time to be reckon'd one of them; if not, he was to be cashier'd,[72] and fined Twenty Marks for the Use of the CLUB, as a Just Punishment for his Impudence, in pretending to what he durst not go thorough-stitch[73] with; but Sir *John* most Heroically saved both his Money and Credit, having the Honour to begin the Health himself. Sure the Liquor must be hot where the *Devil's* the Toast; and the Health very Ridiculous, where the BEING is Denied: But the saucy Watch[74] interrupted their Diabolical Mirth, or rather they disturbed the Watch; by giving the first On-set, who proving a Parcel of sturdy Fellows, fell on without many Words, and routed the whole Herd; some they took Prisoners, and some took to their Heels. Sir *John* was among the Runaways, and made his Escape, saying, The *Devil* might have had more Manners than to see them routed by a Parcel of Scoundrels, while they were shewing so much Civility to him. He was now arrived at the End of his One and Twentieth Year, and had by that Time run the Gauntlet through every Vice of the Town, which is not improperly so called, since every Vice has its Lash, and chastised him as he went: His Drinking made him sick, his Gaming made him poor, his Mistresses made him unsound; and his other Faults gave him sometimes Remorse, though as he had neither innate Principles of Virtue, or the Prejudices of a Good Education to wear off, or struggle with, he in the main made himself very easy: And one Day, as he was going through a certain Street, he saw an Old Lady of his Acquaintance, call Mother *N—d—m*,[75] standing at her Door, She blessed herself (which was very rare) at the sight of Sir *John Galliard* who she began to Reproach for his long Absence. He excused himself by saying, he had now left off all those Things, was resolved to live Honest, and only keep just one Lady or two for his own Diversion, and have nothing to do with any more. But she, Good Creature, was not willing they should part so; and therefore threw the Old Bait in his Way, told him, she had a Curious Fine Girl in the House, that was just come out of the Country, brought by a Fellow that would feign have Ravished her, but she was resolved there should be no such Disorderly Doings in her House: so she believed he was gone to take a Lodging for her; and if Sir *John* would walk in, he should see her, and try to gain her Favour. This was a Temptation too strong to be resisted by the Knight, he struck in after the Baud, who conducted him upstairs to a little Room, where, before they enter'd, they heard the poor Young Creature cry most pitifully; the *Old* One enter'd first and after her Sir *John*, the Girl in Tears thought it had been her Ravisher, return'd and cry'd, kill me, kill me, for I'll never be your Wife, I had rather be torn to Pieces than marry my Brother's Footman.

No my sweet Child (said old *Jezabella*) this is not the Rogue that would have ravish'd you, this is a fine young Gentleman that is come to help you: At that the young Lady turn'd her blubberd Face towards him, and on a suddain got up, ran to him with open Arms and cry'd aloud, my Brother, my Brother. This was extreamly surprizing to Sir *John*, who knew her not, her Face was so disguised with her Tears, he stood some Time to consider her and asked her many Questions before he could believe it really was his Sister, all which she answered so pertinently that he no longer doubted the Truth, then he enquired how she came there, and what Rogues Hands she was fallen into. She said one Evening just after she and the rest of the Misses had supp'd, *Tom* that was once his Footman, and afterwards her Mamma's Steward, came to the Boarding-school where she was placed, and told her Mamma had sent for her to go home for a Week or a Fortnight, I was glad (continued she) and got ready presently, he took me up behind him, no body suspecting but that he was sent as he said, and at Night after he had rid very hard he brought me to an Inn, and said Mamma was gone to *London*, and he was to carry me after her, I still was better pleased and never doubted but he told me true, so he brought me to this House three Days ago, and asked me if I would marry him? Then I spit at him and asked for Mamma, he told me she was at *Galliard-hall*, and if I would marry him he would carry me back to-morrow Morning, but if I refused him he would ravish me and then sell me to the *Turks*, and he would have been as good as his Word if this kind Lady here had not come to help me; he is now gone to get a Lodging, where he said he would do what he pleased with me, and if you leave me I am sure he will kill me. No, (replied Sir *John*) you are now very safe, but I would fain see how far this Dog's Villany will go, I am resolved to abscond when I hear him coming, and desire you will behave as if you knew of no Help at hand. O (said the poor young Lady), I tremble to think I shall ever see him more, I hear his Voice, he is just coming. Sir *John* and the old Woman stept into a Closet in the Room, and *Tom* came up-stairs. Come Madam (cry'd he) I am now provided of a Lodging, where I may do as I see fit, and will now tell you 'tis neither Love or Lust that makes me desire either to marry or lie with you, it is sweet Revenge that spurs me on, and you alone are destined for the Mark. Revenge, she said, why what have I done to you? Nothing Madam, answered *Tom*, you are innocent, so was my poor Wife, and yet she suffered by your Mother's faulty Hand, and so shall you by mine, make no Noise, if you do I shall find a way to silence it, come prepare, put on your Geers[76] and submit your Neck to the Yoak I have provided for it: Stay (answered Sir *John* coming out of the Closet) and prepare your own for that Halter which will certainly fall to your share, Villain what hast thou said, and what are the Grounds of thy Accusation?[77] Speak quickly or thou hast spoke thy last, Dog make haste I cannot hold my Hands. *Tom* was so confounded at the unexpected Sight of his late Master that he stood like one struck dumb, but fear of loosing a worthless wretched Life gave his Tongue its usual Motion, and he begg'd his Master to suspend his just Resentment till he could lay before him all his Wrongs which required a more private Place than that they were now in. But Sir *John* who could consider a little upon Occasion fear'd he should hear more of what he knew too much already, and that the Fellow might have too just a Cause for Complaints, and therefore thought good to dismiss him with no other Chastisement than a broken Pate. This was the first Time Sir *John Galliard* ever commanded his Passion, and it must stand as a Monument raised to his Prudence, since a higher Resentment would have set the World upon enquiring after the Cause, which would only have spread a Mother's Infamy and brought a Slur on a Sister's Character, he therefore stayed where he was, Night came on to favour the Escape of the latter out of a very scandalous House, the Principle of which (though a notorious Baud) he was now forced to have some value for, because her Invitation (though a criminal one) had saved an only Sister from a very black Design; as soon as it was dark his Footman brought a Coach to the Door, and he conveyed the Lady to his Lodgings, where she was no sooner arrived than she begg'd to go to Bed, for her late Fright and Want of rest had left her no Spirits. Her Lodgings were immediately got ready and she was soon got into them, where a quiet Mind lull'd her to that Repose which a troubled one had for some Nights deprived her of. Sir *John* after the young Lady retired sat a while to consider of the late Adventure, which soon work'd it self off, to make Way for something more pleasing, his darling Diversion was intriguing, which he carried on with so much Address that he had a Mistress in almost every street in Town, which impaired his Estate as well as Constitution and left both in a declining Condition, but he is now undisputed Master of a fine hereditary Estate, which he made a little too bold with in his Nonage,[78] yet a future good Management will retrieve all. He now sat considering with which of his Madams he should spend the rest of the Evening, when his Man came up and told him a Lady in a Coach at the Door enquired for him. She is come (said he) in a very good Time to end my Disputes, pray bid her come up, not doubting but it was one of the fair Ones he wanted. She no sooner entered than he saw it was Lady *Galliard*, with a look spoke the inward Troubles of her Mind and e're he could approach her burst into Tears.

It is certain that faulty Ladies past Behaviour had taken away very much of that Love and Duty which is due from a Child to a Parent, but Sir *John*, conscious of his own innumerable Faults, would willingly at that Time have cry'd quits, and though his brutish Way of Living had almost unman'd him he yet felt some Returns of Nature pleading in behalf of his disturbed Mother, the Cause of whose Distress he knew, and pleased himself to think he soon should end it, he ran to her and took her in his Arms, saying, Why Madam are you thus afflicted, am I the unhappy Cause? Or does some new Misfortune wait upon your Hours? Believe me Madam, I will contribute to your Ease if I have it in my Power, and beg I may share the heavy Load in hopes of making yours the lighter. Lady *Galliard's* Weight was great indeed for she lay under the Pressures of a wounded Mind, and often told herself the Misfortunes that attended her Children were heaped upon them for her Faults. Sir *John* (said she) my Troubles flow from too many Foundations, and if I complain of your Conduct I shall doubtless hear of my own, I confess I am ashamed of one and grieve for both, I wretched I, am destined to Misfortunes, your Sister is irrecoverably lost, conveyed away, but spare my shame and ask me not by whom. No Madam (replied Sir *John*) I need not ask by whom, I know much more of that Affair than you imagine, dry up your Tears, your Daughter is safe and under my Protection, her better Genius sent me in a very critical Hour to her Rescue, which saved her from a Chain of Ills design'd her, but how were my Ears filled with Horror when I heard a Mother accused for something that sounded much like Murder. How! said Lady *Galliard*, and did my Accuser go away with Life. F—th Madam (return'd Sir *John*) I was once going to stab the Rascal, but considered 'twas pity to take his Life for complaining of his Wrongs, but no more, this Subject must needs be ungrateful to us both, and I beg it may drop, my Sister is in this House, to whom I will convey you after some Repast: In the mean Time I must enquire after my Country Acquaintance, How does Mr. *Friendly* and all his Family do? Do, replied Lady *Galliard*, have you never heard of their Misfortune, I own I was not willing to send you word of it, because I would not spread the poor young Lady's shame, but she has now a Child, and to compleat her wretched Character and make herself a Jest to every body, she says and persists in it that no body got it, and both she and her Maid tell a most silly Story of some sleepy Sweet-meats sent by no body knows who, with so many other Circumstances that poor Mr. *Friendly*, when they first found out she was with Child, went back to the Inn where it seems the Scene was lay'd, to enquire a little into the Matter, but the Maid who brought the Bait was gone away with Child and no body knew where. This was so far from giving our poor Neighbour any Satisfaction that it doubled his Grief, and he now languishes under such a profound Disorder that the whole Neighbourhood is in Pain for his Life, which most People think will soon be ended. At this Account Sir *John* turn'd pale and trembled exceedingly, which Lady *Galliard* took Notice of and said, I see your Gratitude to that good Man in your Concern for him, and am pleased at it, because I know he loves you almost equal to his own, defends your Faults when he hears you blamed for them, calls them the Follies of Youth which your Reason, when grown a little stronger, will suddainly banish; calls you his dear Sir *John*, and always names you with the Tenderness of a Father.

At this Sir *John* in spight of Manhood and his Love to Vice, dropt a conscious Tear, which when he had wiped away he thus proceeded, but how Madam (continued he) does the young Lady behave under her Misfortunes? Have you seen her lately? No (returned Lady *Galliard*) she has put herself into half Mourning, keeps her Chamber, cries continually, and sees no body but her heart-broken Parents, her Maid and Child, her Brother was sent to travel before the Thing was known, so that he is happily a Stranger to it all. Would I were so too, replied the Knight, for I feel the utmost Pangs of Grief for that dear wretched Family. Lady *Galliard* now grew impatient to see her Daughter, whom she was loath to disturb, but after a light Supper Sir *John* conducted her to the young Lady's Bed, they met each other with a mutual Joy and Lady *Galliard* took a Lodging with her for that Night. Sir *John* return'd to his own Apartment and flung himself upon his Bed, where Gratitude, Humanity, Good Nature and Pity began to take their Places in his Breast. O *Galliard*, said he, wretched *Galliard*, what hast thou done? And how hast thou for a few Hours of brutal Pleasure entail'd an Infamy upon a whole Family, nay upon a Family that always loved thee even in spight of my own Demerits, and with a tender Care endeavoured to wash out the Stains of thy Character, and hast thou in return of so much Goodness branded theirs with an eternal Disgrace, had I taken the lovely Creature's Jewel by her own Consent she had shared the Crime with me, but to violate her Honour without her Knowledge is laying her un-der *Cassandra*'s Fate,[79] always to speak Truth but never be believed, for who will credit a Woman that says she has a Child which never had a Father, so that base as I am, I have not only laid her Innocence under the Character of a Whore, but have made her a Jest to all Mankind, when she asserts so great a Truth as that she never knew a Man.

But then as if he had a War within his Breast betwixt his good and evil Angels, he started up and cry'd avant, ye tender Motions of my Soul, and leave me free as Air to Revel in some new, some fresh Delights, the force of which may bear superior Weight and crush the poor relenting Thoughts of Pity, it is more than sufficient I have destroyed their Peace, I'll now endeavour to preserve my own— but then the dear injured Girl— Why, what of her— Again he cry'd, is she not a Woman and was she not made for the Pleasure and Delight of Man, away fond Thoughts I'll hear no more nor give a farther

Audience to thy impertinent Harangues, be gone I say and trouble me no more. We may here see the strugles betwixt Nature and a loose Education, each arm'd with Weapons to defend it self, and sometimes one and sometimes t'other's Victor. The next Morning Lady *Galliard*, whose Mind was much easier since the Recovery of her Daughter, would fain have persuaded Sir *John* to make her perfectly happy and go with her into the Country to take a full Possession of his fine Estate, but that was a Work required more than a little Time to finish, a single Persuasion was not sufficient nor any Arguments strong enough to remove our Knight, which when Lady *Galliard* saw, she resolved to take her Daughter and be gone without him, but first she paid off his Debts, both of Honour and Extravagance; after which she made the following Speech: You are now Sir *John* set free in the World both from Debt and all Restraint, sole Master of a large and disentangled Estate, which one would think impossible for one single Person to encumber, but that I am forced to leave to your own Discretion, for if you contemn'd[80] my Advice while you were yet a Minor, I have little Reason to believe it will meet with a ready Acceptance now you are perfectly your own Master, yet if my Intreaties could be of any force, I should urge them in your own Behalf and beg you would not live without thought. Madam (return'd Sir *John*) if I make an excusive Answer it will certainly be attended with some Reproach which I would fain avoid. It is certain that very few People's Lives are concluded without some faulty Scenes which may perhaps leave a sting behind, and yet for my Part I must grow weary of Pleasure before I leave it, and to strike into Rules of Gravity while we are Boys, is to be born old and never know the Pleasures of Youth. I find Sir (answer'd Lady *Galliard* with some Disorder) the guilty are to be no Instructers, yet they that make a Trip once need not stumble as long as they live, nor is it necessary that he who steals an Egg for his Dinner should be an Accomplice with one who breaks a House, I am far from excusing my own Failings of which I shall ever be ashamed, but you may remember when you convicted me, how full of bitter Invectives you were against me, and yet your Behaviour since has only shown that we are readier to spy small Faults in others than great ones in our selves, I am sorry there is any to be found between us, but since you would hint that Example goes so far, let that of Contrition find a Place and leave your Faults by the same Example you act them. Methinks Madam (returned Sir *John*) it gives me a little Pain to hear you call your Actions small Faults, and hope you will please to consider the vast Disparity betwixt both our Ages and Sexes, there are a thousand Things perhaps not very innocent which I may act and no Notice taken of them, which in you would draw the Eyes of every body towards them, Women are naturally modest, Men naturally impudent, and in short there is no comparing the Actions of one with the other.

This Dialogue which admitted of something pretty sharp on both Sides, was interrupted by a Voice below enquiring for Sir *John*, Lady *Galliard* withdrew and the Stranger was introduced, on whose Face Sir *John* no sooner cast his Eye than he saw it was the little Gentleman with whom he had had an Intrigue at the *Bagnio* some Time before, and now again in Man's Apparel, Sir *John* received her with some Transport and Warmth, which she return'd with bare good Manners and a modest Indifference: The Knight told her he was a little impatient to know the Effect of their last Meeting, and whether it answered the wish'd for Intent. She told him no, she could not say it had, though there was a Child, but it proved a Daughter. Sir *John* was not long before he kindly offered his Service to get a Son, the Lady told him she was very ready to comply, with only one Proviso, you are to know Sir *John*, my Errand to you now is very different from my last, and as I then tender'd you my Honour I would now recall it, and give you in its Place my Heart, which is now by the Death of my Spouse at my Disposal, he has left me a very plentiful Estate, and the present Question is, do you like my Person, Face and Fortune well enough to take me for your own, with no other Fault than what you are a sharer in, if so you will find me Mistress of Fifteen Hundred Pounds a Year and your self Master of both. Sir *John* look'd a little queere at the Proposal, and told the Lady he had no Objection against either herself or Circumstance, but Matrimony was a Monster he should never have Courage enough to encounter with, said he should be glad to serve her in any other Capacity, and should take the Sight of his Child as a very particular Favour, but Z——s Madam, continued he, a Husband is a d——d Name for a Man that hates Confinement and loves Variety as much as I do, beside Marriage is the direct Road to Indifference, where we travel a few Days and then strike into that of Hatred, Variance, Strife, Noise and the D—l and all. No Madam, if we design to love let us live single, a Man may preserve an Appetite that takes only a Snack by the *by*, but a full Meal very often gorges the Stomach and turns to lothing and surfeits. Sir *John*, replied the Lady with some Emotion, I would not have your Vanity swell too high upon this Occasion, nor fancy the Offer I have made you proceeds from any extraordinary Liking I have to your Person, but entirely from the Reflection of your being the undoubted Father of my Child, since I never came into a Bed with my Spouse after I had been with you, for at my Return I found him ill of a Fever, which increased till it killed him, I then

forbore to write to you till I saw the Event of the foolish Action I had committed, and then resolved either to be the lawful Wife of Sir *John Galliard* or never
know a Man again. Why upon my S—l Madam, (return'd the Knight), I must
own myself obliged to you that you are so very willing to give up all your
Charms intirely to me, but as my Person is not the Inducement, I hope no
violent Action will ensure from my Refusal, but prithy Widow let me see the
Child, F—h methinks I long to look at something that may prove my Manhood, come I'll give it a Whistle and Bells.[81] Your Child Sir *John* (replied she)
wants no Whistle, but is far from hence and so am I when I am at home, and
since your Principles hang so loose about you, I shall think it very fit to keep
her at a Distance least their Infection should reach the tender Bud and blast
each Virtue as it grows up in her. O Madam, (replied the fleering Knight), the
Girl I warrant you will never want Virtue while the Father and Mother are so
well stock'd. That Answer put the poor Lady so deep that she burst into Tears,
told him his Reproach was very just and what her Folly well deserved, then left
him. As soon as she was gone Sir *John* called a Servant and bid him dog the
Gentleman who was just gone out, and find his Lodgings, but to keep at such
a Distance as that he might not perceive he was after him. The Footman follow'd
and the Lady had not gone far before she call'd a Coach, but the Man being
not near enough to hear the Order where to go, as soon as the Gentleman
(which he took the Lady for) was got in he whipt up behind, and the Coach
stopt at the *Black Swan* in *Holborn*, from whence Stage Coaches go to more
Parts of the Kingdom than one, as soon as the Coach stopt the Fellow got
down and slipt aside till it drove off, then return'd and went to the Inn, he
pull'd off his Hat with an Air of great Respect to one of the Drawers, and
desired a Mug of *Nottingham* Ale, which when he had brought he desired he
would please to sit down and take share on't: The Drawer was surprised at all
this Civility from a Footman, who seldom have any for those above them,
much less for their Inferiours; Pray Master, (said *Dick* the Footman), what do
you call the little Gentleman who came in here just now.

    I fancy (said the Drawer) by your Manners and Ignorance you are just
come out of the Country, do you think we trouble our Heads with the Names
of our Guests? No, Child, our Business is to give them what they want, and
see they don't run away in our Debt: But this Gentleman you ask after, came
last Night in the —— —— Stage Coach, and goes away again To-morrow-
Morning; he is this Minute with the Book-keeper entering his Name. I was a
Drawer here myself (said *Dick*) about—— let me see—— How long have you
lived here Brother? Lived here, (said the Drawer) why, I have lived here, come

the fourth of *June* next, just four Years. Aye (said *Dick*) 'tis just so long since I left it; And what do you think I was turn'd away for? Egad! because I would not nick my Chalk, and score two for one;[82] a squeamish Conscience never does well in those Publick Houses; but they repented their parting with me, for I writ a very good Hand, and always put down the Passengers Names. Can you Write, Brother? If you will fetch me the Book out of the Bar, I will shew you my Hand in Forty Places of it; and I'll lay you a Bottle of Cyder—— You have some Profit in the Cyder, Brother, have you not? that you say mine is the Best Hand in the whole Book. Why (said the Drawer) As you say, I have some little Advantage from the Cyder, and I'll bring the Book on Purpose to win the Wager; for there is a good deal of my own Hand there, and the D—l's in't, if I vote against myself. The Book was brought, and while *Dick* was looking for his own Hand, which he was sure he should never find, he call'd aloud for *The Cyder, the Cyder* saying, Whoever paid for it he would help to drink it; and while the Drawer went to fetch it, *Dick* turned to the Names, and found the last set down for that County was Mr. *Venture-all*. A *Dutch* Man[83] I warrant (quoth *Dick*) but here comes the Cyder. Well done Brother (said *Dick*) here take thy book; for I had rather pay for the Liquor, and treat thee generously, than give myself any farther Trouble to find out what you at last will deny. They drank the Cyder, which when out, *Dick* paid for it, and Brother Drawer and he parted. *Dick* posted home (like *Scrub* in the *Stratagem*)[84] with a whole Budget of News, which came at last to nothing, for Sir *John* soon knew the Name was a feigned one; but did his Servant Justice in owning he took a very clever Way to find it out: sometimes Sir *John* had a Mind to go to the Inn, and enquire for this Mr. *Venture-all*; but then he considered the Lady frankly declared, the greatest Motive she had in coming to him, was to make herself as near an Honest Woman as her Fault would admit, which he thought a very bad Reason why he should hope for any further Favours from her, and for complying with her Proposals, he found himself as inclinable to the other Part of Destiny, where an Halter cuts the Thread, and ends our Woes at once. Lady *Galliard* tried a few more Persuasions to get Sir *John* into the Country for a While; but the Wild Oats he had so long been sowing came up a-pace, and he resolved to stay and reap the Crop, she then return'd herself, and took her Daughter with her, leaving Sir *John*, because she could not help it, to trifle away both Time and Estate as the D—l and he could adjust Matters. Lady *Galliard* was no sooner gone than he began to think of setting up an Equipage,[85] which was no more than what with Reason might be expected, because every Man according to his Ability ought to support and maintain his own Grandeur, as well as to help and encourage the Trading Part of Mankind in their Honest Labours and Industry. But as most young Heirs are apt to over-do Things, his Liveries were profusely Rich, his Attendants extravagantly Numerous, to which I may add a Train of Lavish Jilts, daily gaping for Unreasonable Supplies from his Bounty, or to give it a more proper Name, from his Folly. Those sort of Creatures know no Bounds, when they think they have a Purse in View that will answer their Impudent Demands: An instance of which we may see in what follows. Sir *John* among many Mistresses had One who proved a sort of a superior Favourite, and kept her Ground much longer than any of her Rivals had done, but she proved a very Chargeable[86] One; and Sir *John*, at last, found her bestowing her Favours on some-body else, which he would by no Means believe she did. A little odd that a Man should expect a Whore to be honest. However, it incensed him so far, that he turn'd her off, and saw her no more for some Months; but one Day about *Mall*-Time Sir *John* accidentally met her in the *Park*:[87] she soon saw him, and gave herself some very Grand Airs as she passed by him, which set the Knight a-laughing, and looking after her, cry'd Madam, you have dropt your Handkerchief, which was his own, he had thrown down on purpose. She resolving to lose nothing, though she knew it was not hers; and hoping to renew her Acquaintance with him, turned about to take it up, when Sir *John* with an Air of Gallantry stooped, and presented her with it, saying, Madam, you know this is not yours, you once had the Heart of the Owner, why did you throw it away for a Trifle? A Trifle, Sir (said Madam) Why, 'tis my Business to barter for Trifles, and if I was willing to part with your Heart, why that was a Trifle too; and I would have you to know any-body's Trifle that comes with Money is as welcome to me as yours is: Beside, I never knew you had recalled your Heart; it was so much a Trifle indeed, that I have not once asked my self, What was become on't. Ah! *Betty, Betty* (said the Knight) this is all Grimace; for, if you had not been Angry at parting with my Heart, you would never have turn'd about to Angle for't again. Come, I don't care if I Dine with you to-day, that we may talk over all with less Passion and more Love. Well (said the half-yielding Nymph) I am ashamed to think how tender my poor Heart is, which would not so readily soften into a Compliance, but that I have a Mind to hear what you can say for yourself; so if we must Dine together, tell me where, and may be, I may come, but I won't promise neither. Sir *John*, who once did like her, and had been long enough from her to fancy her new again, told her he would meet her at the *Fountain-Tavern*; and bid her go and bespeak what she herself had a Mind to. They then parted, and Madam went to the *Fountain*, and ordered a Dozen of the largest and fattest Fowls they could get to be Roasted for Sir *John Galliard* and his Company, which was accordingly done. The Hour of Dining being come, Sir *John* and his Lady met, as appointed, when, to his great surprise, he saw two Drawers enter the Room with each a Dish and six large Fowls apiece; and, according to the Lady's Order, Roasted crisp and brown. Sir *John* stood staring to see two such Dishes of the same Food, and told the Drawers, they had mistaken the Room: Ye Couple of Blockheads (said he) do ye think two People can eat up the Dinners of twenty Men? Or, Do ye expect the Poor of the Parish to come and dine with us? Nay, nay, Sir *John* (answered the Lady) they have not mistaken the Room; set down the Fowls, (continued she) and bring up some *Burgundy*, a Bottle of *Rhenish*, and another of *German*-Spaw.[88]

The Drawers run to obey the Lady, while Sir *John* sate looking sometimes at her, and sometimes at the Monstrous Feast without any manner of Variety in it: Madam (said he) Did you in Reality order this Dinner? For my Part I am fill'd with the sight on't, and am in full study to find out the Hieroglyphick, for certainly there must be one in it; what the D——l can it mean? I'll soon explain the Riddle (cried the Luxurious Monster) you must know, Sir *John*, I have a great While longed to fill my Stomach with the Skin and Rumps of Roasted Fowls; and that is all I shall eat of these: Now, as you bid me bespeak what I liked, I hope you will not grudge it now 'tis here; but they cool, and then they are good for nothing. So to 'em she fell, and had got nine of them flea'd before the Drawers could return with the Wine, Sir *John* sate with much Patience, making some inward Reflections upon the cursed Extravagancy of such Drabs,[89] till he saw the eleventh Fowl seiz'd, without so much as one single Invitation to him to taste: And seeing that flea'd like a Rook, and the poor remaining one in Danger, said, I am sorry, Madam, you did not bespeak two dozen instead of one, that I might have dined with you: But since I find here are short Commons,[90] I beg you will let me have a Wing of this unexcoriated Animal, and the next time we dine together you shall flea me; sure the whole Race of Whores are the Offspring of *Epicurus*.[91] I do not believe (replied Madam) he was any Relation of mine, because I never heard of him before; but if he was one that lov'd a Good Dinner, I am sure he has left a very numerous Family behind him. Why sure Sir *John*, now you are come to your Estate you grow covetous, or you would never make a stir about a poor Forty Shillings Reckoning:[92] I dare say that will pay it; and if it won't, you may take your Guinea again which you gave me a little While ago to help out. Sir *John* told her, he never club'd with his Wench; paid the House, and left her, with a second Resolution to see her no more. The New Coach was now mounted on the Wheels, and the Splendid Knight began to make his Appearance in all Publick Places, the Drawing-Room, the Park, the Mall, the Opera, the Buffet-Table, the Play-House, and every-where (except at Church) where there was Hopes of being very much seen. It must be own'd, Sir *John Galliard* had many Advantages both from Nature and Fortune that Thousands wanted; his Person perfectly agreeable, his Sense much too good for the Use he put it to, his Temper flexible and easy, even to a Fault; his Dependance centred in itself, and his glaring Equipage finished his Charms. The young Gay Part of the Female World had an Eye upon him from every Avenue, and no Art lay idle that had Hopes or Prospect of drawing him into the Nets and Purlieus which were spread in every Corner to catch the Game; but the Bold Knight stood Arm'd Cap-a-pe[93] in his own Defence, bidding Defiance to all Attacks, and firmly resolving to keep his Foot out of the Stocks of Dreadful Matrimony: so that the poor Ladies had the Mortification to see all their Artifices intirely baffled, and their Blooming Charms despis'd. Sir *John* had now been a great While reduced to the low Mercenary Drabs of the Town, and was clog'd, and grown weary of them, resolving to leave them all, and hunt out Nobler Game. He was one Day at the Ring admiring the Ladies, where he saw in her Father's Coach the young Miss *Wary* formerly spoken of, accompanied by a Beautiful young Girl, whom he had never seen before: she pleased him much, and he lick'd his Lips, and told himself, he could be very happy in her Embraces for a few Hours; and resolved next Day to visit her Companion, in order to find out who she was, and how he might gain Access. Next Morning before he was up, Sir *Combish Clutter*, an Intimate of Sir *John's*, came to his Lodgings, or Levee,[94] and finding him in Bed, cry'd Z——s, Knight, What the D—l dost thou do between thy Sheets at this time of Day? Why, 'tis now six Minutes three seconds past One o'Clock, and it is impossible thou should'st get dress'd by Dinner-time: beside, I would feign have your Company in the Afternoon to see my Mistress, who came to Town but two Days ago, though I must Article with thee, *Sir Jackey*, not to Rival me, and yet I am apt to believe thy Persuasive Faculty will hardly go much Farther than my own— Gad she's a Fine Creature, and if you do not say so when you see her, you are a Son of a — Hold, Sir *Combish* (return'd his Friend) and be assured I will do Justice to the Lady's Charms; but if they prove too strong to be resisted, you must give me Leave to try whose Persuasive Faculty has the most Force: but he that does not like his Friend's Choice, under-rates his Friend's Judgement; and that, Sir *Combish*, is worse than making Love to his Mistress: but where is this Sunbeam? And what do you call her? Thy Questions (return'd *Clutter*) will meet with no Answer; but get up, and let us dine together, then follow me. Sir *John* was always ready for a Walk where a Fine Lady stood at the End on't, and therefore, without Hesitation, got out of Bed, was presently dress'd, and away they went to Dinner; which when over, and the Hour of Visiting come, Sir *Combish* conducted his Friend to the Lodgings of his Mistress, which proved to be at Mr. *Wary's*, and the Lady the same he had a Desire upon at the Ring. He secretly gave himself Joy of his Success, and did not fail to promise himself a great deal from the happy Circumstances of her being in a House where he had some Acquaintance (though not much Interest since the *Bagnio*-Exploit) and being introduced by her Lover, as a second good Omen from his propitious Stars, and resolved to ply her with Love the first Opportunity that kindly offer'd, which he swore should never slip thro' his Fingers, he carrest[95] her even before her Lover with the extremest Gallantry, and she must have had a Load of Cupid's Dust blown in her Eyes, had she not seen a very considerable Difference betwixt Sir *John Galliard* and Sir *Combish Clutter*, the latter of which shortened his Visit, not only to prevent the Exchange of Glances between Sir *John* and the Lady, but to humour his Impatience which was in a woundly Hurry to have Sir *John's* Opinion of his Choice. They adjourn'd again to the Tavern where Sir *John* told him his Choice was his Master-piece, and he had never shewn his Judgement to so much Advantage before, but I always understood (continued he) that you were utterly averse to Marriage, and yet I fancy the little Angel expects nothing more than honourable Love.

Why aye, (return'd Sir *Combish*) there it is the D—l enters with his Horns to push us from our easy Happiness, 'tis d——d hard that if we lie with a fine Woman once we must be forced to do so as long as we both live, but I don't know— the pritty Fool loves me, and I think it is a pitty to break her Heart, though I believe a Months Enjoyment will change my Mind, for a surfeited Stomach does not care if the D—l had the Dish that overcharged it. Nay Knight (replied Sir *John*) you out do me abundantly for as well as I love Variety, I dare say I could be constant to that Lady twice as long as you speak of, and retire at last without one nauseating Thought, but where the D—l didst thou pick up that lovely Girl? Prithee marry her, and let me (when thou art weary) have her a while, I'll show my Humility by being content with thy Leavings. Aye b—g—[96] Knight, so you may (return'd Sir *Combish*) for I have taken up with yours more than once, tho' it was through Ignorance, for had I known it I should as soon have taken a Bone you had pick'd for a Repast as a Mistress you had discarded for my Diversion, but what the D—l didst thou see in me to make thee fancy any Woman that has once been familiar with me, could ever have a Tast for any body else, no, no Knight I shall never have one uneasie Thought about that Affair, e'ne win her and wear her b- g—, but I bar forestalling the Market, no Attempts till after the Consummation, and then— But I must leave thee Sir *Jackey*, for I have an Assignation upon my Hands at *Greenwich*,[97] which I must answer this once though only to take my Leave of a rare brisk Girl, and if I thought the Jade would listen to my Proposal I did not much care if I resigned her over to thee, f—h she has two good Qualities, she is sweet and sound but a little humersome and pretty expensive. Sir *John* thank'd him, said he loved to choose his own Whores, of which *(Venus* be praised) there was very good store: and then the two Knights parted, one to *Greenwich* and the other to Mr. *Wary's* again, under Pretence of enquiring after a stray Snuff-box.

Sir *Combish* had with his conceited Speeches a little picqued him, which when joyned to the liking he had for the Lady, made him very industrious to get into her favour, nay, he was so set upon Revenge that he resolved to offer Marriage rather than loose the Pleasure of it, as doubtless there is a great deal in baulking a Coxcomb. He found the Ladies at Picquet, and told them if they would change their Game he would make one at Ombre[98] for an Hour or two, which they were pleased with, and to Ombre they went, but while the Knight's Fingers were busied with the Cards his Eyes had other Imployment and were hard at work darting a thousand kind Things at the Lady's Breast, which aimed at nothing but her utter Ruin. She understood their talk and return'd as much as Modesty and a short Acquaintance would admit of. Sir *John* well read in Women's Looks, beheld all hers with Pleasure, and being a little willing to sift her Inclinations somewhat farther said, I am glad Madam I happened to return again and hope I have help'd to drive away some of those Melancholy Minutes that sometimes hang upon a Lady's Hands in the Absence of a favour'd Lover. Sir (replied the Lady, whom I shall call by the common Name of *Belinda*) you would be kind in explaining yourself and telling us who you mean by a favour'd Lover, for my Part I brought a Heart to *London* entirely disengaged, and till I see something of higher Merit than it can hope to deserve, am resolved to keep it so. Sir *John* was pleased at the favourable Declaration and hoped it would joyn with his Design, but made the following Answer: If your Heart Madam be disengaged, what will become of poor Sir *Combish*, whose Hopes of you I have some Reason to believe is in a very florishing Condition, and do you now say your Heart is disengaged. Sir *John* (return'd *Belinda*) if you are well acquainted with Sir *Combish Clutter* you must needs know him for a Man of too much Vanity to believe his Offers can be rejected wherever he vouchsafes to tender them, I must own he has been so very condescending as to tell me he liked my Person and Temper, which doubtless he design'd as a very particular Favour, and when I have acknowledged it as such and given him my Thanks accordingly, he has then all the Return he must ever expect from me. I think then, answered Miss *Wary*, since you are so indifferent you had best make a Deed of Gift to me of Sir *Combish*, methinks your Ladyship sounds so prittily upon the Tip of every Tongue. Aye Child (return'd *Belinda*) the sound is well enough, but if the Man that gives us the Honour is nothing but sound himself, in my Opinion one had as good be tied to a Drum, and for giving you Sir *Combish*, I am very glad it is not in my Power, for I never give away any Thing but what's my own, and I here faithfully promise I will never have a Title either to him or from him while I live. Sir *John* was giving himself a vast deal of secret Pleasure at the hearing of all this, when *Belinda*'s Maid came in with a Letter in her Hand for her Lady, which she look'd upon and knew it was from her Sister, she begg'd Leave to withdraw while she read it. Sir *John* with his usual Gallantry told her, he had much rather dispense with a little Breach in foolish Decorum than loose the substantial Pleasure of her Company, though but the short Time of reading a Letter, beside Madam I see it is a Lady's Hand which can neither raise a Blush in your Cheeks or Jealousy in my Breast.

Jealousy Sir *John* (return'd *Belinda*) you surprise me greatly, I thought that silly Whim had never taken place any where but in the Breast of a Lover, nor there neither unless he saw violent Signs of Encouragement given to a Rival— but since you tollerate ill Manners I will read my Letter which I own I am a little impatient to do: She opened it and found what follows:

> *MY trembling Hand is now imployed to tell you, my dear Child is extremely ill, and you well know I share the Malady, fly to see it while alive and help to comfort a distracted Sister.*
>
> P.S. *Dear* Bell *make hast.*

Sir *John* who with inward Delight beheld *Belinda*'s fine Face, saw it alter and grow pale, he asked the Cause of her Disturbance, she made no secret of the Contents of her Letter, said she would be gone next Morning, but Miss *Wary* told her that was impossible unless she hired a Coach on purpose, for the Stage went not out till the Day after, she answered, no Consideration should retard her Journey, there were Coaches enough to be had for Money which was a Trifle compared to the Peace of a Sister. Sir *John* had now an excellent Opportunity of shewing his Complisance[99] by offering his Coach to the Lady and himself to be her Convoy, which he did with an Air of so much Sincerity and good Manners, that the young Lady hardly knew how to refuse the Compliment, though she urged the Trouble it must needs give him, and that so great a Favour could no way be expected from one so much a Stranger to her, begg'd he would excuse her Acceptance and give her Leave to take a Hackney Coach, but Sir *John* liked the lucky Opportunity too well to loose it, and therefore most strenuously urged his Coach might convey her home. She at last consented and Sir *John* posted home to give Orders for a Journey in the Morning. When he was gone the observing Miss *Wary* who was no way his Friend, told *Belinda* she wish'd her a safe Deliverance from him, said a Woman's Honour in his Hands was in much greater Danger than a Ship in a Storm, for there was a Possibility of one being saved while the other must inevitably perish, and when she had said so much, she told her the Reason why she had so low an Opinion of him. But *Belinda* was now prejudiced in Favour of Sir *John* and thought Miss *Wary*'s Invectives proceeded rather from a little Envy than any real Demerit in the Knight, she saw nothing in him which displeased her and was resolved to trust to her own Virtue and his Honour, but Miss *Wary* who had not her Name for naught, and who well knew the advantagious Offers Sir *John* had often had if he would have resolved to marry, was in too much Concern for her Friend to let her Advice drop, till she had given it a little farther, she much fear'd Sir *John*'s Designs were not honourable, and therefore proceeded thus: Suppose *Belinda* any Misfortune should attend you in this Journey do you not think your Prudence would be a very great Sufferer, which ought to tell you, Sir *John Galliard* is in the first Place a perfect Stranger to you, and next that he is a Libertine; remember you have warning given you by one that has known him some time, and what Danger may not a young Girl as you are, apprehend from the Power of one who never denied himself any Satisfaction in Life, and what is your Maid and you in the Hands of him and all his Servants, I tremble for the Danger you seem to be in, and beg of you to stay another Day and take the Stage-Coach. But *Belinda* was now very sure that all Miss *Wary*'s Care proceeded from Jealousy, that she had a Mind to Sir *John* herself and could not bear the Thought of his Civility to her, she therefore answered thus: That I am a Stranger to Sir *John Galliard* I very readily own, but cannot believe him a Man of so much Dishonour as to commit a Rape and I know myself too well to fear I shall ever consent to any Action which cannot reconcile itself to Virtue, I have, you know, but one Sister in the World, and she is very dear to me, her only Child whose Life is hers, is in danger, and can I be so cruel as to loose one Hour in posting to her? No, I would if possible, fly with the Wind to her Comfort, and beg you will have no Concern for my safety of which you shall hear as soon as I get home. Miss *Wary* resolved to say no more; but when they had supp'd they went to bed: *Belinda* was soon stirring in the Morning, and got ready by that Time the Coach and Owner came to the Door. Breakfast over they set forward, and Sir *John* had now Time to make Love without Interruption; a Work he was so well vers'd in, that he knew how to model his Tale to every Taste, and where he foresaw a Difficulty, the Hook was baited with a little Touch of Matrimony. But how resolved soever *Belinda* was to reject Miss *Wary's* Counsel, it put her however upon her Guard, and she kept a constant Centry[100] at the Door of her Virtue, armed with Resolution to defend it for ever. Sir *John* soon perceived it, and began to fear he had a Piece of Work upon his Hands, which would take some time to finish. The Introduction to his Amour was an Endeavour to raise her Vanity, by chiming continually in her Ears, the Multitude of Merits she was invested with, and how impossible it was to view her Charms, without everlasting Captivity. Sir *John* (replied the Lady) your Love, like a Thunder-shower, comes on too violent and too hastily to last long; but I beg you will lay the subject by till I have seen my Dear Sister, and know how her poor little Girl does; for till she recovers, I shall never be in a Humour gay enough to listen to Love.

Why Madam (return'd Sir *John*) do you enjoyn me a Task impossible for me to observe? Do you imagine I can sit near *Belinda*, and be insensible of her Charms? Or— No more, for Heaven's sake (interrupted the Lady) for who, that has ever taken notice of a Modern Husband's Behaviour, can with Patience listen to a Modern Beau making Love; the latter all Adoration, Praise, Rapture and Lies; the other Jarring, Discord, Indifference, and down-right Hatred; one breathes nothing but Darts, Flames and soft melting sighs, the other cries— Damn you, Madam, you are my Aversion, we have been too long acquainted, a stale Face is the D—l, prithee take it from my sight. That, Madam (replied the Knight) is owing to our Law-givers, who force us into Fetters, and then expect we should hug them for ever. No! *Belinda*, Love is a Generous Noble Passion, values Liberty, and scorns Confinement and Restraint, is not a voluntary Gift infinitely more valuable than one that is wrenched and forced from the Donor, Come, my Charmer, let you and I make a Freewill-Offering of our Hearts to each other, they will soon take Root, and fix in our different Bosoms: And if yours, through the Natural Inconstancy of your Sex, should ever desire to remove, mine shall break to give it Liberty; as sure it must whenever it comes to know the Fair *Belinda* is lost: Oh! come, my lovely Charmer, streight pronounce my Joy, and say I shall be happy.

Belinda now saw with Open Eyes at what Sir *John* was driving, but thought it best to sooth his Hopes, lest a Resenting Denial should make him desperate, and while he had her in his Power, take by Force what he could not gain by Intreaty and Stratagem: she therefore told him, she saw nothing in him that was any way Disagreeable; but so short an Acquaintance could not in Reason expect a Positive Answer to the first Request: Beside, Sir *John* (continued she smiling) I would not have you engage your self too far till you have seen another Lady, to whom I will introduce you at my Journey's End, one of superior Merit, and a much better Fortune than I can boast of. Sir John told her, he desired no greater Merit than she was Mistress of; and for Womens Fortunes he never enquired after them, because he never intended to trouble his Head with them. The Lady's Person (pursued he) is all I aim at, and that I'll use as Love and Gallantry inspires me. Come *Belinda*, lay by these Virtuous Airs, Women were made to be enjoyed; and I expect your Inclinations will concur with mine, and give you to my longing Arms this Night: Great is the Addition to our Joys which a Ready Compliance brings; it saves a Man Ten Thousand Oaths and Lies, which are nothing, compared to the loss of Time spent in a fruitless Attempt; shall a Bull or Horse command a Thousand Mates, while Man the Reigning Lord of all stands cringing at his Vassal's Feet, begging to be admitted to his own? Would all Mankind assume their own Prerogative, we should soon divest ye of your pretended Virtue, and let ye see your Pride and Scorn are Weapons only turned against your selves. I am sorry, Sir *John* (replied *Belinda* with a scornful smile) to find you take your Example for Plurality of Mistresses from the Brutes, I always thought Man a Creature above them; One that had Reason to regulate and govern his inordinate Passions, though I confess, the Comparison is very just in those Humane[101] Monsters, who neither can, or will endeavour to subdue them; but if every Man were to choose as many Women as he likes, and take them as his proper Vassals, as you are pleased with much Civility to call us, I cannot but fancy it would destroy the whole system of life, and the best Oeconomy must be turned upside-down. But Oh! I am now too sensible of my own Obstinate Folly, which made me spurn at the Advice of a Friend, whose Kind Persuasions would have kept me from the Danger I now see myself in; but I took Sir *John Galliard* for a Man of Honour, which I now fear I shall not find him; I will therefore lay that aside, and sue for my safety to your Pity and Good-nature: You know, Sir *John*, the Basest Action in life is to Assault an unarmed Adversary. In such a case (returned the Knight) Honour only is concerned, and that you think me intirely divested of, and have laid yourself under my Pity and Good-nature for Protection, which Qualities, when they have served myself, shall certainly shed their Influence over you, but Charity, my Dear, begins at home; I must first pity my own sufferings, which my Good-nature persuades me to; and then, Child, I will consider of yours.

Belinda's Maid during all this Discourse kept nodding, and pretended to be soundly sleeping, though she heard every Word of her Lady's Danger. They were now arrived at the Inn, where they were to dine, and Sir *John* kept a watchful Eye over his Prey, lest she should by any Means give him the slip; nor would he suffer the Maid to come near her, who, having slept false all the Way, was now contriving her Lady's Escape from the Ruin she saw threatening her. She considered they had a six-Mile Forest to go over in the Afternoon, which would be too good an Opportunity for the Performance of any Ill, she therefore went to the Landlord, who she had often heard was a very honest Man, and told him the whole Matter. He seemed to be much concerned for the young Lady, and advised to force her out of his Hands, by a speedy Application to the first Justice of the Peace; but the Maid opposed that, and said, such a Thing would be too publick, and the Noise of it would spread every-where, and blast her Lady's Credit, she rather desired he would try to provide four sturdy Fellows well Arm'd, and well mounted to convey them safe over the Forest, and they should have their own Demands answered, let them be what they would.

The Host told her, he could easily provide her such a Number of Men, but advised her to take them quite through the Journey, for it was very likely, if the Gentleman found himself baulk'd upon the Forest, he would find some Way at Night to renew his Attempt. She approved of what he said, begg'd him to lose no Time, and tell the Men they should meet with a Reward above their own Wishes. While the Maid was thus honestly and carefully employ'd for the Good of her Mistress, the poor young Lady herself was in the utmost Consternation and Perplexity, being denied the sight of her Servant, lest they should, when together, contrive their Escape, which he was resolved they should not do till he had gained his Point, and then— Farewell Love and all soft Pleasure[102]— till another Fresh Beauty presents itself, and a fresh Opportunity of acting the same Villany over again. Dinner over they again took Coach, which, as they were doing, *Belinda's* Maid had the Pleasure to see their Guard well mounted, and ready to follow them, which they did at some Distance, tho' none of the Company knew their Design but herself. An Hour and half's

Riding brought them to the Forest, where Sir *John* had never been before, though his Coach-man had, and knew the Way exactly. He now began again to urge *Belinda* in Favour of his own Desires; at which she could no longer command her Tears, which flowed from her Eyes in a very plentiful Manner. Base and Degenerate Sir *John Galliard* (she cried) who has no sense of Honour, or even of the bare Rules of Hospitality, which you have most basely infringed: Am I not under your Roof and Protection, brought hither by the Kindest Invitation; and do you, at last, use me worse than a Robber would do? Had I fallen into the Hands of the veriest Scoundrel upon Earth, I might have hoped for better Treatment, I only beg for a little Time to consider before I consent to my own Undoing. He told her, Consideration was a perfect Enemy to Love, bid her look round, and see the very spot of Ground they were then on, how many Invitations (by Privacy and Solitude) it gave them to their Joy, then bid his Coach-man stop. I believe, Sir (replied he) we shall be forced to stop, for we are pursued by four Men well-arm'd. *Belinda* was glad to hear of any Interruption, though she expected to be doubly robb'd both of Honour and Coin. Sir *John* was never in such Haste to get rid of his Money, as at this Juncture, and much rather have parted with ten times the sum in his Pocket, than the promising Opportunity that flatter'd his Hopes; he therefore bid his Coachman once more stop (which he did) and had pulled out a Handful of Gold ready to bribe their Absence: But when the Coach stopp'd the supposed Pursuers did so too, which surprised every-body but the Maid, who knew the Reason of their Halt. Sir *John* then ordered the Coach to go on, which drew the Attendants after it, he made it stop again, and so did they; the Experiment was try'd several times, and the same success attended it, till at last provoked with the Fear of losing so fair a Prospect of Bliss, he flung himself out of the Coach, dismounted one of his Attendants, and rid up to the Fellows.

Pray Gentlemen, (said he) have you any Business with me, or Design against me, that you dog my Coach all this Afternoon? By what Authority (said one of the Men) do you examine us? Have not we the same liberty to travel this Road that you have? Can you say we have either Assaulted, or Molested you, or your Company? And if we have not, go back and be quiet; we are resolved to go our own Pace, and either ride, or stand still, as we see Occasion. Sir (said another of them) to be plain with you, we have a very considerable Charge under our Care, and keep up with your Coach, lest we should be Robb'd on't; be assured we will offer no violence to any of you, provided you offer none yourselves, but we must have our Liberty, as well as you.

While Sir *John* was holding a Parly with the Men, *Belinda*'s Maid let her

Mistress into the whole Welcome secret, which raised her spirits to so much Courage, that when Sir *John* returned, she was quite another Thing; and so was he too, though different Reasons made the Alteration: she was pleased at the very Heart to think herself safe; he, mad at his, to see his Hopeful Project baffled, he stepped into the Coach all cloudy and sullen; muttered some Curses between his Teeth, and sate for some time as if asleep. I fear, Sir *John* (said *Belinda*, after a long silence) those Men have Robbed you, else whence proceeds this sudden Chagrin? I thought the Gay Sir *John Galliard* could never have been out of Humour; say, Sir *John*, what can be the Cause? You are very merry, Madam, and have guessed right (replied the Knight) the Dogs have Robbed me of something very considerable, but I may yet recover it perhaps. No Matter (said the Lady in perfect Good-humour) though they have Robb'd you, I have escaped; and I warrant I shall find Money enough to last till To-morrow-Night, and then you shall be furnished with what sum you please. He hardly thanked her, or made any Answer, he was so thoroughly vexed at such an Unlucky Hit in so Convenient a Place for his Ill Design; but sate some time with his Eyes shut contriving new schemes. They were now off the Forest, when Sir *John* hoped the four Gentlemen would take another Road, not once suspecting the Truth of the Matter; but they still continued to follow the Coach, which still increased his Vexation: An Hour before Night he complained he was weary of sitting, and asked the Lady, if she would alight, and walk a quarter of a Mile? She desired to be excus'd, said, she was very easy, and never loved Walking in her life.

Then Madam (said the Knight) will you not think me Rude if I do? No, Sir *John* (return'd *Belinda*) you cannot be Rude, unless you repeat what is already past. He went out, and called his Valet to alight, and walk with him; to whom he gave Order, to Ride before, and take up the first Blind Ale-House he came at, and to bid his Coach-Man say, his Horses were tired, and would go no farther. In the mean Time, the Lady in the Coach had leisure to talk a little to her Maid. O! *Nanny* (said she) I fear there is some new Mischief hatching, Heaven, of its Mercy, blast it, and send me well out of the Paw of this Lion, and may the next devour me, if ever I trust a strange One more. Fear not, Madam (returned the Maid) I have ordered the Men behind to keep within sight and call; and when we come to the Inn, if you please to go to Bed, we will all sit up at your Chamber-door, and guard you all Night. But here is Sir *John* coming already; let us not look concerned. The Knight re-entered his Coach, and seemed a little better humour'd than when he went out, which added to *Belinda's* Fears. About a Mile farther they came to a sorry Hovel, at the Door of which stood the Valet, by way of signal to the Coach-man, who call'd (as ordered) to his Master, told him, his Horses were tired and could go no farther that Night. Sir *John* pretended to be in a very great Concern, that they should be forced to take up with such Ordinary Accomodation as such a Pitiful Hole could afford them; but begged the Lady to bear for once with Inconveniences, since Disasters would happen sometimes. This put *Belinda* and her Maid a little to a stand, and they knew not well how to manage. They were both assured the Pretended Accident was all designed, and kept an Eye upon their Guard, with whom they saw Sir *John's* Valet deeply engaged in Talk; and to their great Dismay and Terror, saw two of them ride away. *Belinda* changed Colour, and Sir *John* conducted her into the House, such as it was. I hope, Sir *John* (said she) you do not pretend to take up here all Night; if your Horses are a little tired, which must be false, an Hour's Rest will surely make them able to go two Miles farther to an Inn, where both they and we may have Good Entertainment; but I see too plainly what your Design is: You are, 'tis true, a Baronet by birth, but your Mother has been some Base, some Faulty Sinner, has violated a Chaste Marriage-Bed, and you are the Abominable Product of her Vice, the Spawn of some of her Footmen. Nothing but a Channel, nay, a Common-shore of Base Plebeian Blood, could put a Man upon such low Dishonourable Actions. Villain (she continued) for thou deservest no other Name; hast thou left a shole of Common Strumpets behind thee to persecute me with thy Detestable Love, as thou hast falsely called it. No, Monster, e're thou shalt accomplish thy Devilish Designs upon me, I will let out Life at Ten Thousand Port-Holes, and my last Breath shall end with a Laugh to see thy Baffled Disappointment.

Sir *John* was never so stung in his life before, as he was now at her bitter sharp Invectives; but that which touched him the nearest was her Just Remarks upon his Mother, from whence Ten Thousand Vexatious Thoughts crouded about his Heart; and (as he afterwards own'd) began to ask himself, Whether there was not more than a bare Probability of his being what she at Random called; his supposed Father he knew was a Man of the strictest Honour and Virtue, from whence then (thought he) does it come, that I am so differently inclined; and am I then (continued he to himself) the Offspring of a Nasty Curry-Comb, or Horse-Whip, at last? Why, if I am, I cannot but think I have many Brethren in this Nation, that look as high as I do, and act exactly like me; yet methinks, I am not pleased to tell myself, I am the Son of a Scoundrel. His private Meditations over, he again accosted the Lady, Why, Madam (said he) are you so very tart? Your Words touch'd me to the quick;

and I now own to you, they have given a Turn to the Design I had upon you, it is true two of them are Disserters bought off for a little Money, the other Pair seem to be honest and resolute, but trust me *Belinda* you shall have no Cause from me to try their Valour, you may now with the greatest safety dismiss them, for all the Love I had for you is vanish'd. Which as you well observed was false, and is now turn'd to Esteem and Respect, which shall for the future regulate all my Actions towards you. No Sir *John* (returned *Belinda*) you have too much Cause to blame my Conduct already, for giving myself up to the Honour of a Stranger, but shall not have a new one to accuse me with by casheering my only safe-guard, but if you relent and are changed as you would persuade me you are, shew it by leaving this dismal Abode forthwith, and take the two Men into your own Retinue, for with me they shall go till I see the inside of my own Habitation. Sir *John* with much Readiness complied, and they all went on to the Inn.

Belinda's Heart was now restored to its former Quiet, and her Fear and Anger were both banish'd, for she saw the Looks of the Knight so much alter'd that she no longer doubted but his Designs were so too, and her pleasant good Humour began to return, which Sir *John* perceiving, he suddainly threw himself at her Feet, and with a penitent Look told her he would never rise till she kindly gave him her Pardon for all the vile Behaviour he had been guilty of towards her, believe me this once (he said) tho' my Words are invalid, I am ashamed of what I have done, and which is more, you are the first Woman that ever made me so. It would be a Complement to tell you, if I could persuade myself to a whole Life of Captivity I should offer you Marriage, which is, I own, what I am utterly averse to, and what I dare say you are very indifferent to, since a Woman so well qualified as you are must needs have Choice in every Place you come at. Sir *John* (answered the good natured Lady) do but forbear to repeat your Fault and you shall see I can now forgive it, as well as thank you for the Esteem you have for me, but when you talked of Marriage you had not asked my Consent, which I take to be pretty material, but no Matter, we are now or at least seem to be upon very good Terms, so desire you will be pleased to order something for supper, since Dinners uneaten never lie on the stomach. F—h Madam (replied Sir *John*) you have starved my Appetite. And it would be but Justice to do as much by yours, yet to shew that good Nature, to which you once referr'd yourself, I will go myself and see what's to be had. Sir *John* was no sooner gone from *Belinda*, than poor *Nan*, who knew nothing of the Reconciliation and good Agreement that was betwixt them, came in to bid her Lady have a good Heart, for there was another Coach and

Six just come to the Inn. *Belinda* was just going to tell her how Matters stood when Sir *John* return'd, and said, Madam you will surely dismiss your two Attendants now, because you have much better just come in quest of you, I believe I shall be forced to hire them for my Preservation now, for I saw Sir *Combish* trip out of his Coach as nimbly as a weather-cock at the Turn of the Wind, and with him Squire *Cock-a-hoop*, as he always desires to be call'd, who will refresh your spirits after a harrast Journey, and give you some Diversion. He is a Thing just got loose from an old ill-natured Governess, who was first his Nurse, then his Maid, next his School-Mistress, and at last his Governante. The Woman it must be own'd has been very just to him, and taught him as much as she knew herself, which was bad *English*, false Sense, ill Nature and worse Manners. They know not we are in the House, but must e're long because both Sir *Combish* and his Servants know my Livery, and if *Belinda* to relieve her late Distress will consent to a little sport, I dare answer she may have it from the Comedians now ready to act their Parts, and I will bring both my Rival and his ridiculous Companion to kiss your Hand. She who had suffered more Fatigue and Disorder than she could well bear, was very ready to consent to any Thing that would refresh her spirits, and told him with some Pleasantry, since he had declared against Matrimony himself, it was Time for her to look out for one of more Compliance, and desired the new Comers might be admitted. Sir *John* ready to attone for his past Faults, ran to enquire for Sir *Combish*, who was just bullying the Cook, because she refused him a Brace of Partridges Sir *John* had already bespoke. —— you Hussy (he said) you deserve to be basted with all the Dripping you save in a Year to teach you how to use People of Distinction, here you are going to send up a Brace of Birds to some Fools, who perhaps may take them for Crows and be angry if you reckon above three pence a piece for them, and we that know better Things must take up with a Neck of rotten Mutton stew'd till the Bones drop out, which was ready to drop before the silly Animal was kill'd. ——when they are enough I shall make bold with sword in hand to seize them, and show me the Man that dare dispute the Matter.

Well said my Bully (cry'd Sir *John* clapping him on the shoulder) come Knight, if you will be content with a Limb or so, you shall have it without fighting for't, but thou know'st I am a true-born *English*-Cock and love to defend my own Property. Sir *Combish* who knew the Voice turn'd about, but did not readily know how to behave whether as a Friend or a Rival, and putting on a solemn Air cry'd, Z—s Knight where's my Mistress? And who the D—l desired so much of thy Civility as to tramp after her a matter of seventy

Miles, sure you did not expect to be overtaken or you would have made more haste, I thought you had been at your Journeys end by this Time, and was posting after to see whose Title was best. The last Thing (returned Sir *John*) that a Man parts with is the good Opinion he has of himself, and while Sir *Combish* keeps that, he cannot fear a Rival, your Mistress is in this House, and the Reason why I trampt after her (as you call it) was because you were gone after a more inferior Fame, and as her Occasion called her back sooner than either you or she expected, I thought it a very good Way of confirming our Friendship, to shew that Respect to her which was due to you, believe me Sir *Combish*, your Mistress is very safe and I have too great a Value for her Vertue to assault it; I wait your Commands to conduct you to her, and will with Pleasure give up my Care of the Lady to one who must need be more concern'd for her safety. B— g— Knight (replied Sir *Combish*) thy Words are Apocryphal,[103] and it is seven to four but I let thee keep thy Charge, for I never knew thee willing to part with a Woman till Matters were fairly adjusted betwixt you; now though I might perhaps share a Wench with a Friend, I must insist upon keeping a Wife to myself, because I should not care to mix my Breed. I am sorry Sir *Combish* (returned young *Galliard*) to find your Opinion of the Lady runs so very low, but am yet more surprised to hear you confess a Flaw in your own Merit, which you certainly do if you say it wants Force to secure her to your self, come don't be a Fool and loose her by a groundless and false suspition of her, by all that is vertuous she is so for me, and I believe for all Mankind. A Plague on't (return'd Sir *Combish*) I had much rather you had called her Whore, for then I should have thought her ill Usage of you had raised your spleen, but z—s so much Commendation is just as much as to say— now I have had her I'll bring her off as well as I can. However I will go to her and shall soon guess at her Innocence by her Looks, but where's my Friend *Cock-a-hoop*, if the worst happens she will serve him at last, methinks I would not have her baulk'd now she is set on a Husband. *Cock-a-hoop* was called and they all went to *Belinda*, who saw them coming and met them at the Door, *Clownish* thrust in first, and taking her about the Neck gave her a smacking Kiss and said, she was a good hansom Woman, b— *G——e*[104] he would have another, which when he was going to take, *Belinda* cried hold Sir 'tis ill Manners to help yourself twice before the rest of the Company are served, beside I am here by way of Desert which always comes after a full Meal and consequently should be used sparingly. Sir *Combish* who was ready to boil over with Jealousy answered thus for his rustick Friend, How sparing you have been of your Desert Madam, to some that shall be nameless, you best know;

some perhaps are cloy'd, and some again don't care for sweet-meats, so you may as well give my Friend *Clownish* another Taste before they mould on your Hands. *Belinda's* true Taste for good sense spoiled her Pallat for the relish of a Fool, and she told Sir *Combish*, whoever she surfeited with her Favours she would be sure to take Care of overcharging his Stomach, lest he should disembogue[105] and they should all be lost; but why Sir *Combish* (continued she) do you think me so very lavish, I am neither old, ugly, poor, or a Fool, and a body may pick up a Coxcomb any where, who if he prove not grateful for what we give, will at least receive it though only to brag of among his fellow Puppies. Sir *Combish* told her with a fleering Insolence he thought Women's Favours too low to be boasted of, and when he offered her so great a one as Marriage he did not see how she could make too thankful a Return for it. This made Sir *John* and *Belinda* laugh, and *Cock-a-hoop* thought it a very good Time now they were quarreling to set up for himself, Come young Women (said he) b— G——e I like you well and am resolved I'll have you, so never trouble yourself about Sir *Combish* any more, for though I am at present but an Esquire I intend to be knighted soon, and then I can make you a Lady as well as he, so let us strike up the Bargain with a Kiss, which he was just going to take when *Belinda* not in a very good Humour returned his Love with a sound box on the Ear, which for ought I know the civil Esquire would have sent back with Interest had not supper interposed: They had not half finished their Meal when they heard a bussle at the Door and a Woman's Voice say, I will come in you Dog, I will see the Rogue your Master. Sir *Combish* heard and turn'd Pale, at which Time the Virago entered and flying at him, arm'd like a Cat clap'd her fierce Tallons into each of his Cheeks, crying aloud, *Betty Dimple* revenge thyself and tear the Villain's Soul out, Sir *John* got up and rescued the half worried[106] Knight, though not without some Danger to himself. Poor Sir *Combish* was no sooner relieved than he ran down stairs like fury, ordered his Coach to be got ready that Minute and drove away as fast as Fear and six good Horses could carry him, which in all Probability he had not done so quietly, but that Madam *Betty*, half-choak'd with Gall, was fallen senseless into a Chair, and gave him Time to make an easy Exit. *Belinda* and her Company were very merry at the Tragy-Comedy, and let her sit to recover at her own Leisure, knowing her Distemper was nothing but Passion, which would soon work itself off. By that Time supper was over and the Cloath taken away the furious *Betty* came to her senses again, and looking wildly round her, cryed where is the Monster, the Hell-hound that has robb'd me, plundered me and left me to Misery, Dispair, and Ruin. O cruel Man (she said to Sir *John Galliard*) why have you put a stop to my Design and hindred me from glutting myself with such Revenge as suits the Wrongs poor *Betty Dimple* has received, O where is he, shew him to me, O I rave, I die for my Revenge.[107] You rave indeed, (answered *Belinda*), I would fain have you cool your Boiling Resentment and let us know the Cause on't, since your Revenge is so publick your Injury may be so too. Cool it Madam (answered the Woman) it is not possible for me to cool my Rage, since every Breath I draw heats and inflames it more, no, nothing will ever quench my burning Wrath, but the Blood of him who first set it in Flames, but Madam as you are one of my own sex perhaps you may have a little Pity for me, and therefore you shall hear my Tale: As for my Father and Mother it is not at all to the purpose to tell you who they were, or what they were, since they both died while I was yet an Infant, and left me to the Care of a Grand-father, whose Daughter brought me forth. While I was young I had I'll warrant you forty fluting Lovers, with their fine Speeches and filthy Designs, who were ready enough to offer Services they had little Reason to believe would be accepted of, but what signifies that, I kept my Ground as firm as a Rock, and stood stoutly to defend my self from them all, at last one of the trouble Houses that was always after me, told me if I would not comply he would take young *Bateman*'s Course and hang humself at his own sign-post.[108] So you may (said I) if you have a Mind, and least your Rope should prove too short, I'll lend you my Garters to lengthen it. Well Mrs.[109] (said he) you'll meet with your Match I warrant you. So he walk'd off, and I never saw him again, or so much as heard he kept his Word and hang'd himself. The next was a lumping Looby[110] that weighed about eighteen stone, and he poor Man was for drowning, but I persuaded him to stay till I got him a couple of Bladders to tye under his Arms for fear he should sink, and all the Thanks he gave me, was to call me a jeering Bitch, and went home as dry as if he had never been drowned at all. The next was a Barber, and a cunning Shaver was he, for I as surely thought one Night he had cut his Throat as I was sorry afterwards I was mistaken, but the Rogue deceived me as all the rest had done. The next was an Apothecary's Apprentice, who had threatened so often to poison himself that I did not know but some Time or other he might do as much for me, so broke off my Acquaintance with him as soon as I could before I began to swell,[111] and yet a Year after I saw the Whelp with as wholsome a Look as if his Master had not a scruple of Mercury in his Shop; well I'll swear 'tis a melancholy Thing to tell ourselves there is no trusting in Man for any Thing but our own undoing. When I had lived a Year or two longer and had got more Wit, a new sweet-heart presented himself to me, he was a Neighbour's Child and one with whom I used to romp when I was a little Girl, but he was grown so fine with his laced Hat and shoulder-knot that I had much ado to know him, humph *Will* (said I) you are very fine, I'll warrant your Father is dead, and you have given all he left you for those fine Clothes: And what are you married? Married (said he) no, no, if I were married I should have no Business here, for I am come to offer my service to you, as my Master says to the Ladies. My Father indeed is dead, and has left me his Farm with a good stock upon it, and I intend to leave my Master and go and live upon it if you will have me, and help to manage it, I have lived these two Years with one Sir *Combish Clutter*, who has lately had a honey Fall of a thousand a Year dropt into his Mouth, some of your great Wits call him Coxcomb, but whatever he is, I have had a main good Place on't, and would not leave it but for thy sake, dear *Betty*, so take a short considering Time and let me have an Answer to morrow. Nay, nay, *Will* (said I) you may as well take it now, what you and I are no Stangers to one another, we have no Acquaintance to scrape at this Time of day, and the less we spend in Courtship the better, but my Grandfather must be told or else he will give me nothing, and then, for all your fine Speeches you won't care a Louse for me. In short my Grand-father liked the Match, and promised to make my Portion equal with his, so *William* gave his Master Warning and told him he was going to be married. A Pox on thee for a Fool, said his Master, is not the D—l in thee to leave a Place of Plenty for a starving Hole of thy own, with half a scored naked Bastards about thy Heels, which in all Probability will either go to *Tyburn* or a Brothel-house.[112] No Sir (said *Will*) I hope not, I was not the Son of a rich Man myself and yet I have escaped the Gallows, beside if there were no poor Men in the World who must wait upon such as you Sir? My Wife and I betwixt us shall be better worth than two hundred Pounds, and that with a little Industry and good Management will keep our Children from Nakedness. Why then (return'd Sir *Combish*) you are very rich I find, though your Father was not, and pray where does this Wife elect of yours live? Why Sir (answered *William*) your being a Stranger in this Country where your new Estate is, makes you so to all the pritty Girls here about, she lives not far off and a tid Bit[113] she is, if your Worship will give me leave I will invite her to sup with us in the Hall, she'll be no disgrace to the best among us Servants: At Night I was brought to the House, and the House-Keeper conducted me in with as much Ceremony as I deserved; but that D—l, Sir *Combish*, was at a Dining-Room Window, from whence he saw me, and thought me worth a Night's Lodging, which he designed to honour me with. A Day or two after, he asked *Will*, when he was to be Married. He said, As soon as we were Three times Asked in Church, which would be Next Sunday.[114] Well then (said the Knight) your Wife may depend upon me for a Father to herself, and a Godfather to her first Child: And for thy Part, since thou hast proved a Good Honest Rascal, I will not only wish thee Joy, but I will give thee some, by adding a Good Close to thy Farm, which will make thee a Free-holder, and qualify thee for a Vote against I want one. But before you leave me you are to do me a private Piece of service, which none but you are to be trusted with. You must know, as much a Stranger as I am on this side the Country, I have an Intrigue with a Girl not far off, that is, I would have one, but the Jade is cautious, and though I do her an Honour, she refuses it, unless I Marry her. Now to gain my Ends, I have promised to Marry her, but d— me if I keep my Word, though I intend to confirm it with a Letter to her, which you shall copy, for you write a Good, Careless, Gentleman-like Hand; and I believe you spell like the D—l, as well as myself: But she is no Judge, nor does she know my Hand at all; so yours shall go for mine; that if ever I am called to an Account for it, I may with safety deny it, and justly say, I did not write it: Call upon me half an Hour hence, and I will give you what I would have you transcribe. *Will* thought to himself, if the Girl did not know his Master's Hand, he was sure she did not know his; and for the Spelling-Part, it was perfectly indifferent to him whether it was right or wrong. The Time was come when he was to wait his Master's Commands, he then gave him the following Lines to copy, which are too well impress'd on my Memory to lose one Tittle of them.

> *I Thought, my Dear, to have seen You this Evening, but am prevented by Company coming in; however, I cannot sleep till I communicate a Secret to You: Though I fear it will be late before I come, let all be quiet, and no Light; for we have had the D—l to do here. But no more of that till we meet.*
>
> *Yours.*

When *William* had writ this over, his Master took it from him, saying, Now have I a Mind for a Frolick, and will go and deliver this Letter myself; but if I do, it shall be in your Cloaths, *Will*: so slip on your Frock, and give me your Livery. Poor *William* obeyed without Delay, and was then sent on some sleeveless Errand,[115] which was to take up some Time, while another Servant was sent with the Letter to me; which I made no Doubt came from *William*, because I knew his Hand, though there was no Name. I was very impatient to know what the Matter was, and never wished more for my *William*'s Company than at that time. My Grandfather and all the Family were gone to Bed, except myself, who sate, as ordered, in the dark, till I heard some Footsteps in the Yard, I then ran and opened the Door, where by Starlight I saw *Will*, as I thought, in his Livery; he came in, and whispered very low, asked, if all were a-bed? I told him, Yes. He then told me I was False to him, and had Reason to believe I was going to be Married to another. Who, I, *William?* (said I) What do you mean by such a groundless suspicion? I love you too well, to think of any Man in the World but yourself, and am so just to you, that if your Master would have me, I would not change you for him. Say no more (replied the Counter-feit *William*) for nothing shall ever convince me you are true, unless you give yourself up wholly to my Arms this Night. I loved my *William*, and made no scruple to cure his Doubts, though at the Expence of a M————d,[116] which I had always kept for him: so we crept up-stairs, and to-Bed we went in the dark; but while we were there *Will* returned from the Walk he had been sent, and found all the Servants very merry, but no Master to deliver his Message to, nor could any Account be had of him. He staid a-while at home, and thought to himself, Sir *Combish* was gone, no Doubt, to the poor deluded Girl with the Letter he had writ for him; And now (thought he) I will go for an Hour or two to my *Betty*, who is doubtless in Bed, but I know she will rise, and let me in. I was so eager to clear myself of the Falshood and Stuff he laid to my Charge, that I went up to Bed without fastening the Latch, *William* came easily in, and directly up to my Room; but fearing he should fright me, he spoke just at the Door, and said, Do not be frighted, *Betty*, it is only I. Only you (cried I trembling) Who are you? What (answered he) do you not know the Voice of your *William?* If you are *William*, (said I) Who have I got here? Go fetch a Candle, for I am undone for ever. He ran down to light a Candle, while I jumped out of Bed, and got my Clothes on; *William* no sooner ad-vanced to the Bed-side with a lighted Candle, than Sir *Combish* threw his Night-Cap at it, and put it out again: But *Will* was so enraged to have his Place supplied by another, that he ran to the Bed, and so jumbled his Master, that after he had battered his Face not fit to be seen a Month after, he cried out *Murder!* which roused my Grandfather, and all the House beside, who came with Candles in their Hands to my Room, and discovered the whole Matter. Sir *Combish* lay still, but cried, G— d— thee *Will*, thou haste given me a Beating that no Dog in *England* would have given to a Porter; Curse thee, go home and fetch my Clothes; take thy own, and let me see thy Dog's Phiz no more. But poor I had more than a double share of a Plot I never help'd to contrive; for when *William* came back with his Master's Clothes he refused to hear me justify my self, took a final Leave of me just then, and I never saw him since. My Grand-father, as soon as the Knight was gone, refused to hear me, likewise turned me out of Doors the next Morning, and I never saw him since neither. Every-body believed I was designedly a Whore; and I have lived ever since in the utmost Contempt on what my Needle and Wheel could bring me in. I have an Aunt in this Town, to whom by an Invitation I came three Days ago, and was sitting at her Door, when I saw that Infernal Sir *Combish* driven in, whose Villanous Soul I would have separated from his Cursed Corpse, had not this Gentleman most Cruelly prevented me; but I hope, it is not yet too late, he is doubtless in the House still; and it shall go very hard but I will have the other Tugg with his D——lship. Sir *John Galliard* at this Recital had two or three inward Qualms, and he often thought of poor Miss *Friendly*, whose Wrongs only he felt Compunction for. But *Belinda* was a little upon the smile, and said, You know not, Mrs. *Betty*, how well you have Revenged yourself already; for I assure you, Sir *Combish*, by your Appearance, is driven from a Mistress he followed from *London*, to which Place I dare say he is by this time returning; for my Maid whispered me in the Ear just now, and told me, his Coach and he were gone off: But let him go, he is a worthless Animal, and has used you basely, yet I believe it will soon be in my Power to do you some service. How long is it since *William* and you parted? And what sort of Man is he? she then described him, and said, It was above a Year since she heard of him. Have you a Mind (asked *Belinda*) to be reconciled to him? If so, provide to go with me, for I fancy your *William* lives with a Sister of mine: And I am the more ready to believe it is he, because Sir *Combish* came with his Addresses to me soon after the time you speak of, and the Fellow pretended to be sick all the while he staid, and would never appear: Now as I am almost sure this is the Man, I am as well satisfied it will be in my Power to make up the Breach betwixt you, if you do but once meet. Mrs. *Betty* said, she was willing to wait upon her any-where, but could never hope to see *William* again with any satisfaction. Next Morning they again took Coach, Sir *John* and Squire *Clownish* who had slept all the while *Betty Dimple* told her Story to *Belinda* and her Maid: As for Mrs. *Dimple*, she came jogging after on a Trotting Horse, who first dislocated her Joints, and then set them right again. After they had been some time in the Coach, Mr. *Cock-a-hoop* asked *Belinda*, when she designed to beg his Pardon for the Box on the Ear she gave him; and assured her, that if Sir *Combish* had not been frighted out of the House, and forgot to take him with him, he should hardly have been so civil, after such an Affront, to wait upon her home. *Belinda* told him, whenever he thought fit to ask her Pardon for the Occasion of the Box, she might perhaps condescend to an Answer of the same Kind; but as for his Company, she found no great Reason to thank him for it, because it was a Piece of Civility forced upon him, and yet she was glad of it, because Sir *John Galliard* must have gone back alone had not Fortune left him behind. Sir *John* sate all the Morning with his Head, as it were, in a Cloud, gloomy and silent; his Thoughts employed on different subjects, which entertained him with no pleasing Variety: sometimes he was vexed he had miss'd his Design on *Belinda*; sometimes ashamed he had ever attack'd her Honour; one Minute he called himself a Thousand Fools, for jaunting after a Woman that would not be his Harlot at last; the next he persuaded himself to Marry her: But that raised a Mutiny in his Breast, crying out *Liberty! Liberty!* In short, he liked *Belinda* so well, that he was forced to stand at Bay with his own Inclinations, keeping them always snub'd, to divert them from what he had always declared against. *Belinda* again took Notice of Sir *John's* silence, and said, Have Courage, Sir, your *Purgatory* is almost at an End, and a few Hours will give you to your self again. Madam (answered the Complaisant Sir *John*) it is my Heaven that is near at an End, and my *Purgatory* will not begin till I leave *Belinda*; who, if she knew at all, has more to boast than any of her Sex ever had before her; for she has brought it to a single Vote, whether I shall Marry, or no. Nay, Sir *John* (returned *Belinda* laughing) a single Vote can never do in a Matrimonial Affair; there must be a joint Consent, or we shall make a sad Botch of what would otherwise be very clever; But I beg you will lay by all your Gravity, and consider, Travellers should be always merry, else methinks, we look as if we were counting how many steps our Horses take in an Hour. By G——e (said *Cock-a-hoop*) and so we do: Bobs, I love to be merry. Come Mrs. *Bell*, I will sing you a *SONG* I made myself; and a good one it is, though I say it.

> *My Whoney SUE, give me thy Haun,*
> *I Love Thee, as I'm an Honest Man;*
> *My Hoggs, my Cows, my Plow, my Cart,*
> *To Thee I value not a V—t:*
> *And yet, Odzooks, Thou art so Coy,*[117]
> *Whene're I Court, Thou sayest me Noy.*

Then *SUE* Answers.

> *Forbear Your Foolish Suit, Good JOHN,*
> *For I must have a Gentleman,*

Can Compliment, and go more Gay
Than Thou upon a Holiday;
Can Kiss, and a-la-mode can Wooe,
While all Your Courtship's High-Gee-Ho.

Then He again.

Aye, marry Gep, are You so stout?
In my Heart I love for to Jeer and Flout,
Ads Watrilaits, were I in Bed,
And Wrestling for —— ————[118]

Oh! for Heaven's sake (cried *Belinda*) no more of your Poetry, we are just at our Inn. A P— o' the Inn (said he) the best is to come; and I am resolved to sing it out.— Ads Watrilaits, you had best have a Care, *Cock-a-hoop* (interrupted Sir *John*) the Lady's Fingers are as nimble as ever, and if your *SONG* does not please her Ear, 'tis six to four but she finds the Way to yours again. By G——e (replied *Clownish*) but if she does, she sha'nt come off so well as she did last time; and I am resolved I'll sing my *SONG* too. They were now all in the Room together where they were to Dine, when *Betty Dimple* standing at the Window saw a Coach coming, and her old Lover *William* Riding before. Madam (said she to *Belinda*) I believe your Sister is come to meet you, for here is my Runagate,[119] full well I know him. The Coach drove into the Inn, and *Belinda* and Sir *John* ran out to see the Lady alight. But Oh! the Ungrateful Interview, when the Lady in the Coach knew Sir *John Galliard* for the Father of her Child then with her, and he the Lady for the same he had had once in the *Bagnio*. The Confusion that appeared in both their Faces was too great to be disregarded by *Belinda*, who looked alternately at them, and whose share of the Amazement was equal to their Surprise. Sir *John* saw it, and did all he could to recover himself, so took the Child in his Arms, and carried her into the House. The Mother cried out, Oh! my Child, my Child! fearing Sir *John* would have taken her away from her. Pray Sister (said *Belinda*) let us go in; methinks, I long to know the Cause of your Disorder. The Lady got out of the Coach, but desired her Child, and a Room to herself: And while she was going in, a Thousand Fears filled her Breast; sometimes she thought Sir *John* had not Honour enough to conceal the Intrigue that had been betwixt them; sometimes again she thought *Belinda* and he was married; then the Fear of losing her Child hurried her to Despair, till she got into the House, and then she begged *Belinda* to bring her little Girl to her, for she could not rest till she saw her again, because she had been so lately ill. Why, Madam (answered *Belinda*) are you so strangely ruffled, you give me at once Pain and Amazement, have you ever seen Sir *John Galliard* before? The Widow was a little Nonpluss'd at that Question, but resolved to deny the Acquaintance; and therefore asked her, who was that? *Belinda* said, It was the Gentleman that took Miss out of the Coach, in whose Hands she was sure the Child was very safe. However, she would go that Minute, and bring her from him. She immediately returned with her, which removed one of the Lady's Fears; but there was yet two more, which hung heavy on her Mind: Nor durst she ask *Belinda*, whether she was Married or no, lest her Answer should stike her dead: But as she knew it must come out, she trembling said, *Belinda*, Are you Married? Married! (replied *Belinda*) what, in a Week's Time? No, Sister; if your Concern proceeds from your Apprehension of losing me, calm your Brow, for the Gentleman you saw with me is too much a Beau to be noosed, as they call it: And I would feign have you joyn the Company, or you will lose a very Pleasant Scene betwixt your *William* and a Mistress of his, which I accidentally pick'd up; the Story is too long for a present Repetition, and will serve to fill up a dull vacant Hour another Time. While they were discoursing in one Room, Sir *John* was considering in another, and told himself with much Ease the Reason why the Widow would not come to them: He therefore called for a Pen and Ink, and writ as follows:

> *IT was an Accident, Madam, that brought us first together, and We are now met by another. I plainly saw Your Concern, and shewed too much of my Own to be disregarded by the Piercing Eyes of Your Sister. If You would prevent her farther Observation, look easy, and view me with the same Indifference You would have done had You never seen me before: And since nothing but a Return of that Indifference can secure us from being discover'd, You shall find my Behaviour (as directed by Prudence) answerable.*
>
> Yours.

When Sir *John* had writ his Letter he gave it to a Servant, bid him enquire where *Belinda* was, and tell her, he begg'd the Favour of her Company for a Moment, and as soon as she left the Room, to convey the Letter into the Hand of the new-arrived Lady. *Belinda* answered the Knight's Summons, and the Servant delivered the Letter, as ordered. The Lady read it, and approved so well of the Advice there given, that she resolved to act accordingly. *Belinda* returned to her Sister, told her, Dinner was just ready, and desired once more to know whether she would go to the rest of the Company, or they two should Dine there alone. The Lady told her, since Sir *John* was so very obliging to give her his Company so far, it would be highly Rude to Rob him of hers; and for that Reason she would go with her. They went, and Sir *John* received the Strange Lady with much Civility, but guarded Looks; she used the same Caution, and managed hers so well, that all Observations were now at an End. They were all sate down to Dinner, and the Servants called in to wait; among whom was *William* so lately spoken of: He stood some time at his Lady's Back before he minded his Landabrides[120] at the Table with them, who cast many a wishful Eye at him unregarded: At last Sir *John* drank to her, which drew his Eye that Way; and no sooner saw her than he colour'd with Resentment, and was going to leave the Room, when *Belinda* said, Stay, *William*, I have somewhat to say to you as soon as Dinner is over. He staid, but with the utmost Uneasiness, not being able to bear the sight of his Unfaithful *Betty*, as he thought her: But when they had done, and the rest of the Servants dismiss'd, *Belinda* asked *Will*, if he knew the Young Woman that sate there? He answered, Yes; he had too many Reasons to know her for an Ungrateful Base Baggage as she was. Harky, Mr. Rogue (said *Betty*) don't you pretend to Abuse me before all this Good Company; for, if you do, I shall make the House too hot to hold you, as I did for the Rascal your Master not long ago. Were not you one of the Basest Dogs alive to send me a Letter writ with your own Hand, and then let your D——d Knight come in your Clothes for an Answer to it; and when you had done, came in with an Innocent Air to find me out in the very Roguery you yourself had contrived: And now, Forsooth, you pretend to put on a Look of Ignorance, as if you knew nothing of the Matter; that so your Load of Villany might be heaped up at my Door, like a Base, Treacherous Whelp as you are. I cod (said *Cock-a-hoop*) you have got a D——d Tongue in your Head, which, if I were your Husband, by G——e I should wish at the D——l. Why, what a P— you scold as if you got your Living by it. And hear me, Young Man, if you know when you are well, by G——e I think you have a good Riddance of her. Oh! no, Sir (said poor *William*) she has Reason for all her Anger; which I never knew before: My Eyes are now open, and I plainly see both her Wrongs and my own. Oh! my *Betty!* we have both been Abus'd, and let us pity one another. No (returned *Betty*) I will neither pity you, nor myself, till I have taken the Law of that Base Transgressor of it: Why must a Poor Man be hanged for stealing a Sheep, and a Rich one escape, that takes away by Force or Trick what is much more valuable from us: I am resolved to make both himself and the World know what a Rogue he is; and I'll see him hang'd before he shall wear the Best Jewel I ever had, and not pay a Good Price for it. Here she fell a-crying, and it wanted not much that *William* kept her Company, till Sir *John* and *Belinda* laughed them out of Countenance: And the latter told them, she saw no Cause for Tears, since they were in so fine a Way of recovering one another's Favour, which in a little time they did. Our Travellers now began to think of finishing their Journey, which a few Hours compleated: But how were they all surprised to find Sir *Combish* got there before them; who resolving not to lose *Belinda*, crossed the Country a little Way, and got again into the Road, designing to be at her Sister's as soon as she; and there to be free from the Fury that paid him so well at the Inn for his past Recreation. But what was his Terror and Confusion, when he saw enter with the rest, not only the Cheated *Betty*, but the Wronged *William* too. —— Z——s (he cried) I am haunted; prithee Widow, dear Widow, send for thy Parson to lay these two Infernal Spirits, and chain them down for Life in the Bonds of Matrimony; or—— I shall never be quiet for 'em. Come *Will*, consume thee, I'll give thee a Farm of Ten Pounds a Year for thy Drab's M————d, and I think it is very well sold; but I will have it inserted in the Contract, that she shall never come within ten Yards of my Person: And the D——l take me, if ever I come within twenty of hers, if Riding forty Miles round it will prevent it. Why, by G——e you are in the right on't (replied the 'Squire) Zooks Man (contined he, turning to *William*) it will be a Folly to wish you Joy; for if thou hast a Soul in thee she will tear it out in a Week's time. By *George* our Champion, I would not Marry her, if *GEORGE* our King would give me his Crown for her Portion.[121]

Well, well, Sir (replied *Betty*) you may give your self as many scornful Airs as you please; but by G——e I had rather have *William* with his own Farm, and that Sir *Combish* has promised, than you with your Great Estate; every one to their Origin: I was never cut out for a Gentleman, nor you for a Milk-Maid; for what say you *William*, shall we take Sir *Combish* at his Word? *William* scratched his Head a little, and then consented; so Married they were, and there I leave them, because after Marriage (like Cheese) comes nothing.[122]

Yes (says a Fleerer at my Elbow) Children, Noise, Charge,[123] Discord, Cuckoldom (may be) and often Beggary comes after. But this spiteful Remarker had the Misfortune to miscarry himself; and who would mind a Prejudiced Person? When the Wedding was over, and the Couple gone, Sir *Combish* began to renew his Addresses to *Belinda*, who received them with a very cool Indifference: For as she never had any Real Value for the Knight, it was not very likely his late Behaviour should make any Addition: and being pretty well tired of his conceited Impertinence, she resolved to give him a final Answer, in

Order to a speedy Deliverance, which the very ensuing Afternoon favoured; for it happened to prove a very pleasant one, and drew them all into the Gardens. Sir *Combish* resolving to take hold of the Happy Opportunity, conducted *Belinda* to a little shady Grove, which he thought a Scene fit for Love; and resolving to improve it while he was separate from the rest of the Company, he first filled the Lady's Ears with his own Profound Merits, and then told her how willing he was to bestow them all on her: Sir *Combish* (returned the Grateful *Belinda*) I shall always acknowledge the Favour you have done me, in acquainting me with your Best Qualities; our Worst, I must own, we neither love to speak, or hear of: But as I am a Person who must always be wholly disinterested both in your Worth and Demerits; All I have to do is to thank you for the Honour you have offered me; and to tell you without Reserve, I cannot accept of it. Now may I be speechless (returned Sir *Combish*) if I know whether I hear well or no: Did you say, Madam, you could not accept my Offer? — I cannot credit my Ears. I never eat my Words, Sir (answered *Belinda*) but beg you will keep your Temper, since nothing spoils the Oeconomy of a well-set Countenance like Resentment and Anger: You know, Sir *Combish*, our Passions are not at our Command; and if we hate when we should love, it is owing to a Depravity in our Fancies, which we may strive against, but can seldom master: This is just my Case, I have tried to subdue my Inclinations, but a superior Force keeps them under; and where our Power is defective submission is our only Choice. Why sure (return'd the Vain Sir *Combish*) my Ears or Understanding must be defective too. Did you really say, you could not accept of my Offers which is Honourable Love; and what at first I did not design, and perhaps more than some People deserve: But since your stomach is so squeamish, you may e'en try to strengthen it three or four Years longer, and then coarser Fare will go down.

Nay Sir *Combish* (replied *Belinda*) my stomach was never sharp set towards nice Bits, nor did it ever relish Palates or Coxcombs; my Taste lies towards cheaper Food, which I think wholsomer too. Sir *Combish* with an Air of Contempt wish'd her a good Digestion, and told her, she that lik'd a Piece of Neck-Beef better than a Pheasant, might perhaps prefer a Foot-man before his Master. Why truly, Sir *Combish* (answer'd *Belinda*) if we did but make some Alllowance for the Paultry Name on one side, and the Good Estate on the other, the Man is very often preferable to his Master. But here comes your Friend the Esquire with a Hare in his Hand, I see he has been a Coursing.

Come (said he) and tell me how you like my Game, b- *G——e* 'tis better hunting Hares than Whores, for here have I in half an Hour got one, and was half a Year in pursuit of the other Bitch and lost her at last, so we will have this Puss for our supper, and let the D——l take the other for his. The D——l (replied Sir *Combish*) owes thee not much for thy Deed of Gift, since thou hast offered nothing but what was his own before, a Pox on thee for a Fool, the whole sex was design'd for him at the Creation. Mercy on us! (cried *Belinda*) Why Sir *Combish*, what do you mean? You make Love till you grow perfectly rude, I beg you will be advised, and when you leave a Lady secure her good Word by a civil Exit, and then perhaps, though she despises you herself, she may have some worthless Acquaintance to recommend you to.

B- G——e (answered our Friend *Clownish*) you may talk of Civility as much as you please young Woman, but I think you practise it as little as he does, come, come, come, your Tongue and your Fingers are flipant alike, what a P— who is bound to take your Blows and your Fromps?[124] B- G——e if Sir *Combish* would stand by me, I would return both his Abuses and my own with Cent per Cent b- G——e. *Belinda* laugh'd at the Fools and left them singing a Piece of an old song— *Why how now Sir* Clown *what makes you so bold.*[125] But while they like the Cats were growling out Love to one another, Sir *John* and the Widow Lady were doing it with more good Manners at another Part of the Garden, he told her he was so out of Countenance at the Reflection of his own Behaviour to her when she was last at *London,* that he wanted Courage to ask her Pardon, but begg'd she would forget it, if only for the sake of his dear little Girl, for whom he declared an Affection and Tenderness equal to what Nature gives us for our own. If you Sir *John* (returned the Lady) are discountenanced at your Behaviour, what Confusion and Remorse must attend mine? I do assure you without flying to any other Interest than that of my own Quiet, I have long since endeavoured to forget my Fault and had most happily banish'd the Remembrance of you, and my own Weakness from my Breast, when all was again recall'd at the sight of you so near the side of my Coach, I must own I had much to fear from the inward tremulous Perturbations of my fluttering Heart that a Discovery would ensue, but I had a Sister to deal with innocent herself and loving me too well to think me guilty, and yet she had much ado to account for my Conduct at such a perplexing Juncture, but thanks to Fate it is now most happily over, and if Sir *John Galliard* will but promise two Things I shall know no more Distress. Name them Madam (replied Sir *John*) and may I never know Ease myself if I refuse (as far as my Power goes) to contribute towards yours, bar Matrimony and command me in every Thing. As for that Clause (answered the Lady) 'tis perfectly needless, and I promise never to put your good Nature to that Trial again, all I beg is, that you will keep my secret and be my Friend; as for a double state of Life, I am now as much adverse to it as you are, and it is because I believe you will never clog yourself with a Wife, that I do not add a third Request to the former which would be, never to address *Belinda*, because abominable Incest shocks my Soul and gives my Blood an Ague. Sir *John* told the Lady he own'd himself a Man of Pleasure but was not quite so bad as she unkindly thought him, *Belinda* he acknowledged was a fine Woman, but Madam (continued he) she is your Sister and Rival only to your Merit, I have already declared my sentiments of Wedlock, and for any other Attempts I here faithfully promise to dismiss them. No Madam, I am now resolved to grant what you have asked, and will for the future love you both, with the same inoffensive Love as if you were my sisters, and when I lay you open to the Censure of the World may I loose both Memory and Reason to prevent a just Repetition of my Fault. This Promise was just made when *Belinda* came in some haste to desire their Protection, saying she was never in so fair a Way for a good Beating in her Life before, pray Sir *John* (continued she) will you tell me (for you are his old Acquaintance) how many Degrees is Friend *Cock-a-hoop* removed from a Brute? Nay Madam (answered Sir *John*) if it was he that was going to beat you, I think you should ask how many Degrees a Brute is removed from him, since the very fiercest among them never fight their Females.

I confess he has put me a little out of Countenance at being one of his Acquaintance, and would resent his rude Behaviour, but that he is in strictness the Guest of Sir *Combish*, not mine, beside I am sure *Belinda* would rather laugh at his ill Manners than see it chastised, especially in this Place. I will tell you Ladies (if you'll give me leave) how he once served me: When I was first acquainted with him, I happened to have a slight Intrigue with a Lady whom I obliged more out of good Nature than Inclination, because she had the Misfortune of being a little stricken in Years. She had one Day invited herself to dine with me at my Lodgings, and as she was a Lady of some Quality I resolved to be very civil to her, when that rude Monster came abruptly into the Dining-room, and looking at her, cried, Why, what a P— Knight art thou reduced already to the Assistance of a Baud,— Man what doest thou do with this Piece of Fripery,[126] in her Curls and her Patches, and her old Coquetish Airs, simpering and leering like a Girl just come from her sweet-heart, peeping into her Bosom to see whether her withered Bubbies heave or no,— a young Coquet is the D———l, but an old one is his Dam, by *George.* You may easily guess Ladies how this blunt speech mortified the Lady, who past for a Maid too, and what Confusion it put me into for an Excuse: she coloured so much with the Extemity of Resentment that it appeared through the Vernish of her Face, though none of the thinest lay'd on, I was forced to shake my Head and cry, poor Mr. *Cock-a-hoop,* I wonder how he has got loose from his Confinement, Madam (continued I, a little out of his hearing) this unhappy Gentleman has for some Weeks been disordered in his Head, and I beg you will take no Notice of what he says. O pray then (said she) let me be gone, and convey me safe into the street, for I neither love to be abused or converse with mad Men,— Sir *John* you keep strange Company, I wonder where you pick them up. My rude Companion catch'd her last Words, and answered, the D———l should pick her Skeliton before he would pick up such an old Yew[127] as she was, who for ought he knew was the first that rotted after the Flood. The poor Lady made the best of her Way down stairs, and swore she should never come near me again unless I banish'd my Mad-man: I confess though *Cock-a-hoop's* Behaviour vex'd me and I let him know it did, yet at the same Time it brought me a Deliverance from one I did not much delight in, for which Reason I forgave his ill Manners, and if *Belinda* will but consider, it is impossible to make a Brute a Man, I am sure she will do so too, to-morrow I design to set my Face towards *London,* and in order to your speedy Deliverance will offer him a Place in my Coach, tho' I fancy he will hardly leave you till Sir *Combish* does, when that will be you, Madam, can best guess. If (said the Lady) one may guess at his stay by his Treatment, I am of Opinion he will not continue long after you, and indeed it would be a little hard if he should, since no body cares for the winnow'd Chaff when the substantial Grain is separated from it, but do not grow vain, Sir *John,* (continued *Belinda* with a Blush) I only hint at your superior share of good sense; I see no room for being proud of your Compliment Madam (answered the Knight) since you only allow me a little more Wit than a couple of Fools. Nay Sir *John* (replied the Widow Lady) I think you are too severe, they are neither of them Fools, but the Vanity of one and the ill Nature of the other gives a Turn of Contempt to rob them of the finest Quality ever given to Man, and I wish Sir *John Galliard* may always preserve his Talent from every Mixture that may rob it of its Lustrue.[128] Sir *John* received the Lady's kind Wishes with a Bow, though he knew they were attended with some secret Reproach, and said he was too conscious of his own Demerits to think he could deserve them, but now Madam, said he, addressing *Belinda*, (though what followed was designed for both) we are now within a very little Time of parting (possibly) for ever, I therefore beg an Act of Oblivion[129] may pass betwixt us, and let us forget every disobliging Thing that has been said on either side, try to mend your Opinion of me, and I will endeavour to deserve it. Here the Widow Lady left them to pluck a ripe Orange she saw, when Sir *John* went on thus: The World you know Madam is divided into four Parts, so are the Inhabiters of it distinguish'd by four Characters: Coxcomb, Fool, Knave and Man of sense; now as we that live in *Europe* reckon it the least Part of the World, but the best, so must Men of sense be allowed the superior Character though infinitly the inferior Number, no wonder then if you Ladies are persecuted with three Intollerables for one Agreeable, as for the Coxcomb and the Fool I see them coming towards us, but which of the other two Epithets will *Belinda* give to me. Ah Sir *John* (replied the Lady laughing) I wish you could as easily acquit yourself of one of the remaining Characters, as you have an undisputed Right to the other, but you cannot blame me if I say you have enough of the best Character and too much of the Worst, yet since you desire and I have partly promised that all should be forgiven, I will now go a step farther and endeavour to forget it too. Sir *John* took her Hand and kiss'd it as a return of thanks, which was all he had Time to do before they were joyn'd by the other two Gentlemen, he then asked Sir *Combish* if he might expect his Company to *London* in the Morning? Ask the Lady (replied the Knight) her Vote must determine the Matter, if she says I am welcome to stay, you go alone, if otherways I am at your service, but I thought by the Kiss you gave her Hand just now, you had been returning Thanks for leave to stay a little longer yourself. No Sir (returned *Belinda*) Sir *John Galliard* need not ask leave to stay any where, his Company will always be desired, but since he is resolved to rob us of it to-morrow, I think it pity he should want Company, for it is dull travelling by ones self. Friend *Clownish* was just going to make some notable Repartee when the Lady of the House came to them, and said, she believed it was Tea-time, so desired they would all walk in. How they imployed themselves the rest of the Day I know not, but next morning the two Knights and the growling Esquire took leave of the Ladies and returned to *London*, where every one fell to the Exercise and Diversion they best liked. Sir *John* had not been many Days in Town before he received a Letter from Lady *Galliard* as follows:

YOU shew'd so much Concern when I was last at London, *for Mr.* Friendly *and his Family, that I imagine it will not displease you to hear farther from it, last Week I went to visit Mrs.* Friendly, *but did not expect to see Miss who has had a most melancholy Time ever since she came from* London, *but as she is very young and of an easy, cheerful, sweet Temper, she begins to recover her quiet a little and desired to see me, she told me I should see her little Mackroon (as she calls the Child) which when brought, methought I saw every Line and Feature of Sir* John Galliard's *Face in his, you know best whether you are the Father, every Body believes you are, but the Mother who says you were not in the Nation at the unhappy Conception of it. I wish you would come and see yourself in Epitome, for if you are not Father to this, I am sure you never will be to one more of your own Likeness. I should now reproach you for your long Silence, and twenty other Things, but as I am fully determined to bury your Faults, this shall be the last Time I will (if possible) ever think of them, so you will but come to a Mother impatient to see you, and who will receive you with Transport and Pleasure.*

B. Galliard.

Sir *John* who never heard Mr. *Friendly's* Family named, since the Injury he had done it, without some Concern, trembled as he read the Letter, and could not prevent a Sigh or two which forced their Way from a disordered Heart, sure (said he to himself) this one Action of my Life must be the worst because all the rest wear off while this alone sticks to my Mind, and brings an ungrateful Remembrance along with it. Poor *Nancy Friendly*, indeed I have done thee wrong, and such a wrong as nothing can repay, at least I know but one way and that I never can consent to. No *Hymen* forbid I should, and yet methinks the Girl has vast Desert, and I could wish my Fault undone— Why?— F—th I believe only to have the Pleasure of committing it again, well what must be, must be, and I could gladly see this little Likeness of mine, but how to face the charming Mother—— No, it must not be, for I should either discover myself by a foolish Concern, or fall a Victim to my own Tenderness and marry the Girl to redeem her Honour while I intail a Slavery upon myself for Life— No thank you *John* (he said) she it seems begins to be easy, and I will be so too, may a separate Blessing attend us both, and now I'll go to a Lady that cannot marry me in order to forget one that would. He had now an Intrigue with a new H——t,[130] whose Husband was very much a Man of the Town himself, but was not very willing to give his Wife the same Liberty he took, which made him look a little displeased when a certain Beau made pretty frequent Visits to her; it was by this Spark's Interest that Sir *John* had gain'd Admittance to her, and he happening to be the finest Man of the three, both

Husband and Gallant were dispised, and Sir *John* fix'd in her Favour till some-thing new supplanted him, as he had done his Predecessors, for Women are whimsical as well as Men and sometimes love Variety as well as they can, but the poor— C——d[131] must I call him? 'Tis an ugly Name, but it is much better than his Wive's, he I say found his Stomach grew squeamish, and could not digest the gross Proceedings of his Partner, who had now cured his Jeal-ousy by Certainty, and made him resolve to chastise the Interloper that shared his Bed without his Leave. Poor Sir *John* who was but just admitted, and had never yet an Opportunity of receiving one single Favour above leave to make a Present or two, fell into the Trap, and paid not only for his own intended Faults, but the repeated ones of him that shew'd him the Way to it. The Hus-band, however, knew nothing of Sir *John Galliard*, nor had ever seen him; his Design was laid against the Notorious Offender, whose Insolence grew so intolerable, that he began to insult him in his own House: Of whom to be Revenged he let his Man into the Secret, and by his Assistance, carry'd on the following Design.

The Lady was gone in the Afternoon to the *Park* for Air, when the Good Man taking the Opportunity of her Absence, provided himself of an Ounce or two of Gun-powder, with which he made about Thirty Crackers, and placed them on a Row on each side the Stairs, but so dextrously, that they were not to be seen. As soon as he had done, he went to his Closet, and writ a few Lines, to be given to his Spouse at her Return.

> *I Am going, my Dear, this Evening with three or four Honest Fellows to eat fresh Oysters at* Billings-gate,[132] *it is very likely it will be late before I Return; let this desire you neither to expect me home, or be anxious for my Stay.*
>
> Yours.

As soon as he had writ this Kind Epistle he gave it to his Lady's Maid, and bid her deliver it at her Return: And when he had given his Man a Key of a Closet at the Stairs-head where he was to act his Part, and farther Directions about the Affair in Projection, he really went, as said in the Letter. The Lady returned, read it, and immediately dispatch'd away her Emissary to let Sir *John Galliard* know of the favourable Opportunity that offered itself to promote their satisfaction. The Knight who was never backward at paying his Devoirs to a Fine Woman, promised to be with her in an Hour, being till then en-gaged. The Man that was left at home to execute his Master's Revenge lay snug in the Closet, where he could hear the first step set upon the stairs. The Hour was now expired, and the Visiting-Knock alarmed the Scout, who that Minute made ready to fire his Train, which as soon as the Punctual Sir *John* had advanced three or four steps, he did, and made such a D———e[133] Noise about the poor Knight's Ears, that he was not only scared out of his senses, but his Hands, Face and Bosom very much scorched; He stood the shock of the Ambuscade on the Middle of the Stairs till it had spent its Force, not knowing in the Fright whether he had best go forward or backward; while the Expecting Lady in the Dining-Room stood staring and surprised at the unusual Noise, full of Wonder from whence it came; but it was now over, and she ventured to the stairs-head, where she saw Sir *John* like a smoked Flitch of Bacon, and burning his Fingers to put out his Flames, which were so perfectly extinguish'd that the poor Lady never had any share of them; for the Knight supposing she had a Hand in the Contrivance turned from her, and went with the utmost Precipitation out of the House to his Lodgings, where he sent for a Surgeon, and was forced for some Weeks to keep his Chamber. O poor Sir *John!*

The Lady whom he left at the stairs-head, when she saw her greatest Beloved vanish, as it were like the D———l with smoke and stink, began to inquire the Cause, and what it was that made such Ratling Doings in the House? But no-body could satisfy her Curiosity. While she was disputing the Matter among her Maids, not a little vexed at her Disappointment, the Fellow in the Closet made a shift to convey himself privately out of Doors, and went with Tidings to his Master, as order'd. He was both surprised and vex'd when he heard the Person that received his Noisy Revenge was not the Man he expected. I find (said he) my Wife provides against Disappointment, and lays in a stock of Lovers against a Dear Year; Do you not know who the New Stallion is? I know no more of him, Sir (return'd the Man) than that he has been twice at our House, and I once heard my Mistress call him Sir *John*. O very well (reply'd the Husband) she has been dealing among the Officers and Merchants ever since I Married her, and now she begins to aspire to Quality. Well, I hope Sir *John*, as she calls him, has got enough however; Come Sirrah, since it is so, go you and fetch me a fresh W——— if she proves a Fire-ship,[134] I'll carry her Present to my Dear Wife, that she may disperse it among her Multitude, that so their Crime may be attended with a certain Punishment, and every one share alike: 'Tis a compendious Revenge, and reaches all, like a Feast of Poison to a Crowd of Rats. The Man obey'd, brought the S—t,[135] and conducted her to a private Apartment; the Consequence I never inquir'd after, but may guess it prov'd as intended. The Gentleman then repair'd to his Dwelling, who was met by his Wife in the Entry, My Dear (she said) our House is haunted.

I know it, my Life (return'd the Loving Spouse) it has been so a great While with the spirit of Concupiscence, which I fancy you are too fond of to endeavour to lay. I know not what you mean (answered the Innocent Lady) but I really believe the D——l has been here he left such a stink behind him; and for a Minute I thought he had been taking the House along with him there was such Thundering Doings on the stairs. Good lack (said the Tender Spouse) why here has been sad Doings indeed: But if the D——l had taken the House, so he would but have left the stairs and the Stallion upon them I dare say your Good-nature would have pardon'd the rest of the Damage, and promised your Soul as a Reward for the great Civility. Lard! Child (reply'd Madam) you are strangely out of Humour to-Night; indeed I did see a Gentleman on the stairs, but did not know his Name was *Stallion*; and I was so frighted I never asked it. Bless us! how came you to know on't, I am afraid you deal with the D——l, and dare say he wanted you.

I believe he did (return'd the Spouse) for you and I are one: Pray what Colour was he of? Colour (said she) he was so black I should have taken him for the Fiend that made the Noise, but that I saw a Full-bottom'd Wigg in Flames; and I never heard the D——l was a Beau.

Verily, my Fair One (reply'd the scoffing Husband) you grow strangely ignorant, I never took you for a downright Wit; but methinks, your small Understanding begins to dwindle into nothing: Come, let us to Bed, and try if Sleep can recover what seems to decay.

Poor Sir *John* was now doing Pennance, and the Fiery Trial he had so lately gone through made him believe there was a *Purgatory* in this World, whatever there was in another. He had had a Long Voluptuous Reign, without any considerable Disturbance till this last Engagement, which proved very mortifying; and upon which he had Leisure Hours to make the following Remarks.

He said to himself, A common Woman, like a common Thief, was best to deal with, because nothing worse than what we may reasonably expect can happen from either; but a sly lurking Whore or Thief, steals upon us insensibly, and draws us to Ruin in the midst of security, where we can have no Defence because we fear no Danger. Again, to intrigue with a Married Woman was (as Experience had lately taught him) a very unsafe Thing, because the Love or Jealousy of the Husband often makes him watchful; while the Policy of the Wife, to establish her Character in his Opinion, sacrifices the Lover to her own Designs, and brings him in the whole Criminal, when he should only have been a sharer with herself.

These Thoughts, and some other of the same Kind made the Knight resolve against a Married Mistress for the Time to come, tho' he often said, the best Way to shew a Man his Folly in running into Matrimony was to lie with his Wife, and let him know it. While he was thus entertaining himself with Thoughts, one of his Servants brought him a Letter, which contained something a little unusual.

Dear Knight,

AS Partners are, or should be always Friends, I hope the sharing of a Woman betwixt us will make no Difference, at least, when I am sole Proprietor, and yet willing to give up Part of my Right to One I never saw. Business, which You know must be done, calls me away for a few Days; and as my Dear Wife may have Business too, I beg You will assist her in it till my Return: Women, You know, when alone, are but indifferent Contrivers; and if I leave my Spouse a Good Assistant in the Person of Sir John Galliard *(for that I hear is Your Name) I shall expect at least Your Thanks for the Favour, and a Positive Answer* per Bearer, *who will tell You how to Direct it, or at least convey it safe to the Hand of*

Your most Affectionate,

Humble C——d.

Sir *John* had so many Humble C——ds all over the Town, that, being a stranger to the Hand, he could not possibly tell from whom the Kind Invitation came; and was at a stand-still till he called for, and Examined the Messenger, who made no scruple (as by Order) to let him know he came from the Master of the last House he had been at. Sir *John* being persuaded the Wife was the Contriver, at least an Accomplice in the Cracker-Scheme, was resolved, by way of Revenge, to answer the Letter as little to their satisfaction as the Visit was to his; he therefore order'd the Fellow to wait, and writ what you may read.

Dear C——d,

THOU art certainly one of the Civilest Cornutes[136] *I ever had yet to deal with; and to let Thee see I have some Good-Manners, I here send my Thanks*

for the Kind Invitation You have sent me, but am forced to tell You, the Feast
is too luscious, and has cloy'd me more than once. I therefore desire You will
enquire after somebody that has a stronger Stomach, and a better Digestion,
to eat up those Orts you Keck[137] at Yourself. And now, by Way of Postscript,
Thou art to know, that I should have sent Thee another sort of Message, but
that I think it a little hard to lye with Thy Wife, and then kill Thee for it.

J.G.

I might here tell the Reader what Effects this Letter had upon the Loving Pair it went to: But as Domestick Jars are trifling to those that have nothing to do with them, I shall say no more of the Matter, but go back to Sir *John*, whose Mortification daily increased, when he considered he was not only confined to his Lodgings, but to a Parcel of stale Mistresses, of whom he had long been tired, and no present Hope of Dear Variety: Beside, he saw himself a standing Jest to them, and every one made an Invidious Remark upon his Misfortune, though none of them knew how he came by it. Lard! Sir *John* (cry'd one of the Queans) you look as if you had got a flap over the Nose with a French Faggot-stick. Another said, he had burnt his Fingers playing at Hot-Cockles with the Drabs[138] of Drury. A third said, she believed his Heart had got a Fever, and his Stomach had been blister'd for it. All which, for the present, he was forced to bear, but resolved to leave the Town for some time, as soon as his Face was fit to be seen, which took up more Weeks than he was at first aware of. But what is Resolution without Inclination to keep it? Sir *John* was no sooner in a Condition to go Abroad, than he began to despise the Thoughts of the Country; He was now once more at liberty to cater for himself, and seek out New Game, after a surfeit of the Old. He had one choice Companion, among a great many more, whose Name was *Bousie*, and had been his Adviser and Assister in most of his Irregular Actions. This Gentleman was one Night at the Drawing-Room with a Good, Clever, Pretty Woman, when Sir *John* came there: And as he was always quick-sighted towards a New Female, he presently singled her out for his own, that is, till he had enough of her: He therefore made towards *Bousie*, and after the common Compliment, asked him aside, what Lady he had got? *Bousie* told him, it was his Sister; and hoped that Information would be sufficient to prevent all farther Inquiry after her, since he believed Sir *John* was too much his own Friend to marry any Woman, and too much his to debauch so near a Relation; but farther declar'd, that if he ever did attempt her Honour, he should meet with all the Resentment his Sword or Arm was capable of shewing. Sir *John* laugh'd at his Threats, and

said, Why, how now *Bousie?* I have often heard you say, nay swear, there was
not an Honest Woman within the Four Seas: And what the D——l is thy
Sister more than the rest of her Sex? Or, what is my Fault, that I may not have
her as soon as another? Keep your Temper, Sir *John* (reply'd Bully *Bousie*) while
Peace is the Word Bilbo[139] sleeps, but War will ensue, if you rouse the Dragon.
You will have need of one (return'd Sir *John*) to guard your Golden Pipkin,[140]
for you may depend upon it, I shall attack, and with some Fury too. *Bousie*
said, the Place they were in admitted of no Dispute; turned away, and went
again to the Lady.

Sir *John*, on the other side, Entertained the Fine Females of his Acquaintance with his usual Address and Gallantry, which *Bousie* observed, and took
that Opportunity of carrying off his Sister, as he called her; but was in Reality
an Innocent Girl, on whom he had Honourable Designs. However, they did
not get so cleverly away, but Sir *John's* watchful Eye catch'd their *Exit*, and
immediately made his own to keep within View of them, tho' they knew it
not, or ever once imagined he was near them.

But mark the Fate which Curiosity and Love of Variety brings upon us;
Sir *John*, fond of a New Face, which he resolv'd, if possible, to be better acquainted with, dog'd both her and *Bousie* into a Tavern. They took up a Room,
and Sir *John* the next to it, into which he convey'd himself without Noise or
Light, by a Wink on the Drawer, who, by the Force of Half a Crown, was
drawn to his Interest, and there heard all that pass'd betwixt them; but another
of the Drawers, who saw him go in the dark, and was in Fee with Mr. *Bousie*,
whisper'd him in the Ear, and told him where Sir *John* was. He nodded his
Head, and bid the Fellow be gone. He then took the Lady to the other End of
the Room, as if to shew her something writ upon a Pane in the Window; and
there begg'd of her, that when they return'd to their Seats she would seemingly
comply with whatever he propos'd to her; and he would give her his Reasons
another time. She consented, and they went again to the Fire. *Bousie* then
ask'd her how she liked the Drawing-Room, and the Fine Ladies she saw there?
Nay, Mr. *Bousie* (answer'd she) that Question ought to have been put to you;
mine should have been, how I liked the Fine Gentlemen? But who was that
you Talked to while we were there? I think he was much the Handsomest Man
in the Room.

Bousie was not a little vex'd to hear her say so, because he knew Sir *John*
did so too; but told her, that Gentleman was a Baronet, one who had had a
general Fund of Love for the whole Female World, and there is not a Woman
in this Town that has Youth and Beauty to reconcile her to his Notice, but he

either has had, will have, or would have an Intrigue with. I durst lay five Pieces, he is this Minute at my Lodgings enquiring after yours; for which Reason, if you will oblige me in so small a Matter, you shall change them this very Night, and lye in your Aunt *Hannah's* Bed till she returns from *Hamstead*: But don't you dream of the Knight, for them very Lodgings were his once; and it was there I knew him first.

The Lady stared at what she did not understand, but seem'd to comply. And when they had Supp'd, away they went: But Sir *John* was before-hand with them, who no sooner heard how the Lady was to be dispos'd on, and preserv'd from him, than he got out of his Hole, and went off, in order to secure her.

When he lodg'd in the House *Bousie* spoke of, he lost the Key of his Bed-Chamber-Door (the same the Lady was to lye in) and got another made; but he having left the first at a Friend's House, he got it again, and laid it by, lest he should happen to lose the other: The fair Opportunity of getting to the Lady soon reminded him of it, and he went directly home, put it in his Pocket, and then took his way towards *Bousie's* Lodgings; where being well known, he went directly up-Stairs, without any Questions ask'd, or Notice taken, as if he had been going to *Bousie*, with whom he us'd sometimes to lye; and by the Help of the Key, he convey'd himself into the Chamber, where he expected the Lady, laughing in his Sleeve, to think how he should mump[141] poor *Bousie* with all his Blustering; and when he had fix'd himself to his own liking he lay Perdue,[142] waiting for the Happy Approach of the Lady.

Mean while *Bousie*, who well knew Sir *John* would leave no Attempt untry'd to get to his Mistress, conducted her safe to her own Lodgings, and then went to an Old Madam of his Acquaintance, and desired her to put a Girl into his Hands that had not lately been under the Surgeons. In short, he would have one (he said) that could pepper, tho' she was not Pepper-Proof.[143] The B—d understood him, and accordingly supply'd him; he gave the Girl her Q,[144] told her what to say, and conducted her to the Chamber-Door, where he bid her Good-Night, and left her. It was now *Bousie's* Turn to laugh, who knew Sir *John* had a Key to that Door, and did not doubt but he had already taken Possession, when he heard he had been up-Stairs, and nobody saw him come down again.

This Rencounter proved the very worst that ever poor Sir *John* was engaged in; for tho' he had had many Skirmishes with the Ladies, they had hitherto prov'd light ones: But in this last Battle he was almost Mortally wounded: And it gave him such a thorough Mortification, that he swore to himself, if ever he got well again, he would demand Satisfaction of *Bousie*, and then retire into the Country, where he design'd to continue some Time before he saw *London* again.

Bousie, on the other Side, who knew a Quarrel would ensue, plaid least in Sight till Sir *John* was laid up pretty safe for a while, and then got the Girl's Consent to marry her, which when over he went directly into the Country to her Father's House; and I never heard Sir *John* and he met afterwards; for he thought it not worth his while to follow him, and so the Breach heal'd itself. But the Knight grew extreamly impatient; and tho' he could not reach *Bousie* with the Point of his Sword, he sent many a Curse after the Cause of his Sufferings, and more Intolerable Confinement: but Time recall'd his former Health and Liberty; neither of which obstructed his Design of going into the Country, because he began to be tired of the Town.

The next Post he sent Lady *Galliard* a very welcome Epistle, with his Resolution of making her a Visit in a few Days. She immediately prepar'd for a Sumptuous Reception of him in the Country, and he in Town for a Speedy Journey to her. In Three Days he arriv'd at *Galliard*-Hall, from whence he had been Four whole Years. His Mother receiv'd him with Open Joyful Arms; and making bold with a Line or two of Mr. *Cowley*'s, said,

> *Go let the Fatted Calf be Kill'd,*
> *My Prodigal's come home at last.*

May I, Sir *John* (continu'd she) repeat the Two next Lines?

> *With Noble Resolution fill'd,*
> *And fill'd with Sorrow for the past.*[145]

But before Sir *John* could make any Return to what Lady *Galliard* said, the poor disconsolate Mr. *Friendly*, who expected him much about the Hour he came, enter'd the Hall to make him a Kind and Early Visit, but with Looks so alter'd, that Sir *John*, conscious of the Cause, beheld him as well with a Pitying, as a Guilty Eye; he saw a Man, once Happy in his Family and Fortune, Reduced to the utmost Disquietudes, and laid under the Heavy Pressures of a continu'd Uneasiness; he observ'd his Eyes grown languid, his Cheeks pale and thin, the whole Man wasted, lean and old with Trouble; when at the same Time he was forced to Reproach himself, and secretly say— Ah! *Galliard!* Thou art the Cause of all. Mr. *Friendly* (said he, taking him to his Arms) I cannot say I am glad to see you, because I can hardly persuade myself 'tis you:

Believe me, Sir, a good-natur'd Tear steals to my Eyes to see so great an Alteration in you.

O Sir *John* (reply'd that worthy Man) you see, in me, a Wretch depriv'd of Joy, of Ease, of Comfort; one, whose daily Reflections on his own Misfortunes make a Havock of his Peace, and is in continual Struggles with my Heart to rend its Strings asunder. I cannot look back to the Happy Time, when I could have told myself, none upon Earth enjoy'd more, or greater Tranquility than I; none was surrounded with greater Blessings: And when I tell myself how great a Change succeeded all my Bliss; it withers all my Reason, blows a blasting Vapor over my Philosophy, and makes me wish I had been born wretched, to prevent the Knowledge of what I have lost.

I see Sir *John* (continu'd he) you pity your poor Afflicted Friend, your Eyes declare the Sentiments of your Heart for one, who, if he has any Remains of Content, it is to see you again in Safety at your own House; and may the Return of your Reason recall your scatter'd Resolutions and force them to joyn in the firmest Bands to make you my Reverse: May Kind Heaven shower down all those Blessings on your Head, which it has seen good to deprive me of.

These Words were succeeded by a pretty long Silence, and some Tears on both Sides, when Sir *John* raising his Eyes from the Ground, found a sudden Alteration in his Breast, Honour, Pity, Gratitude, and every Noble Passion of the Mind, had seiz'd the whole Man, as if they had combin'd by Force of arms to rescue his Soul from all their own Opposites.

He could not hear such Kind Expressions from a Man he had so greatly injur'd, without the utmost Remorse; and as he now began to look upon his past Life with some Contempt, he felt the Dawnings of a secret Impulse, to do the Injur'd Justice.

Come Mr. *Friendly* (said the Knight) call up your Courage to your own Assistance, and try to banish this corroding Grief that preys upon your very Vitals. I confess I am not much acquainted with the Decrees of Heaven, nor have I ever much concern'd myself about them: but if there be any such Thing, they will certainly disengage your Innocent Heart from that black Cloud which eclipses all your Joy, and taints all your Morsels with the worst of Bitters: you have often, and I believe with much Sincerity, declar'd yourself my Friend; I now give you here my Hand, as an Earnest of a most Faithful Return; and promise, in the Presence of an unseen BEING, that I will do all I can to restore your Ease—— Nay, do not look surpris'd; that Promise has Weight and Energy in it, and will do more than you at present comprehend. Tell me, may I see poor *Nancy Friendly?* Your Words Sir *John* (reply'd the Father) thrills through every Vein, and reaches my Afflicted Broken Heart: Oh! say, but say it soon, Are you the Father of her Child? And will you do her Justice? Tell me I conjure you, was she consenting to her own undoing, and has she lied thus long, in saying she knew not when her Shame commenced. Mr. *Friendly* (returned Sir *John*) it is a little uncustomary as well as unnatural to accuse ourselves, but I dare venter to excuse her, and believe her a Woman of strict Virtue and Honour, nor did I ever propose any Thing to her that could touch either, which I am satisfied she will confirm if she will give me leave to see her, and that I earnestly desire to do. You shall freely have my Consent to see her (replied Mr. *Friendly*) but she has never seen the Face of any Man but mine since her Child was born, who is now turn'd of two Years old, and has, I must needs say, the very Face of Sir *John Galliard.*

If you see her, at least if she sees you, it must be by chance, she often walks in the Garden, which is her utmost Limits, and if you come in an Afternoon and rush in abruptly upon us, she will have no Time to abscond and then you must see her of Course, but Sir *John*, the answers you have made to my past Questions seem a little ambiguous; if you are what you have promised to be, my Friend, you will at once end those Sufferings which I now must believe you have created, and if so, 'tis doubling your Cruelty to procrastinate my Ease. When we are once possest our Malady is incurable (answered Sir *John*) a few Minutes make but a trifling Addition, and there is no Happiness so exquisit as that we are surprized into. I desire Mr. *Friendly* will dine with me to-morrow, and at your Return home this Night, take no Notice of my Design, convey my Service to your Lady and Daughter, but give them no reason to expect a Visit so soon. Mr. *Friendly*, as desired, dined the next Day with Sir *John*, whose Impatience to see the young Lady made him both hasten and shorten his Meal, which when over, Mr. *Friendly* went back to get his Daughter into the Garden, and had not been there ten Minutes before the Knight appeared. Miss *Friendly* blush'd extremely at the Sight, and look'd with some Displeasure at the Freedom he took, which he would not mind, but going up hastily to her gave her a Country-kiss, and cry'd, *Nancy*, how dost Girl. That very Minute Mr. *Friendly* was call'd in to hear a Cause (for he was a Justice of the Peace) betwixt two well-bred Scolds, whose Tongues had given place to their Fingers, and Blood-shed and Battery ensued. But the poor young Lady was in double Confusion when she saw herself alone with Sir *John*, and said, I cannot give you Sir the common Compliment of saying, I am glad to see you, because I am glad to see no body, for Gladness has left my Heart ever since I had my little Boy: I have got a little Boy Sir *John*, did you never hear of it, but he is a fatherless one, for no body will own him, and I can lay him to no body's Charge, all People say he is like Sir *John Galliard*, but I am sure he is no way concerned in his Being, because he was gone to *France* when my little Mackroon was begotten. No matter Madam (replied Sir *John*) where I was, since he is so much my Likeness, I'll adopt him and take him for my own, whoever is the Father, *Nancy Friendly* is undoubtedly the Mother, and I will never be ashamed to father her Productions. Will you give him to me? Give him? Sir *John* (returned the Lady) do you think I want a charitable Hand to take my Child off mine? No! As you have already observed, I am certainly the Mother, though I can still say some unknown Chance bestow'd him upon me, and it is very possible you, with the rest of the World, will laugh at me when I affirm it, yet it is true, and perhaps he may yet live to recompence those melancholy Hours his Birth has given me. When he first made his Appearance in Life, I had an Abhorrence of the very sight of him, but Nature pleaded strongly in his Behalf, and I must own he is now so dear to me that the Wealth of the Universe should not buy him from me, but see where the little Chance-ling comes. Sir *John* at Nature's Call, ran to meet it, took it to his Bosom and embraced it with a Father's Love. It is indeed my Representative (said the real Papa) and what have you called him? *John* (answer'd the Lady) after my own Father. And after his own Father too (return'd the Knight) for ought you know, since you are at a Loss to find out who that is. That is too true (return'd she) I am so unhappy as to be a perfect Stranger to him that wounded my Honour, blasted my Fame, and left my Mind a continued Chaos never to know either Form or Regularity more, don't you pity me Sir *John?* Yes I am sure you do, for our Fathers always loved, and you and I have never quarrel'd: You make me melancholy Madam (replied the Knight) upon my S—l[146] you do, but come my *Nancy* I'll get you a Husband shall banish all your Shame and re-establish that Peace in your Mind which seems at such a Distance. Ah Sir *John* (returned she) I do not want a Husband for my self, but a Father for my Child, and till he is found I will never know a Man, as for my Shame it is too well establish'd to be displaced, 'tis entail'd upon my wretched Days for ever, and Peace is become so great a Stranger that if it were to make me a Visit I should look surprised and cry I know you not. But suppose *Nancy* (return'd Sir *John*) I should chance to be let into this grand Secret, and can tell you who the Father of your Child is, suppose he should prove an inferior Rascal, and I, in pity to your Wrongs, and instigated by Friendship, should offer to marry you, which would you take? Neither Sir (replied the Lady) for I have already declared against any but the Father of my Child, and I should soon declare against him too, if he should prove what you have described, No, I'll never think of Marriage, even that will never retrieve my lost Credit, the good natured World knows my Fault, and it will be sure to keep it in continual Remembrance. You wrong yourself Madam (answer'd Sir *John*) when you own a Crime you are not guilty of, you say you know nothing of the Fault laid to your Charge, how then are you culpable?

Alas Sir (answered she) is not my Child a living Demonstration against me, and who do you think will believe me when I urge Innocence and Ignorance. I will my dear *Nancy* (said the Knight, snatching her to his Arms) I know your Innocence, I am the Brute that wrong'd you of what you held dear, that plundered your Honour and caused your Shame, the Father of your Child, and the Ravisher of his Mother, but— Hold Sir *John* (interrupted Miss *Friendly*) you have said too much already to be believed, this condescending Confession must proceed from your Height of Friendship, you love my Father and would take a bad Bargain off his Hands, he, as well as I ought to acknowledge the Favour, but it would be the worst Return in Life to believe Sir *John Galliard's* Soul could be guilty of so poor, so low, so base an Action, no, in pity to yourself unsay it all, and keep up that good Opinion I always had of your Merit. Look'ye *Nancy* (returned the Knight) this is too nice a Point to be entered into with much Examination, and I have certainly done Things since I was born which perhaps I should blush at now, but if I am willing to own my Fault and make you Restitution I would not have you give yourself Airs, but take me at my Word when (Liberty forgive me) I say I will marry you, and if your lost Honour be what you lament, I will restore it with the Addition of a Ladyship and a good Estate. The poor Lady trembled with Resentment, but recalling her Temper said as follows: Your barbarous Usage Sir *John*, might very well countenance a firm Resolution of seeing your Face no more, which I should certainly make were I only to suffer for it, but I have a Child which is very dear to me, and in pity to him I will close with your Proposals, provided you will promise to order Matters so, that he may be the undoubted Heir to your Estate, I know it must be the Work of a Parliament,[147] and you must expose yourself on such an Occasion, but as you are the only Aggressor you must be the Sufferer too: These are the Conditions, Sir *John*, if ever you and I meet again. Madam (said the Knight) I have promised to marry you, and if I can but keep in that mind till the Deed confirms my Word, I shall never after deny you any thing; your Child I am sure is mine, and it would be a pitty to let him suffer for my Faults: No! *Nancy*, I'll find a way without the Legislature, to make him Heir to all, but here's your Father coming, whose Advice I will always follow for the future, let us meet him and go in.

Miss *Friendly*'s Affairs look'd now with a very propitious Aspect, and Sir *John* who had for many Years indulged an Aversion to a settled State of Life, was now resolved to hasten his new Design least a returning Qualm should rise to stop his generous and honourable Intentions. The very Night before the Nuptials young *Friendly* return'd from his Travels, a most compleat, clever Gentleman, to the unspeakable Joy of his glad Parents, it was whispered that a Love-Suit commenced betwixt him and Miss *Dolly Galliard*, but as they were the very Reverse of one another I dare not affirm it, but shall leave their Story to that grand Tell-tale old Father TIME to begin and finish.

As for Sir *John Galliard* I would have him acknowledge the Favour I have done him, in making him a Man of Honour at last, but withall I here tell him I have set two Spies to watch his Motions and Behaviour, and if I hear of any false Steps or Relapses, I shall certainly set them in a very clear Light, and send them by Way of Advertisement to the Publick.

FINIS.

APPENDIX

~

FROM *The Grub-street Journal* NUMBER 80,
THURSDAY, JULY 15, 1731.

From the PEGASUS *in Grub-street.*

To Mr. Bavius,[1] *Secretary to the Grub street Society.*

Cambridge, July 29.

Much respected GRUB,
The gentle usage with which you treat all your Members (except your Orator)[2] hath embolden'd me to address you in this manner, and forbids me to despair of receiving the decorum due to my Sex, as well as the respect due to me as a member. *My Plays, my Novels, my Wit (of which the young Students here can testify) I think may sufficiently entitle me to this illustrious character; yet that I may be owned and recorded so in one of your Journals, is the occasion of this Epistle: —— You must know then, dear BAVY, that finding this a very bad place for one of our Society to live in by their Wit only, I frugally resolved, in imitation of a late Brother[3] of ours, to turn an additional penny, by selling an inspiring cup, not of your insipid Parnassian Water, but true Heliconian Punch.[4] How much even your Society owes to my Punch, I appeal to our famous Jonian Punsters, Orators and Poets.[5] — My scheme succeeded, and to the character of a Wit, having that added of being a perfect Mistress in the finesses of love, my house was not only filled with Freshmen and Under-graduates; but learned M.A.'s and reverend D.D.'s[6] have received not a little delight and profit from my instructions. My success in this way

also exceeded expectation; I have made a young Fellow Commoner just come from kissing his Mothers maids, a perfect master of intrigue in a week; a northern Jonian paste his wig,[7] and with a tolerable assurance, hand an Alderman's Daughter to St. Mary's his first Sunday. Nay, the polite Trinitonians[8] allow I'm perfectly instructed in the rudiments of Love, tho' they will not grant me the character of a Wit. From this last article, BAVY, all my misfortunes flow: for on the repute of my being a Wit, part of my business arises; and to obtain of them to pronounce me a Wit, I pronounc'd them so. What was the consequence of this? Why, immediately they set up for Wits, quitted their smart dress (for which they were so fam'd) for a wit-like slovenly air; they used me like Wits, left off admiring my writings, and wrote themselves, especially Satyrs and Sonnets; they run a tick,[9] and never paid me; if I sent never so handsome a letter, they were not at chambers. In short, they set up for all the polite accomplishments of your modern London Wits. What could I do? If I spoke to 'em myself, they put me off with something they would have pass for wit. At last, upon arguing the case with some of the greatest of these Wits (i.e. those who had the greatest scores) they agreed, if I would own myself a Grubean, and get myself inroll'd in one of your next Journals, they'd immediately pay off their ticks.— Tho' I myself have the greatest veneration and esteem for the name of a GRUB,[10] I must confess it bears no great character here: and by this artifice of theirs, I'm brought to this Dilemma, I must either own myself a Wit, or I must disown my debt. I can ill bear to lose either: I can't afford to give 'em my debts; and on the reputation of my wit, part of my trade subsists. Yet after many serious considerations (if you'd entitle me to my debts and record me a Member, by inserting this) I rather chuse to be a Grubean with my money, than have only the name of Wit without. I am (on admission) your Sister,

PHILOGRUBAEA.[11]

* *Mrs. D. wrote several bawdy Novels, and the Northern Heiress.*

FROM *The Grub-street Journal* NUMBER 81, THURSDAY JULY 22, 1731.

From the PEGASUS *in Grub-street.*

For Mr. ——— to be left at his Chambers in Grub-street.

SIR,

Tho' my Hand trembles and my Eyes are allmost blind, I can not forbear sending you my best thanks for the *True* Grubean Letter you publish't last week in my name, it is certainly so very full of wit that you have done me too great an Honour and I can not tell how to get out of your debt, and yet I fear part of the obligation is due to a second Person, for one single Head could never find *Stuff*[12] enough for such a worthy and learned Epistle, I therefore fancy you call'd in the assistance of Glib Tongued wife of a certain Gentlemen *Tailor* who fancys like your dear self She has wit enough to serve a whole Parish, but I will now lay by the wit and come to the Malice of it which is I own inimatable and there I believe she helpt you again, but as you are a Friend I do not much care if I give you the Merit of that intirely to your self.

As for the Licquor you speak of, had it been Eleemosynary[13] it wou'd have had no fault and had I never desired to be paid for it I should have had none neither but a Dun is the Devil and I was the Devil upon Dun.[14] The *Novels* may e'ne fight their own Battles all I shall say for or against them is, that they are too unfashionable to have one word of Baudy in them, the Readers are the best judges and to them I appeal; it is a pitty any Gentleman shoul'd make himself a Lier where so many are ready to confute him, but he is doubtless a Great Man, and yet by my troath, I think he has very little to do now the Grand affair is over, however he has written a speech that make every body Laugh tho' there is not one jest in it.

Cambridge, July 29, 1731.

Notes

1. Bavius] A Roman poet who is remembered today because of his role as an enemy of Horace and Virgil, the great poets of his day; Pope uses him in "The Epistle to Dr. Arbuthnot" as an illustration of "a rule, / No creature smarts so little as a fool" for despite everything he has said about the grubs, "Whom have I hurt? . . . Does not one table Bavius still admit?" (lines 83–84, 94, 99).

2. your Orator] John Henley (1692–1756), included in the list of dunces in "The Epistle to Dr. Arbuthnot" (see n. 1, above) and in *The Dunciad,* 3.195–212.

3. a late Brother of ours] Ned Ward (1667–1731), who died in June, just a month before the "letter" was published. He is chiefly known for *The London Spy,* a monthly journal published between November 1698 and May 1700, but he wrote many other works besides, describing and satirizing the people and places of contemporary England. His less-than-reverent approach to the powerful of his day frequently got him into trouble, which included time in the pillory and a spot in Pope's *Dunciad.* By 1713 he had earned enough money by his writing to set himself up in an alehouse. Information from Ned Ward, *The London Spy,* ed. Paul Hyland (East Lansing, Mich.: Colleagues Press, 1993). The comparison is not one Davys would have welcomed, since she repeatedly sought to establish the respectability of her own position.

4. Parnassian . . . Heliconian] Parnassus was the home of the muses in classical literature; Helicon was a mountain in Boetia sacred to the muses; two rivers, the Hippocrene and the Aganippe, flowed from it. Punch: a drink composed of a mixture of some form of alcoholic beverage with spices and sometimes milk or water.

5. Jonian Punsters, Orators and Poets] The undergraduates of St. John's College, Cambridge; see introduction, and the preface to *RC.*

6. D.D.'s] Doctors of Divinity, usually clergyman.

7. paste his wig] Transformation of a country boy into a city beau, wig and all.

8. Trinitonians] Members of Trinity College, one of the wealthiest of the Cambridge Colleges.

9. run a tick] Keep a running (unpaid) bill.

10. GRUB] The Grubs were the impoverished hack writers who were looked upon with disdain by writers such as Swift and Pope who satirized them in works like *A Tale of a Tub* and *The Dunciad.* The satire continues in *The Grub-street Journal,* which reflects Pope's view of the hacks.

11. Philo-Grubaea] "Love of Grubs."

12. Stuff] Generally a term of contempt, and not used in our more neutral and generic sense of "matter"; it therefore sharpens the irony of the previous compliments.

13. Eleemosynary] "Of the nature of alms; given or done as an act of charity; gratuitous" (OED).

14. See British Museum Catalogue of Prints, item no. 1039 (1672) for a broadside entitled "The Devil upon Dunn: or the Downfall of the Upstart Chymist: Being the Second Edition of a Late Song: To the Tune of Smoak us and Choak us," which suggests that Davys is being allusive here.

Notes on the Novels

Abbreviations

AR	*The Accomplished Rake*
FL	*Familiar Letters Betwixt a Gentleman and a Lady*
DNB	*Dictionary of National Biography*
McBurney	*Four Before Richardson: Selected English Novels, 1720–1727*, ed. William H. McBurney (Lincoln: Univ. of Nebraska Press, 1963)
OED	*Oxford English Dictionary*
RC	*The Reform'd Coquet*

Notes to *The Reform'd Coquet*

1. The title page gives the title as *The Reform'd Coquet; A NOVEL*, while the first page, and the headers in the body of the novel, call it *The Reform'd Coquet; or Memoirs of Amoranda*. The novel does not consist of memoirs as we understand the term, that is the reminiscences of a life presented by the central personality. Instead, "memoirs" here is used in the sense of "memories of."

2. "provided with a Racket to strike it from themselves"] The witty Gentleman is Jonathan Swift. Preface to *A Tale of a Tub:* "'Tis but a *Ball* bandied to and fro, and every Man carries a *Racket* about Him to strike it from himself among the rest of the Company." He is not, however, speaking of vanity, but of the inefficacy of Satyr addressed against abstractions: "But Satyr being levelled at all, is never resented for an offence by any, since every individual Person makes bold to understand it of others, and very wisely removes his particular Part of the Burthen upon the Shoulders of the World, which are broad enough, and able to bear it."

3. One of the mysteries of Mary Davys is her finances—while she kept her coffeehouse going throughout most of her life in Cambridge, she complains on more than one occasion of lack of funds. This reference implies that she had more money prior to 1724, and she may have turned to writing to support herself when the coffeehouse became less profitable. Her pejorative reference to the South Sea bubble (see below, n.

9) might be another clue, although castigating the South Sea project was common practice at the time. Claiming to be forced into writing and publication by dire necessity was another convention; the excuse of idleness, also a convention, seems somewhat unlikely, given the demands of running a coffeehouse.

4. The Rev. Peter Davys was buried on 6 November 1698, at St. Patrick's Cathedral (see introduction). "The Gown" is the cassock, or clerical robe, and thus is a metonymical reference to the clergy.

5. The Rev. Dr. Burnet] Not the celebrated historian, who died in 1715; possibly his son, also named Gilbert (1690–1726), prebend of Salisbury and chaplain to the king, although the DNB does not indicate that he ever received the D.D. It is most likely, however, that this is the Reverend Dr. Thomas Burnet, who died in 1750, and who certainly did receive a doctorate. He was (confusingly) also a prebend of Salisbury and wrote religious treatises.

6. Martha Blount (1690–1762)] Friend of Alexander Pope, to whom he dedicated several works.

7. Alexander Pope (1688–1744) and John Gay (1685–1732)] With Jonathan Swift and others, members of a collaborative group of writers who called themselves the Scriblerus Club. Thus, while Swift's name is absent from the list of subscribers, his influence can be seen in the generosity of his friends, whose names would add literary cachet to Davys's volume. Pope also subscribed to *The Collected Works* a year later.

8. byass] Bias, influence.

9. The South Sea bubble was a speculative venture, originally for investment in Spanish America, which, when it collapsed in 1721, caused the ruin of many people. It developed into a run of investments in many impossible and crack-brained schemes, and its name became synonymous with risky and foolish financial speculation.

10. A condensation of the Stoic philosophy which denies human suffering and pleasure, and privileges the spiritual and intellectual.

11. Clandestine marriage] Secret marriage, generally an elopement to avoid disapproving parents, and notoriously difficult to prove. See Laurence Stone, *The Road to Divorce* (Oxford: Oxford Univ. Press, 1990), 96–120, for legal definitions and implications.

12. Note the discrepancy in the names of the two brothers—the younger signs his letter "Traffick" (below, p. 25). While it is a good allegorical name for a merchant, it means his last name is different from his brother's. The device of East-India Merchant brother as potential financial angel is one Davys also uses in *The Merry Wanderer*.

13. Babies] Dolls.

14. Jackanapes] A foolish or silly boy.

15. "Poor *Amoranda*, what will be thy Fate? / So soon to like the Love, the Lover hate"] In keeping with Davys's use of dramatic form to shape her novels, this couplet resembles those used by playwrights such as Congreve to mark the end of an act. Davys uses the couplet to punctuate her remarks on Amoranda's behavior.

16. Davys did have a sister (see introduction) but there is no way of knowing whether this incident is autobiographical or merely a cautionary tale told in the voice of the narrator's persona.

17. Interregnum] Literally, between the reigns. Used historically to refer to the period between the reigns of Charles I and Charles II, 1649–60, when England was a republic; here the image is domesticated to refer to the time when Amoranda is living without a guardian.

18. Jessamine] Jasmine.

19. Helen ran away with Paris rather than being raped in the sense that we understand the word; the term "rape" included the sense of abduction as well as sexual assault. The scene is "unlike his own design" because he has no intention of running away with her much less causing an international incident; far from launching a thousand ships, he merely wants to seduce Amoranda and leave her behind.

20. From *The Old Batchelour*, 1.1, by William Congreve (1670–1729): "I thought a Contemplative Lover could no more have parted with his Bed in a Morning than a' could have slept in't."

21. Lard] Lord.

22. Hue and Cry] To raise a hue and cry is to make a public announcement of a search for a criminal or missing person.

23. Halter] Stone says that the kidnapping of heiresses was a penal (or criminal) offence (*Road to Divorce*, 99), and all felonies were capital offences. Not only was it a capital offence, but the offender could not claim benefit of clergy (prove literacy) and escape the gallows. Callid and Froth's plan fits all the criteria: the motive is clearly money, they intend to carry her away against her will, and one of them plans to marry her.

24. Cuts] "Applied to a ready way of casting lots, by the chance drawing of sticks or straws of unequal length" (OED).

25. what a cold Bed is to a Melon-Seed] In addition to making an obvious sexual remark, Lord Lofty is using an accurate gardening metaphor. Melons, being heavy feeders, must be planted in a bed that is well covered with dung or compost in order to thrive; it is called a "warm bed" from the action of the compost. Thus, the starvation in a cold bed. I am indebted to Douglas Chambers for this information.

26. Lud] Lord.

27. positive] Dictatorial.

28. Gripes] "Spasms of pain, pangs of grief or affliction" (OED).

29. Purlieus] Borders; in this case, metaphorical—Amoranda is being accused of attempting to make all men her "subjects."

30. drubbing] Beating.

31. Closet] A small private room.

32. take up the Cudgels] Cudgels are clubs, but the term was used colloquially to mean entering into a dispute.

33. pull him by the nose] Again, a colloquial usage, implying initiating a fight by insulting behavior, in order to teach the opponent a lesson.

34. Seer-cloth] Normally spelt "sere," it refers to cloth that has become worn and thin with age and is used for bandages (see OED "sere" 2).

35. Desert] Dessert; also a pun on "deserve" in the sense of getting one's just deserts.

36. Catterpillars] Caterpillars. While generally referring to the larva of the moth or

butterfly, the word's meaning can be extended to other insects; the OED also notes a figurative meaning: "a rapacious person; an extortioner; one who preys on society."

37. Argus] The one-hundred-eyed watchdog sent by Hera to guard Io so that Zeus could not seduce her. The plan was foiled when Hermes lulled Argus to sleep with music.

38. "Desperate Disease must have a desperate Cure"] Guy Fawkes's justification for his involvement in the Gunpowder Plot: "Desperate diseases require desperate remedies"; Antonia Fraser believes it must have been a catchphrase among the conspirators (*Faith and Treason: The Story of the Gunpowder Plot* [New York: Doubleday, 1996], 174). Shakespeare also picks it up (see *Hamlet*, 3.9) and it may have been proverbial by this point. Davys does not present herself as one likely to be a plot supporter (see reference to the Jesuits below, n. 67).

39. Buttery] A pantry, which originally got its name from being the place in which butts of beer were stored, but quickly became the designation for general storage of food.

40. Scrutore] Escritoire, a small writing desk, sometimes small enough to be portable, although Altemira's appears to be a stationary piece of furniture.

41. in *Foro Conscientiae*] According to his conscience; he means that they have a kind of contract marriage. See Stone, *Road to Divorce*, 67–95.

42. Friend] In the sense of patron and benefactor, not of companion or equal.

43. Hymen] Greek god of marriage.

44. Patches] Small pieces of black fabric or plaster, used among the fashionable as a means of highlighting and ornamenting the face; they were also used to cover the face sores of persons with venereal disease.

45. Quean] Prostitute; woman of no virtue. Also used, as in this case, as a general-purpose pejorative.

46. Zouns] Generally spelt "zounds"; a common expletive deriving from a contraction of the phrase "God's wounds."

47. Sir Roger de Coverly] Sp. Coverley; recurring character in Addison's and Steele's *Spectator Papers*. See *Spectator* 109 (5 July 1711), describing the plight of three sisters, who were members of his family. Two of them never married because the middle (homely) one had their dowries added to her own and ran off with a fortune-hunter. Sir Roger remarks "Misfortunes happen in all families."

48. canonical hours] Amoranda is quite right: the hours at which the canons (laws of the church) allowed persons to marry were from eight in the morning to noon.

49. License] Valid marriages required that banns, an announcement of the intention of a couple to be married, be read aloud in their parish churches on three successive Sundays; failing banns, a couple in a hurry or wishing to avoid publicity could get a license. Note the disapproval of Parson Andrews in Henry Fielding's *Joseph Andrews* when Joseph and Fanny ask to be married by license, an action which he considers representative of indecent haste (vol. 4, ch. 8). But it was much easier for the aristocracy to get a special license than it was for the lower classes like Joseph and Fanny because it cost money, and one had to approach a representative of the bishop to get one. See Stone, *Road to Divorce*.

50. her own name] That is, she must give her true name instead of Amoranda's when she makes her vows so that the marriage is not invalidated by her using an assumed name; on the other hand, she must be quiet enough so that Lofty does not catch on and halt the ceremony before the marriage is irrevocable.

51. "throw the Stocking"] A custom very like ours of throwing the garter and the bouquet; these bedside wedding night visitations were traditional.

52. Sack-Posset] A warm alcoholic drink. Sack is a Spanish wine very like sherry; a posset is a drink made with milk, sometimes with sugar and spices (and in this case, sack) added, "formerly much used as a delicacy, and as a remedy for colds or other affections" (OED).

53. "Work of my Grandmother" refers to the hangings and bedspread. But obviously the bed itself is quite large as well. The Great Bed of Ware, which measures 10 feet by 11 feet, got its name from the town in Hertfordshire where it was part of the furnishings of the inn and was meant for multiple occupants. It is now in the Victoria and Albert Museum in London.

54. Desarts] Deserts. Uninhabited, uncultivated wilderness, rather than today's connotation of barren sand and aridity.

55. Trapan'd] Entrapped. Not to be confused with the more generally understood sense of boring through bone with a surgical instrument. The OED lists the word as Davys is using it as a separate meaning with unknown derivation, possibly thieves' slang.

56. Viands] Cooked meats.

57. Screech-Owl] Because owls were believed to be blind in daylight, they were considered symbolic of those who denied the truth (light) and turned to falsehood (darkness). See T.H. White, trans. and ed., *The Bestiary: A Book of Beasts* (New York: G.P. Putnam, 1960). Their cry was thought to be an omen of death.

58. his Men] The pronouns are confusing here; although his own attendant has every right to be exasperated with him, Biranthus is killed by one of the stranger's servants.

59. In modern French, "Je ne sais quoi," trans. "I do not know what," sometimes used to mean "that certain [ineffable] something."

60. fit] "Fit you for this" means "get my own back," as in "I'll pay you back for this."

61. I-cod] By God.

62. flat Bottom] The bargeman is making an unflattering comparison between Jenny's anatomy and the construction of a barge.

63. cricket] "A low wooden stool" (OED).

64. The banter between the servants looks back to similar scenes in Shakespeare and is a precursor to the conversations in the servants' hall in Fielding and Sterne. William H. McBurney includes Jenny and the bargemen among Davys's borrowings from the dramatic conventions ("Mrs. Mary Davys: Forerunner of Fielding," *PMLA* 74 [1959]: 350).

65. Elogiums] Tribute or tomb inscription; anglicized to "elogy" and often confused with "eulogy" and "eulogium" (OED).

66. "To turn them off" is a term frequently used for the action of hanging criminals; the execution was sometimes accomplished by having the prisoner climb a ladder with the noose around his neck, and then removing the ladder (similar results were gained by having the accused stand on a cart). Formator is clearly seeing the rape in terms of theft of property—he speaks of "stealing our Heiresses." Both the verb and the pronoun are instructive.

67. "your Master's a Papist, and you are his Chaplain in disguise . . . the Evasions of a Jesuit"] Because Roman Catholicism and the presence of Roman Catholic clergy were illegal in England at this time, the Catholic aristocracy frequently sheltered their clergy in their houses under the guise of servants; in equating the Jesuits, or members of the Society of Jesus, with evasive and misleading speech, Davys reflects the standard English distrust of Jesuit equivocation, that is, speech which says one thing and means another. On the other hand, Formator/Alanthus does show himself an adept at equivocation, as the conversation among him (as Formator), Amoranda, and Maria displays (see below, pp. 73-74).

68. "'Tis a work Nature requires of us."] Davys refers to the controversy over whether or not Ladies should breast feed their own children or hand them over to a wet nurse (see Laurence Stone, *The Family, Sex and Marriage in England 1500–1800* [New York: Harper and Row, 1977], 426–32; and Ruth Perry, "Colonizing the Breast: Sexuality and Maternity in Eighteenth Century England," *Journal of the History of Sexuality* 2 [1991]: 204–34).

69. "if I had follow'd Nature"] Jenny's response refers to the unnatural aspect of a life of enforced chastity spent waiting on a young woman when the maid is in her prime child-bearing years.

70. gennet] A small Spanish horse (so the expression "Spanish Gennet" is redundant); usually spelt "jennet."

71. Man of Mode] A fashionable gentleman; also the name of one of the most famous restoration plays, *The Man of Mode, or Sir Fopling Flutter,* by Sir George Etherege (1632[?]-91[?]).

72. "I am free, and will be so"] Not traced. By "old song," Davys may mean a frequently repeated wish, a common refrain.

73. habit] Riding suit.

74. a great person, who always had one by him, to put him in mind he was a Man] Juvenal's tenth satire (*On the Vanity of Human Wishes*) in describing a triumphal procession adds "*et, sibi consul / ne placeat, curru servus portarte eodem*" (lines 41–42, Loeb Classical Library edition). Thomas Shadwell (1642–92), in his translation of the satire, presents these lines as "Not pleas'd too much must the great Consul be, / With him a slave to check his Pride we see" and adds this instructive note: "This Servant rode behind the Triumpher in the same Chariot, and put him in mind of Instruments of punishment affix'd to the Chariot, and cryed out to him, *Respice post te memento te esse hominem,* Look behind you, remember you are a Man, and bid him mind the Whip and the Bell." He gives Lubin and Farnaby as his references. Davys might have

known this particular translation (she refers to Shadwell's play, *The Virtuoso*, in *Familiar Letters*) but it was also the kind of commonplace with which the wife of a schoolmaster might well be familiar. For use of it among the Scriblerians, see Swift, *The Examiner*, 7 July 1711; and Pope, *The Dunciad in Four Books* (1742), 4.133–34.

75. attractives] Attractions.

76. The fox complain'd of acids] Amoranda refers to Aesop's fable of the fox and the grapes. After a number of unsuccessful attempts at a bunch of grapes that hangs temptingly out of reach, the fox walks away muttering, "They were probably sour anyway."

NOTES TO THE PREFACE TO *The Works of Mrs. Davys*, 1725

1. Because *Familiar Letters Betwixt a Gentleman and a Lady* had no publication other than its inclusion in the *Works*, I am using the preface to the latter work to introduce it. It is set in italics in the original; I have reversed them.

2. It is difficult in the face of Eliza Haywood's enormous popularity in the 1720s to understand how Davys can make a case for the novel's moribund state, unless she is doing so ironically, as the reference to ladies' taking up improving history and travels may suggest. She may be thinking in terms of the French romances which she berates at the beginning of the next paragraph; she is also making a case for her own writing being superior to what has gone before, both in technique and in moral tone.

3. See Aristotle, *Poetics*. Aristotle is clearly the prescriptive critic Davys has in mind, with her emphasis on the unity and probability of plot and the just treatment of virtue and vice.

4. Published as *The Amours of Alcippus and Lucippe* (London, 1704), the volume in fact did have a preface and a dedication. See the introduction, and Frans De Bruyn, "Mary Davys," DLB, 39:33. De Bruyn notes that it is possible that the novel might have had a 1700 printing without preface and dedication, but if so it is entirely lost, and the 1704 volume does not indicate that it is a second edition; its reference to "first fruits" would seem to argue that it is the first.

5. one hundred and fifty Miles *Northward*] York.

6. Her Grace the Dutches of Norfolk] Written in a contemporary hand in one of the Bodleian copies (vet. A4 2608). Not all copies have the list of subscribers; see the textual note. I am very grateful to Antonia Forster for transcribing the list for me.

7. *Mrs.* Johnson] Possibly Esther Johnson (1681–1728), to whom Davys dedicated *The Fugitive* (1705). Johnson, also known as Stella, was one of the central figures in Jonathan Swift's life and correspondence. He mentions Davys in the course of the *Journal to Stella*.

8. *Mrs.* Stanton] Possibly Davys's sister, whom Swift refers to as Roda Staunton (letter to Benjamin Motte, 4 November 1732; *The Correspondence of Jonathan Swift*, ed. Harold Williams, 5:83).

Notes to *Familiar Letters Betwixt a Gentleman and a Lady*

1. Jointure of the greatest Part] The jointure, or annuity assigned in the marriage contract to the wife should she outlive her husband, was generally based on what she brought into the marriage. A wealthy husband was indeed being generous to arrange for her to have most of his estate if she had a relatively modest fortune because dower (the common law right of interest in her husband's real property), for which jointure was substituted, would have given her a claim on only one-third of the estate. See Susan Staves, *Married Women's Separate Property in England, 1660–1833* (Cambridge: Harvard Univ. Press, 1990).

2. Female Engineer] A female contriver.

3. Birth of a Young Prince] Letters from the Gräfin zu Schaumburg-Lippe speak angrily of the obstetrical practices of the English doctors, which resulted in the stillbirth of a son in 1716. Another child, George William, born in 1717, lived only a few months (Hatton, 132, 168 n). See the introduction for the identification of the prince, and below, n. 20, for a discussion of the dating of the novel.

4. Grums] The OED lists an adjectival use, "morose or surly," and notes that the word first appears in the seventeenth century, probably formed by a combination of such words as "grim, gruff, grumble."

5. Union] Refers to the Act of Union, 1707, joining England and Scotland.

6. The birth of an heir on English soil will placate those who view the German Hanoverians as interlopers. George I succeeded in 1714 on the death of Queen Anne, the last Stuart, who died without heirs.

7. "The Poison of Asps is under their tongues"] See Romans 3:13–15. The Stuarts, whom the Tories—like Artander—supported, were Roman Catholics, and Berina suggests with this reference to poisonous rhetoric that they attempted to persuade their followers to subvert "their Religion and Laws."

8. English Annals] The historical records of England; a narrative in which the historical events are organized year by year.

9. "Those Men, from whom the Name first took its Rise"] The first people to be called Whigs were members of the Covenanter group of Western Scotland, extreme Protestants. Popular culture located the origin of the word in the Whigamore raids of 1648, when the group marched on Edinburgh, but the OED disputes the claim because "whig" was in use before then.

10. Artander refers to the actions of Cromwell and the Puritans: the execution of Charles I, the execution and imprisonment of Church of England clergy during the Republic, and the vandalism in the churches, including the destruction of windows and statues.

11. T—k—l] Thomas Tickell (1685–1740), contributor of verse to *The Spectator*, *The Guardian*, and other papers. Since Tickell caused a breach between Pope and Addison, it is perhaps appropriate that he has this rather Grub Street-like presentation in a volume to which Pope subscribed. There is no evidence that he wrote the dedication here described.

12. Devoirs] Respects.

13. Hoop-skirt] Hoop skirts were popular for over a hundred years, beginning in the first decade of the eighteenth century, and were a constant target of satire, complaint, and pulpit rhetoric. See Kimberly Chrisman, "*Unhoop* the Fair Sex: The Campaign Against the Hoop Petticoat in Eighteenth-Century England," *Eighteenth-Century Studies* 30 (1996): 5–23.

14. Plaister] Plaster; medicine spread on fine cloth and applied to the skin to soothe and heal injuries.

15. Mary I (Tudor) reigned 1553–58; her attempt to restore Roman Catholicism to England became a standard feature in the Church of England's recitations of Catholic cruelties, as did the Irish massacre of 1641. Because the latter was used as propaganda, the numbers were usually exaggerated.

16. flea'd] Flayed.

17. Refers to the belief that the Roman Catholic Church encouraged its members to assassinate Protestant rulers.

18. The theory, which still has proponents today, that the Gunpowder Plot was invented by the Earl of Salisbury to discredit the Roman Catholics in England and cause the laws against them to be tightened; and that Guy Fawkes and the others who were executed for their involvement were framed. Since the Gunpowder Treason was a central plank in the Church of England's anti-Catholic platform, any attempt to dismantle it was charged against the Jesuits who (in the Anglican scheme of things) devised it in the first place.

19. *Caesar his Due*] "Render therefore unto Caesar the things that are Caesar's, and unto God the things that are God's" (Matthew 22:21).

20. Eight and Twenty Years] James II was forced to abdicate in 1688, at which time his infant son, who would normally be the successor, was passed over in favor of his eldest daughter Mary, who was safely married to William of Orange, a Dutch Protestant. William arrived in England on 5 November 1688 and was constitutionally accepted and crowned in 1689. The infant, James Edward, became known as the old Pretender (see below, p. 100); there was an attempt by the Jacobites to place him on the throne in 1715, and another in favor of his son Charles Edward, the young Pretender, in 1745. The reference suggests 1716–17 as the period in which the text was written; the announcement of the prince's birth makes the matter less certain. See the introduction.

21. cricket] A trivet, or three-legged stand for holding pots or kettles in the fire.

22. Diaper napkin] Diaper is a coarse, inexpensive fabric used for bibs and napkins, as well as wrappings for infants.

23. *Scotch*-cloth Pinners] Scotch cloth is another inexpensive fabric, this one resembling fine linen. A pinner is a form of headdress that had long flaps that came down in front and wrapped around the chest; here Artander is using the term to refer only to the flaps.

24. Pasteboard] He probably means a wooden board on which pastry is rolled out, rather than cardboard formed by gluing together several sheets of paper. Either mean-

ing is congruent with the picture of ungracious miserliness. Pease-pudding is a kind of porridge; a Black Jack "A large leather jug for beer, etc., coated externally with tar" (OED); a squab "a sofa, ottoman or couch" (OED "squab" *sb.* 4); and Bacon Swerd is bacon fat.

25. Mahometan] Mohammedan, Muslim.

26. neuter] Neutral.

27. nos'd with C——] Catholicism. To "nose" is "to confront, face, or oppose (a person, etc.) in an impudent or insolent manner" (OED).

28. Vertuoso] Virtuoso, used pejoratively, that is, one who fancied himself an expert, especially in scientific or arcane studies.

29. Sir Nicholas Gimcrack] The central character in Thomas Shadwell's play, *The Virtuoso*; a form of mad scientist.

30. Quixote, cave of Montesinos] *Don Quixote,* pt. 2, ch. 23. The Don is lowered into a cave by Sancho and a student; he falls asleep and dreams of wonderful adventures, which he is convinced actually happened.

31. Virtue an innate qualification] Artander is supporting Descartes's theory of innate ideas, that is, that we are born with certain qualities and ideas within us, as opposed to the Lockean belief that everything we know we have learned through the association of ideas acquired through experience.

32. Scandal] Gossip.

33. Quinsy] An inflamed throat, sometimes caused by tonsillitis.

34. Black Guard] While a blackguard, all one word, indicates an unprincipled person, the OED indicates that the sense of a group, used by Davys here, refers to the lowest menials of a household or military camp. The two meanings tend to elide— there is definitely an underlying fear that the doctor may be in the hands of thugs.

35. Farthing-candle] A small, inexpensive candle (a farthing being one quarter of a penny). The cheap candle would also probably be made of tallow or animal fat, which would smell horrible, unlike the more fragrant beeswax. Thanks to Isobel Grundy for the gloss. See below, p. 112.

36. ——] Chamber pot.

37. Goal] Early spelling of the still-current spelling "gaol"; jail, prison.

38. Chymer] The OED gives a poetic connection to one meaning of the verb "to chime": "to rhyme or jingle." While the definition sounds deprecatory, the quotations (one from Cowley) do not. There is no citation of "chymer" or "chimer" as poet, good or bad.

39. Public Prints] Newspapers.

40. Royal-Society] An institution chartered in 1662 for the purpose of scientific discovery and experimentation.

41. fit of Chagrin] Bad temper or melancholy.

42. quick silver] Mercury; a mercurial temperament is slippery and changeful.

43. *Miss Hoiden*] Miss Hoyden; character in *The Relapse* by John Vanbrugh (1664– 1726); described in the Dramatis Personae as "a great fortune," Hoyden is a tomboyish young heiress from the country.

44. brass Crown . . . *Sterling*] The brass crown would be counterfeit (true crowns were gold coins), although not necessarily an intentional deception on the part of the father. The other heiress's money is "all Sterling," that is genuine. A crown was worth five shillings, and was therefore a small portion of an entire fortune.

45. Mummy] The equivalent of the modern expression "beaten to a pulp." Ointments made by pulverizing material from mummies were used medicinally, but the word "mummy" was also used as a slang expression for dead flesh or any ointment-like substance.

46. Reduction of Light Horse] See Berina's reference above, p. 100, to George I's reducing the number of his guards; she refers to public events and then presents a mock-apology for straying beyond the Tea-Table.

47. Three Score witches . . . Flamsteed] John Flamsteed, 1646–1719; clergyman and distinguished astronomer. After the death of Queen Anne in 1714, and the resulting changes in government, he was given 300 of the 400 copies of a previously published and inaccurate edition of his book *Historia Coelestis*, or *The History of the Heavens*, by order of Sir Robert Walpole. The book had been published in 1712 against his wishes and he had spent the intervening years attempting to have it recalled. He burnt all the copies, except for ninety-seven pages in each, the accurate transcription of his own observations (DNB). The "Blazing-Star" suggests the name of an inn or coffeehouse, often used as convenient meeting places for public events, but here it refers to the subject matter as well, since it is a comet. Davys has thus produced a reference that is both topical and complex: the burnt witches represent scientific, not religious, unorthodoxy.

48. Longitude] At this time there was no accurate method of calculating longitude; as a result maps and marine navigation were unreliable and sailors were understandably eager to correct the problem.

49. Sir Harry Wildair] A character in Farquhar's *The Constant Couple* (1700), and the eponymous hero of its sequel (1701).

50. Dog in the Manger] Aesop's fable in which the cow begs the dog to move out of the manger so that she can eat; he refuses. The story became proverbial for the selfish hoarding of a commodity for which another has a genuine need.

51. *"Who cares for any body that has more wit than themselves"*] Congreve, *Love for Love*, 1.1.129–30.

52. Pug] Common name for a pug dog or a monkey; the dogs were more frequently lady's pets. We may thus surmise that among his other affectations Artander keeps a monkey.

53. Artemedorus] Artemidorus Daldianus, fl. 138–179 C.E. in Rome; wrote a four-volume work on the interpretation of dreams (*Encyclopaedia Britannica*, 1937).

54. Babies] Dolls.

55. as much Estate as will qualify him for a vote] In the eighteenth century suffrage was determined by property holdings.

56. *"How happy he, that loves not, lives!"*] Sir John Denham (1615–69); "Friendship and Single Life against Love and Marriage," line 16.

57. *Quevedo's Vision of Loving-Fools*] Francisco Gomez de Quevedo (1580–1645), Spanish; his *Visions* was translated into English by Sir Roger L'Estrange (1616–1704) in 1668.

58. An echo of Shakespeare, *Julius Caesar*: "The Evil that men do lives after them / The good is oft interred with their bones" (3.2.75–76).

59. Proteus] The Greek god who had the ability to turn himself into any size or shape, and therefore could not be restrained or restricted.

60. Breach of Promise] For all Berina's anger, she is also being playful, since breach of promise is a legal action by a woman or her family against a man who has reneged on his promise of marriage—the opposite of her situation. Berina continues the legal language by referring to his letter as testimony. Artander shows his own facility with legal language below, (p. 117: "no Man lies under a Necessity of keeping a Promise any longer than he has it in his power."

61. Wast] Waste.

62. Obedience] Berina is insisting on the authority of the husband as codified in the marriage ceremony; see introduction, and Lindy Riley, "Mary Davys's Satiric Novel *Familiar Letters*: Refusing Patriarchal Inscription of Women" in *Cutting Edges: Postmodern Critical Essays on Eighteenth-Century Satire,* ed. James E. Gill, Tennessee Studies in Literature, vol. 37 (Knoxville: Univ. of Tennessee Press, 1995), 206–21. I think Riley overstates her case—Davys is less radical than she indicates—but the article gives a good indication of the range of issues in this very short novel. Berina's statement is interesting in the context of Mary Astell's call to women to reject marriage and submission to patriarchal control in favor of a life of study and good works in a community of women.

63. Oh! what foolish Things are we Mortals!] Echo of Shakespeare, *A Midsummer Night's Dream*, "Lord, what fools these mortals be!" (3.2.115).

64. "my false foolish Heart!"] Abraham Cowley (1618–67), "The Heart Fled Again," line 1, from *The Mistress*.

65. Basilisk] Mythological creature, also called the cockatrice, whose gaze turned mortals to stone.

66. One of the two copies of the *Collected Works* (Harding M 78, 19) in the Bodleian library contains much (ungrammatical) emendation and addition by one of its eighteenth-century readers, including the following couplet written at the conclusion of this novel: "Love is a God that always takes Delight / To tiranize poor Mortals with his Spite."

NOTES TO *The Accomplish'd Rake*

1. The verse is from the title page; Davys probably wrote it herself since she is generally conscientious about attribution.

2. Beaus] Those men whose main concern was their appearance; dandies.

3. Scruple] A tiny measurement of weight, 1/24 ounce, according to the OED; one of the quotations describes it as "twenty barley corns."

4. Rake] A man whose preoccupations include sex and gambling and who pays little attention to virtue; according to the OED, it takes its origin from "rakehell." Davys's description of Sir John's character and behavior as the novel unfolds is as good a definition as any, and the dedication develops the distinction between the beau and the rake.

5. Spaniards] McBurney (*Four Before Richardson*, 239 n. 1) refers to "the virtual state of war with Spain which had resulted from Townshend's alliance of England with France and Prussia by the Treaty of Hanover in September, 1725."

6. Billet-doux] Literally, sweet notes; love letters, containing, in modern terms, sweet nothings.

7. Barley-Water . . . Burgundy] One an infusion of barley soaked in water, used to lower fevers and reduce irritability; the other a strong red wine.

8. *Gentilshomme des Amour*] Gentlemen of Love.

9. The dedication is unsigned.

10. Knight of the Shire] "A gentleman representing a shire or county in Parliament" (OED). The description, "one of the largest Counties in *England*" suggests Davys's former residence, Yorkshire, which is the largest county.

11. Genius] Spirit, gift, brilliance. The eighteenth century used the term slightly differently from our sense of innate intellectual capacity; significantly, the usage was "to have a Genius" rather than "to be a Genius." Below, p. 175, the word is used in the sense of guardian spirit: "her better Genius sent me in a very critical hour."

12. Libertine] A person, usually a man, of loose morals, who rejects both sexual and religious restrictions.

13. Joynture] See *FL*, n. 1, for an explanation of jointure.

14. Sampson] Samson, the biblical strong man. The men of Judah bind Samson with "two new cords" so that they can hand him over to the Philistines, who mock him. At this point "the Spirit of the Lord came mightily upon him, and the cords that were upon his arms became as flax that was burnt with fire, and his bands loosed from off his hands" (Judges 15:13–15).

15. Month's Confinement] The traditional seclusion of the recently widowed. See Lady Booby, in Fielding's *Joseph Andrews*, bk. 1, ch. 5, for a similarly satiric description of the widow's grief. The reference to the permanence of the darkened room, however, links Lady Galliard's confinement to the treatment of the mad, who were kept in darkness since it was thought to calm them.

16. Baronet] The lowest hereditary rank; according to the OED, a baronet is a commoner, that is, he does not sit in the House of Lords. Davys also calls him "the Knight" but they are in fact different titles; knighthood is not hereditary.

17. *That Manners makes the Man*] "Manners makyth man": the motto of William of Wykeham (1324–1404), founder of Winchester College and New College, Oxford; responsible for the fourteenth-century remodeling of Winchester Cathedral.

18. gold clockt stockings, and a Tupee] Stockings that have an embroidered pattern on the sides; gold thread would make them particularly fine. "Tupee" is an obsolete form of "toupee," according to the OED, meaning "a curl or artificial lock of hair on the top of the head, esp. as a crowning feature of a periwig." It is thus a fashion accessory and not intended to hide hair loss.

19. King's Evil] Scrofula, a chronic swelling and enlargement of the lymph glands. Traditionally, the cure was thought to lie in the touch of the monarch, but that is not a possibility for Davys's characters because Queen Anne, the last monarch to do so, died in 1714.

20. "Train up a child in the way he should go: And when he is old, he will not depart from it" (Proverbs 22:6). The book of Proverbs is traditionally thought to be by Solomon, the biblical "wise man."

21. acquired Quality] See *FL*, n. 31, on innate and acquired qualities.

22. guest] Guessed.

23. Brilliant] Precious stone, such as a diamond.

24. Even you yourself . . . his Majesty's Health] These words would appear logically to belong to Mr. Friendly although there is no speech tag to suggest so; McBurney emends the text by adding "said Mr. Friendly" (248).

25. Dulcinea] Don Quixote gives the name "Dulcinea del Toboso" to Aldonsa Lorenzo, who lives in the neighboring village of Toboso, and whom he designates his lady love (see Cervantes, pt. 1, ch. 1).

26. in the Mind] Take advantage of his inclination to go to Cambridge.

27. Moliere] Jean-Baptiste Poquelin Molière (1622–73); his comedies target particular flaws in society, personified in the central characters. Isobel Grundy has suggested to me that a book that keeps the reader awake far into the night might more likely be a novel than a play, and that the novel in question would therefore be *Les Memoires de la view de Henriette-Sylvie de Molière* (1672–74) by Marie-Catherine Desjardins, Madame de Villedieu (1640[?]-83). This is an intriguing prospect, for Davys would be depicting one of her most respectable and admirable characters reading a genre that was considered frivolous and possibly even immoral.

28. Fame's Trumpet] Juvenal 14.152, "quam foedae bucina famae" translated "How loud the blast of evil rumour" in the Loeb Classical Library edition. The eighteenth century translated "fama" as Fame in the sense of notoriety; see Swift, *Tale of a Tub*, sec. 10: "whether she [Fame] conceives her Trumpet sounds best and farthest, when she stands on a *Tomb*, by the Advantage of a rising Ground, and the Echo of a hollow Vault."

29. within the little Dining-room] That is, the bedroom opens off the dining-room.

30. height of Passion] In this case, anger; the term passion indicates any strong and uncontrolled emotion.

31. swound] Swoon, faint.

32. Hudibras] From the poem of the same name by Samuel Butler (1612–80); the central character is based on Don Quixote and is a satire of the Puritans. According to McBurney, the lines are from pt. 2, canto 2, 385–87, quoted slightly incorrectly.

33. Goust] Appetite.

34. Scriveners . . . Reversion] See OED, "scrivener," def. 3; a moneylender who acts as intermediary between those with money to lend and those who wish to borrow. Sir John is planning to borrow money against his inheritance, which he will be able to control when he reaches twenty-one, the age of majority (see below, p. 155).

35. *Medes* and *Persians*] Proverbial expression for inflexibility of rule or purpose.

36. Dark-lanthorn] Dark-lantern. A device well-designed for intrigue, since it is possible by means of a sliding panel to conceal the light without actually putting it out—as Tom's wife does.

37. Phyz] Physiognomy, face.

38. prised] Prized, or appraised; valued.

39. his Accompts] As Steward, Tom is in charge of the household's finances; in order to resign, he must give up his account books.

40. Court-End] Westminster, closer to the end of town where the King's Court resided, where he could become more involved in the fast pace of living from which to this point Teachwell and Friendly have protected him. The Friendlys seem to live in the old city of London, which is the financial district.

41. gentile] Genteel.

42. Sir *Combish Clutter*] His name resembles Sir Fopling Flutter, Etherege's Man of Mode. As McBurney points out (279 n. 7), the 1756 edition of the novel makes use of this similarity to change his name to Sir Tony Flutter, one of several alterations which serve to link the work more closely to the theater. "Combish" suggests "coxcomb," and thus the strutting of a rooster.

43. *Cockahoop*] The various meanings the OED gives for this word produce a sense of ungoverned and often noisy high spirits.

44. stooking Gamster] McBurney connects the phrase with "thieves' cant for handkerchief, hence *stook-hauler*, a pick-pocket" (279 n. 8). The reference to "Gleanings" below, however, suggests that Davys is using "stook" in its agricultural sense of a pile of hay. Neither explanation seems quite satisfactory.

45. flurt] Flirt; waves her fan flirtatiously; "that" a few words on, refers to the movement of the fan.

46. Duce] Devil.

47. "Liberty is the Soul of Living / Every Hour new Joys receiving / Neither taking Hearts nor giving"] Untraced.

48. F—th] Faith. It is a convention to blank out oaths, even when they do not seem particularly obscene or profane; see "By George," below, p. 196.

49. Baulers] Bawlers.

50. Galliard's description of the unmusical singing, and the congregation's joining in the absolution, which church doctrine reserves only to ordained ministers, suggests he has gone to an evangelistic or dissenting parish and not to the mainstream Church of England.

51. Masquerade] A fancy dress ball, to which the guests wore costumes and masks. It is associated with a freedom of behavior brought about by the release from everyday

identity due to the anonymity facilitated by the costume and mask. Miss Friendly and Miss Wary enter into the spirit of the event by switching costumes and disguising their voices, further intensifying the carnival confusion.

52. chairs] Sedan chair, a vehicle, designed for a single occupant, that is mounted on poles and carried by two men.

53. Squibs] Firecrackers.

54. Boufet] Buffet.

55. Tom Thumb] A tiny hero of folk tales whose "heroic" adventures include being eaten by a cow. In 1731 Henry Fielding made him the hero of his *Tragedy of Tragedies*, a satire of heroic drama.

56. Bagnio] Public bath; but as Miss Wary explains below, p. 163, often a places for illicit sexual encounters.

57. Poynant Sauce] Poignant; a sharp-tasting or acidic sauce, thought to increase the appetite.

58. Punctilio's] Insistence on form or etiquette; in this case fulfilling the terms of the challenge. The usage is ironic when one considers the kind of skirmish Sir John has had with the "little gentleman."

59. Apothecary] Pharmacist, who functioned in some ways as a physician, since he both prescribed and provided medication. The implication in "a different Nature from anything he had ever served him in yet" is that Sir John has been treated, perhaps frequently (a few sentences later he is described as "an excellent Customer") for vene-real disease.

60. Mole under-ground] This reference to the burrowing animal so destructive of lawns may also be an allusion to Shakespeare: "Well said, old mole! Canst work in the earth so fast?" *Hamlet*, 1.5.162.

61. Mackroons] Macaroons—sweet biscuits flavored with ground almonds.

62. Quantum] Total sum of his being.

63. B——] Bitch.

64. *incog.*] Incognito; unknown; disguised.

65. Shampain] Champagne.

66. Groom-Porter's] "The Groom-Porter was an officer in the Royal Household, whose duty it was to tend the King's apartments and see that it was supplied with cards, dice, and other gambling appurtenances;" he also occasionally set up a place of gambling for his own profit (McBurney, 299 n. 11). Ned Ward in *The London Spy* (1698–1700) also describes visits to the Groom-Porter's.

67. Recruit] More money.

68. Z——s] Zounds; contraction for "God's Wounds."

69. Tedder'd] Tethered.

70. HELL-FIRE-CLUB] McBurney (300 n. 12) notes that there was more than one Hell-fire Club; one was put out of action by George I in 1721; another, better known, was founded by John Wilkes in 1745. Both were atheistic and devoted to the kind of pranks portrayed here.

71. *St. Martin's*] There are several St. Martin's both inside and outside the city of

London; this one is probably St. Martin's-in-the-Fields, now in Trafalgar Square, but then distinctly rural.

72. cashiered] Dismissed, expelled.

73. thorough-stitch] Completely, thoroughly.

74. Watch] Official patrol of the area, alert to prevent crime.

75. N—d—m] Mother Needham, a notorious procuress; Dolly displays her innocence by calling her a "kind lady" (below, p. 173).

76. Geers] Clothing, probably meaning her hat and cloak.

77. See *RC,* p. 20 n. 23.

78. Nonage] The years in which he is a minor (i.e. before he is of age).

79. Cassandra's Fate] Cassandra, Princess of Troy and beloved of Apollo, was given by him the gift of prophecy; when she refused to sleep with him, he turned the gift into a curse by condemning her always to speak the truth but never to be believed. She attempted to warn her countrymen against the wooden horse, but was ignored, and when Troy fell she became part of the conqueror's loot which Agamemnon took home to Argos. There she was murdered along with Agamemnon by Clytaemnestra and her lover Aegisthus.

80. Contemn'd] Condemned.

81. Whistle and Bells] Child's toy; conventional present, and rather thoughtless and insubstantial a gift from the child's father, who normally would have to support her.

82. nick my Chalk] The running tab for drinks was kept on a chalkboard; if a piece of chalk has a nick down the center of it, it will produce two lines instead of one, thus doubling the bill. Davys, as keeper of a coffeehouse, was no doubt fully aware of all the dubious practices of the less respectable members of the trade.

83. *Venture-all* . . . a *Dutch* man] A play on the Dutch prefix "van," intended to emphasize Dick's simplicity in not recognizing the name as a pseudonym.

84. like *Scrub* in the *Stratagem*] George Farquhar, *The Beaux Stratagem,* 3.1.55: "Madam, I have brought you a packet of news." McBurney points out that the scene resembles another one in the same play, 3.3.1–116 (McBurney, 312 n. 15).

85. Equipage] Galliard plans to get a coach and horses, a great expense, since it involves purchasing the equipment, stabling it, and hiring men both to drive the vehicle and attend to the horses. The next few lines demonstrate the expenses he is required to cover.

86. Chargeable] Expensive.

87. *Mall*-time . . . the Park] McBurney identifies the time of day as late afternoon, and the Park as Hyde Park (313 n. 16), although it could equally be St. James's or Green Park.

88. *Rhenish* . . . *German*-Spaw] Rhenish: a wine from the Rhine area; German-spaw: mineral water from the Low Countries, now Belgium.

89. Drabs] Prostitutes.

90. short Commons] Little to eat from the shared feast; Davys's use of the phrase may reflect her coffeehouse clientele, since it especially refers to college fare.

91. Epicurus] Greek philosopher (4th Century B.C.E.) who believed in the indulgence of the senses.

92. Some indication of the extravagance of this feast can be gained from Day's observation that in the first quarter of the eighteenth century, "wages for a skilled laborer might go no higher than two shillings and sixpence a day" (*Told in Letters*, 71).

93. Cap-a-pe] Head to foot.

94. Levee] An audience held while the host is getting dressed for the day, thus generally in the morning; usually a time when a nobleman hears petitions from his tenants and others who wish his help.

95. carrest] Caressed.

96. b—g—] By-God.

97. Greenwich] Suburb of London.

98. Picquet . . . Ombre] both are card games. Picquet is played by two persons, ombre by three, which is why they must change games in order to allow Galliard to play (see OED). See introduction for a discussion of Davys's allusion to Pope's *Rape of the Lock* (1714) through the references to ombre and Belinda.

99. Complisance] Complaisance: courtesy, politeness, the characteristic of being agreeable.

100. Centry] Sentry.

101. Humane] Human.

102. Farewell Love and all soft Pleasure] From the pasticcio opera *Thamyris, Queen of Scythia* (1707), words by P.A. Motteux, tune A. Steffani. Many thanks to Linda Veronika Troost for sharing her research with me.

103. Apocryphal] The Apocrypha contains the books of the Old Testament not originally in Hebrew and excluded from the Protestant Bible at the Reformation; thus, Sir Combish is expressing strong doubt about Sir John's veracity.

104. b— G——e] By George.

105. disembogue] Vomit; Belinda is using the term in a figurative sense, which the OED acknowledges, although none of its examples describe the violent emptying of the stomach's contents. The primary meaning is "Of a river, lake, etc.: To flow out at the mouth; to discharge or empty itself; to flow into."

106. worried] Mauled.

107. In keeping with the tragi-comic strain of the encounter, Betty's language mimics the heightened strain of heroic drama. She describes herself in true heroine fashion, undercut by the circumstances of her life: while an orphan, her parents were not of a class to make them worth mentioning, and the cluster of suitors is far from a gathering of lovelorn knights and noble courtiers.

108. Young *Bateman*] McBurney notes: "From a ballad beginning or entitled, 'A godly warning to all maidens.' A chapbook version appeared in 1710, *Bateman's Tragedy: or, the Perjur'd Bride Justly rewarded. Being the Unfortunate Love of German's Wife and Young Bateman*" (337 n. 21). The designated spot—"at his own signpost"—suggests that the lover was in trade, and owned either a shop or a pub.

109. Mrs] Abbreviation for Mistress, a courtesy title for adult women; its use in the eighteenth century does not necessarily denote married status.

110. Looby] An awkward fool; at eighteen stone he is lumping indeed, since a stone is fourteen pounds.

111. swell] A reference to the effects of poisoning, but a double entendre, since she is also clearly referring to pregnancy—in other words, she escaped without injury to person or reputation.

112. *Tyburn* or a Brothel-house] Tyburn was a place of public execution; Sir Combish is predicting a criminal future for Will's unborn children of both sexes.

113. tid Bit] Tidbit; dainty morsel.

114. Three times asked] They will be married when the banns are read. See *RC*, above, n. 48.

115. sleeveless Errand] An errand that cannot succeed; a wild goose chase. Thanks to Isobel Grundy.

116. M————d] Maidenhead.

117. Mr. Clownish's song is, as McBurney points out, in a Somersetshire accent (344 n. 23); whoney] Honey; V—t] Fart; Odzooks] God's hooks, a common exclamation, reference to the nails of the cross—surviving today in the expression Gadzooks

118. Noy] Nay, no; Ads Watrilaits] The components translate as following: ads: a corruption of "God's"; watri: an obsolete form of "water;" laits: dialect form of "lights" or "lightning;" but I can find no instance of the combination in the OED or the English Dialect Dictionary; ———— ————] Your maidenhead.

119. Runagate] Renegade, deserter.

120. Landabrides] "Lindabride was a lady in the romance, *Mirror of Knighthood*. The name was used allusively for a lady-love, a mistress" (McBurney, 347 n. 24).

121. Davys's linking of the two Georges, the patron saint and the king of England, reflects the consistent support of the Hanoverians in her post-1714 writings, even from the mouths of country clowns. The king is George I, who died in June 1727, three months after *AR* was published (see McBurney, 234, for the date of publication).

122. after Marriage (like Cheese)] Cheese is traditionally the last course in the meal, marriage traditionally the end of the story.

123. Charge] Expense. A "fleerer" is one who sneers and disparages another person.

124. Fromps] Frumps: "sulks, ill-humour" (OED) rather than dowdiness.

125. "Old Song": "Why how now Sir *Clown* what makes you so bold"] Untraced.

126. Fripery] Frippery, a gaudy trifle.

127. Yew] Ewe.

128. Lustrue] Luster.

129. Act of Oblivion] In 1660, the first Parliament after the Restoration passed an Act of Indemnity and Oblivion, granting a general pardon to all those who participated in the Civil War and the Interregnum; the Act covered the period from January 1637 to June 1660, although it contained a long list of exceptions, which allowed Charles to prosecute the ringleaders (*English Historical Documents*, vol. 8,

ed. Andrew Browning, ser. ed. David C. Douglas, [New York: Oxford Univ. Press, 1953], 164–65).

130. H——t] Harlot.

131. C——d] Cuckold.

132. Oysters at *Billings-gate*] The location of London's fishmarket; also a place to find whores, and the oysters have their usual aphrodisiac association, so that the entire letter is a sustained double entendre.

133. D——e] Damnable.

134. Fireship] Infected with venereal disease.

135. S—t] Slut.

136. Cornutes] A scientific term referring to horned animals, which here refers to the cuckold's horns, the traditional sign of the deceived husband.

137. Orts you keck at] Orts: scraps, leavings, especially of food; in general Dialect use in Britain; keck: to refuse with disdain (North Yorkshire; [*The English Dialect Dictionary*, Oxford Univ. Press]). The OED defines "keck" more directly as gagging, or making a sound as if to vomit.

138. The bawdy talk links Sir John's injuries with syphilis, the more usual result of promiscuity; thus the "French faggot stick" harming the nose refers to the ravages of the disease, and the "hot cockles" of the Drabs refers to infected prostitutes.

139. Bilbo] McBurney notes that "Bilbo" was "originally a sword made in Bilbao, Spain." It became colloquial speech for a bully (363 n. 26).

140. Dragon . . . Golden Pipkin] The eleventh labor of Hercules was to acquire the golden apples of the Hesperides, which were guarded by a dragon.

141. mump] Fool.

142. Perdue] Hidden (the French actually means "lost").

143. one . . . that could Pepper] He is looking for an infected prostitute. The reference to pepper continues the association of venereal disease with heat, a common one since the early stages of the disease include burning urination and sores.

144. Q] Cue.

145. Mr. Cowley's poem] "The Welcome" by Abraham Cowley, from *The Mistress*. The imagery alludes to the parable of the Prodigal Son.

146. S—l] Soul.

147. Work of a Parliament] There was no means of retroactively legitimizing a child whose parents had not undergone any form of marriage before his birth, and only legitimate offspring could inherit titles. Thus the child could probably inherit Sir John's property if the latter adjusted his will, but could not ascend to the baronetcy. Davys seems to be rewriting the law in order to assure her happy ending.

BIBLIOGRAPHY

CONTEMPORARY EDITIONS

The Reform'd Coquet; or, Memoirs of Amoranda. London, 1724.

The Works of Mrs. Davys. London, 1725; includes *The Reform'd Coquet* and *Familiar Letters Betwixt a Gentleman and a Lady.*

The Accomplish'd Rake, or Modern Fine Gentleman. London, 1727; unsigned.

MODERN EDITIONS

Backscheider, Paula R., and John Richetti. *Popular Fiction by Women, 1660–1730.* New York: Oxford Univ. Press, 1996. Includes *The Reform'd Coquet.*

Day, Robert Adams, ed. *Familiar Letters Betwixt a Gentleman and a Lady.* Augustan Reprint Society, no. 54. Los Angeles: William Andrews Clark Memorial Library, 1955.

Grieder, Josephine, ed. *The Reform'd Coquet (1724) and Familiar Letters Betwixt a Gentleman and a Lady (1725) by Mary Davys; and The Mercenary Lover (1726) by Eliza Haywood.* New York: Garland, 1973. Facsimile.

McBurney, William H., ed. *Four Before Richardson: Selected English Novels, 1720–1727.* Lincoln: Univ. of Nebraska Press, 1963. Includes *The Accomplish'd Rake.*

Stefanson, Donald Hal. "The Works of Mary Davys, a Critical Edition." Ph.D. diss., 2 vols., Univ. of Iowa, 1971. Contains all works included in *The Works of Mrs. Davys,* 1725.

CRITICAL STUDIES

Bowden, Martha F. "Mary Davys: Self-Presentation and the Woman Writer's Reputation in the Early Eighteenth Century." *Women's Writing* 3 (1996): 17–33.

Craft-Fairchild, Catherine. *Masquerade and Gender: Disguise and Female Identity in Eighteenth-Century Fictions by Women*. University Park: Pennsylvania Univ. Press, 1993.

Day, Robert Adams. *Told in Letters: Epistolary Fiction Before Richardson*. Ann Arbor: Univ. of Michigan Press, 1966.

De Bruyn, Frans. "Mary Davys." *Dictionary of Literary Biography*, 39:131–38.

McBurney, William H. "Mary Davys: Forerunner of Fielding." *PMLA* 74 (1959): 348–55.

Perry, Ruth. *Women, Letters, and the Novel*. AMS Studies in the Eighteenth Century, no. 4. New York: AMS Press, 1980.

Riley, Lindy. "Mary Davys's Satiric Novel *Familiar Letters*: Refusing Patriarchal Inscription of Women." In *Cutting Edges: Postmodern Critical Essays on Eighteenth-Century Satire*, ed. James E. Gill, 206–21. Tennessee Studies in Literature, vol. 37. Knoxville: Univ. of Tennessee Press, 1995.

Spencer, Jane. *The Rise of the Woman Novelist: From Aphra Behn to Jane Austen*. Oxford: Blackwell, 1986.

Turner, Cheryl. *Living By the Pen: Women Writers in the Eighteenth Century*. London and New York: Routledge, 1992.

SUGGESTED SECONDARY READING

Hunter, J. Paul. *Before Novels: The Cultural Contexts of Eighteenth-Century English Fiction*. New York: W.W. Norton & Co., 1990.

Gallagher, Catherine. *Nobody's Story: The Vanishing Acts of Women Writers in the Marketplace, 1670–1820*. Berkeley and Los Angeles: Univ. of California Press, 1994.

Grundy, Isobel, and Susan Wiseman, eds. *Women, Writing, History, 1640–1740*. Athens: Univ. of Georgia Press, 1992.

Perry, Ruth. *The Celebrated Mary Astell: An Early English Feminist*. Chicago: Univ. of Chicago Press, 1986.

———. "Colonizing the Breast: Sexuality and Maternity in Eighteenth-Century England." *Journal of the History of Sexuality* 2 (1991): 204–34.

Richetti, John J. *Popular Fiction Before Richardson: Narrative Patterns: 1700–1739*. Oxford and New York: Clarendon Press, 1969, 1992.

Ross, Ian Campbell. "'One of the Principal Nations in Europe.': The Representation of Ireland in Sarah Butler's *Irish Tales*." *Eighteenth Century Fiction* 7 (1994): 1–16.

Schofield, Mary Anne, and Cecilia Macheski, eds. *Fetter'd or Free? British Women Novelists, 1670–1815*. Athens and London: Ohio Univ. Press, 1987.

Staves, Susan. "British Seduced Maidens." *Eighteenth Century Studies* 14 (1980–81): 109–34.

Stone, Lawrence. *Road to Divorce: England 1530–1987*. Oxford: Oxford Univ. Press, 1990.

Tobin, Beth Fowkes, ed. *History, Gender and Eighteenth Century Literature*. Athens and London: Univ. of Georgia Press, 1994.

Todd, Janet. *The Sign of Angellica: Women, Writing and Fiction: 1660–1800*. New York: Columbia Univ. Press, 1989.